Praise for

'Hunter's ancient Britain is a brilliantly realised world of imperial ambition and native resistance and the inevitable clashes that arise. Faustus is a fascinating character and it's a treat to see how he negotiates the challenges he faces. His duties in the service of Rome comprise a truly Faustian pact!'

Simon Scarrow

'I loved it. Wonderful, distinct characters – I adored Faustus and Constantia in particular. Great sense of humour throughout. This is a terrific read'

Conn Iggulden

'*Shadow of the Eagle*, a very fine novel about Agricola's campaign in the Highlands in AD 83, has all the ingredients for a first-class, page-turning, well-researched Roman historical adventure. There is a bit of love to be enjoyed along the way, a nice, bloody battle or two, some excellent dialogue and fine, delicate characterisation. Highly recommended!'

Angus Donald, author of *The Last Berserker*

'I only need one word to describe this stunning novel: masterful' Anthony Riches, *Sunday Times* bestselling author of *Wounds of Honour*

'Enthralling and authentic historical Roman fiction, that brings the period to life and keeps you turning the page'

Alex Gough, author of *Emperor's Sword*

Shadow of the Eagle

Amanda Cockrell, writing as Damion Hunter, is the author of seven previous Roman novels: the four-volume series The Centurions, concluding with *The Border Wolves*; and *The Legions of the Mist* and its sequel *The Wall at the Edge of the World*. *Shadow of the Eagle* is the first in The Borderlands, a new Roman series. She grew up in Ojai, California, and developed a fascination with the Romans when a college friend gave her Rosemary Sutcliff's books to read. After a checkered career as a newspaper feature writer and a copywriter for a rock radio station, she taught literature and creative writing for many years at Hollins University in Roanoke, Virginia, where she now lives.

www.amandacockrell.com

Also by Amanda Cockrell writing as Damion Hunter

AMANDA COCKRELL WRITING AS

DAMION HUNTER

SHADOW OF THE EAGLE

CANELO

First published in the United Kingdom in 2022 by Canelo

This edition published in the United Kingdom in 2023 by

Canelo
Unit 9, 5th Floor
Cargo Works, 1-2 Hatfields
London SE1 9PG
United Kingdom

A CIP catalogue record for this book is available from the British Library.

Ebook ISBN 978 1 80032 666 8
Royal Hardback ISBN 978 1 80032 667 5
B Format MMP ISBN 978 1 80436 101 6

Look for more great books at www.canelo.co

Printed and bound in Great Britain by Clays Ltd, Elcograf S.p.A.

1

For Tony

Characters

Abudia: madam of a whorehouse in Isca

Aculeo: guard commander in Faustus's sixth century

Agricola: Gnaeus Julius Agricola, consular legate and governor of Britain

Arion: Faustus's troop horse

Arrius Laenas: new legate of the II Augusta

Atticus: Aulus Atticus, prefect of I Batavian cohort

Aulus Carus: primus pilus of II Augusta

Bassus: legionary in the fourth century, Ninth Cohort, II Augusta

Clio: woman in Abudia's whorehouse

Constantia: daughter of Silanus

Cornutus: former optio of II Augusta third century

Demetrius of Tarsus: grammarian and scholar sent by emperor to study British religion

Domitia Decidiana: wife of Agricola

Domitius Longinus: legate of II Augusta

Faustus: Faustus Silvius Valerianus

Gaia Valerinani: formerly Guennola, Faustus's mother, deceased

Galerius: centurion of the fourth century, Seventh Cohort, II Augusta

Glaucus: deceased; Faustus's predecessor in the II Augusta

Indus: member of First Batavian Cohort

Ingenuus: proprietor of the Capricorn tavern in Isca

Julia Agricola: daughter of Agricola, wife of Tacitus

Lartius: Lartius Marena the Younger, tribune attached to Second Augusta

Lartius Marena: Lartius Marena the Elder, father of Lartius

Livia Tulla: wife of Aulus Carus

Manlius: husband of Silvia

Marcus Silvius: Marcus Silvius Valerianus, deceased; father of Faustus

Marcus Silvius Minor: Marcus Silvius Valerianus Minor, deceased; older brother of Faustus

Mucius: drillmaster at the army training camp

Pandora: Faustus's dog

Paullus: Faustus's slave

Popillia Procula: Constantia's aunt

Publia Livilla: Aunt Publia, distant relative of Governor Frontinus

Rutilius: commander of the Fleet expedition to Orkney

Sallustius Lucullus: new governor of Britain

Septimus: optio in Faustus's century

Silanus: Constantius Silanus, senior surgeon of the II Augusta

Silvia: sister of Faustus

Sulpicia: Faustus's former betrothed

Tacitus: Publius Cornelius Tacitus, historian, son-in-law of Agricola

Tarpeius Naso: primus pilus of the II Augusta after Aulus Carus

Tubertus: helmsman of one of Rutilius's ships

Tullius: centurion of third century, Seventh Cohort, II Augusta

Ursus: Caesius Ursus, commander of the Seventh Cohort, II Augusta

Varus: legionary in the Ninth Cohort, II Augusta

Adaryn: village girl on High Isle, sister of Cari
Aelwen: wife of Calgacos, and sister of Rhion
Aregwydd: sister of Goewyn, married into Emrys's clan
Bleddin: son of Calgacos
Boduoc: one of Eirian's brothers
Cadal: chief of the Ordovices
Calgacos: Caledonian chief
Cari: village girl on High Isle, sister of Adaryn
Catumanus: Orkney priest
Celyn: one of Calgacos's Kindred
Ceridwen: daughter of Calgacos
Coran: harper of Calgacos's household
Curlew: girl from sidhe of Llanmelin
Dai: one of Calgacos's Kindred
Efa: wife of Rhion
Eirian: Orkney girl
Emrys: chief of rival clan of Caledones
Eogan: one of Eirian's brothers
Faelan: father of Eirian
Goewyn: younger daughter of Maldwyn
Guennola: original name of Faustus's mother
Hafren: Damnonii girl stolen by Idris
Idris: one of Calgacos's Kindred
Kite: one of the highland Old Ones, of the sidhe of Bryn Dan
Lorn: trader
Madoc: Orkney innkeeper
Maldwyn: smallholder of Calgacos's Kindred, neighbor of Idris
Nemausos: Druid of Emrys's clan
Ossuticos: chieftain of the Venicones

Otter: one of the highland Old Ones, of the sidhe of Bryn Dan

Rhion: one of Calgacos's Kindred, brother to Aelwen, and husband of Efa

Salmon: Curlew's brother, of the sidhe of Llanmelin

Selisoc: young smallholder of Calgacos's clan

Tuathal Techtmar: exiled claimant to high kingship of Inis Fáil (Roman Hibernia)

Ula: young smallholder of Calgacos's clan

Vellaunos: Druid high priest

Wren: one of the highland Old Ones, of the sidhe of Bryn Dan

Prologue

Spring, 831 ab urbe condita, from the founding of the City, in the ninth year of the Emperor Vespasian

The hired mourners trailed behind the carriage with the casket, wailing women in black who set Faustus's teeth on edge. The procession followed the wagon road from the house to the line of yews along the avenue, where generations of his family lay in their urns and marble boxes, topped with votive stones, the oldest of them slowly being swallowed by the grass. Faustus, in a dark gray mourning toga, with his sister Silvia beside him in a somber gown, followed the casket ahead of the shrieking mourners. He had not wanted them but Silvia had insisted. What would people think if they didn't hire professional mourners to see their father off? They had had them for Mother, of course, not two months since, but Father had directed that funeral as he had directed everything else on the farm.

Now he was dead and Faustus had two choices – accede to Father's dying wishes and let the farm swallow him too, rooting him inexorably into the ground like the tombstones, or flee. The appointment to the army's Centuriate training camp in Rome was tucked into the gray folds of his toga, a talisman against changing his mind.

Two days after the funeral he signed the bill of sale that extricated him, despite Silvia's weepy protestations. The chickens in the farmyard bobbed about his ankles in a little brown-feathered tide as Faustus threw them a last handful of grain to remember him by.

I

"You didn't have to sell it. Manlius would have married me without a dowry." Silvia twisted her mantle round and round her hands until they looked like a chrysalis, or some hapless infant swaddled by a murderous nurse.

Faustus unwound her. "Of course he would." He wouldn't and Faustus knew it. Manlius wanted Silvia but he couldn't afford to marry a woman with no money.

"The farm has been in our family for two hundred years," Silvia sniffled, now using the mantle to wipe her nose. "What would Father think? It was his life."

"I don't know what Father thinks because he hasn't popped up from the Underworld to tell me." Father had been going to borrow money to get Silvia married. If Faustus had done that, he would never have got free.

The price of the farm had taken care of a dowry, and Silvia was to be duly handed off to Manlius, up-and-coming quaestor of Narbo Martius. Faustus had kept just enough cash to buy a good horse. The slaves would go with Silvia, except for Paullus, who regarded the change as an improvement on tending cows.

The Silvii had been well enough off by Gaulish provincial standards until Faustus was nineteen, when Silvius Valerianus had made a few investments that he had later described as unwise, and his wife had called insane. She had died shortly thereafter of a fever, and Faustus's father had followed, as if her loss was a final dispiriting event that he could not manage. His parting words had invoked his wife's name, with more loss in his voice than Faustus would have expected. Faustus had loved his mother but she had not always been an easy woman. She had come into the household as a slave after Claudius Caesar's invasion of Britain. Silvius Valerianus had bought her for a housekeeper, and then freed and married her. Faustus's father had been big-boned and ruddy, with light brown hair and a heavy brow. His mother was pale and dark-haired with a fine-boned face like a cat's. Faustus had his father's height but he owed much of his looks to her, as well as the promised post in the army. She had taught her children her language, despite his father's objections, telling Silvius that she wanted someone to speak to in her own tongue when he complained that she was a Roman now. Being a Roman was much better than being a Briton, Faustus had had to agree with that, but there was something lyrical in his mother's speech that had made him want to learn it. And as it happened, that had proved useful.

Theirs was neither a family of equestrian rank nor one with a tradition of army service and he would likely have had no chance at an immediate commission but gone in as a rank-and-filer to work his way up, except for the fact that he spoke his mother's language. There was a need for British-speaking officers now that Agricola, new governor of Britain, was planning to finish off the conquest of that province.

–

"All right, you lazy worms, take those jumps again, this time bareback. An officer who can't stay on his horse in an emergency doesn't belong in the army! Anyone who hasn't fallen off, line up for pilum practice afterward, and then we'll have a nice march down to the harbor. You've got six months for me to turn you into Centuriate material."

Faustus took his horse over the last jump and arrived still mounted, unlike a number of his fellows. If there was one thing to be grateful to the farm for, it was that he could ride practically anything. And any exercise, even a twenty-mile march along the Tiber to Ostia harbor and back, was better than a life spent trying to be the brother who had died young, the one who should have inherited the farm, the one who had wanted it. Instead Faustus now served a great Empire to which everyone from the seal people of the northern islands to the little djinns of the eastern desert paid fealty. Or so he was told daily during training by Mucius, a muscular centurion who looked as if he had personally conquered all of it, though he had perhaps exaggerated a bit about the northern islands, now the goal of Governor Agricola's campaign.

There was only one small fly in his wine cup. On his first night in the training barracks in Rome, Faustus had been too exhausted to move, thanks to Mucius, and too excited to sleep. The combination induced a dreamlike haze in which he imagined what his father would have had to say about it all and, possibly as a result, saw his father standing at the foot of his bed. He was dressed in a toga, one arm slightly raised, the image of the paterfamilias. His form was transparent, like the first wash of a painting with details to come later, but his voice was clear.

"You have disgraced us."

Faustus lay perfectly still and whispered, "Go away."

"Two hundred years, Faustus. Two hundred years that farm has been in our family, and you have sold it to an upstart with no breeding to go and play soldier." The buyer had been a freedman looking to come up in the world. Despite his wife's status, Silvius Valerianus didn't approve of other people changing their station in life.

Faustus sat up, now more irritated than afraid and pretty sure the apparition was imaginary. "That's what Silvia said. Go haunt her." Paullus, asleep on a pallet at the foot of his cot, was snoring lightly and seemed oblivious.

"I shall never find rest," his father said dolefully, "because of you." He faded into a wisp of mist and then disappeared entirely.

In the morning Faustus was not entirely sure what he had seen, and Paullus gave no indication of having heard anything. On the other hand, Paullus was bound to feel that it was no part of his duties to talk to ghosts, particularly not the old master. Any further contemplation was swiftly dispelled by Mucius, who set them to hacking with wooden swords at straw men and then at each other, finally with real swords once he thought they could avoid accidental death. They learned to shoot a bow and arrow and use a sling, on the theory that an officer should be able to do anything that the men under him might

4

be trained to do. Those who couldn't swim learned. Most of the legions' ranks couldn't, but an officer was expected to rise to any occasion. Growing up on the farm gave Faustus an advantage over the City-bred candidates there as well, and Faustus won Mucius's grudging approval.

"You're to be posted to Britain. I was there twenty years ago, under Agricola too, when we put down the Iceni uprising. The cursed place is almost all water, between rain and bog and a river in the way anywhere you want to go. Your mother was British, wasn't she?"

"Yes, sir."

"Well, that'll be a blessing or a curse, take your pick." Mucius's eyes snapped suddenly to the helmet in Faustus's hand. "Where's your cap?"

Faustus made a feeble attempt to conceal the helmet behind his back. "It's hot, sir." They had been sweating on the drill field in the summer heat. The padded helmet liner was soaked and made his head itch.

Mucius glared at him. "And the first time someone manages to land a blow on you, your head will ring like a gong, or better yet you'll have a rivet through your skull. Go put it on and do three runs around the field to fix that in your mind."

Faustus, penitent, set off at a jog while Mucius propped himself against the wall of hay bales his charges had been besieging, and watched to make sure he did it. It was the first of a number of lessons Faustus imagined he was going to thank Mucius for later, assuming he survived.

I

Isca Silurum

Autumn

Six months later, Faustus Silvius Valerianus, newly minted centurion of the lowest rank, leaned his arms on the railing of the transport *Salacia*, goddess of the salt water, and watched the British coast, marked by the tower of Rutupiae Light, rise across the gray swells as *Salacia* pitched in the Channel current.

Paullus had seemed impressed by their adventures so far, particularly since cows were not involved, although just now he was throwing up over the railing. The thundering from below deck was probably Arion the horse expressing his own displeasure at the sea voyage. He was a sturdy bay with one white boot and a blaze that looked as if someone had poured milk down his face, and ordinarily had the unflappable nature of an equestrian statue, but he didn't like boats.

The *Salacia* docked at Rutupiae to deposit a military tribune posted to the Ninth Legion at Eburacum. It then backed oars and put out again for the coastwise journey around the westward tip of Britain to the Sabrina estuary and the new fort at Isca Silurum, destination of most on board.

Paullus pushed a shock of wheat-straw hair off his forehead and gave the sea, and Faustus, a baleful glare, which Faustus discounted since Paullus had been lounging around the training barracks for months with nothing to do but polish armor, while Faustus had been getting whacked in the ribs with a wooden sword when he didn't get his shield up in time.

6

"Don't look at the water, look at the coast. It helps." He waved an arm at the white chalk cliffs and the twin lighthouses rising imposingly from the headlands as they sailed past Dubris.

"It doesn't," Paullus said. "Likely I'll die and then where will you be?"

"Polishing my own armor." Faustus grinned. "So don't." The fact that he wasn't seasick himself convinced him that he had done the right thing. If he hadn't, surely he would have been? Westward past the shoals off Vectis the chalk cliffs began to change to stone and farther on along the rocky western shore there were dolphins in the water. That was probably a good sign too; dolphins were lucky. Life would be more promising for Faustus than ever before, were it not for the fact that his father had continued to talk to him, usually at night.

By the time *Salacia* headed up the Sabrina estuary on the incoming tide, Paullus had failed to die and was even acquiring some semblance of sea legs and a return of his natural cheerfulness, despite the fact that it was raining and had been since they had rounded Belerium Promontory. They both looked curiously through the rain at the pale green lowlands that slid by as the ship made her way upriver, and at the darker green hills lifting into mist above them where the Isca River flowed into the Sabrina. Here they took aboard a river pilot who brought them into the harbor at Isca Silurum in the late afternoon, after a swearing match with the helmsman of a liburnian from the Fleet. The passengers, mostly auxiliary recruits, began to be collected by their commanders and shouted into formation. The dock was crowded with sailors unloading oil jars and wine, and taking on tin from the mines. Faustus collected Arion from the hold and Paullus shouldered both his own belongings and his master's.

Isca Fortress, home base of the Second Legion Augusta, was new and raw looking but imposing, built of stone and timber, and roofed with tile. Its vicus, the civilian settlement that accreted to almost any military base, spread about its feet in a ragtag hem of taverns, food stalls, whorehouses, and sellers of almost anything else a soldier might want, from bronze pots to sheepskin leggings. The town was well enough established that a parade of gray tombstones lined either side of the road, resting places of civilian and military alike. Burial within inhabited land was forbidden by law and every Roman settlement was soon edged with its own gravestones. The paved streets were slick with runoff but the rain appeared to be doing nothing to slow the usual business of Isca. A cohort of the Augusta splashed its way through the fortress gates in parade formation, returning from patrol along the eastward road from Venta Silurum, new capital of the recently pacified Silures.

At the gate, the sentry on duty returned Faustus's salute, fist to chest, and passed him through on inspection of his orders. At the Principia at the fort's center he presented the orders again to the optio in charge, who thumbed the tablet open, squinted at the emperor's cypher and welcomed him to the Second Legion. "You'll find your century in barracks, I think, so look up your commander, that's Caesius Ursus, and let him know you're here."

Caesius Ursus, commander of the Seventh Cohort, seemed pleased to have him, which was gratifying until Faustus discovered that it was because his predecessor had fallen into a bog and not been found.

"Your quarters are at the end of the last row," Ursus said, having delivered this information. He was a stocky man somewhere in his twenties, with a disfigured ear and a more impressive scar running down the side of his neck into his scarf. "There's a stall for your horse there or you can stable him in the vicus. Your century's assigned patrol to Burrium and back tomorrow. They've been allowed to grow lax so be sure you get them properly under your thumb at the start. Always begin as you mean to go on, Centurion Valerianus." He nodded a clear dismissal.

The quarters proved to be a trio of small whitewashed rooms, with a bed in one and a desk in another. The third appeared to be the horse stall. The room with the bed also contained a brazier, presumably for cooking since the floor was warm, indicating that the barracks were heated by hypocaust. That would be useful since Paullus was learning to cook, or at least to get things hot. Faustus gave him a handful of coins to buy provisions and sat down on the bed, wondering uneasily what on earth he had done.

A head poked itself around the doorframe. "You're the new one for the sixth century," it said. "I'm Galerius, fourth century." The head came all the way into the room attached to a lanky frame topped with a dripping shock of dun-colored hair. "Welcome to West Britain, where the rain falls all year. I hear you're half British so you may not mind."

"I don't think it's an inbred preference," Faustus said. "Will you sit?" He pointed at one of the rickety chairs that also furnished the room.

Galerius settled in it gingerly. "Glaucus was hard on chairs. Your predecessor. A portly man. No wonder he sank so fast." He caught Faustus's appalled expression and grinned. "He was awful, he let his men go slack because they curried favor with him. He had pets who brought him little presents, and too heavy a hand with the vine staff on the rest. You'll have your hands full, but frankly we aren't mourning him. That kind of thing endangers the whole legion."

"The commander said something about beginning as I mean to go on," Faustus said.

"Sound advice. We've just gone into winter quarters so you'll have several months to bring them round. In the mean-time, consider me the welcome committee. You'll want to eat. Leave your slave to settle you in, and we'll get something and I'll show you the sights."

Accompanying Galerius seemed as reasonable a thing to do as any, and he was hungry. Faustus shook the water off the scarlet woolen folds of his cloak and put it back on. The rain let up as they passed through the western gate, and Galerius

9

turned them toward the river in the late summer twilight, as a skein of starlings swooped overhead and then settled noisily to roost in the trees and under the bridge that linked the fort to the opposite bank. Near the bridge a tavern sign sporting the Capricorn badge of the Augusta hung from an oak tree and the squat timber building beneath it appeared to be a favorite of the legion and the Isca auxiliaries. Galerius ordered a cup of wine from the heavyset man behind the counter, probably an ex-legionary, and Faustus a cup of native beer and a bowl of the stew that was simmering in a pot set into the counter. They sat and Galerius introduced him to various passers-by while he ate his stew, an aromatic mixture thick with chunks of venison, barley and vegetables.

He met several other officers of the Augusta, a prefect of the Batavian auxiliaries, and a tall youngster with a lordly attitude whom Galerius introduced as "Tuathal Techtmar, high king of Tara in Hibernia… if he can only get back there."

Tuathal, a dark-haired boy in a civilian tunic and checkered cloak of good wool, gave Galerius a look that said he was tiresome and his jokes were old.

"Oh, sit down and tell Valerianus your tale," Galerius said. "It's a good one and mostly true."

Tuathal pulled a chair over and sat, propping his elbows on the table and his chin on his long pale hands. Faustus saw that he was wearing a pair of gold armbands enameled with the figures of running horses that looked to be worth several years' pay, and wondered if the boy was safe out here alone.

Galerius seemed to read his thoughts. "Aside from being Agricola's pet, he's handy with a knife. He also plays latrunculi with the frontier scouts and wins. I wouldn't play rota with them."

Rota was a child's game. Faustus remembered Centurion Mucius's parting advice: *Don't gamble with the frontier scouts.*

"It is all true," Tuathal said with dignity. "Elim mac Conrach overthrew my father with the help of the lesser kings when I was an infant, and my mother fled home to her people among the Epidii, taking me before he could maim me. She sent me to your governor here some two weeks ago when she was dying."

"Maim you? Why not kill you?"

"He risked the gods' anger already by killing the true king. All he would need do would be to put my eye out or cut off a finger, and I would never rule. The kings of Inis Fáil are the land and the land is the king. A maimed leader brings a soured land – crops fail, the fish leave the rivers, and the cattle dry up."

"Meanwhile he petitions Agricola to restore him to his throne," Galerius said. "We don't know what Agricola thinks about it but he hasn't thrown him out of the camp."

"Agricola keeps me as something between honored guest and hostage, while we both think how we may be useful to the other." Tuathal raised his hand and a girl with a long brown braid and an apron over her woolen gown set a cup of wine in front of him. She didn't ask for money and Faustus suspected that Tuathal's tavern bill ended in the governor's account book.

Faustus thought about kings and land while he drank another cup of beer. "If Agricola – if Rome – should put you on the throne at Tara, will that not obligate you in certain ways?" he asked.

"There is always a price, Centurion."

"Indeed there is." Faustus thought about more beer but fortuitously the mailed sandals of the Watch clicked by outside the open door. Faustus and Galerius both rose.

"It's late and the *Wake Up* trumpet comes early," Galerius said.

Faustus put a hand on Tuathal's shoulder for a moment. "I am sorry for the loss of your mother." Tuathal looked startled.

"Thank you. No one thinks of that usually."

"Mine died not so long since," Faustus said.

While Galerius made his final round through his century's barracks, Faustus did the same to announce his presence among them and the coming patrol in the morning. Ten or twelve of them were gathered on the barracks floor, betting on a dice game. They seemed unimpressed by his arrival.

"Who is optio?" he inquired. A century's optio was second-in-command.

One of the men in the ring looked up. "Isn't one."

"What do you mean there isn't one? And stand up, all of you." Faustus hefted his vine staff with some meaning behind it and they straggled to their feet.

"Dead."

"And your centurion didn't replace him?"

No one answered.

"Go to bed," Faustus said. He looked at the jumble of armor and gear that cluttered the barracks haphazardly. "I expect to see you in proper kit tomorrow, so if that needs work, hop to it."

Faustus turned on his heel and returned to his quarters, where he found his father's shade sitting at the head of the bed.

Paullus was asleep on his pallet at the foot of it and seemed as oblivious as he had been during previous visitations. The form on the bed was translucent, pale and nacreous as mother-of-pearl, like a figure molded in glass.

"Two hundred years," said his father's shade. Or his own hysterical mind, Faustus was never sure which. "That was our land. Our purpose."

The kings are the land and the land is the king. "It was my brother's purpose," Faustus protested.

"Your brother is dead."

Faustus had been ten, his brother thirteen, with Silvia between them. Marcus Silvius Valerianus the Younger had dived into water that was shallower than it looked and broken his neck. Faustus, whose name ironically meant fortunate, had become the heir.

It had been one of those crystalline days that glowed around the edges. There had been a drought and the dry air somehow polished everything. The surface of the swimming hole was gilded with it. The fish below flickered like little coins among the stones at the bottom.

"Look! Look at me!" Marcus capered on the top of their diving rock, an upturned pillar that rose from the scrub willow along the banks. "I am Horatius Cocles on the Pons Sublicius and all the world belongs to me!"

"Marcus, come down from there!" Silvia shouted at him. "It's not very deep today!"

"Get out of my way! It's always deep enough." He poised on his toes, waved his arms at the sky, and dove down through the shining air.

Afterward, Faustus remembered only the two of them pulling Marcus from the water, and the slow, cold realization that he was dead. Then the wailing and the mourning and the funeral and his mother's weeping. And his father's lecture: Now he, Faustus, was the heir, and it was all up to him. He was the end point of all the Silvii and their ambitions. The ancestors would look to him to raise the family even further in the world; he felt them settle on his shoulders like leaden birds.

"We couldn't have kept it," he said now to his father's shade.

"You could have." That was true and Faustus knew it. It would have been a struggle, but it could have been done. Instead he had sold it and run.

"It was too much," he said pleadingly. "The farm. And Sulpicia." Sulpicia was a lovely girl, beautiful, suitable, and the thought of spending his life with her made his skin itch. Her father had broken it off when the money had been lost.

"Sulpicius would have come around," his father said. "When you had done your duty."

Faustus knew that. Sulpicius's daughter had been just another tendril of the family bindweed reaching out for him. He glanced at Paullus, half expecting him to wake, but he didn't. He looked back at the head of the bed but his father had disappeared in the way that he always had when his point had been made.

Faustus was awake before the morning trumpet, itchy with the coming day. He dressed with care, noting gratefully that Paullus, who gave no sign of having observed anything untoward in the night, had polished every speck of rain marks from his lorica, greaves and helmet, and dried and brushed his cloak. He slipped his tunic over his head and held up his arms while Paullus dropped the leather harness tunic over it. Faustus buckled his lorica on, adjusting his scarf so it padded the edges of the plates. Paullus fastened his greaves and handed him his helmet, topped with a centurion's crosswise crest, and Faustus knotted the strap under his chin.

Paullus gave him his vine staff too, and Faustus tucked it under his arm. "Saddle Arion, but then I want you to come with me to take him back to the barracks. I have a point to make."

It was cold and the river and camp were layered with a dank fog like the breath of Boreas. The sixth century was formed up raggedly in the mist, an unsettling welcome for an officer with his first command. A century held eighty men and the sixth was largely up to strength with a paper count of seventy-seven. One of those was in the hospital with a broken jaw, undoubtedly from a tavern brawl. The missing three had appeared on the Dead List after the last skirmish with the Silures, and three was a disastrously large number for one century to lose when Roman casualties had been otherwise light. The remainder eyed their new commander sullenly as he regarded them from Arion's back.

"Form up!" he snapped, and the uneven lines straightened somewhat. "You're appalling. We may march to Burrium twice if you can't get the hang of it." His eyes roved over them. "The man in the rear with his chin strap untied has until I can count to two to get it fastened." The culprit hastily fumbled the straps into a knot. "What's your name?"

"Septimus," he said. And "Sir," as Faustus glared at him.

14

Faustus dismounted, handed Arion's reins to Paullus, and hefted the vine staff. "March! Patrol formation!" A centurion fought on foot with his men in the line but he generally rode on the march. Since Faustus wanted to make a point, he intended to march with them. "One! Two!"

They set out in not particularly good order, but he had their attention. Faustus strode beside them, calling cadence from midway down the column, being disinclined to put all of them at his back. He had wondered once or twice if Glaucus had had any help getting into that bog.

Their way followed the Isca valley west of the river, part of the network of roads and forts built by Agricola's predecessor, Julius Frontinus. It ran between low stony hills, cleared on both sides to a prudent distance and tufted with late summer grass going to seed, but beyond the cleared land, forests of oak and ash swallowed everything. Fog wreathed the surrounding slopes and masked the ridge before them as the road rose up it, so that it felt as if they might be marching into some Otherworld. There was no sound but hobnailed boots on stone, the chink of armor, and Faustus counting cadence at the steady twenty-mile-a-day pace of the legions. Septimus, he noted, didn't seem able to keep in step, and dropped his pilum twice. A sparrowhawk perched on a milepost was the only other being they saw, although Faustus thought of the recently pacified Silures, whatever grudge they might nurse, and the darkness of the woods.

The fog burned off into a sky of shifting cloud like oystershell by the time they crested the ridge and descended again toward Burrium. As they came to the river a family of otters popped their heads up from the bank, bristly faces curious, and then slid into the shining silver water. Faustus envied them their lithe grace, unarmored, unadorned, unworried.

Burrium, once the Twentieth Legion headquarters, was now a works depot for the iron mines, housing only a small auxiliary garrison. Faustus reported their arrival to the commander there and turned his men loose to eat a noon meal of army biscuit and dried meat.

"Any trouble on the way?" the commander asked.

"None," Faustus said. *Except for my century.* They had all pulled their helmets off, which was forbidden in enemy territory, or indeed when on any patrol at all. He shouted at them to put them back on.

"Those are Glaucus's lot, aren't they?" the commander asked, noting the century standard resting against the wall of the ironworks baths. "I heard what happened to him. It was up by Blestium. Frankly I was surprised they didn't all blunder in after him. You'll have your hands full."

"Undoubtedly." Faustus swung around as a spate of angry voices erupted from the men lounging against the wall. Two of them dove at each other, thrashing on the ground in a clatter of armor plate.

"Stop that and form up!"

They ignored him and he saw Septimus wade into the fight and pull one of them loose from the other by the back of his helmet. The second sat up, spitting out a tooth. Faustus laid about him with his vine staff, first one and then the other, and then roared "Stand up!" They got up and he glared at them.

"Are you Roman soldiers or unweaned puppies? Get into formation, all of you. I don't care whether you've eaten or not. And if you have to piss, you can piss down your leg while you march."

He turned on Septimus. "Septimus, do you want to live until your enlistment is up?"

"Not likely I'm going to, is it?" Septimus gave him a black look. "We lost three last battle…" – he paused, just long enough to be insubordinate – "…sir."

"You won't if you don't stop fucking around," Faustus informed him. "I know you're able to keep step. If you drop your pilum again I'll ram it up your ass. Now march!"

They were halfway back to Isca, coming down the slope of the ridge above the fort, when one of the men in the rear shouted at him. Faustus turned around in a fury, ready to use the vine staff again.

"Look, sir! Behind us!"

He pointed and Faustus squinted his eyes. Somewhere in the mountains to the north there was a beacon burning on a signal tower, and the faint glow of another behind it. While they watched, a courier on a lathered horse went by them at a gallop.

They marched back at double time and when they got to Isca, Faustus took the century standard and pulled its insignia off: three gold medallions of honor, the century's number, and the open silver hand that represented loyalty.

"When I think you deserve it, you'll get this back," he told them, handing the empty pole to the signifer. He strode off with the rest under his arm.

The fort seemed extraordinarily busy and Centurion Ursus's optio met Faustus at his quarters. "Commander wants to see you," he said. "Five minutes ago."

Faustus nodded. That courier had not been carrying good news. He put the century's insignia on his bed. Paullus raised his eyebrows. "Hide those."

Ursus looked up from his desk as Faustus came through the open door. "Centurion Valerianus, close that please, and sit down. I need to have a conversation with you."

Faustus saluted and sat. The cohort commander's quarters were somewhat larger than his own and contained chairs that did not threaten to disintegrate, but were otherwise equally spartan. Ursus's armor and helmet hung in the corner and a slave was cleaning mud from a pair of his boots. Ursus dismissed him.

"The Ordovices attacked a garrison to the north of here, and the governor is pulling us out of winter quarters to go after them. Are those men of yours going to hold? Or should I leave them in Isca?"

Faustus swallowed. "Is 'I don't know' an acceptable answer? I've only had them for a day." *And this is my first command, Mithras help me.*

"It's an honest answer, which is what I expect from anyone under me."

"May I ask you a question in return, sir?"

Ursus nodded.

"Why didn't you replace Centurion Glaucus?"

"We try not to second guess junior officers. It's bad for cohesion. In any case, he replaced himself." Ursus sighed. "But I should have."

"They'll hold, sir. I'll see to it." If he stayed behind, it would haunt the rest of his career. And if they didn't hold, he probably wouldn't be alive to know about it, so there was that comfort.

Faustus headed for the barracks. The men jumped when he appeared, which he thought was progress. "Septimus!"

Septimus put down the armor he had been polishing.

"Come outside."

The fort was like an overturned anthill now, frantic with preparation. Faustus pulled Septimus out of the path of a catapult carriage. "We're going into the line. I had it from Ursus, and I don't intend to disgrace the legion I just joined. Why didn't Centurion Glaucus replace the optio who was killed?"

"Played us all off against each other," Septimus said disgustedly, "waiting to see who he'd pick."

"Who should have been next?"

"Aculeo. He's your guard commander. He's the one in hospital."

"Oh, for Mithras's sake." Faustus considered. Septimus was the only one who had shown initiative of any kind, even if it was mostly to see what he could get away with. "All right then." He pointed a finger at him. "You're promoted. Now straighten up and help me get this century into shape."

–

Julius Agricola, consular legate and governor of the province of Britain, spread a sheaf of maps across the table in his office in the Isca Principia. He had a strong-boned, fox-like face, narrow at the chin, with dark heavy brows, knitted just now not in irritation but because he was listening carefully. Domitius Longinus, legate of the Second Augusta, bent his muscular shoulders over the map.

"Ordovice territory is here." Longinus swept two fingers north and northwest above Isca, across the inverted V's of mountains. "Cadal's fortress is here, at Bryn Epona. You will need siege weapons to take it, but it can be done. We sewed up the last of the Silures here in the south last year and this summer the legions out of Deva and Viroconium have made a start on fencing in the Ordovices in the same way. My guess is that Cadal heard that the governorship has changed and he is seeing what he may try with the new one."

"That will be a mistake," Agricola said. "What is the relationship between the Silures and the Ordovices? Julius Frontinus's report spoke of some attempt at alliance in the past."

"Not now," Longinus said. "They are old enemies and spent most of their councils plotting to betray each other until it all fell to pieces. They share a common tongue, like most of Britain, but the Silures are other somehow. It's said they intermarried at the beginning with the little dark people who live in the hills, and you can see that in them. But their last king gave up the kingship to the current one in a way that can't be broken, in exchange for peace with Rome."

"Frontinus told me about that," Agricola said. "It made my skin crawl."

"It's an old ritual," Longinus said. "The death of the king to buy life for the tribe. But at any rate, the Silures won't trouble us."

"Very well. I intend to take a sizable detachment of the Second under your command, please, and to pull the bulk of the Second Adiutrix and the Twentieth out of their winter beds as well. Plus the Batavian auxiliaries." He rolled up the map.

"What about our young guest?" Longinus inquired.

"Bring him along. It may be instructive."

When Longinus had left, Agricola unrolled another map, this one of the entire province to anyone's best guess. It faded into questionable accuracy in the north, the coastline, if there was one, uncertain. The mapmaker had drawn a trio of sea serpents frolicking in the margins. Whatever was up there Agricola intended to bring it into the Empire and under Roman governance, a campaign likely to require equal parts of military persuasion and diplomacy. On his first posting to Britain as a young tribune he had seen what happened when the natives were mishandled. That was not a mistake that would be made again. Settling the Ordovices in a way that made them more content to look to Rome than to their defeated Silure enemies would be the start.

The next morning Faustus paraded his charges in the pouring rain for pilum practice, followed by a ten-mile march at double time with full packs. Septimus called the cadence in a tone of exaggerated rectitude, but he never missed a beat. On their return, they did an hour's extra drill while Galerius's fourth century hooted at them and asked where they had lost their standard.

"When you no longer look like a troop of drunken maenads, you may have it back," Faustus informed them. That would have to be soon since word was that they were to march in three days. A relief column had gone out immediately, but to ready an entire army for campaign was not an instantaneous affair. Faustus said a grateful prayer to Minerva, goddess of war and strategy, for that.

The next day they drilled again, on the rough ground beside the northern road, Faustus calling rapidly alternating commands for line formation, wedge formation, pull back, advance, tortoise, circle, and fall back, until they were hopelessly tangled. Then they did it again. By the end of the following day they were beginning to eye their centurion with considerably more respect.

Galerius found him in the fortress baths at nightfall, soaking aching muscles in the hot pool.

"You're the talk of the cohort," he commented. "When are you going to give them back their standard?"

"Tonight at prayers," Faustus grunted. "I'll have to, if Ursus's information is right, and I am told it always is."

"It is. My watch commander came back with the orders an hour ago."

"That reminds me. Aculeo is out of the hospital. Do I break him and give his post to someone else? I don't know him." He was reluctant to put that decision on Septimus.

"I'd try him out," Galerius said. "From what I've seen of him, he's the type that just needs a steady hand and an assignment. Glaucus didn't give him either, so he took to getting drunk instead."

Faustus grinned. "He should be cured of that by now. The surgeon wired his teeth together. Today's the first day he's been able to drink without a straw."

"All the same," he informed Aculeo the following morning, "one misstep and I will break you down to regular pay, and you'll need your jaw wired again, am I clear?"

"Yes, Centurion." Aculeo looked pious and attentive. He had no doubt been briefed by Septimus.

The century was gathered with the rest of its cohort and the others of the Second Legion for evening prayers at the standards. The great gilded Eagle of the legion rose above the rest, wings swept back as if about to take flight. The standard of the sixth century of the Seventh Cohort stood among the rest, although its signifer had been greeted with snickers from the other standard-bearers. The legate, who was fully aware of the sixth century's trials, glared at them and they subsided. With the governor, he made the legion's invocation to Jupiter Best and Greatest, to Juno and Minerva, and to Mars, the ancient god of war and mythological father of the Roman people.

Faustus had always given the Empire's official gods their due, but there was something about the prayers at the standards that went deeper. The army was a country in itself, one to which he now belonged more surely than he had belonged to the land in Gaul.

When it was over, and the haruspex had pronounced the omens good for the coming battle, he went with Galerius and a few other officers to the Temple of Mithras outside the fortress walls to make prayers there as well. Faustus's worship of this soldiers' god had begun during his training days, and he had found in the mysteries of the Bull-Slayer and Unconquered Sun a sense of belonging that was new to him. Like the prayers of the standards, it had felt like slipping on another piece of armor. Mars was every soldier's god, who ruled over War itself, but the worship of Mithras was personal.

The last light of the day sifted through the oculus in the ceiling to light the figure above the altar, sitting astride the great bull, his knife in his hand.

"Unconquered Sun, Redeemer, grant us your aid and inter-cession, and take our pleas before the Lord of Boundless Time. As you slew the Bull for our sakes, take now our sacrifice, freely given, and grant us strength." The cloaked and hooded figure of the Sun Runner made the sacrifice of a hare, newly caught, and the worshippers went in twos to dip their fingers in the blood, Faustus with Galerius.

"Mithras, lord of armies, grant us victory."

"Mithras, let me do right by them."

By the time Faustus went back to his quarters, it was full night, with a thin horn moon low in the sky. *Go away*, he thought at the faint opalescent figure that hovered in the doorway. *This isn't your business*. It dissipated, as if in agreement.

II

Demetrius of Tarsus

Governor Agricola ate a late meal in the Praetorium of Isca Fortress with his wife and daughter and the tribune Cornelius Tacitus, whom his daughter Julia had recently married. Domitius Longinus, the Augusta's legate, had joined them as they were for the time being sharing the commander's quarters in the Praetorium. Extra couches had been pulled about a communal table laden with small dishes and the officers had removed their breastplates in deference to the upholstery.

"Are you positive you don't wish to go to Aquae Sulis, my dear?" Agricola inquired of his wife one more time.

Domitia Decidiana shook her head. "Julia and I will be much happier not shifting house three times in a season," she said firmly and Agricola let it go. A long and affectionate marriage had taught him when an opinion was not going to alter. His first posting to Britain had been before he was married but since then she had followed him, even when Julia was a child, to every country to which the Empire had sent him.

"Constantius Silanus's daughter and her aunt are here," Julia said. "They've said we will be quite comfortable." She dipped her fingers in a dish of olives and baked fish. "Particularly now that Theodosius has arrived." The governor's cook had followed the family with the rest of the household and a mountain of trunks.

"Her standard of comfort may be somewhat laxer than yours," Longinus said, "given that she's followed her father

23

about his surgery since she was old enough to walk. I think she was twelve when her mother died and the old aunt isn't a match for her, frankly. But she's a nice girl."

Tribune Tacitus still looked dubious and Julia decided to nip in the bud any excessive pretensions of authority, as her mother had advised. "We will be equally comfortable here with you in the field as with you in residence," she said, "since your presence, although pleasurable, does not magically change the surroundings. And really, it's quite nice." The floor was pleasantly warm and tiled with a pattern of African beasts and geometric borders, and the walls were painted with fool-the-eye columns and draperies.

"Give up, my boy," Agricola said, holding out his cup for a slave to add a measured amount of wine and water. "And yes — what is it?"

A headquarters optio had put his head around the dining room door. The Praetorium was not normally his territory and he looked apologetic. "There is a person, Governor."

Agricola raised his dark brows. "What sort of a person?"

"A person who tells me he has been sent by the emperor, and has, I regret to say, a letter to prove it."

"Oh dear. Well, you had best send him in."

The diners regarded the optio's retreating back with interested speculation, tempered by a certain unease. Whatever the emperor wanted the governor to do with this person, he would have to do, however inconvenient, and it was practically assured to be inconvenient on the eve of a campaign.

The optio reappeared with a small man in a traveling cloak and a felt hat.

"Greetings to the senatorial legate of Britain! I am Demetrius of Tarsus, scholar and historian." The visitor held out a wooden tablet with a papyrus sheet enclosed between its covers.

Agricola's eyebrows went a bit higher as he read the message and duly noted Emperor Vespasian's personal seal. "The emperor requests me to give you all possible assistance to undertake a study of — native religion?"

24

"Indeed. I am to conduct research into all native gods but most particularly into Druidism, and to prepare a thorough report."

"Why?" Agricola asked.

Demetrius looked surprised. "Why, for the sake of knowledge."

"There have been many reports on the Druids," Agricola said. "From Governor Frontinus and others." The Druids were an ongoing nuisance, one of the few religions that Rome proscribed, for their constant incitement of rebellion.

"Military reports are often not conducted with a scholar's precision. I am, for instance, an expert on the cult of Apollo at Tarsus, my home city."

Agricola's eyes slid toward his wife. "We are marching in the morning on a difficult campaign. If you will await our return we will be happy to give you assistance."

"Certainly," Domitia said, with a certain sense of gritted teeth. "I feel sure we can make you comfortable in Isca. There are many good inns."

"No, indeed!" Demetrius looked excited. "If there is a campaign afoot, the timing is perfect. I shall accompany it. Where better to learn about the natives in their natural state?"

"The natives are quite dangerous in their natural state," Tacitus said.

"The pursuit of knowledge requires bravery of the heart," Demetrius said. "I shall go with you."

–

In the morning Demetrius appeared at daybreak astride the horse provided him from the cavalry barns, and seemed reasonably comfortable in the saddle. Agricola began to have a certain admiration for his tenacity. He suspected that Vespasian had acquiesced in Demetrius's request for an official letter mainly to get him out of his own helmet feathers. He made an odd companion beside Tuathal Techtmar, who seemed amused by his presence. Tuathal, in a red-and-blue checkered cloak, saffron shirt, and scarlet breeches, looked like an exotic bird beside the dark gray-green of Demetrius's cloak and hat. The prince's long dark hair hung down his back, confined at his forehead by a gold fillet. He had made no protest at accompanying the column, although he was probably aware that the governor was making a point about the inadvisability of crossing Rome.

Faustus sat astride Arion at the head of the sixth century, its standard newly restored, and watched the column form up around them. Nothing in his training had prepared him for the complexity of a Roman army on the march. The Batavian auxiliaries guarding the scouts and engineers were followed by the bulk of the Second Augusta detachment, more than half the legion, a sea of scarlet and polished steel under its gilded Eagle, bristling like a hedgehog with the deadly points of pila. The governor and legate rode at the detachment's head, with Tuathal and the odd little scholar who had attached himself to the governor. Behind the legion came the baggage carts, the hospital wagons, and the rumbling catapult carriages with the deadly machinery of the bolt-throwing scorpions and the great stone-throwers fastened to their beds.

The frontier scouts who had come and gone all week, appearing at dusk in disreputable native breeches and most sporting the brushy mustaches favored by the Britons, had reported that Cadal's warriors were gathering into the fortress at Bryn Epona and the outlying hold of Caer Gai, high in the wild territory of the Ordovices. Agricola had ordered the Second Adiutrix to move in from the north and the Twentieth Valeria Victrix from the east. The Augusta, the farthest away, would march up the lower river valleys to meet them. Between the three they would stitch a net to encircle Cadal's forces, and after that where there had once been an Ordovice hold, a Roman garrison camp would rise.

That was the speech that Faustus gave his century on the first night in camp, painting a picture of inevitable victory and the spoils that would accompany it, as the Ordovices were a wealthy people. The men of the sixth century had outwardly shaken off their sloth and sullenness, but the question was whether it would stick when it came to battle.

In the morning they pulled down the camp and slighted the defensive walls and ditch. The army left nothing behind it that might be useful to an enemy, current or future. Walls and ditch were easily built and dismantled again by five thousand men with shovels.

The farther northwestward they went, the wilder the land grew. Cadal's territory was a ragged, alien world stitched with swift, rocky rivers and sudden upthrust slopes whose peaks were suitable only for those creatures with wings; a land where a tribal lord might hold off even Rome, for a time. But during the months Cadal had argued over treaties and numbers and sureties with the Silures' king, the Romans had pushed their outposts farther and farther into his uplands. And Cadal's people had not got their grain harvest in before their king had decided to test the new governor. The villages they passed on the march were empty now, small gatherings of round, reed-thatched houses amid deserted fields and pastures. What the Roman army didn't reap from the abandoned fields they trampled under boots and hooves.

Couriers came and went between the three arms of Agricola's force and slowly the net wove tighter. Where they could they used the Ordovices' own trails, but those were often wide enough only for chariots or along a route too easily ambushed. Elsewhere the column followed the pioneers who cut trees and undergrowth. Behind them the legion dug the beginnings of a road, smoothing the way for the wagons through the emerald trees and water. There was water everywhere, in small streams and sudden unexpected falls, the ground under their feet covered with fern and soft moss like fine green wool. Oak and birch, hazel, rowan and ash filtered the sun through a green veil. Between them lay mounds of moss-covered stone like cobbles set by giants. As they neared Caer Gai, it rained as it had off and on along the march.

"There'll be moss on us in another day," Septimus said, sinking a pick into the wet ground.

Faustus leaned on his shovel to wipe the rain from his eyes. "Think of it as making it easier on the way back," he said. "And dig."

Septimus swung his pick again while beside them Aculeo leaned on a digging bar to uproot a rock the size of a goat. There was no point in arguing and in any case the centurion was down in the mud with them, which was a thing old Glaucus wouldn't have done.

—

Caer Gai sat on a low shoulder of land above a river, guarding the ford that opened the way north to Bryn Epona. An earthen bank and ditch surrounded it, and then an inner wall of stone encircling a cluster of round thatched buildings. Smoke rose above it, indicating a garrison waiting for them.

Ordinarily the auxiliaries began a battle, retiring when they had blunted the enemy's charge to let the legions come up for the finish. This time Agricola put the cohorts of the Augusta into the front line to make a short, swift point and give any who escaped something to tell Cadal. Faustus sent Arion to the rear with Paullus and took his position with his century in the second rank. *Mithras let me do right by them.*

"First time?" Galerius had asked that morning as the cohort was forming up. "You'll do. You've got them well in hand now, and you've got good instincts. Military family?"

"Farm boy."

Galerius's eyebrows had gone up into his helmet. He grinned at Faustus. "You'd be wasted on a farm."

Faustus didn't elaborate, but Galerius's words allayed some of the cloying fear that maybe he couldn't do this after all.

The first charge of Britons was always with chariots, Galerius had told him earlier, a terrifying avalanche of thundering horses and baying war horns that was designed to shatter the enemy's nerve. "We've learned a thing or two about chariots since they tried it on Julius Caesar," Galerius had said. "You just lock shields. Horses won't run into what looks to them like a solid wall." Nevertheless, Faustus had to remind himself of that as the Britons swept from the gates of Caer Gai, nearly naked but for blue war paint, howling war cries like demons out of Tartarus. Each chariot carried a spear-armed warrior and a driver capable of turning his lithe, maneuverable vehicle around on a pinpoint.

A sharp intake of breath from someone in the ranks made Septimus say, "Stow it. You've seen chariots. Get worried when they dismount. Lock shields."

"Hold your ground," Faustus said, trying to sound as if he too had done it before. There was a tight place in his stomach where Phobos, god of battle fear, had chosen that moment to twist his guts into a knot. He willed it to undo itself.

The front rank locked shields; the ranks behind locked them over their heads. The Ordovice spears rained down with very little effect except deafening noise when the line didn't shift and the chariot ponies shied away from the shield wall. The knot loosened just a little.

Now, Faustus thought as the chariot drivers retreated to the rear and their spearmen dismounted to rally the Ordovice foot soldiers moving up behind. Cadal's horsemen tangled on both flanks with the Roman cavalry, the bellowing of their war horns shattering the air. Faustus glanced at the century standard held above the signifer's head, and the cohort standard to their right, watching for signals from Ursus, who would be watching for signals from the legate. The Ordovices flung themselves against the line and the Augusta moved doggedly forward, their short stabbing swords at the advantage in close combat, their formation never shifting. If a man went down, he moved back through the ranks, on his own feet or with help, and a man from

29

the next rank moved up. The Britons were given to heroics in battle, each striving to kill the greatest number of the foe, to take heads and gain glory. It made them vulnerable, and once they were loosed on the enemy nearly uncontrollable. The Romans strove only not to break ranks and to move forward. Any man who broke from his comrades to be a hero would hear from his centurion afterward, if he lived.

Now Faustus found his focus narrowed to his century, and within it to the men at his left and right and the signifer beside him. A Briton with flaming hair and a torso painted with tribal marks hurled himself at Faustus, and Faustus brought his shield up to block the wildly swinging, longer sword of the Briton, stabbing with his short sword, the military gladius that was so efficient in close quarters, the muscle memory of his training blessedly instinctive. The Briton caught the blow on his own shield, smaller than Faustus's and round, with a shining gold boss. He had gold at his throat and on his arms as well, the sign of a lord, who took pride in wearing their wealth into battle. The Briton slammed his shield into Faustus's. It shuddered under the blow but it held. Faustus tilted his own up and caught the edge of the Briton's just enough to pull it slightly askew before the round edge slipped away. He got his sword up under the edge and stabbed. The Briton went down, and another took his place. Faustus stabbed at the new enemy, stabbed and took another step forward, while all around him the rest of the Augusta was doing the same, stab and step forward, stab and step forward.

The momentum began to shift. The Britons in the front ranks were being driven slowly back, and then not so slowly. Then they were in retreat. Agricola's point was made and the Roman trumpets sounded the *Pursuit*.

Even hunting a fleeing enemy, a Roman army did not break formation. "Hold your line!" Faustus shouted and to his gratification his men obeyed. Chasing a defeated enemy was the most likely time to lose them; Mucius had told him that.

When the call to *Halt Pursuit* sounded, the army made camp inside Caer Gai, its last before besieging Bryn Epona, where no doubt the final stragglers had gone. Septimus came to Faustus, as the smell of cooking meat, appropriated from the cattle pens of Caer Gai, filled the air. "I thought you'd want to see this, sir. Centurion Ursus has signed off on it already, grinning like an old fox."

Faustus held out his hand. It was the Dead List and there were only four names on it out of all the Augusta detachment, none of them from his century or even the Seventh Cohort.

Faustus grinned too. "Tell them all I am proud of them, but it's not to go to their heads." They had held. And so had he.

–

The next day they followed a native chariot track from Caer Gai to converge with the legionary detachments of the Twentieth and the Second Adiutrix and their auxiliaries below Bryn Epona.

Cadal's hold was impressive. Set into a ragged slope, seven concentric rings of mud-and-timber wall rose through six courtyards to the top level, linked by a banked chariot track which passed through each of the seven gates. Within were cattle pens and pony sheds, granaries, smithies, ovens, and a water supply from the stream that rushed down the slope, passing through the mid-level of the hold on its journey.

Agricola inspected it, nodded, and gave his orders. There wasn't time to starve them out. They would have to be provoked.

The stone-throwing catapults were unfastened from their beds and set up on a slight rise, and because a good trajectory required an uncomfortably close proximity to the defenders, a shield wall of auxiliaries was stationed in front with the legions to the rear. This detachment dug in behind "ship's prow" tortoises, triangular defenses designed to deflect anything rolled downhill from the besieged fortress. Faustus watched the preparations with interest, while standing a good way back. The onagers, named for the powerful and occasionally unpredictable kick of a wild ass, required expertise to handle the tension in the torsion springs against the weight of the stones they threw. Miscalculation had been known to cost their operators a finger or hand.

The first shot took out a piece of the lower wall to make entry easier, and the second a piece of the upper wall to aggravate Cadal. A third took the head off a watcher on the ramparts. After that a bombardment began in earnest to break down the lower wall. The effect was to send Cadal's army pouring out of Bryn Epona in a fury. The battle was short and fierce, mainly against the auxiliaries, and the victory a matter of both tactics and numbers. By the time the legions moved up, they were through the gates of the lower level and halfway up the track to the upper courtyard. Faustus's century pushed steadily upward behind Ursus. Grinning skulls of ancient enemies looked sightlessly down from Cadal's walls above gates now torn open. Cadal's men fought them at every gate and their archers rained arrows down from the topmost walls. Faustus gave the order for his rear ranks to raise shields over the heads of those in front and the column pushed its way like an armored centipede up the spiral track that circled Bryn Epona. As they came into each level and the way opened out, Cadal's warriors tried desperately to push them back with sword and spear.

The Ordovices made one last desperate stand in the upper level but they had lost the better part of their war band, and when it was obvious that it was useless, Cadal himself came out through the high gate with a green branch.

Faustus got a glimpse of him: tall, tawny-haired and battle-scarred, with a gold torque around his neck and the blue spiral of the king mark on his forehead. Cadal had a practical side and he consequently got the best possible terms in the circumstances. Since Agricola wished to leave a pacified territory behind him

32

when he marched north in the spring, they were not far from what he would have granted had Cadal surrendered to begin with: grain tax to be paid, roads to be built and maintained, hostages and gold handed over, and the slighting of the defensive walls of Bryn Epona. Agricola was aware that while they were negotiating, a number of Cadal's diehards had slipped out of Bryn Epona rather than face the inevitable. He put an outlaw bounty on those and forced Cadal to agree to it.

Demetrius had observed the battle from a position near the onagers, with an optio assigned to keep him from getting in the works since he was endlessly curious, and the governor had no wish to send him back to the emperor in two pieces. He pronounced himself disappointed that they had captured no Druids, but since Druids were outlawed in any Roman jurisdiction and subject to execution, that was not surprising. They had no doubt fled with Cadal's holdouts into the hills.

"They appear to dislike being interviewed," Domitius Longinus said. "We caught one once. He killed himself somehow before we could question him. We never could figure out how. He just muttered something and dropped dead. It gave the officer in charge the fits."

"Fascinating." Demetrius scrabbled in the case at his belt and took out a small tablet. "I must note that."

Tuathal, who had been listening quietly, slid away from the conversation. The Druids were ancient and powerful and Demetrius's scholarly attempt to dissect their ways made him nervous. He found the half-blood centurion whom he had met in the tavern drinking beer by his fire with Centurion Galerius and settled there instead.

Faustus produced a third cup and offered him beer. "I thought you would be in the governor's camp, but you are most welcome among the lowly."

"It's pleasant to speak a tongue other than Latin," Tuathal replied in British. "I find Latin a stiff, annoying language. Not unlike the Romans themselves."

"Now we are insulted," said Galerius, who had been attempting to learn the local speech.

"No, that means 'cursed' not 'insulted'," Tuathal said. "Some insults are only rude, some are curses. This is the word you want." He enunciated it carefully.

Galerius repeated it after him. "A useful distinction."

"Is the speech of Hibernia greatly different from what is spoken here?" Faustus asked.

"In the main, yes," Tuathal said. "My mother made sure that I could speak the tongue of Inis Fáil, but I am not fluent. She likened it to what is spoken in Gaul, but I have never been there."

"Will the difference make a barrier to welcoming you as king?" Faustus had no idea how the Hibernians decided matters like that. Probably with spears.

"Blood matters more than speech. That and my father's sword, which my mother took with us when she fled." He touched the scabbard at his belt, which Faustus realized he had never seen him without. The scabbard was fine bronze, bound in strips of red leather that had darkened with age, and between the bindings was the repeated figure of a crow. "In Inis Fáil, which you call Hibernia, they will know both." He drew the blade out and laid it across his knees. "The sword of my father Fiacha Finnolach, and his father before him."

Galerius and Faustus both drew in their breath. The leaf-shaped blade was old as well, dark and lovingly polished. The hilt was a human face with staring gold eyes beneath a gold crown. Below it, on either side of where the tang would run, were rows of seals' teeth. The blade below shimmered with a dark flame.

Faustus eyed it with respect. Some things were holy and he thought this was one of them.

Tuathal slid the sword back into its scabbard as Aculeo came round with the evening watchword. "Mars Ultor," he said. "Also I think we're off in the morning. A pair of border wolves

34

just came in looking as if they had a tale to tell, and the legate's still in the governor's tent."

The border wolves were the elite of the frontier scouts, spies who melted into the countryside and the local populace with ease and went by ways that only they knew into enemy territory, and what was more came back out again. Whatever they had to say, Agricola would listen.

—

The governor heard them out, and nodded. "Very well. If they've gone anywhere, it's clearly Mona. We'll really have to put a stop to that."

The island of Mona lay offshore of the northwest coast of Ordovice territory and was a stronghold of the Druids as well as home to a centuries-old colony of holy women. A previous governor had attacked it nearly twenty years ago in an attempt to wipe out the Druids' influence on the mainland natives. He had cut down their sacred grove and burned the wood, executing any he could lay hands on, but a disastrous rebellion among the Iceni had drawn his attention away. In the years since then Mona had grown once more into a Druidic sanctuary and a refuge for dangerous malcontents from the mainland tribes.

"Will we wait for the Fleet, Governor?" the legate of the Second Adiutrix asked.

"Late in the season for waiting," the legate of the Twentieth said.

Agricola prodded a finger at his map. "The strait is barely more than a quarter-mile. The Batavians could swim that in full armor with bowls of soup on their heads." The Batavian auxiliary came from the marshy lowlands around the Rhenus, where you swam to get to most places at high tide. They were even fonder of fighting than most Germans and were the only people whose tax and tribute to the Empire was paid solely with military recruits.

In the morning Agricola's army marched north, leaving a detail to see that the walls of Bryn Epona were taken down by the remaining Ordovices under Roman supervision. Cadal was allowed to remain a client king to forestall the kind of succession conflict that often resulted in a new rebellion. Caer Gai would become a Roman outpost under a detachment sent south, and two more were seeded in Cadal's hills as the main army passed through.

At the coast they halted where the blue-gray water of the strait was narrowest. The Batavians, a mixed cohort of infantry and cavalry, tied their weapons to the horses' backs at low tide and swam beside them, six men to a horse, and arrived without wetting the fox-fur caps that perched atop their helmets.

The defenders had expected ships and seeing none had prepared no defense, choosing instead to quarrel with each other for precedence. The Druids peered into their bronze bowls and at the patterns of birds overhead and chanted curses to sink any Roman warships, while Cadal's men waved their spears and shouted for one last stand to take Roman heads and die with honor, until the Batavians came up out of the surf like waterborne banshees.

Agricola followed as the surrender was being taken. The troops who had not taken part in the attack he arrayed on the mainland shore to make it clear that there were more where the Batavians came from.

The scholar Demetrius accompanied him by the simple expedient of getting onto the boat commandeered from the Druids and refusing to get off. He was practically bouncing with excitement. "This is an opportunity of a lifetime, Governor. Not to be missed. Simply not to be missed. I must speak to the Druid high priest."

Agricola considered him. If they gave him a chance to speak to a Druid, assuming they could keep one alive long enough, would he then go home? The governor doubted it. Demetrius had more unanswerable questions than the Sphinx.

"I am told there is a temple of holy women on the island. What is their relation to the Druids? Are they like Vestals? Do any of them have sexual congress or are they celibate? Druids' knowledge is never written down. I *must* speak to one. I shall need an interpreter."

The governor found that he had developed a headache by the time the little boat was beached on the shore. "There's a junior officer in the Second Augusta's Seventh who speaks British," he told an optio. "Go fetch him, please."

He sent the Batavian second-in-command to sort out a Druid from the prisoners, and a guard to stand watch while the scholar asked his questions. If the Druid blasted his interrogator into shards with holy fire, that was Demetrius's lookout and Agricola would write a nice letter to the emperor.

Only one Druid had been taken alive but he showed no signs of killing himself. This one was dragged out for Demetrius to interview, an ancient man with a white beard like uncarded wool. A gold sun disk that was probably worth more than any chieftain's ornaments hung from his neck. Faustus regarded him hesitantly. A Druid's curse was said to be particularly effective. At his first question, the old man spat at him.

Demetrius said, "Perhaps he doesn't understand that I am trying to preserve his knowledge for the civilized world," and the man spat at him too.

The guard gave the old man a shove and he pulled a dagger that had not been there before – the guard swore it afterward – from his ragged gown and stabbed himself in the chest. That ended the interview.

When the chained prisoners had been loaded into transports, the Druids' grove was once more obliterated, and the stumps of the young oaks that had replaced the original ones dug out with shovels and pry bars. They left the holy women alone. They were said to be priestesses of the Mother, not of the sun god the Druids served, and Agricola had developed a healthy regard for the Mother in all her guises during his previous service in Britain. He went to pay his respects to the chief priestess.

The holy women had their home on a smaller island that lay across a winding channel of tidal waters from the northwest coast of Mona. Agricola took with him Faustus and a bodyguard of ten men from the First Cohort, and arranged for Demetrius to be occupied elsewhere.

They beached their boats on a shore edged with salt marsh and eel grass, sending flocks of terns and oystercatchers scattering in a flurry of feathers. A heron hunting beside a drying tide pool watched them warily. The priestess of the Mother sent a slave, or maybe a novice, to meet them, a girl who eyed them much as the heron had.

"You are to follow me."

They trooped behind her obediently, through an apparently uninhabited landscape where the forest came down to the marsh edge. Inside the forest it was dim and the trees so thick it was clear they had not been cut since an ancient people had built the moss-covered burial mounds they stumbled over, and set the gray standing stones to watch over them.

"Place gives me the horrors," one of the guard said and made the sign of horns.

On the edge of a grove of old oaks she halted. "No weapons." She pointed at the bodyguard. "They can't come." The legionaries bristled and put their hands to their sword hilts, understanding that well enough, but Agricola shook his head at them. He untied his scarlet general's sash and unbuckled his sword belt, set them on the ground with his dagger, and tucked his helmet under his arm. He motioned to Faustus to do the same. The girl inspected them and nodded, and they followed her between two pillars of dry-stacked stones. Through the trees they could now see scattered circular, reed-thatched houses like those of the mainland.

The holy mother was young. That was a surprise. Like the girl and the other women Faustus glimpsed moving through the trees to well and cowshed, she was draped in a gray woolen tunic and rough black mantle. Her black hair hung loose, long enough to reach her waist, and she was small-boned and sharp-eyed, like a hooded crow.

She sat on a stool piled with deerhides, her feet on a cow's skull. "Why do you wish an audience with me, Commander of the Eagles?" she inquired. "If you wished, you could have slaughtered us by now as you did the others."

"The others were rebels from the mainland," Faustus said, translating. Her accent reminded him of his mother's. "And Druids fomenting rebellion."

She turned her head to Faustus thoughtfully. "What are you?"

He blinked at her. "The governor's interpreter, Lady."

"And a soldier of the Eagles. That may come back to bite you."

Faustus translated that for the governor, although it seemed unnervingly and personally directed at himself.

"Tell her that as long as she does not harbor Druids here, we will offer the priestesses of the Mother no harm," Agricola said.

"The Druids serve the sun and stars," she said. "Our allegiance is to the Goddess. I am her body-on-earth."

"And she has no interest in war with Rome?"

"The Goddess is in everything, Eagle lord. Everything earthly. In the birth of a child and in the scream of a hare in the hawk's talons. In the grain rising up in spring and in the death of men in battle. It is not a matter of interest."

"Nonetheless," Agricola said, "will you give me assurance that you will not give shelter to those who fled the battle three days ago?" According to the border wolves, there had been more Druids than the dead accounted for.

"As to that," she told him, "you have no need for my assurance. There are no men permitted on this island. I have made an exception for you and yours, but it would be well not to linger."

Agricola bowed his head to her, and Faustus followed, somewhat startled. Only the emperor, father of his country and representative of Jupiter Capitolinus, could command that. But the Goddess was older than Jupiter, and older than Rome, and he could well believe that she resided in the black-haired woman on the deerhides.

–

"They've gone to Inis Fáil, governor," Tuathal said.

"They are priests, not sailors."

"If you live on an island you can handle a boat. Now is the time to hunt them down."

"And restore you to your throne in the process, no doubt," Agricola said. "That may be, and likely is, I admit. But they are harmless there and we are overdue for winter quarters. I have no wish to be caught at sea in bad weather."

"Samhain is coming, Governor, when the High King at Tara marries the Goddess." Tuathal leaned over the camp desk, palms planted on the governor's map.

"The High King's relations with the Goddess are all one to me," Agricola said. "I made my peace with her this afternoon."

"The marriage seals the kingship," Tuathal said insistently. "If I come in time to stop it, it will serve us well."

"As I understand that this ritual takes place yearly, you have ample time to interrupt the next one," Agricola said, exasperated.

"This is the fourteenth year since Elim mac Conrach slew my father. The seven-year cycle is holy," Tuathal said. "Before we worshipped the Sun Lord, the old king died at the seventh year, slain by the new one."

"In the process of wedding the Goddess?"

"Yes."

Agricola thought of the goddess-on-earth on her holy island. That prospect made the hair stand on the back of his neck.

"We do not do that now, but it would be symbolic. My people believe in destiny."

"Mine also." Agricola wasn't certain that he would want Tuathal's destiny. "But our needs are not the same and I cannot provide you with your opportunity just now. When we have taken the north of this province, *then* we may turn our attention to Hibernia. Take that or leave it, Tuathal. I will not be hounded." *And you are only fourteen, no older than your usurper's kingship. Wait for the next seven-year and it will serve you better.* He didn't say it. What fourteen-year-old ever wished to be told to wait half again his lifetime? Agricola, in the thirty-ninth year of his own, had been given the chance to bring the entire island of Britain — he was certain it was an island and he would prove it — under Rome's dominion. That was *his* destiny. He would seize it. He had supported Vespasian's claim to the purple through the long dreadful year of civil war that had cost so many lives, including his own mother's. He had paid in blood for it.

III

Bryn Caledon

The old priest saw it in the fires of the forge. Unlike the Druids of the mainland, his eyes were fixed on the human world, on the handful of islands flung across the sea north of Britain, the gods who lived in their waters, and on the words that the fire spoke. And so he talked with the traders when their ships docked at High Isle, and then thought on the invaders they had described, who had been few at first in the far south but now multiplied like ants in the larder.

When he had seen all it had to show him he went back to his work, because the priests of the Orcades were merely ordinary men who could see farther than most into deep waters, but had a living to make in the meanwhile. After a while, as he had thought, Eirian came with a plow blade to mend.

"Boduoc was dreaming and ran it into a cleft rock and got it stuck and then beat at it with another rock," she said. Her pale brown hair was tied up under a kerchief and she wore an apron smeared with flour and grease. "And so I needs must carry it to you, because he is very occupied with something important."

"And because I called you," Catumanus said.

"I thought you had." Eirian perched herself on the work-table, pushing his tools out of her way.

"What do the seals say in the dusk this evening?"

"That the fishing is good." Eirian smiled. "Not much else. Except – there is something coming."

"Have you told your father?"

Eirian shook her head. "He doesn't like it, even when I am right."

Catumanus snorted. Those who could hear the seals, tease out the meaning from voices so like human ones, were touched by the gods but also feared. Eirian was twelve and she had been talking to the seals since she could talk at all. Her aunts had tried to beat it out of her until Catumanus intervened. Her brothers mocked her for it and her father refused to acknowledge it the way that he refused to acknowledge that he had ever had a second wife who had gone back to the sea one spring morning.

"Keep listening," Catumanus told her. "The seals will know when it comes."

Eirian thought about that, walking home from the village with the mended blade. The wind blew the seals' voices up from the rocks on the shore, across the nearly treeless heath. When it did come, she still wouldn't tell her father Faelan, or Boduoc or Eogan either. Whatever it was, they would no doubt find it out without her. She gave Boduoc the blade, stuck her tongue out at him when he didn't bother to thank her, and went to start their supper. The old aunts had stopped coming to help keep the house, scold Faelan for a fool – and inspect at the baby's fingers – as soon as Eirian was old enough to do the work herself. *Something coming*, the seals cried again. *Something coming*.

–

Autumn came to the mainland highlands around Bryn Caledon in a tide of red and bronze, burning its way across the green slopes. Calgacos suspected that Lorn, the trader who had come up the track with his wagons and his ponies in the morning, was looking for a place to burrow in through the coming snows. An offer of hospitality was required, but Calgacos would be happy to have him. Lorn brought not only the bronze pots, fine goldwork, Roman glass and cures for eye disease that the southern tribes sent in trade for Caledone wool and hides, but was also a harper in a small way. He had already provoked Coran Harper into a fit of temper, so their competition over an evening's meal promised entertainment.

He had brought news as well, of an unsettling sort, events that seemed both far enough away to be the stuff of hearth-side fable and at the same time at Calgacos's doorstep, as the Morrigan counted distance. It would be necessary to think on that later, but for the time being, the cattle were coming down from the high pastures and must be sorted out, each to their owner's smallholds for the winter. The women had driven the pigs into their autumn forage as well, and slaughtered any that would not live through a hard winter or were simply needed to feed mouths until spring. Calgacos could see Aelwen, her skirts tied up above her knees, a kerchief over her red braids and a sacking apron over her woolen gown, scraping a scalded carcass beside the vat of boiling water with the rest of the household women and slaves. Ceridwen, just turned six, stood beside her to fetch and carry and get underfoot. *I will buy her that bronze pot she wants*, Calgacos thought. Aelwen hated hog butchering, but never shunted the task off on her women just because the headman's wife could have done so.

A cluster of cattle thundered by with two of the Kindred and Bleddin, who was ten and permitted his first drive, behind them churning up great clumps of mud from the last rain. Aelwen's women flapped their aprons at them and shouted to keep clear. It was going to rain again soon, Calgacos thought, looking at the sky, iron-colored and lowering. With luck they would finish the butchering and get all under roofs before it started. He went to meet the horsemen driving the cattle down the track to the low pastures.

"How is the count?" he asked, mentally tallying the young ones as they went by and calculating possible summer gain.

"A bit higher with some of Emrys's," Rhion laughed. "It may be we mistook a few for ours."

Calgacos grinned. "That will put him in a temper if he notices." Calgacos's clan and Emrys's were the most powerful of the scattered, related tribes of the Caledones. The feud between them, sometimes but not often amounting to blood feud, was of long standing, long enough that no one was certain of the start of it. The people of the mountains surrounding Bryn Caledon were smallholders, each grouped about a headman through kinship or marriage. A slight to one in a clan was a slight to all, and cattle raids were a recognized method of responding to insult without open warfare.

The hold built on the lower slopes of Bryn Caledon was overfull as night fell, with the lords of the Kindred gathered for the bringing in of the cattle. The presence of Lorn and his goods was an added inducement to stay and feast on the headman's hogs before going home to butcher their own. They crowded around the great table in the dining hall, while their hounds, tall, lean dogs with rough iron-gray coats, squabbled with each other for bones in the straw beneath it. A kitchen slave went round with pitchers of beer, filling and refilling the cups held out to him, and the air within the hold's stone walls was close with woodsmoke and the smell of butchered meat. Outside, as predicted, it had begun to rain again, falling softly and steadily on the cow byres and pony shed, making a small lake of the yard. The water below Bryn Caledon was wreathed in silver.

At the table, Rhion was still gloating over the theft, which made Aelwen want to ask her husband if his Kindred were grown men or boys fighting a neighbor hold's children for their toys, but she held her tongue. The tale grew in the telling and was putting everyone in a cheerful mood, which might soften the news the trader had brought with him, clinging to his wagon like bindweed on a tree.

Calgacos sat back in his chair, beer horn in one hand. Barley-colored hair hung loose down his back, and the heavy gold torque around his neck and the twisted gold armbands at his wrists spoke of a wealthy household by northern standards. His heavy woolen breeches were checkered green and brown and his shirt a deep blue wool. A bronze buckle cast with a stag and a baying hound fastened a belt of scarlet leather. His wolfskin cloak hung drying by the door.

Aelwen, beside him, thought that he looked very fine, and also like a man anticipating trouble. She had changed her bloody apron and gown, let down her hair in a wave of red like a vixen's pelt, and put on her best gold necklace and ear drops as befitted her husband's standing. His status as headman rested on his wealth and good name and a little on birth. His mother had been the old headman's sister, and having no sisters of his own, another man in the female line was more like to follow him than Bleddin, who would shortly go to be fostered in Rhion's hold as sister's-son to Rhion. Despite being the Sun Lord's people, inheritance was mostly matrilineal. That was just common sense. There was never a question as to who someone's mother was.

The rules were not unbreakable. If Calgacos proved an unsuitable headman, another man might fight him for his place, or even another clan like Emrys's. He was not anticipating that sort of challenge tonight, but Lorn's news was making them all itchy.

"So the Romans have fought the Ordovices," Celyn said finally, because the subject had been hovering in the air like a wasp and he was tired of waiting for Calgacos to swat it. "What is that to us?"

"Nothing necessarily, lord," Lorn said. "I only bring news. If the meaning is unclear, then that is for someone else to interpret."

"There is more," Calgacos responded. "Lorn, no one will blame you for bad tidings. Out with it!"

The trader set down his cup. "I have spent most of my life on the road, here and there, selling this and buying that. Because of that, people talk to me, and so the tavern talk comes to me. This new governor of the southern lands has ambition to take Roman rule to the north. To your hunting runs and beyond."

"A fool's tale!" Celyn snorted. "If they can find their way through our passes it would be by magic."

"So the Ordovices thought," Lorn said.

Dai stood and stretched, prodding a dog out from under his chair before sitting back down again. "The south is many days' ride away, with bad country in between. I don't believe it."

Lorn shrugged. They would no doubt believe it if they had seen the army that had flowed up Cadal's mountains like the Sabrina at high tide.

Idris slouched in his chair. He bit into a small apple after inspecting it for worms, showing white teeth behind a thick blond mustache. "How are Romans a matter for a headman of the Caledones to fear?"

"What do the gods say?" Calgacos asked Vellaunos Chief Druid, ignoring that. The old man had sat silently, wolfing down more meat than Calgacos would have thought anyone that frail could hold. His beard and white gown were splotched with it down the front.

Vellaunos bit the end of the best cut of pork off his knife. He chewed and swallowed before he answered. Calgacos eyed him with some irritation, which was best left unspoken. The Druids generally spoke only to the stars, but their word when it was pronounced was law, and a Druid's curse could kill. They had precedence even ahead of kings. Anyone in their right mind was afraid of Vellaunos.

"That is a matter for the headman to ask the gods himself." Vellaunos stabbed his knife into the table and held out his hands for a slave to bring him a wet rag. "War is not the business of the Druids."

"It will be if Romans dig you out of your sanctuary at spearpoint," Rhion said.

"Lorn, tell my Kindred what you have seen since then," Calgacos said hastily. "On the trail between the southern lands and here."

"Roads, lord. Stone-paved and straight as a spear flies. Forts that come up like toadstools overnight. Patrols tramping lordlywise over anything in their path. Romans, lord. That's what I've seen."

47

"And did you sell them your goods?" Dai asked with a grin.

"Certainly. They are prone to cheat, but no more than most men. They buy dice and gameboards and such, and fairings to take back to their women in the villages outside their forts."

"Do they bring their wives here too, from Rome?" Celyn asked. That seemed to him more worrisome. A war band looking for plunder, or even tribute, was one thing. Invaders who settled on the land were another matter. That was how Celyn's people had displaced the Old Ones.

"Most of them don't come from Rome itself," Lorn said. "There are Germans and Gauls, or even men from the East. But they are Romans when the army gets through with them. But as to your question, mostly no, except for the officers. The regular soldiers aren't allowed to marry. They take up with women from the southern tribes and make the marriage legal when they retire."

"When they are too old to fight?" Idris demanded, then smirked at Lorn. "And too old to do much with a woman either."

"Not necessarily. They pledge themselves for twenty-five years. At the end of that they leave the army with money from Rome to buy land or start a trade. A man who signs on at twenty can retire at forty-five, if he survives."

The only way a man of Calgacos's people stopped fighting was at the end of a spear or when he was too old to lift one. Dai spat into the straw at his feet to indicate his contempt for Romans.

"Pah!" Celyn grunted. "Men who fight for pay!"

"You are puppies," Rhion said to both of them. "They are not cowardly."

"They are without honor!"

"And retreat like slaves if their commanders order," Idris added.

"And you are foolish to underestimate them because of it."

A slave went around with more beer and Calgacos decided that they had argued it enough for the night, or someone would start a fight just out of beer and boredom. "Coran, give us a song for the night. And Lorn, I'll buy that overpriced pot from you if you can sing us something Coran doesn't know."

The slaves cleared the dishes and bones from the table and more beer went around while Coran sang them the story of how the Sun Lord's people had come over the water in the old days and mastered the people of the mountains, becoming rulers of the land. Harpers were Druids at a minor level and could sing the clan's history. The songs were only a small part of the Druids' knowledge passed from mouth to mouth and never written down, but in that Coran was something above Lorn, who had learned his music in taverns and village fairs, and sang only for men's amusement.

By the time they had traded songs, and a few insults, and Calgacos had intervened to squelch that, the question of Romans had been abandoned, at least for the night.

Aelwen brought it up in the dawn light, combing out her hair while her husband stretched and splashed water on his face from a bowl by the bed. "What of this talk of Lorn's? Do you think he really knows what the Romans will do, or is he only making himself interesting?"

"If he plans to spend the winter among our holdings, he doesn't think the Romans are on our doorstep, that much I know. Lorn has a care for his own hide."

"But he thinks they will come?"

"He does. And sorry though I am to say it, so do I."

Aelwen began to braid her hair in swift, practiced movements, and then came to comb her husband's. "What will you do?"

"I am thinking on that. *If* they get as far as our mountains, they will have needed to go through more lands than the Ordovices' and they will not be welcome in all of them. The southern lands may be clients of the Romans but the lowland peoples north of them are no friends. They will have to fight their way through those. We have time yet."

She tied his hair back and watched him finish dressing, pulling a heavy shirt on over the lighter one and buckling his belt. His arms were marked with intricate tattoos, as all the Caledones were, each clan with its own pattern and small differences for each household. Her own arms and breast bore the spiral and sun rays of her brother Rhion's house.

"You will need time to bring the Kindred round," Aelwen said. "Celyn and Dai think that because the Romans have no honor, they are not dangerous. *I* think it makes them more so."

Calgacos pulled his boots on. "You are wise. It may be that if I send one of them south to see the Romans for themselves, it will be useful."

"Now? On the edge of winter?"

"No. In the spring, with Lorn. But for now, I need them to take *me* seriously, if not the Romans, so I am going to call a treaty council with Emrys. That will be the shouting you hear in a moment or two."

When he had gone, she tucked up her skirts and went to the kitchen. They might all be in a temper but they would need to be fed.

Calgacos waited in the outer doorway while the smell of hot porridge drifted from the kitchen, and he waylaid Celyn and Dai as they emerged from the guest house.

"I have it in mind to send to Emrys with an invitation to council," he told them, and waited for them to argue with him.

"For what reason?" Dai demanded.

"To make treaty with a wolf?" Celyn spat. "Never."

They were spear brothers of the same year. Dai was taller, with brown hair and mustache to Celyn's straw color, but somehow everyone thought of them as much alike. Just now they stood, arms folded, feet planted in the muddy yard, and glared at the headman.

"Because if the Romans come north," Calgacos said, "the only way to stop them is to ally with the other clans, all of them, even the seal people of the islands, if it comes to that."

"They keep to themselves," Dai replied. "And are maybe not human anyway."

"They are Cornovii, like their kinsmen across the firth," Calgacos said.

"Barely."

"Emrys is the most powerful headman aside from myself, so I will start with him. If he joins us, the rest will follow."

"If you make a treaty with Emrys, someone will challenge you as headman," Celyn said.

"You, Celyn?"

"No," Celyn said. "But someone will. We have been blood foes with the men of Emrys's kin for generations. Generations, Calgacos! Generations of stolen cattle and stolen land, snares laid in our hunting runs, men killed, and women taken."

"And have we not got our own back in that time?" Calgacos asked.

"We have," Dai retorted. "And the more reason not to trust a wolf like Emrys."

Calgacos stood his ground while they glared at him. Rhion came out of the guest house yawning, and seeing them, came to find out what the quarrel was.

"He wants to hold a treaty council with Emrys!" Celyn snapped.

"I have no love for Emrys," Calgacos said. "But we are kin in the bone to them, and the Romans are foreigners. The Romans will do more than steal cattle."

"So will Emrys if we turn our backs on him to fight the Romans," Dai said. "A man of his stole a girl out of Maldwyn's smallhold not twelve months ago."

"Her father cried rape, but the girl denied it," Rhion said. "To be fair, I don't think we can count that against Emrys."

"I still say we should have taken her back."

"She didn't want to go back, and she isn't a cow," Calgacos said. "The Druids ruled, and I ruled. Let that go." Dai rarely let go of anything that gave him an excuse to fight someone.

"The Romans will never come this far north," Celyn said. "And if they should try, how will they gain authority over hundreds of holds that can dig themselves into the mountains and are as used to fighting as breathing?"

"That, no doubt, was what the Ordovices thought," Calgacos said. "And the Iceni. And the entire south of Britain."

"The Iceni burned the Romans' city at Londinium," Rhion said.

"And where are they now?" Calgacos asked.

No one bothered to answer. The Iceni's rebellious queen had ended by suicide and the Iceni's territory was firmly in Roman hands. Even as far removed from Roman lands as they were, they knew that.

"I will send to Emrys to ask for a council," Calgacos said. "You will attend it, along with the others of the Kindred. Anyone who does not like that may fight me for it."

"Just watch your back and count your cattle," Dai said to that, and stalked off, followed by Celyn.

Calgacos looked at Rhion, who was brother to his wife and would be foster father to Bleddin. "Will you back me on this?"

"I don't know," Rhion said. "I will back you on your wish to take council with Emrys. That much. And if someone challenges you as headman. On alliance, I don't know."

"That is fair enough. Neither Celyn nor Dai will challenge me. Idris may."

"Idris has an eye to anything that may give him some advantage. You should not have let him take his father's hold."

"There was no one else. It would have come to blood if I had put up anyone not in the family for it. You said so yourself."

Rhion sighed. "I did. I have regretted it."

"If Idris challenges me, Idris will regret it." Calgacos put his arm on the other man's shoulder. "Come and eat and see Aelwen before you ride out. Time enough to worry about anything else when I see what message Emrys sends back."

A request for council from Calgacos was so unusual as to be unnerving and so Emrys agreed to it. Calgacos was not afraid of Emrys and so he must be afraid of something else, and anything that could make Calgacos afraid was to be taken seriously.

They met in the flat upland meadow where Lughnasa Fair was held each summer. The highland clans gathered yearly midway between the solstice and the equinox to pay tribute to the Sun Lord, Lugh Bright Spear, to trade and make marriage contracts, and all feuds were set aside for three days. Now, as winter settled in, the surrounding mountains were gray and leafless, dappled with dark patches of pine, and the meadow was cold and empty of the summer tents and wagons, the singing and the scent of roasting meat.

According to mutual agreement, Emrys brought ten of his own Kindred, and a Druid somewhat younger than Vellaunos but with the same air of a man who speaks to the invisible and ineffable. Like Vellaunos he wore a white gown and a heavy gold sun wheel on his chest beneath a brambly beard. Emrys was tall, with a scarred cheekbone and pale hair cut short and lime-bleached to near white, his skin almost as pale beneath the clan marks. His wrists were encircled with heavy gold cuffs set with carnelian.

The day was fair if cold. They tethered the chariot ponies to graze on the drying grass and squatted in a semicircle about the sacred stone at the meadow's center. The Druids greeted each other palm-to-palm and then stood silently to either side of the stone.

Calgacos spoke his piece and watched Emrys's eyes. His expression was unreadable but Calgacos saw his eyes slide round to the men of his clan. They murmured to each other, too low for Calgacos to hear.

"And are your clan united in this proposal of alliance?" Emrys asked when Calgacos had spoken. He regarded Calgacos with yellow-brown eyes like an osprey's.

"Not as yet," Calgacos admitted.

"Not while I breathe," Dai said.

"Possibly," Rhion said.

"The headman has yet to convince me," Idris added, "of his wisdom in this."

"*If* the Romans come, yes," Celyn said, with a glance at Dai.

Vellaunos thumped the grass with his staff and nodded at the younger Druid, Nemausos. "We will consult with each other." He walked away and Nemausos followed.

"My Kindred have not had time to think on their opinions," Emrys said. "And as yours are not behind you, why should I make treaty?"

"For the reason that enmity between us favors the Romans when they come. *If* they come," Calgacos added. "But do you wish to chance that? The southern tribes could not put aside their own disputes to unite against the Romans. They all bickered and quarreled and fought each other instead, and now their walls are torn down and their governing overseen by Romans. What happened in the south will happen here if we do not do differently."

"The south had little natural defense," Emrys said. "Our mountains are our defense."

"So thought the Ordovices," Calgacos said.

"Those are not mountains. Those are hills. I have been there once." Emrys held his hand a few inches above the grass to indicate the Ordovice hills.

"Lorn Trader has been there recently," Calgacos retorted, "and the walls of Bryn Epona are torn to rubble and Roman roads run through their fields."

"That is little to me."

"Lord Emrys is wise," Idris said. "What are the southern lands to us?"

Celyn glared at him. He might be in agreement but a compliment to Emrys was uncalled for.

"If the Romans come," Calgacos said, "we are like to find out. And there will not be leisure then to sort out an alliance, or the command of a war band to stop them."

Emrys raised a pale eyebrow. "And it is you who would command?"

"Only as regards the Romans," Calgacos said.

"And what have the stars told you?" Emrys inquired as the two Druids returned to the circle and stood leaning on their staffs.

"We see nothing in the stars to say that they will come," Vellaunos answered. "Nor in the flights of birds. Nor in the fish of the rivers." All things were foretold in the movements of the heavens and the patterns of earthly beings. The Druids read those things and interpreted for the rest.

"And I see nothing in the stars to say I should put my war band under Calgacos," Emrys said, "and maybe find that he has too much liking for that power afterward."

"Make peace between you if you will," Nemausos said. "Or do not. That is not yet our affair."

"Where the Romans have overrun, the Druids have been quick enough to espouse war," Calgacos retorted. "You have heard what happened on Mona."

"That is very grave," Nemausos admitted. "But they have gone over water to Inis Fáil."

"What was left of them." Whatever secretive methods of communication the Druids employed, Calgacos had never known their factual information to be incorrect.

"We do not die," Vellaunos said. "Not as other men do. They will take pupils and the order and the knowledge will regrow, as all things do."

"You may have need to fly to Inis Fáil yourself, if you do not wish to die in your current body," Calgacos snapped, which was as close as he was willing to come to direct confrontation.

Emrys's men were growing restive. One of them murmured something to Emrys and Emrys stood. "I have thought on this," he told Calgacos, "because I agreed to council. But there will not be peace between us. Our clans have been enemies for longer than Rome has been a power in the world. We will not bow to your word, and I smell a trick in this." He nodded to his clansmen and they stalked across the grass in a cold wind to the waiting chariots.

"A trick!" Rhion spat. "Fine talk from a wolf like Emrys."

"It may be that Emrys is wise," Idris said lazily, unfolding himself from the ground.

"And what does that mean?" Dai demanded.

"Do we, who are the headman's Kindred, even know the headman's mind?" Idris asked.

Calgacos stood. "You don't even know what you mean by that, Idris, you only mean to be insulting."

"I meant no insult," Idris said. "It was a compliment, mind you, to the headman's cleverness."

The wind was growing stronger and the sky growing steel-colored, with the smell of snow in it.

"Mount!" Calgacos snapped. "Before we are caught in a storm. And Idris, keep it in your mind that *you* are not half as clever as you think!"

Rhion caught Idris by the arm as Calgacos untethered his ponies. His fingers dug through the fur cloak and woolen shirtsleeve. "Watch yourself, Idris, or I may do what the headman will not!"

He gave Idris a shove and stalked away to step into Calgacos's chariot. "That one is going to make you trouble," he said, "and then whatever you do about it, it will cost you the men of his hold one way or another. You should challenge him now."

"Because I have been insulted?" Calgacos asked. "That's a thin excuse, from headman to smallholder." He shook out the reins and set the ponies up the track toward Bryn Caledon.

Rhion braced himself against the chariot's rim as the wickerwork body shifted with the ruts in the road. Behind them the others came two by two, Celyn with Dai and Idris with

Maldwyn, a smallholder whose land bordered his. "I warn you, Calgacos," Rhion said, "if you don't do it, I will, sooner or later. Idris is dangerous."

"I will take care of Idris. You are not to. Am I clear on that?"

–

"You should have listened to my brother," Aelwen said the next night in bed, buried in furs and blankets against the cold. Calgacos stuck his head out from under them, where he had been investigating her right breast. Apparently Rhion had stayed long enough to tell his complaint to his sister.

"The Morrigan take Idris. If I'm lucky, she will. He picks a quarrel with everyone."

"And everyone will do better without Idris. Especially if you are right and the Romans come, when you will need the clans behind you without any doubts about it," Aelwen said. "Idris could make a mare doubt her own foal. It's why I wouldn't have him. He thinks everyone is a cheat because he is."

"Idris wanted you?" Calgacos sat up now, dragging the furs around his shoulders.

"Not for long," Aelwen said. "I pulled my knife on him for trying to take me into the woods at Lughnasa and lying to me that my father had agreed. I knew Father would have asked me before he did that."

"That angers me, but it's another reason I can't kill him."

"Some people would think it a fine reason to do just that," Aelwen retorted. Sometimes Calgacos's reasoning seemed to her as inscrutable as the Druids'.

"It was me you married. It would only look like spite."

"Spite drives all our quarrels with Emrys's people," Aelwen pointed out. "Every cattle raid and stolen sheep and poached hare and deer from his glens. I do not see a difference."

Calgacos didn't either, on the face of it, but he was nevertheless reasonably sure there was one. Idris was going to be trouble, but trying to avoid it ahead of time felt dishonorable.

Trouble of that kind had to be met; it couldn't be forestalled with murder. Additionally, there would be purification to be done for a killing within the clan, unless Idris challenged him. The Druids would stroke their beards and look at the sky and decide its form, and the result would be dark and unpleasant. No one sane would court that if it wasn't necessary. And no one honorable – it kept coming back to that – would let Rhion do it for him.

IV

The Sidhe of Llanmelin

Winter

Julius Agricola collected his household and settled into winter quarters at Deva with the Adiutrix, sending half of the Augusta, including the Seventh Cohort, back to Isca to remind the Silures that they were still a client kingdom. Winter quarters, Faustus found, might as well have been summer quarters, only with worse weather. Drills and marches were assigned whenever it wasn't actually freezing. In between, Faustus and his century were assigned to go and inspect the gold mines at Dolaucothi in the Silure Hills, since the overseers were Roman but the miners were Britons, and it was useful for a native speaker to be sure they were not skimming or otherwise cheating their masters. The natives had mined the site for centuries, washing gold from their hills with water from the nearby stream, but Julius Frontinus, an engineer at heart, had begun the installation of modern mining methods before his transfer. Several aqueducts were now installed, with water tanks and a hydraulic trip hammer to crush the ore, and waterwheels to drain the deep mines. Faustus's century was quartered for the duration of their stay in a new camp at Luentinum nearby, an uncomfortable assortment of turf and timber buildings with no heat.

The mine workers were mostly not slaves, but conscripts from the peace treaty made with the Silures, bound to service for varying terms. Faustus watched them with an odd sense of something seen before. They were smaller and darker haired than the Ordovices, fine-boned and stubborn-looking. His mother's people. Their accent was very like hers. They remained unimpressed by his ability to mimic it, and made the sign of horns behind his back every time he turned away, so Septimus reported.

"I don't like them," Septimus said.

"Well, they don't like you," Faustus replied philosophically. "Or me. We're just here to see that buckets of ore don't walk away." He settled on a rock near the shaft being worked and pulled his military cloak more tightly around his shoulders against a dank fog. He fished in his pack for the noon meal he had assembled in the morning – cold venison from a recent hunting expedition and army biscuit, a hard bread that took good teeth to cope with.

The letter from Silvia emerged with it, an unnervingly thick stack of wooden tablets tied with cord. It had caught up with him that morning and he hadn't read it yet, regarding it much as he would a basilisk egg.

"Letter from home?" Septimus asked. "Maybe someone's died and left you money. That's a thick one." He eyed it curiously.

"Go and supervise something, please."

"Yes, Centurion." Septimus saluted and departed, dodging an ore cart coming up from the dark opening in the rock beside them.

> *To my dear brother Faustus Silvius Valerianus, greetings.*
> *We are well and Manlius also sends his greetings. You will be unhappy to know that the farm has been let go to ruin. The new people have not even plowed the south field, and the peach trees have a blight. You know that Father always burned straw in the orchard every spring for that. The cistern is clogged too.*

How on earth did she know that?

> *They haven't made any offering to Ceres or Saturn Ster-*
> *culius either, and you know that Father was scrupulous*
> *about that. I do not know what will come of it all, it is*
> *most distressing, and as I am now expecting a child, I fear*
> *that it will affect the baby in some horrible way. I have*
> *been to the midwife for an amulet and also to the Temple*
> *of Juno Lucina and made sacrifice, and also to Diana,*
> *but I fear the worst.*

How in the name of Fama goddess of gossip did she know what these people were doing? And why was she lurking about the farm? Faustus glared at the tablets. There were six more. He scanned them, hoping for some other news, and sifted out only that the baby was due early in the year. He would send her a present, he thought, and make an offering to Juno himself. Childbirth always required careful management and propitiation of the proper gods, but he was reasonably certain that the state of the farm was not going to affect a baby ten miles away in Narbo Martius. He hoped not. He didn't need something else for his family to hang about his neck.

Faustus bit irritably into the army biscuit and became aware of someone watching him. It took him a moment to see her, a slight dark-haired creature in a ragged shift among the dark trees beyond the mine entrance. He took out a piece of the venison and saw her eyes follow it.

He held the venison out but she wouldn't come to him. After a moment he stood and went toward her carefully, slipping into the deep shade of ancient oaks through drifts of wet leaves. She retreated, but only out of sight of the mine workers, and when he held out the venison this time, she took it and gnawed at it ravenously.

"Are you hungry?"

She nodded. "We are always hungry."

"What's your name?" She was tiny, the height of a nine-year-old, but the thin frame under the ragged shift was that of a girl in her teens. Her brown arms and forehead were tattooed with faint blue patterns, loops and spirals not unlike those of the Silures, but she wasn't one of them. Her eyes were a startling blue.

"Curlew." Her voice was curiously accented and slightly singsong, as if the Silure dialect might not be her native speech.

"Who are your people?"

"Not these." She glanced at the Silure mine workers contemptuously. "We were here before they came, or the tall fair ones either, the Sun People. We will be here when they have gone," she added. "Whatever they think. Or the Romans with their iron swords and shells like turtles." She nodded at his lorica.

Something half remembered that his mother had told him, about the little dark ones, the sidhe-people who lived in the hills, came back to him, misty as a bedtime tale. Maybe it had been.

"I see. Why were you watching me? Was it just the venison?"

She had finished it and wiped her mouth on her hand. "No. I need to tell Grandmother about you."

Someone at the mine shaft cursed angrily and Faustus turned to see what the trouble was. When he turned again she was gone. There was no sight of her retreating back among the trees, just a stillness under the bare branches. The cursing intensified and he gave it his attention.

The Silure mine foreman stood beside the top pair of the monstrous waterwheels that drained the mine. He was shaking with fury. The wheels were motionless, their operators lounging in the lee of the tunnel opening.

"What is the problem here?" Faustus asked him.

"The little beast jammed rocks between the spokes and put it just enough out of true that it hangs up every turn."

"What little beast? And they look all right to me."

"The little beast of a mine slave and not these here, the bottom ones. Of course the bottom ones, so everything's stopped!"

"Let me have a look." Faustus edged past the wheels and another ore cart being loaded from pulley-raised buckets and started gingerly down into the shaft, gripping the handholds carved in the wall. Behind him the great wheels stood still. There were six pairs of them, going stairstep down beside the shaft to drain the workings at the bottom. Each pair lifted water to its own height where it flowed into a sump to be lifted again by the next pair, driven by men walking atop them to turn the wheels with their feet. With the bottom set stilled, the rest sat motionless too, looming over him in the dim light. Faustus had been down one of the mine shafts before but he hadn't liked it. It was too much like crossing the Styx, particularly at the bottom where the water that seeped in everywhere flowed about their feet if the wheels weren't turning. Once into the tunnel that followed the ore vein, the only light came from oil lamps set into niches in the stone.

The problem with the bottom pair of wheels was obvious – a handful of rock had been shoved between one set of double spokes that radiated from the hub to either edge of the wheel and pounded into place with the head of a pick, breaking two spokes and splintering several more. Out of true, the wheel slobbered half the water it caught back into the sump before it got to the top. It would take the engineers to come down and fix it, or it would have to be disassembled and hauled to the top.

The Silure foreman was hard on Faustus's heels. He grabbed a slave who sat shivering in the water beside the wheel, guarded by the other miners, and slammed him against the wall of the tunnel. The slave was small, brown-skinned, naked except for a ragged tunic and an iron collar, and marked on his arms and forehead with spiral patterns in blue woad. He was older than the child from the woods but he had a look of her, Faustus thought. One of the same people?

63

The foreman lifted him to hurl him at the wall again and Faustus grabbed his arm. "Stop it. You'll kill him."

"I don't care. Sneaking little ferret. They're all like that. They do it for spite."

"Well, I care," Faustus said. "He belongs to the mine, and therefore to Rome, and he's not worth anything dead. I'll send the engineer down to see if this can be repaired on site or if you're going to have to take it down."

"You're like to see fish swim by in a half-day if he can't," the Silure man said.

"In the meantime, do what you can with one wheel then," Faustus told him, "before it gets too deep." He considered the slave. If he left him down here the foreman would probably kill him despite his orders. "You follow me up top and I'll decide what to do about you there."

He found Septimus among the crowd gathered around the shaft to offer unsolicited advice on the situation, and handed the culprit over to him. "Hang onto him until I've talked to the engineer."

The engineer went down into the mine with three assistants, sent one of them back up for more tools, and finally came up himself, shaking his head. "I've stabilized her for now but it's a stopgap job and we need to send a new wheel down to replace that one. I've told them to get ready to swap when it gets there. I understand one of their mine slaves did that. What have you done with him?"

"Nothing yet."

"Well, give him a good beating and put him to work breaking up ore or something. Don't send him back down in the works. Once one gets the idea of sabotage, it spreads to the rest and we don't need any more of that."

That seemed like sound advice but when Faustus went to collect the man from Septimus, he was gone.

"Where is he?"

"Right here," Septimus said. "Never left my side. Oh, shit!"

"Has he gone invisible then?"

"He was here, I swear it. He was here just now when I saw you coming over. I was *looking* at him!"

"I suppose they'll dock our pay for that," Faustus said. "Your pay," he added pointedly. The little man was definitely gone, faded into the woods the same way the girl had.

"Not if you don't mention it," Septimus suggested. "It's iffy who he belonged to, isn't it? Us or the Silures? And we're rotating out of this post tomorrow anyway."

Faustus stared into the empty woods, wondering for an instant if the little slave had even been there in the first place. But of course he had. Septimus had seen him and the Silure foreman most certainly had. The sense of invisible things floating about his head might be making him slightly mad, he decided. He had thought that his father's shade had gone back to where it was supposed to be after the fighting at Bryn Epona, but this morning it had arrived at Luentinum along with the letter. He had caught just a glimpse of it, barely visible against the pale plastered wall of the barracks. Paullus had been there and had maintained what Faustus thought was a suspiciously blank expression. He still wasn't sure whether Paullus could see the apparition too, and for that matter whether it actually existed at all.

"If anyone asks you about that slave, you tell them the commander is still making his mind up," he said. "I'm going to be making it up until we leave." The Silure Hills made the back of his neck itch.

When they got back to Isca he paid a stone cutter for a dedication stone to the shade of Marcus Silvius Valerianus, erected it with Paullus's help in a suitable spot among the tombstones that lined the road from Isca to Venta Silurum, and poured a libation of good wine over it. The wine stained the frozen slush about the stone a deep red-gold.

"An auspicious gesture of filial piety, Master," Paullus commented. "The old master is bound to appreciate it."

"Paullus," Faustus said, "do you ever – um—"

"No, sir," Paullus said firmly. "I do not."

"Aha. Then you do."

Paullus looked uncomfortable. "To be honest, I don't know. But it doesn't seem like my business."

Faustus sighed. "All right, go and fix us something for dinner. I'm going to sit here a while and see if the old bastard will talk to me."

"That might not be the best way to frame it, sir," Paullus suggested.

"I'm past caring about that. If he doesn't like it, he can go away." He watched Paullus saunter back down the road to the fort, a carefree man whose dead father stayed dead. When he turned back to the stone, Silvius Valerianus was sitting on it.

"A Roman son's duty lies with his family," the apparition said. "That is the heart and the whole of his obligation."

"I made the sacrifices," Faustus said stubbornly. "I fulfilled every requirement. For you and for Mother. And I have another obligation now that I swore to the army."

"Your mother was a restless woman. You take after her, I think."

"Mother was completely loyal to you!" Faustus replied, outraged.

"In the body, yes. A wife has no choice. For the rest… She used to go to the cowshed and speak in her own tongue with the dairy girl. After we married. It wasn't suitable. You wouldn't have noticed."

Had he? he wondered. Probably not. After Marcus died she had clung to him and to Silvia, and several times he had found her weeping but when he asked if it was over Marcus, she said that the grief of one loss always opened a door for other losses to come through. She hadn't told him what those were and, with childlike self-centeredness, he hadn't asked.

"Are you coming to me over old grievances with my mother?" he asked the apparition. "Go find her and sort them out."

"There is nothing to sort. I suppose she has gone where her own people go. That which we think is ours slips through our hands."

"Are you talking about me or Mother?" Faustus demanded, but the shade vanished. "And you might thank me for the wine," he added to the empty air.

He grumbled his way back toward the fortress gates and dinner. No further apparitions appeared and in the morning he set out with the sixth century on patrol. Their rounds went past the sentry camp at Coed-y-Caerau and then northeast into the hills around the abandoned Silure fortress of Llanmelin. The Silures had left Llanmelin when the Romans first began to build at Isca, and its defenses had been slighted by the Romans afterward, but it was too tempting a spot for hiding small bands of malcontents to be left unwatched. They would camp at Llanmelin for two nights and search for signs of the unauthorized activity that a mild spell in the weather could encourage. Technically speaking, the Silure Hills were now pacified, but that did not eliminate the occasional tree felled across a new road or dead sheep in the water supply.

With the sixth century now displaying exemplary behavior, Faustus chose to exert the privilege of his rank and told Paullus to saddle Arion. Paullus rode at the rear on the wagon carrying their tents and a dozen braziers to provide just enough heat to keep everyone from freezing solid. The woods around Coed-y-Caerau were leafless, black contorted branches against a gray sky and the remains of the last snow. They were crisscrossed with trails, mostly of deer, some well-worn by hunting parties from the sentry camp. An occasional stream flowed through the wet leaves and rock, and here and there a spring bubbled up, fringed with ice. The track skirted a ridge above Venta Silurum to the south and was well kept enough not to need clearing, except for where someone had dug a steep cut across it and then covered it over with branches and scattered moss and leaves. They filled it in before they went on and Faustus wondered who was in the trees watching them.

They came to Llanmelin at nightfall. The broken stone and old earthworks of the hill fort topped a rise where wild grasses and a few young trees were beginning to sprout among the remains of cattle pens and round mud-and-timber houses. The wind was sharp and they set about digging in a small section for a camp, reinforcing a piece of the original walls and ditch. Faustus thought about using the old houses for shelter, but the thatch roofs were mostly rotten and falling in and they pitched their tents in orderly Roman rows among them instead. By full dark they had a fort in miniature, the same rectangular shape as every Roman camp and with the same roads cutting through it. No Roman soldier was ever lost in a new camp at night, and sounding *To Quarters* instantly revealed anyone who should not have been there.

In the morning Faustus formed up the century, with a handful left in the camp to keep the gear from disappearing. Pilfering by natives who viewed any unattended Roman stores as a supply depot was constant. He was mounting Arion when Aculeo waylaid him.

"I found this," he said. "Just outside our dexter gate." Aculeo held his hand out with an iron collar dangling from the fingers. "It was weighing down a branch of dead oak leaves, and a kind of squiggly mark scratched in the dirt. Come and see."

Faustus took the collar and turned it over in his hand. Any slave collar was much like another but he was quite aware of the last time he had seen one. He followed Aculeo to the camp gate and peered at the ground where the collar had lain. The oak branch was still there with its rustle of brown leaves. Three wavy marks were scratched in the wet ground beside it.

"Looks like a message for someone," Aculeo said.

"I think so too," Faustus said. "And it's for me. Let me have that."

Aculeo handed him the collar. It had been recently cut through and twisted open enough to be pulled off. That part of the message was clear. But why leave it at all unless there was something else that needed telling? Something about the mine that had recently been Faustus's responsibility? A warning of further sabotage?

He considered the rest of it. An oak tree. Or an oak grove. And squiggly lines meant water, anywhere. A spring in a grove? That sounded very like a place of the Mother, and if so, very likely of the little dark people. He wouldn't have believed in them if he hadn't just seen two of them, but the iron collar was extremely real. And they had come through such a grove just below Llanmelin at dusk the day before.

"Tell Septimus he's to take the column out on the route we discussed."

"And you're going to go haring off by yourself?" Aculeo demanded. "Out here? Sir?"

"I don't think I'm in much danger," Faustus said. "If I'm murdered, send my pay to my sister. But I don't think so somehow."

He mounted Arion and they retraced the way down the track from Llanmelin to the grove that Faustus remembered. They halted at its edge and he tethered Arion to a sapling before he made his way into the darkness under the trees and settled beside the spring. Oak leaves often did not drop until the new ones pushed them out. These clung to their branches, making a rustle like papery wings in the winter wind. The spring bubbled up from a cleft in a stone outcropping and filled a small bowl carved into the rock below it, then spilled over the edge into a stream that ran away downhill to join the hundreds of other streams that laced the hills and flowed south into the tidal estuary of the Sabrina. Faustus noted that someone had left a glass bead in the bowl, shimmering beneath the ripples like a little green moon. He reached into the pouch at his belt and found a copper coin and dropped it in for the Mother or the *genius loci* or whoever the spring belonged to.

After a moment he realized that the little man was standing beside him. His neck showed the healing gall marks of the collar, but he had shed his ragged tunic for a woolen shirt and a kilt of wildcat's skin. A wolfskin cloak was wrapped about his shoulders.

"I thought you would come," he said. "Grandmother said that you would."

"Grandmother?"

"The Old One. Curlew told her about you, and then I did, and she said you were to come to speak to her."

"Because I was fool enough to let you get away from me?" Faustus asked him.

"Oh, no. If it was only that, you would not have seen me again."

Something else about the mine then, Faustus thought. He had better find out what. "And where is the Old One?"

The little man gestured vaguely to the north. "Not very far. But we must go outside the grove now. Iron is a Wrong Thing and you are covered with it. I should have thought of that. I was only just cleaned of that collar. I have no wish for doing it again." He moved toward the grove's edge and Faustus followed him.

"I am called Salmon, in the Sun People's language," he said over his shoulder. "I will stay where you can see me and you can follow on your horse. It is not far."

Faustus couldn't see anything that looked like a village or even a house in the scrubby winter growth that covered the hillside below the ruined courtyards of Llanmelin. In the distance the tail end of the column on patrol was just visible. The winter sun was still climbing in the east when Salmon halted and said, "You must leave the horse here. And everything iron."

"Here?" Faustus looked about him. There was still nothing to be seen but a hawthorn thicket and a bare hillside topped with trees twisted by the wind.

"It will be here when you return," Salmon said. "None of our people will touch it. I will give you one of our knives to carry if you are afraid of us." He drew the blade from his own belt and held it out. It was bronze, very fine workmanship, leaf-shaped.

"No," Faustus said. "No, I will trust you." He shed his lorica, helmet, sword belt and greaves, and stopped to think if he carried anything else of iron. The rivets in the skirt of his harness tunic were bronze. His boots had iron hobnails in the soles. He pulled them off and stood with the wet soaking into his socks.

"It is dry inside," Salmon said, looking amused. "Come." He pointed at the hillside and finally Faustus saw the thin blue curl of peat smoke that drifted across it. A thicket of wild briars caught at his tunic as he followed Salmon, and beyond the briars a wooden doorframe was set into the hill itself, under the clump of twisted trees. His own patrol could have ridden past and seen nothing.

The doorway was low enough that even Salmon had to duck to go through it and for a moment Faustus almost balked. He had been in Britain long enough to have heard tales of men who went into these hillsides and came out again a century later to find their families dead, their cities only piles of stone. He went through anyway, and stood blinking on the other side while his eyes adjusted to the darkness. The cave was deep, receding into blackness, and smelled like a fox's den. The peat fire at the hearth end, and its smoke hole in the roof, were the only sources of light. There were four women seated on benches around the fire, one of them Curlew. Through the dim light he could see other furniture, chests and beds, and tunnels running off into the darkness, perhaps to other rooms. The women wore woolen gowns of some patterned weave, as ragged as Curlew's, their hair loose about their shoulders, their faces and forearms tattooed with spiraling lines as if vines grew across their skin, their eyes the same startling blue as Curlew's. Curlew was grinding what looked like a very scant handful of grain in a stone quern, and two others tended some kind of flat cake on a griddle over the fire. The smell of it, added to the smoke and the scent of the cave, made Faustus draw in his breath, trying not to cough.

71

Salmon dropped to one knee before the eldest of them, an ancient woman with a cloud of white hair as fine as the peat smoke. All four cocked their heads to listen to him speak in a language that Faustus had never heard. When he had finished, the ancient woman beckoned to Faustus.

He knelt as he had seen Salmon do.

"You have manners, I see," she commented, this time in the Silures' dialect.

"I try to," he said. "Forgive me for what I may do from ignorance. What am I to call you?"

"I am the Old One of the Sidhe of Llanmelin. We have been here since before the Sun People came and built on Llanmelin Hill and buried their kings there."

"That is a very long time," Faustus said.

"We are in your debt for the freedom of one of ours." She smiled faintly. "He tells me that it was unintended, but the outcome is the same."

"How did he come to the mines?" Faustus asked.

"They hunt us." Her expression was grim. "For slaves, particularly in the mines because we are small and expendable."

"I was looking for him," Curlew said quietly, "when I found you."

"If there is something more you need to tell me of the mine," Faustus said to Salmon, "some other damage done, I will be grateful. I am responsible for it to Rome, you see, but I would not blame you."

Salmon looked surprised. "No. I only did that to make them kill me."

Faustus flinched but he couldn't fault his logic. It was better than dying slowly. "Then why have you sent for me?"

"Your responsibility to Rome is all one to us," the old woman said. "We do not particularly care if the Romans and the Sun People kill each other. Their wars have driven the game from our hunting runs and trampled our gardens. When the ravens have come for all of them, we will dance on their graves.

In the meantime we make our displeasure felt as we may, but we also go hungry. I have sent for you because you are one of ours."

Faustus blinked. "No, Old One. My father was Roman. My mother was a slave out of Britain, but she came from the Silures."

"Blood knows blood, soldier of the Eagles."

"I promise you—"

"Look at me!" She held up a small bronze mirror in a thin, gnarled hand. "Come closer to the fire and look at my face beside yours."

For some reason the mirror made his skin crawl and Faustus almost fled out of the cave. She sat waiting and finally he did as she said and took the mirror from her. He held it up beside her cheek and looked from her face to his own. The darkness drew away and as if in daylight he saw them side by side: winged dark brows, pointed chin.

"She was small, even for a Silure, wasn't she?" the Old One asked him. "Your mother."

"Yes."

"That is because her mother, or her mother's mother, went from a sidhe to wed her father. I don't think she went willingly, but it happened all the same."

"From this place?"

"No, or I would know. But someone. We know our own. Curlew did as soon as she spoke to you. I will prove it to you. Look in the mirror again."

He did and his mother's face looked back at him. He flung it from him.

"Why have you brought me here?" he gasped. "I belong to Rome."

"That you may know who you are, Eagle soldier. What was her name?"

"Gaia Valeriani."

"Her own name," the old woman said. "Not what *he* called her."

73

Faustus had to think for a moment. "Guennola." Why had his father chosen Gaia, he wondered. He might as well have called her 'Woman'.

"And what do they call you?"

"Faustus Silvius Valerianus. Faustus in my family. Centurion Valerianus in the army."

The Old One put her hand on his where he knelt in front of her. "Remember us, and that we are in your blood."

"I will try to see that my men tread lightly on your hills," he said. It was all he had to offer.

She was silent for a moment, her thin fingers still on his. "There is something else caught in your hair that you will have to make your peace with," she said. "I think you know about it already."

"If you know how to untangle that, I would be grateful," he said, only half joking.

"No," she said thoughtfully. "That one is not of our world. It will not be easy, to be of two worlds. You must think on the balance."

"The balance?"

"The dark and the light, the living and the dead. The grain that comes up in spring and the harvest in autumn. The cow that eats the grain and the man that eats the cow."

"You are making my head ache, Old One," he said, and meant it.

"Good. That is the first step. Now go back to your Eagles, and tell your General Agricola that if he wants peace at his back to keep his soldiers out of our wild lands until we can feed ourselves again."

When Faustus stepped from the cave mouth into the fresh air he almost gasped with the cleanness of it. The sun had come out too, turning the melting ice to bright glass. He had been terrified to see only a pile of bones and rusted metal on the barren hillside, but Arion was still there, tethered to the hawthorn tree, and Faustus's armor and weapons shone with the polish that Paullus had given them that morning.

V

The Mothers

Faustus reported to Centurion Ursus that his men had seen only minor signs of untoward native activity such as the cut across the track, but...

"But?" Ursus inquired, pausing in his perusal of the duty roster.

"It may be that the Silures are not the ones to be wary of. I met some of the little hill people," Faustus told him.

"Indeed?" Ursus looked interested.

"One of them was a mine slave at Dolaucothi, and I'm afraid he got loose on my watch. He lives near Llanmelin and caught up to me there to thank me. I assure you that it was unintentional."

"That's all one to me," Ursus said. "I don't keep the books for the mines. What kind of doings did you have with them?"

Faustus produced an edited version of his interview with the Old One. "The campaign against the Silures has trampled their land and driven the game away and they're living on the thin edge of hunger. Some food might cut down on the mantraps in the trees and the tainted water."

"Do you think that's their doing?"

"They didn't say so. But I wondered."

"Most of the garrison here have never seen one and don't actually believe in them, and the credulous think they're some sort of fay," Ursus said. "On the other hand, they have been useful before now, when they aren't making the kind of trouble

75

that you never see coming or going, you just find the corpse. You can make your case to the primus pilus at dinner tonight."

"Dinner?"

"One of the duties of presentable junior officers," Ursus said. "Making up an extra at dinner parties in winter quarters. The primus pilus's wife is a social sort and has parties regularly. She likes to give her friends interesting young men to talk to. I volunteered you."

"That was kind of you, sir." Faustus decided that Centurion Ursus had probably pled a cold in the head and offered him as a substitute. On the other hand, the primus pilus no doubt set an excellent table, and otherwise Faustus was looking forward to another of Paullus's stews. Paullus's cooking was improving but he still had a tendency to throw in whatever was handy, not always with edible results.

Faustus sent Paullus to clean and brush his parade tunic and comb the burrs out of his military cloak, and went to make himself presentable. A proper bath house was considered a necessity even on the frontier and the one at Isca included a warm room, hot and cold baths, and an open-air swimming pool. Faustus left his clothes in the changing room and rubbed himself down with his best oil in the warm room, letting the heat soak it into his skin. He got up again before the warmth made him sleep through the primus pilus's dinner, and went to scrape himself clean in the steam chamber. Afterward he slipped into the hot pool and soaked contentedly while he thought about whether a cold plunge would make the weather outside seem mild by comparison or simply freeze his balls off. He decided against it. Clean, newly shaved, in his best tunic and boots freshly polished, he presented himself at the primus pilus's house in the vicus.

Aulus Carus had quarters in the First Cohort barracks in the fortress, but also maintained a house for his wife in the village. Livia Tulla had followed her husband from posting to posting since she had married him and their agreement had been that she need not live in the fort, any fort, no matter how luxurious (by army standards) it might be. The house in the vicus was new, in the Roman style, of timber and plastered stone with a tile roof and a hypocaust for heat, warming the floor sufficiently that the slave who greeted Faustus at the door went barefoot, according to custom. Livia Tulla was Rome-born and she had standards.

Faustus was relieved to see Demetrius of Tarsus among the guests. At least there was someone he knew. There was also less likelihood of being required to make small talk since Demetrius was inclined to hold forth on many subjects for as long as anyone would let him. Constantius Silanus, senior surgeon to the Augusta, was also there, with a young woman who was introduced as his daughter Constantia, and a small gray-haired woman who looked as if most things were too much for her and who was presented as Popillia Procula, Constantia's aunt. The wife of a tribune currently in Deva with the governor completed the guest list.

"I understand that Centurion Ursus is feeling poorly," Livia Tulla said, confirming Faustus's suspicions. "It is kind of you to take his place."

"I am flattered to be invited," Faustus said. "You are most kind."

Livia had arranged her dining room in City fashion, with couches for two surrounding a central table. Faustus found himself paired with Demetrius, with Constantia and her aunt on his other side. The dining room walls were fashionably painted with bowls of fruit and displays of dead hares and ducks, alternating with scenes of family life among the major gods. The food, as he had expected, was excellent, particularly for the frontier. A course of oysters from Rutupiae was followed by lamb boiled in wine, peas in onion sauce, and leeks imported from Rome. The wine was also good, as fine as anything that Faustus's father's vineyard had ever produced. He noted with amusement Aunt Popillia's attempt to add more water to Constantia's cup as the slave went around with the pitchers. Constantia held it away from her with a grin. She was an attractive girl, with a pale oval face touched up judiciously with lip rouge and kohl, and golden blonde curls piled on top of her head, caught with an ivory comb. The blonde hair was plainly natural and made him wonder whether there was Gaulish or German blood somewhere in her family.

She seemed equally curious about him, and whispered, as Demetrius was expounding on the works of Euripides, of which he had made a study and could quote at length, "You're new, aren't you? It was one of your men that Father had in hospital with the broken jaw."

"I'm afraid it was," Faustus whispered back.

"Livia Tulla says you're half British."

"That too," Faustus said.

"And a very junior officer, so I suppose you're poor as a stray cat."

"I'm afraid so," Faustus said, startled.

"Excellent, then you are quite ineligible and Father won't try to marry me off to you."

"Does he do that?" She was probably old enough to be married, but barely.

"He thinks he had better," Constantia said. "Because he doesn't like the man *I* want to marry. Here's the slave with more of those little pie things. Have one, they're really good. Livia has a much better cook than Father." She took two off the tray as it passed and offered him one. Her hands were long-fingered and elegant, the nails cut short. Three gold bangles set with agate encircled her wrist.

Faustus cast a wary eye at Aunt Popillia. "Who do you want to marry? If I may ask."

"Tribune Lartius."

Faustus bit his lip. Lartius was a broad-stripe tribune and ought to have been perfectly eligible. Apparently, however, Surgeon Silanus was aware of his father's reputation, which wasn't lovely.

"Are you sure?" Faustus said tentatively.

"He's been very much maligned," Constantia said. "Lartius is not responsible for his father's actions."

Even in Gaul, Faustus had heard about Lartius Marena the Elder. He was famous for shady lawsuits that were generally found in his favor by judges about whom Lartius the Elder knew something. He could understand Silanus's desire not to be allied with him by marriage.

He was trying to think of a way to put that delicately when Demetrius finally wound down, and Aulus Carus found the opportunity to wedge a sentence in.

"Tell me, Centurion Valerianus, what did you think of the little hill people? Centurion Ursus says you had an encounter with them."

So Ursus had taken it seriously enough to send Carus a note. "I think they may be responsible for some of the missing supplies and other nuisances like clogged water intakes," Faustus said. "I suspect it might stop if we can give them breathing space and some food. They've suffered from our recent campaign."

"Are they actually real?" the tribune's wife asked. "I've heard such fairy tales one could scarcely believe in them."

"They're real enough," Carus said. "They're the people who were here before the Silures and the Ordovices and the other British tribes."

"Are they the ones who raised the great standing stones?" Demetrius asked.

"They say maybe." Carus shrugged. "In the distant past. Or perhaps it was an older people yet. I don't think they know. This is a very ancient land."

"Most interesting." Demetrius produced a tablet from the case at his belt and extracted a small bronze stylus.

"I'll take that thought to the legate," Carus said to Faustus. "Do you know how to make contact with them again? Any time we've looked for them they simply disappear into the landscape. Turn into trees or something."

"I know roughly where one steading is." Faustus hesitated. He felt uneasy about showing that door in the hillside to anyone else, even if he could find it again. If the Romans found it, it wouldn't take much for the army to burn them out if the army decided to. And the army would decide whatever suited its purposes best. "Frankly, I doubt I could get to it again," he said at last. "But I know a place I can leave a message, or a wagon load of grain."

"I will let you know then, if that's decided," Carus said.

"There are more of them than just the one house," Faustus said, knowing that Carus was considering whether it might be more to his advantage to simply let them starve and be rid of them. "If the Silures and the Ordovices couldn't wipe them out, we won't."

"Very well, Centurion," Carus said, and it was clear that was the end of the subject.

"I am delighted to see you again, Valerianus," Demetrius said. "That was a most distressing event on Mona, but educational, of course. I understand that your mother was from this country."

"She was," Faustus acknowledged. "But I'm afraid the only thing I learned from her about Britain was her language. She was my father's freedwoman and thoroughly a Roman by the time I was old enough to remember."

"I expect she didn't have much choice," Constantia said, and her aunt said "Constantia!"

"No," Faustus admitted. Lately he had begun to wonder why he had never thought of that. In the way of children, he had simply thought of her as Mother, with no real identity outside of that.

"The governor suggested that you might be able to tell me the ways in which the natives live," Demetrius said, plainly disappointed. "I am particularly interested in the history of their religion."

I must remember to thank the governor, Faustus thought. He suspected that Agricola had used his junior centurion as bait

80

to satisfy Demetrius with spending the winter in Isca, while the governor himself was in Deva. Deva was a more exposed location than Isca Silurum and the governor would have no wish to write an apology to the emperor for losing his scholar in a border raid. Possibly for the same reasons, Tuathal Techtmar was in Isca as well.

"I should like to see the great stone rings and the white horse that I have heard about that is carved into a mountain," Demetrius said wistfully.

"They are worth the journey," Constantius Silanus said. "Most impressive."

"They are also several days' ride away," Aulus Carus said firmly, "and it is poor weather for travel." He waved his cup at the slave and the water and wine pitchers were produced. "There is excellent fishing here, however, when the weather holds. Do you fish?"

"Inexpertly," Demetrius admitted. "I find I am too distractible. I am always more interested in combing the riverbank for flint arrowheads and such and I frighten the fish away."

"Don't be discouraged," Constantia said. "We'll think of something to show you."

–

Faustus had decided on their first acquaintance that Constantia was a person of considerable determination, but he was still startled to meet her in search of him the next morning. She had Demetrius and Tuathal Techtmar in tow.

"The High King of Inis Fáil and I are going to show Demetrius the Mothers," she told him. "It's a beautiful day." Demetrius seemed excited. He had three tablet cases hung from his belt.

"Father says we can't go without an escort," Constantia went on, "so Centurion Ursus says we may borrow you." She produced a note from Faustus's commander.

"And how did you charm him into that?" Faustus inquired, amused.

"She's a pet of the garrison here," Tuathal said. "She takes deplorable advantage of it."

The Mothers were a ring of three stones near Coed-y-Caerau, and it actually was a beautiful day, one of those clear blue ones that winter sometimes sends. Faustus told Septimus, "Send me ten men I can count on not to tell filthy jokes in the ladies' hearing. And we're supposed to be getting three recruits to actually put us up to strength. If they show, you and Aculeo take them out with the rest for a mixed drill and make sure they know what they're doing."

He collected Arion and their escort and met the others outside the fort gates on the Venta road. He was startled to see Constantia in a pair of military breeches with her gown hitched to her knees, astride a dappled mare. The small feet that dangled below the mare's belly were shod in serviceable leather boots.

"Don't look so horrified," she told him, catching his expression. "I can get away with this on the frontier and I loathe carriages. They make my bones rattle."

"What about your aunt?"

"Aunt Popillia would throw herself from a cliff before she got on a horse. She's in the carriage with the lunch, deploring my behavior." She pointed at a mule-drawn conveyance waiting in the road.

Faustus felt a certain sympathy for Aunt Popillia. Women did not ride horses. He gave his escort a look that said whatever the surgeon's daughter did was not their business. As they set out he took note of the fact that Constantia had no trouble managing her mare and in fact sat her saddle better than many men. The air was bright but chilly and his charges were all bundled in cloaks, and in Demetrius's case a hat jammed over his ears giving him the look of an erudite mushroom. A little wind whipped a flurry of dry leaves about their faces as they climbed into the hills above Isca. Past Coed-y-Caerau, there was no sign of any other creature in the woods, but nonetheless Faustus split the military escort to walk before and behind their party.

At the crest of a hillock the trees thinned and they came out into a meadow with the ring of the Mothers at its center. They were gray stone, slightly tilted and smaller at the top, so that they might have been cloaked figures standing sentinel on the hill. Faustus halted Arion beside Constantia's mare as a thought occurred to him. "I don't suppose Tribune Lartius is planning to meet us?" he asked her.

"What a suspicious mind you have," she said. "And you can relax because he's in Venta with the legate, overseeing a tribal court."

She hopped down from her saddle while Tuathal and Demetrius helped Aunt Popillia out of her carriage.

Faustus told the escort, "Keep your eyes open. I'm not expecting trouble but you never know. Go and see the carriage driver for some food and wine and be sure to thank the lady for it. Have a look at the stones if you like but be respectful."

The Mothers were half again taller than Faustus, set in a triangle on a small rise, with an open space at the center where a stone-lined well had been set into the ground. From the dank smell of it he thought that there must still be water at its bottom.

Demetrius circled the stones, bending over to look at their bases, craning his neck at the tops, peering at their sides for any inscription, of which there was none.

Faustus felt less inclined to enter the circle, remembering what Salmon had said about iron. These stones were not the work of Salmon's people, they were even older and their very mystery made the hair go up on the back of his neck. Someone had been tending them too. The grass and wild briars had been pulled from the stones and the well. If the circle wasn't the work of the hill people, it still belonged to the Goddess, and he suspected they were its caretakers.

"Why are they called the Mothers?" Demetrius asked.

"That's just what the local people say," Constantia said. "The mother goddess here has three bodies, maiden, mother and crone. These are all her, they say."

"Ah. An extension, or triple avatar, of Magna Mater. She is universal. Most interesting. Of course there's no knowing what the people who made them meant by them."

"There may be a burial vault beneath them, or nearby," Tuathal said. "There are old kings in the ground here. It is a place of some power."

Faustus thought of what Salmon's grandmother had said about the kings buried at Llanmelin.

The carriage driver had handed out provisions to Faustus's men and was spreading a blanket on the grass not far from the Mothers for the rest of them. Demetrius could not be enticed away from the stones, but continued to inspect them with an apple in one hand and a piece of bread and cheese in the other. Faustus noted that he left the last bite of cheese on the edge of the well. His interest might be academic, but he took the goddess seriously. Aunt Popillia followed him, listening to his learned commentary on different incarnations of the Great Mother.

Constantia sat down on the blanket with Faustus and Tuathal and opened a cloth-wrapped package of olives to go with the bread and cheese. "Tell me, destined king of Inis Fáil, will you have a magical burial vault like that, and do they have such stones in your own country?"

"We have the Lia Fáil, the king's coronation stone," Tuathal said. "And others, I would suppose. When I am king, I will send for you, brat that you are, and show you."

"I am older than you are!" Constantia said indignantly. "And I am sorry. That was disrespectful."

"It was. But you are a woman and therefore ignorant."

Constantia raised her eyebrows. "You might reconsider remarks like that, right here." She nodded at the gray figures of the Mothers.

84

"If I am to be king," Tuathal said, "I must marry the Goddess, and so she knows me from the bones out already."

"That sounds terrifying," Constantia said, solemn now. "I would not wish to marry a god."

"Fortunately, I do not believe there is a god that would have you." Tuathal stood. "I am going to go and make my respects now that our scholar has stopped bumbling about their feet." Demetrius had settled down at last and was conversing with Aunt Popillia in the carriage.

"Father has suggested three eligible new prospects," Constantia said grumpily to Faustus. "They are not gods, fortunately, and they would all have me. I won't marry Lartius without Father's permission, but I can't bear the idea of marrying anyone else. Do you have a girl?"

"I did have," Faustus said. "My father set it up. When he lost most of his money her father broke it off."

"That's terrible." Constantia looked sympathetic.

"It was a relief. Sulpicia was a nice girl, and still is, I expect, but she had nothing to say. She was Father's choice."

"What made you agree to marry her in the first place? You're a man. Can't you do as you please?"

"Familial duty. A famous Roman virtue." He hesitated and then said, "Beware of it. I'm not saying I think Tribune Lartius is a good idea, but don't let your father push you into marrying someone you don't want just to keep you away from Lartius."

"It's not just that," Constantia said. "He thinks it's not good for me, following the army, hanging about his surgery and seeing wounded and dying men and so forth. He's afraid it will coarsen me. Tribune Lartius feels that way too," she added. "It's the one thing they agree on."

Faustus considered saying that Tribune Lartius was a dog's ass, but thought better of it since Constantia was clearly under his spell. Tribune Lartius had black curling hair and dark, doe-like eyes. He displayed his muscular physique in a gilded cuirass, with silvered greaves on his fine legs. Faustus had considered him a prick since he had heard him chewing out a slave because the tribune's boots, which he had just worn through the mud, were dirty.

Constantia bit the flesh off an olive and flicked the pit into the grass with some emphasis. "At least you could join the army," she observed.

He thought about saying that at least Silanus wouldn't follow her wherever she went if she disobeyed him, being still alive and all. The dead seemed to have more reach.

"Are you going to take some food to the hill people that you talked about at dinner?" she asked him.

"If the legate gives permission," Faustus said.

She looked at him thoughtfully. "And if he doesn't?" She had green eyes, he noted. Not emerald but a yellowy-green like kelp. They were fixed on him with a knowing look.

"You're entirely too intelligent, do you know that?"

"If he does, can I come with you?"

He flung the last bits of his bread across the grass for the crows that were watching them from a stand of alders. "I've already refused to take Demetrius there. These people are not a circus act to be stared at."

"Of course not."

"And what makes you think your father would let you?" Faustus poured a bit more wine into his cup and watered it well. A man dining with Constantia needed a clear head, he thought to himself. "It's an overnight journey. It takes a full day just to get there, particularly with a heavily loaded wagon."

"Now on that matter I have inside information," she said with satisfaction. "Last night, after you left, the primus pilus cornered Father and volunteered *him* to take Demetrius to see the standing stones and the White Horse, because he had encouraged the man and it was very clear that Demetrius isn't going to give up on that. I declined to go on the grounds that I have seen them, and it will snow or sleet the whole way, but Father thinks I want to skulk about the fort and flirt with Lartius. He'll be happy to have me anywhere else."

"Including on an expedition with a century of soldiers? I am not a tour guide."

"He seems to regard you as a suitable escort because I don't want to marry you. I'd have to bring Aunt but she's really not so bad. She's a scholar herself at heart. She carries on a correspondence with Plinius Secundus about his *Natural History*, and she wants to see the ruins of Llanmelin."

"Llanmelin's not old enough to be interesting," Faustus said. "The Silures abandoned it less than five years ago."

"I remember that. Father was posted to the Second around then, when Isca was just being built. I remember being sent off to Aquae Sulis with Aunt twice when things got hot."

"Llanmelin is nothing but the kind of thatched round houses you can see in any native village," Faustus said. "And some earthworks that have been pulled down. What used to be the king's hall is a pile of rubble that's been raided for every barn and well lining in the surrounding hills. The only thing there now is foxes."

"Let us come with you anyway. *Please*. I probably don't have much time left to hare around on a horse before I have to get married and be respectable. Father's already let me get away with more than most fathers would."

She looked serious now and Faustus flinched at her words. The old sensation of slowly smothering in duty dropped over him like a blanket. He wavered. It occurred to him fortuitously that the little hill folk were older children of the same Goddess that the holy mother on Mona served, and that the presence of women beside him might encourage their trust.

"All right," he said, "if the legate gives me permission and your father agrees." The wind whipped up and they watched Demetrius's hat sail across the grass. The sky was darkening and low scudding clouds ran across it. "It will probably snow and sleet all the way to Llanmelin too," he warned her. "We had best start back."

He cast a glance at the Mothers' dark veiled shapes against the gray sky. They were waiting for something, he thought, making some kind of magic around that old well.

VI

A Season of Omens

A warm spell that might or might not hold graced the last days of December, just past Saturnalia and the solstice, and reminded the legate that spring and a march north were coming, and of the desirability of keeping the south quiet behind him. He gave Faustus a chit for a wagonload of grain. Faustus bought six sacks of winter apples and went out with Galerius to hunt down a deer.

On their return, Silanus summoned him to his surgery. Faustus saluted and looked attentive. A senior surgeon held a rank close to that of a primus pilus, certainly the equal of an ordinary cohort centurion. A century commander was a lowly worm in comparison.

"I am allowing my daughter to go on this expedition," Silanus informed him, "on the word of your commander that you are trustworthy and are not a comrade of Tribune Lartius. I do not wish her in the tribune's company while I am escorting our visiting nuisance to view the White Horse. I consider Tribune Lartius to be an unsuitable match."

"I am beneath Tribune Lartius's notice. Also Tribune Lartius is a wart on a toad," Faustus said. "Meaning no disrespect, of course."

Silanus seemed satisfied with that and in the morning they set out along the Venta road, to travel together as far as Coed-y-Caerau. Faustus began to understand Silanus's suspicions when he found Constantia chatting with Tribune Lartius in the shadow of the far side of the grain wagon.

He saluted the tribune. "I'm sorry to interrupt, sir, but we must be moving."

Lartius looked down his nose at him. Lartius was tall, and it was a long nose. "I can't approve of this."

"As I understand it, Surgeon Silanus is the authority on his daughter... sir. I am merely the escort. But we must be going if we're to reach Llanmelin by nightfall and not expose the ladies to a night journey."

"Don't fuss at him, Lartius," Constantia said. "It isn't his fault. We'll be back in three days most likely." She smiled. "Well before my father is."

Lartius kissed her hand.

"You're appalling," Faustus told her as he boosted her onto her mare, enjoying Lartius's look of disapproval. "What do you see in him?"

"For one thing, he loves me," Constantia said. "That goes a long way. Most of Father's 'prospects' just want a wife with a little money and a good family."

"You realize, don't you, that if you marry a tribune, who all go back to Rome to make a political career, you'll be far more restricted by convention than you are now?" Faustus tactfully looked the other way while she adjusted the folds of her gown over the disgraceful breeches. "Political wives might as well stand on a stool in the Forum and invite everyone to critique them, their looks, their clothes, their morals, and what they had for breakfast."

Constantia was silent. He supposed she knew all this. A circumscribed life with a man who loved her or a freer one with a man who didn't; it did not seem like much of a choice.

They parted at Coed-y-Caerau, the party bound for the White Horse heading upriver to the ferry crossing beyond Venta. Silanus and Demetrius and their slaves were on horseback, accompanied by two mules to carry their possessions. There were inns on the way to the standing stones and the White Horse. There were none on the road to Llanmelin and a second wagon carried tents, but Constantia regarded that too as an adventure, and even Aunt Popillia, bundled into a carriage with a hot brick under her feet, seemed prepared to make allowances for the frontier.

Constantia was a cheerful companion, chatty and interested in everything they passed. "We haven't had peace in West Britain long enough for me to have seen any of the country west of the Sabrina," she said, "except for the Mothers and market day in Venta."

"Where were you before this?" Faustus asked her.

"Father was with the Third Gallica in Syria," she said. "And before that in Moesia with the Fifth Macedonica at Oescus. Mother and I trooped after him, until she died when I was eleven. Then Aunt came to live with us. Poor woman, she had just been widowed and was comfortably settled in Antium with her library and a few slaves to keep the house up. Uncle was a dreadful man so she must have been looking forward to a lovely new life."

Faustus laughed. "In that case you're lucky to have her."

"I suppose I am. When I marry she can go back to Antium and be comfortable again. Another reason for my getting on with it."

There didn't seem to be an answer to that. Faustus stopped to split the century into a front and rear guard, and told Septimus, who was in front, "Tread lightly. They will know we're here but don't make a big military noise of it. And if you see anyone, unless they're shooting arrows at you, and I don't think they will, pretend you didn't."

"Got it, sir. Peacekeeping mission."

"Precisely."

They stopped for a noon meal halfway from Coed-y-Caerau. The weather still held but it was bitterly cold. Septimus brought out his flint and made a fire to let Aunt Popillia warm herself at it. "Mind your cloak tails, Lady, you've just got them in the edge of it."

"Thank you!" Aunt Popillia wrapped her layers more tightly around herself. She surveyed the leafless hills. "One can see why they might burrow into the ground, you know," she said. "It's a constant temperature underground, cooler in summer and warmer in winter, and so easy to disguise the entrance. We've probably ridden past their houses before now and never known it. I must write to Plinius Secundus about this."

They came to Llanmelin just at nightfall, bypassing the grove until morning, although Faustus was almost certain he caught a flicker of movement in the trees there. They dug in a small camp as before, inside the old defenses.

"Look how quickly the wild comes back." Constantia pointed at a round house whose thatch had collapsed, with the bare branches of a sapling birch coming up through it. Above, on the tumbled walls of the ruined hold, a crow sat watching them suspiciously. "Can we look inside?"

"Just be careful and make a noise first. There are mice still in the old granary so there may be adders."

"I'll go with you," Aculeo said. "Your father wired my jaw back together, I'd not forgive myself if I didn't give you an escort." He brandished his pilum. "I'll do for any adders."

Constantia and Aunt Popillia looked approvingly at him, and they took a lantern and set out across the hold in the dusk.

"The rest of you get the tents up," Faustus said. "Put a guard on the ladies' tent for the night besides the normal watch, and make sure no animals get at that deer."

After they had eaten and the watch had been set, Faustus sat bundled outside his tent under a full moon and stared at its round eye while Paullus snored inside. Constantia reported, disappointed, that there was nothing in the houses or the remains of the king's hall except mice and one old fox's lair, but that seedheads of spurge and sow thistle had invaded anywhere there was light, patterning the floor and crevices in the stone with tufts of winter-killed leaves. The wild did indeed come back swiftly, a tide of sapling trees and brush covering over the places of man. In ten years, grass and thickets of scrub would have covered the whole of Llanmelin, and in ten more it would be forest.

The old hill fort was silvered with the moonlight and the white patches left from the last snow. Faustus half expected his father's shade to make an appearance, but there was no ripple in the chill air and the only sound he heard was Paullus snoring and the bark of a fox somewhere. Maybe here, in his mother's territory, his Roman father was reluctant to venture. Or couldn't. Although the Old One had sensed him. Both experiences made Faustus's head ache. He waited until the first watch changed and then went inside to sleep, shedding his armor and wrapping himself in his woolen cloak over blankets against the freezing night.

In the morning they unloaded the grain sacks, the deer and the bags of apples, and pulled everyone and everything else out of Llanmelin. Faustus marched the century and the wagons down the hill and halted them outside the grove of old oaks. The trees were black shadows wreathed in mist, their papery leaves still whispering on their branches. He shed his armor and weapons while the women watched him curiously.

"No iron," he told them. "They call it a Wrong Thing and it's not allowed in their places." He had had the presence of mind not to wear hobnailed boots this time.

The grove was silent but it felt inhabited. Faustus put a silver coin in the basin below the spring. "Someone will come," he told the two women.

They waited while the mist-shrouded sun crept higher through the black branches, and then between one breath and the next, Salmon appeared among the trees.

"There is food for you at Llanmelin," Faustus told him. "Grain and apples and a newly killed deer."

"We saw you come last night," Salmon said. "You make a great noise. My brothers are in Llanmelin already, as soon as your Eagle soldiers left. The Old One says to tell you that we are grateful. Who are these women who come with you?" He eyed them with the same curiosity that they were according him.

"This is the daughter of the surgeon of my legion, the chief healer, and her aunt. They wished to see the ruins at Llanmelin."

"If they wish to see ruins, they need only follow your Eagle soldiers," Salmon said. "But the Old One says you are to come with me so that she may thank you." He turned to the other two. "Because you are women, you may stay here in the grove if you wish."

"How will you get the grain back?" Constantia asked him.

"On our backs, Lady. We are many."

"If I'm not back by noon, make camp near here," Faustus told Septimus. "But stay out of Llanmelin."

He followed Salmon and they came to the steading in the hillside before Faustus realized where they were. This time only the Old One and Curlew were there, sitting on the bench by the peat fire, the Old One with a spindle and Curlew with a lapful of wool. Faustus knelt in front of the Old One.

"We are grateful," the Old One said in the curiously sing-song accent that their true speech overlaid on the local language.

Curlew smiled at him and said, "Apples!"

"It is a gift from Rome," Faustus said carefully. "When Rome has conquered a land, it becomes Rome's responsibility to see to its people. That is our law. We did not know that we had spoiled your gardens and hunting runs."

"No, it was the Silures that you meant to starve out," the Old One said. "We are like the hares and the nightjars whose nests you trample unseen. All the same, we are grateful for the food." She nodded to Curlew who set the wool down in a basket and took a pot from the fire. She poured a small clay cup full of something dark and aromatic and handed it to Faustus.

He hesitated only a moment and the Old One said, "I have trusted you with the knowledge of my house. You will trust me that I do not intend to poison you."

"Forgive me, Old One. I have heard tales that are no doubt fanciful."

"Not entirely," the old woman said with the ghost of a smile. "But not now."

The liquid was bitter but not unpleasant, and Faustus found that it warmed his bones.

"I will speak to the other houses," she said. "We will not fight you behind your back as you go north."

"Thank you." Faustus set the cup down. "I will take that to my commander and he will take it to the governor. They will both be grateful."

"If their gratitude extends to another load of grain in the spring, it will not be amiss. But remember that I only speak for the houses of these hills. In the north it may be another matter."

"I will remember."

She nodded what was clearly a dismissal, the white cloud of her hair fluttering in the updraft from the peat fire.

"Grandmother?" he said tentatively, to see what she would do.

"Yes?"

"May I come back sometime? After the campaign?"

"Yes."

Summer, 832 ab urbe condita

They marched with the first thaw, sweeping north through the territory of the Brigantes in two columns. The bulk of the Second Augusta joined the Second Adiutrix at Deva and then the Twentieth Valeria Victrix at Viroconium, while the Ninth Hispana moved north from Eburacum in the east. Between them they knotted a net of new forts and watchtowers designed to keep the troublesome Brigantes on good behavior. The western column was even larger than the one that had marched against the Ordovices in the fall: almost the entire bulk of three full legions behind their Eagles, with the auxiliary cohorts and cavalry in their wake, refinishing old roads laid down by Julius Frontinus and laying down new ones where there had been only rutted wagon paths. They would reach the wild mountainous lands of the Caledones and their mysterious kin before they stopped.

Because this campaign would likely be measured in years rather than months, and the army would winter away from its home forts, many officers' families joined the march, including the governor's. Aulus Carus's wife had firmly kissed him goodbye and gone back to her comfortable sitting room in Isca, but Constantia and Aunt Popillia were among the civilian followers, with Demetrius, Tuathal Techtmar, and at least twenty other officers' wives and households from the Augusta alone, their carriages and carts assigned official spots in the column among the hospital and baggage wagons. Behind the auxiliaries of the rear guard, the unofficial civilian population followed in a raffish array of rolling taverns, whorehouses, and the mule carts of launderers, barbers and others whose income came mainly from the soldiers of Rome. Faustus was pleased to see that Ingenuus, the ex-legionary proprietor of The Capricorn, was among them, his barrels and wine jars loaded on an ox cart. There would be good drink at any rate.

"Abudia's put her girls on a wagon too," Galerius told him. "Did you see it?"

"The purple painted contraption with the yellow shutters?" Faustus asked. "That's not a wagon, that's a traveling villa. She's got rugs and incense burners in there, and the back unfolds into a tent with little rooms."

Constantia had been enthralled by the sight of the wagon and was burning to look inside. Faustus thought it was just as well she couldn't since he had seen Tribune Lartius there. Faustus had taken to stopping by the surgery tent to chat with her when any of his men presented a convenient ailment, partly to prevent malingering and partly for her company. Her devotion to Tribune Lartius remained unfortunately steadfast, but otherwise she was a pleasant change from eighty footsore, grumbling legionaries tired of building road.

By July they reached Brocavum on the edge of the Lake Country, not much more than a day's march from the Ituna estuary, the boundary of Brigante lands and their less settled kinsmen the Selgovae to the north. It was a windy green country with wild gray-blue mountains and water everywhere, and there was a feeling in the raw new outpost of being about to step off the edge of the Empire into something entirely new.

Wherever the army stopped to dig in, they left a garrison behind, and traders' wagons began to frequent the outposts with luxuries that the army supply train didn't provide, from the daily necessities of bath oil, combs, razors and small mirrors, to bronze cookpots, boots, jewelry and knives.

When one such stopped at the Brocavum camp, Faustus remembered that he had not sent a present for Silvia's baby, a boy who had arrived happily unaffected by the predicted bad omens. He would buy something for Silvia too, he thought. One of Abudia's girls, despite precautions, had recently had a baby, and had informed Faustus, while nursing it and cooing at it, what a thoroughly unpleasant process its arrival had been.

The trader laid out an array of bangles, ear drops and necklaces on a black cloth. "From the jewelers at Londinium," he informed the crowd gathering around his display. A muscular assistant with a no-nonsense expression kept watch for the light-fingered, while the trader arranged a second table with sticks of medicine made to be dissolved in water, along with votives of the parts they were supposed to cure. "Remedies for cough and eye diseases from many specialists," he assured the crowd, "and for irritations of the nether parts, as well as charms to bring the favor of the gods and ward off all misfortune." A handful of bright little amulets in silver and stone cascaded onto the cloth.

Faustus saw Paullus examining a small faience figure of Epona, goddess of horses. Faustus had acquired a second horse for Paullus and he was learning, with some falls, to ride it. Maybe the amulet would improve his seat.

Rugs piled with lengths of the luxurious woolens that the northern mountains bred were spread around the wagon and a second assistant with the heavy tattooing of the Caledone tribes heaved an armful of hides onto the ground beside them. He was bare-chested in the summer warmth and his torso was covered with spirals and sunrays in interlocking patterns.

Faustus picked out a silver *fascinus* for the child, a little winged phallus to wear for good luck, and inspected a pair of gold and blue enamel ear drops, turning them to catch the light.

"For the mother, Centurion?" the tattooed assistant asked him. "Give her a bangle for her wrist instead. The child will only pull at the drops and hurt her ears. My wife told me this," he added with a rueful smile beneath his red mustache, "when I bought her ear drops." Faustus cocked his head at the man, listening carefully. His accent was unfamiliar, and heavy enough to be difficult to understand, but intelligible. He came no doubt from the tribes that the governor intended to bring under Rome's command. Faustus wondered what he was doing so far south.

"That is good advice," he told the man. "Clearly I am not a father. These are for my sister."

"You are young," the man assured him. "You have time yet for your wife to conceive. I could show you a stone sacred to Damara for that."

"Nor am I married," Faustus said. "Except to the army."

"Your army commands a great loyalty," the man said thoughtfully. "What do you gain from it?"

"A home," Faustus said without thinking.

"Rhion! Your dogs are loose again!" the trader called and the man turned away. A tumble of half-grown puppies were spilling from the wagon. The man collected them, looped a rope through their collars, and tied it to a stake as three soldiers came eagerly to inspect them. Paullus looked at them wistfully, big-footed gray youngsters with feathered ears and tails.

"We need a dog," he whispered to Faustus.

"Why?" Faustus asked.

"For hunting, when I have learned to ride."

"Centurion Galerius has a dog."

"We need one of our own."

Paullus looked so hopeful that Faustus recalled the farm dogs that had followed the boy everywhere, trotting behind him while he plowed the bean field and sleeping under his cot in the slave house. Paullus had made friends immediately with Galerius's spotted hound, and it still hadn't occurred to Faustus that Paullus was lonely. He made a mental calculation involving his pay, the money in his purse and the cost of a bangle, the *fascinus* and a dog. It might stretch, and what else was he going to do with it? His father's shade appeared to have been mollified by the last sacrifice because Faustus hadn't seen him on the march. Either that or the wind and rain that was an everyday occurrence here had blown the hallucination out of his head. He turned back to Paullus to say, "Maybe," and found him with a wriggling dog in his arms, licking his face. Faustus went to bargain with the man from the north.

Caledone hunting dogs were one of Britain's main exports and hand-raised ones were particularly valuable. They haggled for a bit while the seller assured Faustus of the fine breeding of the ones tumbling at his feet, and Faustus pointed out that you never could tell with puppies.

"Do you trade here on a regular route?" he asked. "Your people are far north of here, are they not?"

The man shrugged. "I am a trader, like my father and grand-father. We have no clan."

Faustus refrained from saying that the man's clan tattooing said otherwise, and produced the amount of silver that they had agreed on.

Rhion watched the Eagle soldier and his slave walk away, with the gray bitch bouncing at the slave's heels on a length of rope. They were not monsters then. He had thought not. The soldier had bought the dog because his slave longed for it.

But the soldier's answer about a home in the army made him uneasy. These men were not a war band raised for one battle or to fight out a feud that had grown out of bounds. They were... he didn't know what the word should be. Someone bound not to his commander in the way a headman's smallholders were, but to the war band itself, permanently. When one battle was won they would not go home to their hearthsides, they would look for another. And then another.

Paullus named the dog Pandora and taught her to follow at his heel and behind his horse, which he determinedly mounted each morning and returned in the evening more and more often still on its back. He had bought the little faience figure of Epona with his own money and wore it around his neck. Tuathal Techtmar, admiring Pandora, said she was a Caledone wolfhound, or mostly, and well worth what Faustus had paid for her. Constantia wanted one of her own and was only forestalled by the fact that the trader had sold them all. Demetrius expounded at length on the association of wolfhounds with wolves and thus with the Temple of Apollo at Tarsus. Pandora came inconveniently into season as they were leaving Brocavum and had to be tethered to Paullus's saddle horn so that he could ward off Galerius's dog and several others who appeared from nowhere. Faustus reflected on his increasing encumbrances.

Tribune Lartius waylaid him at the end of a long day of digging out roadbed. Faustus was slumped in a camp chair outside his tent with his feet in a pan of hot water. His century were likewise in their tents at the sixth's end of the cohort barracks row. Lartius loomed over him, resplendent in a spotless cuirass. Pandora, who was a discerning dog, bared her teeth at him and Paullus hauled her into the tent.

"It would be as well, Centurion, if you were to pay less attention to Surgeon Silanus's daughter," the tribune said. "She is still a child and given to things that cannot befit a respectable woman of Rome, but you sully her name by encouraging her."

Faustus debated not standing up and saluting, but not for more than a moment. He heaved himself out of his chair and the pan of water and did so. "I understand the tribune's concerns," he said with as much tact as a day of heaving rocks had left him, "but she has her aunt for guidance. I would never go against her aunt's directions." *You're afraid I'll tell her I saw you in Abudia's tent.* He thought he'd save that information in case he needed it. Lartius had a reputation for being vengeful.

"I intend to marry her," Lartius said flatly.

"I will congratulate the tribune on that occasion," Faustus said and saluted again. As he glared at Lartius's departing back he heard a snicker from Septimus.

It was well into the late summer twilight and the sixth was cooking its supper. The smell of baking flatbread and stew drifted on the wind. They had been singing to entertain themselves, one of the many songs the legions marched to, and built road to, and traded around fires at night. Septimus started a new one now. It was generally known as "The Legate's Horse" but was often adapted to suit the occasion and its verses were the kind that were made up as the singers went along.

Tribune Lartius had a horse.
The horse was missing a leg,
He fed it oysters and garlic and gorse
But it only laid an egg.

A second singer took up the song.

Tribune Lartius had a pig.
The pig it was the same,
He bought a dress and a new red wig
And took it to the games.

The inference of the missing appendage was both rude and metaphorical, but not easily missed.

Tribune Lartius had a cow.
It only had one horn—

Centurion Ursus came out of his own tent. He was grinning but he said, "That's enough of that. Go and shut them up. He has a short temper."

Faustus did so and the night settled down to a murmur of voices and the calls of the Watch on the hour as the sky darkened to black and the pearlescent smear of stars glowed overhead.

In the morning a military courier caught up with the column, squelching through the rain that had developed at dawn, and his news set the camp into a flurry of speculation and upheaval: the Emperor Vespasian was dead. Governor Agricola was in conference in his tent with his tribunes, the legionary legates, and auxiliary commanders and prefects. There was an anxious wait for more news.

Vespasian had been emperor for the ten years since he had come out on top at the end of the Year of Four Emperors, a civil war that had engulfed the Empire at Nero's death and had pitted legion against legion as each swore for their candidate for the purple. That bloody contest was still a nightmare in the memory of most Romans and no one wanted another.

An optio finally emerged with the announcement that the emperor had died two weeks ago at the spa at Aquae Cutiliae, of undulant fever following a chill. There had been a peaceful succession and the Praetorian Prefect Titus Vespasianus now wore the purple, the first emperor to actually succeed his father to the Principate. And they were all to get back to business, please.

The crowd of soldiers and civilians dispersed slowly, still uneasy.

"Natural causes, they say," a legionary on sentry duty reported to the man he was relieving.

"It's natural to die of a knife in the chest too," the other man said.

Centurion Ursus called his junior officers together, as the other cohort commanders were doing. "Have your command formed up at noon to swear loyalty," he told them. "In their parade armor, or at any rate the best they've got with them."

"Do you think Titus can hold things together?" Galerius asked him.

"Vespasian named him to succeed some time ago," Ursus said. "The Senate may not like the idea of a dynasty but no one wants a war either."

"Is it likely to affect us out here?" Faustus asked. "Unless he recalls us all wholesale and I can't see that that's probable. Agricola supported his father for the purple."

"I've heard he's led a rackety life," Galerius said. "Not that that's my business but the Senate has been asking questions about that Jewish mistress of his ever since that became public. What's he going to do about her?"

"I suppose he'll have to get rid of her," Faustus said. "The Senate won't stand for her now. My father always said she was another Cleopatra, out to ensnare the emperor with her eastern wiles."

"She's led a more rackety life than Titus," Ursus said. "Four husbands, one of them her uncle. *And* she lived with her brother, and there was talk about that."

"The Egyptian court used to make a family tradition of marrying their sisters," Faustus said, "when the Ptolemies were on the throne. To be fair."

"And we're not Egyptians, are we? Nor Jews." Ursus looked disapproving. "When the deified Claudius married his niece it caused Pluto's own row. We won't be having that kind of thing again."

"Whether it's true or not, he'll have to send her away. There are some things the Senate won't put up with, even from the emperor," Galerius said. "More important from my personal and currently impoverished standpoint is will there be a *donativum?"*

"There will if he's wise," Ursus said. A celebratory bonus to the army on accession tended to cement an emperor's popularity. "If possible, keep your men from spending it all with Abudia and Ingenuus."

–

"I swear that I shall faithfully execute all that the emperor commands, that I shall never desert the service, nor shall I seek to avoid death to the dereliction of my duty to the Empire." It was the same oath that they had all sworn on joining, but this one, given in a drizzling rain at the edge of the world, took on new meaning. Vespasian had been emperor for a decade. He represented the stability that had settled on the Empire after the capricious reign of Nero and the subsequent civil war. Now they swore to a new leader of whom all they knew was rumor. Vespasian's sudden death might be a sign that nothing was stable after all. His son's succession might be a sign that it was. No one knew.

Agricola consulted his legates, his tribunes, and his wife, whose opinion he respected. Their consensus was that Titus, rackety or not, was likely to continue his father's policies, and in addition be appreciative of a new conquest to mark his accession. As the summer ended, a final effort pushed the road as far as the Ituna estuary and north into the territory of the Selgovae, before settling into winter quarters that were still to be built. The governor had chosen Luguvalium, the site of an existing outpost, for the erection of a timber fort and extended marching camp. Luguvalium, in territory largely held by the Carvetii, a subgroup of the Brigantes, had been established after the last tribal rebellion. Its enlargement was at least a change from laying road.

In early September, news of a different upheaval reached them with the supply train from the south: Mount Vesuvius on the Bay of Neapolis had erupted in a fiery spew of flame and ash and rock, followed by a deadly tidal wave of poisonous gas. The new emperor had sent humanitarian relief and appointed staff aides to oversee what reclamation could be done, but Pompeii and Herculaneum were gone, their luxurious villas, restaurants, brothels, theater and shopping districts utterly vanished under the deadly cascade. Even Stabiae farther south, its rooftops still showing beneath the rubble, was so damaged that it was unlikely that human residents would ever return.

The Bay of Neapolis was a tourist resort, lined with the beachside villas of the wealthy, its public baths and piers a source of amusement for lesser citizens. The destruction of one of its richest districts seemed a warning of some kind, a word in the new emperor's ear perhaps, from Hecate, from whose underground realm the eruption had spewed. No one knew, and speculation over the meaning of the volcano so soon on the heels of the old emperor's death unsettled the camp. The emperor had indeed sent a *donativum* and, despite their commanders' advice and the enforced saving of a percentage of it in every soldier's account, a restless sense of making the most of life now while the sky wasn't exploding drove a good deal of it into Ingenuus's till, and Abudia's.

Faustus, who would have liked to have a bit more time in Abudia's tent himself, with a dark-haired girl named Clio who knew a number of interesting things to do, instead spent most of his nights prying his men out of her establishment and Ingenuus's before they got drunk enough to start fights.

"Next thing we know, one here'll go up in flames," Aculeo said. "I want a drink first."

"There aren't any mountains just here," Faustus pointed out, since Luguvalium lay on a flat plain not ten miles from the estuary. "And that's what got your jaw broken. Go to bed." He hefted his vine staff and Aculeo departed grumbling.

"They're like horses in fly season," Galerius said, propelling one of his own toward the barracks. "We'd best take them out on a long march tomorrow before Ursus orders something worse. One of mine had a mother in Pompeii and he hasn't heard from her."

Faustus grimaced at that. At least Silvia was in Narbo Martius, well along the Gaulish coast. He looked at the mountains that were barely visible in the distance, gray-blue shapes that might hold anything, even volcanoes. Or the seal people that Centurion Mucius had spoken of. Or the horned god whose image he had stumbled upon, scratched on a rock above the river. They would know in the spring, he thought.

VII

The Third Century

Autumn

"Rhion is back," Aelwen told her husband, unnecessarily since Idris was in the courtyard quarreling with him already. It was Samhain Eve and all the lords of the Kindred were coming into the headman's hold for council. This year the air was thick with more than the awareness of the doors between life and death opening that Samhain always brought. Idris had been among the first to come up the banked chariot track on Bryn Caledon from his own holding. Eager to see what trouble he could make, she thought irritably. Or maybe just eager to get ahead of whatever would be out on the Samhain wind that night. Idris had enough dead enemies to fear them.

Calgacos left her to the spit of roasting meat she was supervising in the kitchen, which had to be finished before the hearth fire was put out at dusk for the lighting of the need-fire. He went out to greet Rhion and detach him from Idris before they came to blows. Since the summer of the council with Emrys, Idris had been prodding his fingers into any rift he could find to see if he could make it bigger.

"Good Samhain to you," Idris said to Calgacos while a cold little wind danced a spiral of dead leaves across the courtyard. "May the need-fire light on the first tinder." Calgacos could tell he was hoping it wouldn't.

"Good Samhain. Rhion, I want you." Calgacos jerked his head toward the hall and Rhion followed him. "Try not to quarrel with him. It's what he wants."

"And it will serve him ill if he gets it," Rhion said.

"A quarrel among the Kindred will serve us all ill." Calgacos sent the slave who was sweeping the old rushes from the floor to fetch beer. "Are you just come home?"

"I stopped at my own hold to tell Efa I am still alive, and then I came to you. We went south as far as the Roman cities at Londinium and Calleva, and back north again to follow the Roman army when it marched. Lorn has found a ready market in their camps. He grows fat with it."

The slave brought the beer and Calgacos waved him back to his task. "Where is the army of the Romans now?"

"On Carvetii land." Rhion took a long drink. "And north in Selgovae territory. And east on the edge of Votadini country. *And* everywhere else between the sea off Inis Fáil and the German Ocean. They have thirty, maybe forty thousand men under arms. You were right, Calgacos."

"I wish I could take pleasure in that." Calgacos poked up the hearth fire. It too would have to be doused at dusk and the hall would chill quickly. "When did you leave Lorn?"

"By the equinox I had seen what you sent me to see, and Lorn was heading south again to winter there. I bought some of his stock to resell and took my time coming north, to see what was being said in the lowland villages."

"And what did you hear?"

"That the Romans will stop where they are. That the Romans will not stop but a treaty with them is no bad thing. That the Romans are soft and one Briton can kill ten of them in battle. That the village smith knew a man who knew a man who had seen houses warmed by hot air in the walls and marshland drained and brought under the plow and all manner of marvels."

Calgacos was silent, thinking. Outside in the courtyard a dozen small hounds, boys in their warrior training, were building the bonfire that would be lit at nightfall. Samhain marked the hinge of the year, when the old year died and the new one came in with the kindling of the need-fire. Coming on the heels of the autumn gathering-in of cattle, it was another of the rituals that bound the households of the clan to each other, and to the house of their headman, but it was also a time of year when everyone felt the next world looking over his shoulder. It was not a good time to present the council with unsettling and uncertain news.

"Also that they are not actually human but demons out of Annwn," Rhion added, "or some other fearsome underworld that has only just now opened to spew them forth. And also that their priests can work great magic and turn a man into a cow; the speaker had a cousin who had seen it happen."

Calgacos smiled a little. "That sounds as likely as anything." He lowered his voice. "On the other hand, I do not think they can be stopped with magic, and neither does Vellaunos Chief Druid, although he won't admit it. The Druids on Mona found that out."

"With a spear maybe," Rhion said. "With enough spears."

"Do you believe the rest?"

"They are not demons. They are men, well-disciplined and very dangerous." He recounted his meeting with the soldier who had bought a dog for his slave and how the soldier had called the army of the Eagles his home.

Calgacos took a deep breath. Roasting meat and woodsmoke mingled with the cold air that came through the shutters, blown on a breeze out of the Underworld. If the Romans weren't demons, they might as well be. If the people of the north did not have a care to them, a whole other world would arrive on their black wings and overwhelm the Caledones as they had overwhelmed the Old Ones who had been kings here before them. Outside came the clatter of wheels and ponies' hooves as chariots streamed into the courtyard.

"If anyone asks your news," he told Rhion, "tell them that I have forbidden you to speak of it until the fire is lit and we have eaten. And I have held council. When I have settled whatever quarrels they bring me, you will speak. I do not want anyone, Idris for instance, telling them what to think beforehand."

—

"And by what right," Idris demanded as a man from each household took it in turn to work the fire drill, waking a spark to kindle the need-fire, "does the headman forbid any free man to speak?"

"By the right of the Kindred, since he may ask what he will, and we may obey if we wish," Rhion said. "I so wish." He knelt to take over the turning of the drill and Idris glared at his back.

Dai put a hand on Idris's shoulder. "It's ill luck to quarrel at the fire birth. Mind your tongue."

Rhion turned the drill with Coran Harper on the other side, while a small hound held tinder to the growing wisp of smoke. There was a faint glow and then a tiny flame. Coran knelt to feed it a tuft of dry grass while the Kindred lords and the villagers of Calgacos's hold held their breath. For the infant fire to die was an ill omen, for it to catch on the first try, a good one. The flame rose higher, Coran fed it again and dropped the burning stuff onto a clay plate.

Vellaunos took it in one hand and with the other raised his staff to the night sky, the light of the little flames turning his white beard and gown to gold. The crowd murmured with relief. There was always the fear that this time the spark might not come, that the fire would not be given back.

When the bonfire was well alight the youngest hounds took torches to relight the fires in the hall, and the dark doorway glowed with light again. A child ran with a torch to each house in the village, and each of the smallholders would take a pot of the need-fire back to his own hold, where the fires there would be extinguished and relit. The world would turn toward the solstice and then toward spring on the great wheel of the year, the same way that the stars turned overhead. Calgacos watched the glowing white ribbon of Lugh's Chain overhead and imagined the Romans looking at it too, like a road in the sky, and wondered how much time he had. "Two years," Rhion said in answer to that when other council matters had been dealt with. "Two years *if* they move at the same pace as this past year."

"How do we know they will come farther?" Celyn asked.

"How do we know the tide comes in?" Coran murmured. Unlike Vellaunos, the harper had a foot more firmly in the world of men. The stars spoke to Vellaunos. A harper paid attention to the human world. Just now he had heard the settling of an evening's worth of grievances, from stolen pigs and misappropriated cattle to a pointless quarrel over a woman who wanted neither of the combatants, and none of it had changed his assessment that if someone wanted something, they would try to take it.

"We are a free people," Idris snapped. "Are we to cower in fear of Romans at the headman's word?"

"Two years," Calgacos said. He looked pointedly at Idris. "We can be ready for them, and if they do not come, there is no penalty for our readiness. If we are *not* ready and they do come, then otherwise. If you cannot grasp this then you are too foolish to be in charge of your holding." There was a veiled threat in that, as there had been in Idris's words. If Idris could challenge the headman for the leadership of the clan, the headman could also remove Idris from his holding.

Calgacos turned to Dai, who kept the tally of the horse herds among the clan. "How many chariot-trained can we breed in two years? And saddle broken?"

Dai closed his eyes and thought for a moment, counting in his head. "A two-year-old is the youngest we can put in the traces, or under saddle. Including this year's crop of yearlings and foals, maybe three thousand, across the whole clan. If every mare foals in the spring, then a thousand more."

"Does the headman intend to order the breeding of our mares?" Idris asked. "Mares which are not his?"

"Don't play the fool, Idris," Dai snapped. "We breed the mares every year anyway."

"And sell the foals if I so choose," Idris said stubbornly.

"Not this year, and not next year," Calgacos said flatly. "Nor any mares. If anyone sells foals or mares, or any war-trained pony out of the clan, they will answer to me."

Idris folded his arms. "And what will the headman do?"

"I will decide that when it happens. Let it suffice, Idris, that you won't like it."

Spring, 833 ab urbe condita

Like Coran Harper's tide, the double column spread up and across the width of Britain in a steady march of scarlet and steel, halting only to drive their stone roads arrow-straight through the half-tamed lands of the Selgovae and the Novantae.

The May air was heady with the smell of spring, the grassy lowlands covered with the small flowers of clover and milkwort and little dog violets under tall white clouds of cow parsley, and not even the translucent flicker that Faustus had caught from the corner of his eye could dampen his giddy feeling of standing on the edge of adventure and the wild.

"Funny," Paullus said, stirring a morning pot of porridge over the fire, "the old master never liked dogs that I recall."

Faustus looked at him suspiciously. "What makes you think about that?"

"Thought I saw him give her a pat," Paullus said.

"What? Now you're seeing him? Stop."

"It's Lemuria," Paullus suggested.

"That's for ancestors who've died a violent, unnatural death," Faustus protested. "Father died of a fever. In his bed." Lemuria covered three alternate days in May, and was held to have been begun by Romulus at the founding of the City to placate the murdered shade of Remus.

"The old master might have thought it unnatural to die when he wasn't planning to," Paullus said.

"I am not going to go stomping about the tent barefoot in the middle of the night, throwing beans at the floor and muttering. Much less let you bang on the cook pots. It would wake the whole barracks and all I need is for them to get the idea that we're haunted, right before a fight. Just saddle my horse and don't contribute to my hallucinations."

There was no further manifestation despite Faustus's reluctance to conduct the Lemuria ritual, and the column moved steadily north. Agricola's strategy was to harass an enemy until they were sufficiently alarmed and then to hold out the inducements of peace and Roman patronage. The Selgovae and Novantae were already technically clients of Rome, although earlier agreements had unraveled. These were reinstated with a show of pila and a request for tribute and hostages. The hostages were generally princelings of the tribe and sent to study Latin and Roman history in the southern cities as soon as they could be given an escort. Tuathal Techtmar watched them come and go with some amusement, being not unlike them himself.

"Although," he said to Faustus over a game of latrunculi at which they were each trying to cheat the other, "sometimes I cannot tell if I am a useful hostage or merely a burr in his blanket."

"You grow wise," Faustus said. "I expect he doesn't know either."

By July they had reached Damnonii lands, joined midway by the Ninth Hispana and its auxiliaries, moving north from the supply base at Corstopitum. Here the Bodotria estuary on the east and the mouth of the River Clota on the west cinched a narrow belt across the province, no more than forty miles from coast to coast. The Damnonii were a tribe who had had little contact with Rome, and made plain their desire to have none now. While the rest of the column made their presence felt among the Selgovae and Novantae, the Second Legion was sent to prod the Damnonii out of their hill forts.

"Get ready, it's coming." Faustus sent Arion to the rear and took up his place at the right of his century's front line. The auxiliaries were falling back and it was their turn. As he spoke, the trumpet sounded and he knelt behind his shield, raised his arm with pilum in hand and waited for the range. The Damnonii chariots swept in as the auxiliaries pulled back, their foot fighters and cavalry behind them. Faustus launched his pilum. The rest of the century, eyes on him, threw their own from staggered ranks, the rear over the heads of those kneeling in front. A Roman pilum was heavy enough to go clear through a man and one that hit an enemy shield stuck fast, weighing it down. Nor could they be thrown back; only the iron head was tempered, so that the shaft bent on impact.

"Up!"

The signifer waved the century standard and the kneeling rank stood while the rear closed the gaps between them, shields locked, swords in hand. The Damnonii chariots were pulling back, their foot fighters rushing the Roman lines, climbing over the wreckage of downed chariots. Their own spears rattled against the legion's shield wall.

By now it was a familiar dance: the staggered ranks, the rain of pila, the tight formation, the sense of being part of a living whole that moved as one great creature to the trumpet calls and the shifting of century and cohort and legionary standards. In a fight, the world closed down to Faustus's own piece of the whole, to the men on either side of him and the individual enemy at his sword's point. The Damnonii left flank was beginning to fall back and the Seventh Cohort moved after them, pushing them slowly up a scrubby hill where the uneven ground put them at a further disadvantage. A river curved around it, the spot where the Romans had forded it dropping off abruptly downriver to a series of jagged banks of stone over swift current.

To his right Faustus saw the third century standard farther ahead of the line than it should have been. The third century whooped behind it, chasing Damnonii fighters now in full retreat. He could feel his own century pushing to follow. Faustus turned to face them, planting his feet.

"Hold your formation!"

He felt them steady but the third century was well ahead of the main line now, chasing the fleeing Damnonii, heads filled with thoughts of being first at the spoils. Faustus looked among them for the red crosswise helmet crest that marked a centurion. The commander of the third, who should have stopped them, was nowhere to be seen. With a growing unease Faustus saw the third pursue the fleeing enemy into a stand of trees along a ridgetop. Around him the rest of the line was fighting with shrieking blue-painted warriors who now gave no sign of retreat. One flung himself at Faustus and Faustus took his attention from the third's pursuit to block a heavy sword swung in a deadly arc at his head. He caught it on his shield and slammed the shield's metal edge in the man's face. Blood streamed down his forehead into his eyes, and Faustus put his sword between the man's ribs.

An insistent trumpet call cut through the melee, the *Hold and Halt Pursuit*; Centurion Ursus had seen the third century break lines. But they paid no attention until the Damnonii broke from the ridgetop trees and came swarming down around them, encircling them from left and right with far more men than had retreated up the slope.

A cohort-level optio appeared at Faustus's shoulder. "Go up there and get them, they're going to be cut to shreds."

Cursing, Faustus took the sixth century up the slope in formation, Septimus and his signifer at his elbow while the rest of the Seventh Cohort closed ranks behind them. Farther down the line Galerius's fourth century was moving up too.

The third came straggling back, all formation lost and fighting desperately as they went, while the Damnonii pushed them sideways now along the slope toward the jagged river banks. Several went down under the spears and long swords of the Damnonii fighters. Faustus stumbled over the body of the third's commander on the way up but there was no time to see if he was dead. A Damnonii warrior leveled a spear at him and drove it past his head, just sliding off the cheek piece of his helmet, while Faustus ducked and then rose to hack open a bloody gash in the man's side. Septimus moved up alongside and stabbed him through the throat as he fell. They caught up to the third's signifer, fighting backward down the ridge with three Damnonii hanging on his flanks. The standard waved wildly as the signifer stumbled down.

"Get that up!" Faustus shouted at him. He swung at one of the Damnonii and then got his shield edge under the man's own and wrenched it away. The Britons wore no armor as a rule, and shieldless, too close in for his spear to be manageable, the man went down in a spray of blood. "Get that standard up and pull your men in!" Faustus shouted again at the signifer. "Now! Where's your optio?"

The signifer looked wildly around him. It was clear that he didn't know.

Faustus turned to Septimus. "Take command of ours, these fools haven't got any officer left. I'm going to try to pull them together, you get the rest ready to let us in."

Septimus saluted and Faustus bellowed, "To me! Third century! To *me!*" across the chaos. They blundered past him blindly and he resorted to grabbing men by the shoulder and shoving them toward their signifer, fighting off the Damnonii as they went. A Damnonii sword caught the neck guard of Faustus's helmet, skewing it enough to blind one eye, and Faustus dropped his shield to frantically right it while he fought off the attacker and shouted at the third century in a fury.

"Formation! Form square and fall back! Hold formation!"

He managed to snatch his shield up again, tangling his opponent's legs with it and closing on him with his sword, his shield arm now dripping blood.

"Third century! Form up!"

A remnant of the discipline instilled by endless marches and drill reasserted itself over panic. "To me! Third century!" he shouted again and miraculously they listened. They began to coalesce, locking shields as each man stumbled into line, pulling their wounded into the square with them, clambering over the wreckage of the battlefield, while Galerius's century formed up around them to hold off the pursuing Damnonii. Faustus began to angle them back down the slope away from the fanged river bank and toward the ford, toward the rest of the cohort and the front ranks of the legion. He cursed them as they went, for fools and undisciplined apes, and slowly they tightened their formation while he bade them remember they were soldiers of Rome.

Ursus called for cavalry support while the bulk of the legion moved steadily forward against the Damnonii, driving a wedge into their ranks and then encircling them. The Damnonii were fleeing in earnest by the time the Seventh Cohort's ranks opened to pull in the shreds of the third century.

Faustus was leaning on his shield, trying to tie his scarf around his shield arm, one-handed, when Paullus came through the aftermath to find him.

Paullus tightened the scarf and looked the rest of him over worriedly. "There's another gash in your neck that's bleeding all down under your lorica. Another finger's breadth over and he'd have got you. Give me your helmet."

Faustus took it off and felt his neck, which suddenly hurt like Hades now that he had noticed it.

"You're getting dirt all in it," Paullus said, swatting his hand away. "Go get seen to. If you die I'll have to go live with your sister and the quaestor."

"I'll free you on my deathbed." But he stood up because both wounds were still running fresh blood and he was getting light-headed. At the hospital tent he was inspected by an orderly, then by an apprentice surgeon, and finally by a junior surgeon who gave him a more efficient tourniquet and a towel to hold against his neck, and put him in a line of minor wounds to wait his turn.

He had never seen the hospital in operation after a fight before and it gave him a new respect for the surgeons. The wounded had started to be brought in from the field even before the Damnonii had retreated. Those who couldn't walk were carried on canvas stretchers and set on the surgery tables. Orderlies pulled the poles from the stretchers, inserted them into the sleeves of new ones, and went for the next man. The air reeked of blood and vomit and men who had lost control of their bowels, and the canvas floor was slick with blood. Screams from an auxiliary soldier whose leg had been crushed by the iron-rimmed wheels of a Damnonii chariot cut through the moans of the wounded and the calm methodical orders and consultations of the surgeons. An orderly held a cup with poppy tears to the man's lips as Silanus began to examine the leg. The soldier gagged at it.

"Get it down," Silanus said. "Your leg has to come off. I'm sorry."

"No!" The man stared at him wild-eyed. "No!"

"You'll die otherwise. And you'll be invalided out anyway. This can't heal. Hold still and I'll be as quick as I can." Poppy, like all painkillers, was unreliable and tricky to administer in the right dose. Too much could kill a man. The surgeons generally only gave enough to make the operation bearable.

Faustus closed his eyes when Silanus held out his hand and an orderly put a saw in it. His arm had ceased to bleed and the towel was growing stiff with coagulating blood. He inspected it gingerly, mainly so as not to think about the saw.

"Here, let me have a look." Apprentices had been going down the line of the lightly wounded, washing sword cuts with vinegar and picking debris out of the shallower spear wounds. Constantia appeared among them with a blood-smeared canvas apron tied over her gown.

She bent over him. "Juno! That came as close as anything to getting you in the throat. You're lucky. Go and sacrifice to

Fortuna to be sure you stay on her good side. And hold still." She dabbed a wet cloth at the blood and then tilted Faustus's head sideways to pour a beaker of vinegar into the wound. It felt like liquid fire. Faustus shrieked, and glared at her, embarrassed.

"You'll thank me later when that doesn't get infected. Hold your arm out."

"I'll thank you now," he said, getting his breath back and obeying. She repeated the vinegar wash on the gash in his shield arm and he clenched his teeth.

"It looks clean to me, but Father will want one of his juniors to have a look, so don't go away. I'm strictly unofficial. And I think that needs stitches."

A moan and a horrible rasping gasp from a man two places down the line caught her attention. "Stretcher!" she snapped at an orderly as soon as she had looked closely. "Now!"

The orderly turned to look too. "Mithras!" He caught an empty stretcher going past and they picked up the man, whose chest was now bubbling blood through the plates of his lorica.

Faustus settled in his place on the bench along the tent wall. He watched another stretcher go by with a limp form in legionary armor. A centurion's helmet sat at its owner's feet. He had a cold fear about who it was but the blood loss was making him drowsy. His head nodded a bit and he gave in to it.

It was full dark by the time a junior surgeon had inspected him and set three stitches in his neck and four in his arm while Faustus gritted his teeth. They tied bandages around both with instructions to change them every day and use the salve he was handed. Faustus asked about the centurion he had seen being brought in, and as he had feared, it was the third century's commander.

"He has a gut wound and a broken arm," the junior said. He sighed. "I don't know. Gut wounds are bad most often. He may live," he added hopefully. "I've known them to."

Faustus said a prayer for the centurion and made his way to his tent by lantern light. Sleep was a long time coming back, the destruction that had resulted from a commander's losing control preying on his mind.

By the end of the next day, the Damnonii had seen the advantages of peace and sent a messenger to the governor by way of a tribal lord carrying a green branch. Agricola sent for Faustus, startling him out of his brooding.

An optio showed him into the Principia tent, and when he tapped his knuckles to his chest in salute, the governor looked up at him from a half-eaten meal and a clutter of maps on a camp desk. He wore only a white undertunic and house shoes, his shoulders draped in the purple folds of his military cloak. A gilded cuirass and his helmet under its eagle feather crest sat on a rack behind him.

"Come in, Centurion Valerianus." Agricola washed the last bite of meat down with a swallow of wine and motioned to a slave to clear it away. "I have need of an interpreter. Ordinarily that's a senior post but my last one has just been promoted out of the province, and you were most helpful on Mona."

"Thank you, sir." Faustus stood at attention. "What can I do?"

"You can tell me when you think the Damnonii delegation are lying, for one thing. Some understanding of these people is critical and it seemed to me that you had that. It's not enough just to know the language."

"Yes, sir."

"I will need a literal translation as well as what you suspect the speaker actually means by it." Agricola paused. "You are from Gallia Narbonensis, are you not?"

"Yes, sir," Faustus said, aware that the governor was born in that province, proof in a purple cloak that provincial birth was no longer a hurdle to a man's ambitions.

"I shall retire there one day, with my long-suffering wife who has followed the army all these years. Do you miss it?"

"No, sir," Faustus said frankly.

Agricola laughed and Faustus had the sense that he was angling toward another subject.

"But your mother was British? Silure, I believe?"

"Yes, sir."

"And I understand that you have some acquaintance with the little hill folk of this province."

"Some, sir, yes," Faustus replied warily.

"My predecessor found them both dangerous and occasionally useful." Agricola poked a finger at his maps. "I would very much like to know where they are. My scouts think they live everywhere, and the scouts aren't generally fanciful, no more than the border makes any man."

"My limited experience suggests that is true, sir," Faustus said. "Although I don't think we will find them unless they wish it. My acquaintance with one household was accidental. Our wars had spoiled their hunting and forage and we gave them some food this past winter, for good will."

"Is there any likelihood that they would make an actual alliance, either with us or with the other Britons against us?"

"I would think not, sir," Faustus said. He paused, remembering the Old One's words, and wondering how far to go. "They are a different people from the ones who are lords in the land here now. Perhaps understandably, they would be glad to see Rome and the Britons both blown back into the sea."

The governor nodded. "Very well. If you should have further encounters with them I wish to know about it. In the meantime, we will meet the Damnonii delegation in three days and arrange matters with them."

When Centurion Valerianus had departed, the governor returned his attention to his maps. There were large blank spots and they were not to scale of course, being based on the frontier scouts' description and scribbled drawings. *We don't even know for certain that this is an island*, Agricola thought. He would bet that it was. The border wolves said so, and so did traders who had been to the north. He would prove it, a new laurel to hang on the new emperor's helmet and something to distract public opinion from an unsuitable mistress and the ominous explosion of the volcano. Agricola had supported Titus's father Vespasian for the Principate and Vespasian had given him his first command in Britain, as legate of the Twentieth, and then after other honors, the governorship. Titus would remember that, he thought, but at this distance the political wind was hard to read.

Agricola's wife came for the evening domestic conference that they held as often in the Principia tent as in his quarters when he was on campaign. After nearly twenty years of marriage she had an instinct for what troubled him but he supposed that tonight it was obvious.

"Have you had any word yet from the emperor?" she asked quietly. She set a cup of hot wine on the table for him.

Agricola sighed. "No. But given events, he might not write just to confirm appointments. Perhaps I should be glad not to have heard."

She settled in a chair beside him and bent to pore over the maps. "We are so far from everywhere else, out here. Anything could have happened weeks ago, even with the military post. It's why I follow you from camp to camp, you know – to be sure you haven't been eaten by sea monsters months before I get the news."

Agricola chuckled. "If I am eaten by sea monsters trying to prove this cursed place is an island you may put one on my tombstone: 'Here lies the breastplate and helmet of the consular legate Gnaeus Julius Agricola, all that was left of him.'" The sound of water made him glance through the narrow opening in the tent flaps. It was raining again. A centurion splashed by, dragging a hapless soul who had done something he should not have. "I saw one just now. Scaly, with teeth. It had a legionary in its jaws."

"Come to bed," Domitia said, pulling him out of his chair.

—

It rained all night and through the next morning. Paullus, suitably inspired by his master's temporary assignment to the governor's staff, washed the ubiquitous mud from Faustus's best tunic and cloak, and polished his armor to a shine as splendid as any tribune's. Even Pandora looked impressed.

"You know that I have freed you in my will," Faustus told him as he buckled the gleaming plates of his lorica. "And you could buy yourself out now if you wanted to."

Paullus grinned. "Currently my status is much risen among the officers' servants, since you pulled Centurion Tullius's ass from the flames. Is he going to live?"

"They still don't know," Faustus said, ignoring the unsuitable disrespect for a fellow officer. "Belly wounds are ugly." He felt some responsibility for Tullius, for convoluted reasons that made no outward sense, and had asked Constantia for information. The auxiliaryman with the amputated leg had died, she had told him sadly, of an infection, and it would be a miracle if Tullius didn't.

The weather cleared as the Damnonii delegation arrived with an escort of spear-armed warriors who were required to stay outside the perimeter. Their chief was accompanied by two of his lords, all three dressed in richly colored tunics and breeches, arms and necks heavy with gold. They wore their hair in two braids beneath horned helmets and were very fine to look at. The entire population of the camp, military and civilian alike, turned out to see their chariots come thundering up the road, which the Roman army was in the process of driving through their countryside.

General Agricola met them in the Principia tent, which had been set up for their meeting with a dais on which the general sat, with Tribune Tacitus and the legionary legates beside him. A trio of chairs were arranged for the Damnonii lords below the ones on the dais.

Faustus suspected that at least one of the Damnonii lords spoke some Latin, but their chieftain left it to Faustus to lay out the benefits of a client state alliance with Rome. Translating for the governor, he pointed out that the Damnonii were greatly outnumbered, and he held out the new prosperity of the peaceable southern tribes as an inducement. Damnonii lands now sat between the inexorable Roman advance and the highland tribes at their backs, with whom the Damnonii fought interminable wars. Rome would now defend them from these attacks.

The chieftain sat silently, stroking his flowing mustache, while Faustus laid out the terms, and at the end he haggled on only a few points.

"It is required that you hand over any Druids within your villages," Faustus informed him.

The chieftain folded his arms across his shirt front. "There are none," he said flatly. "You have agreed to respect our gods. We have agreed to a yearly sacrifice to your gods. That should content you."

"Druids are proscribed," Faustus said.

"Indeed. And for that reason, we have none."

"Very well," Agricola said. "We shall take the chieftain's word on that, trusting to the chieftain's honor." He knew he wouldn't get any further unless he wanted to tear every village and hold to shreds. Druids were politically dangerous but when the entirety of the island was under control they would be easy to find.

Faustus translated and put a little emphasis on "honor" to indicate that he knew the chieftain was lying and it ill became him.

The Roman terms were otherwise strategically lenient. Taxes were to be paid, including a grain levy, and ten men from each village conscripted to help build the roads. Six boys from lordly households were to be sent south to Londinium to learn Latin and Roman law. In exchange, Rome promised peace and protection from all enemies. The army's foraging parties would bypass Damnonii farms and herds, and no one would bother their women. After the Damnonii lords had departed, the governor made it clear to his generals, who made it clear to their centurions, that anyone who disobeyed these latter restrictions would be *very* sorry, "sorry" being on a level with unpleasantly dead. The rebellion among the Iceni twenty years before which had ended with Londinium in flames had begun with a rape.

Against the odds, Centurion Tullius did survive, but his broken arm could no longer bear any weight and he was invalided out with only the small pension that an officer certified unfit could claim. "It wouldn't have happened if he'd kept control of his men," Galerius said, "and not let them run after the enemy like barbarian berserkers." The junior centurions of the Seventh Cohort had gathered to sort it all out among themselves, out of Ursus's hearing.

"He never had a grip on them," the centurion of the second century said. "You need a firm hand and he thought they could be equals instead. Fool." He spat into the fire for emphasis. "We're well rid of him."

"Even when he went down, his second should have held them," the commander of the fifth said. "Instead I heard the optio went howling after loot with the rest of them and barely got back."

The morning after this discussion, Centurion Ursus sent for Faustus and put him in command of the remains of the third century.

"You seem to have a knack for restoring discipline to other officers' messes," Ursus informed him, "so I'm giving you this one. I've put in for reinforcements for you. Ten of the fools are still in hospital. But they listened to you when it counted, so build on that."

"Yes, sir." Faustus thought regretfully of his own well-disciplined century, and of the disaster that the third was bound to be. Catching the eye of his commanders was beginning to seem dangerous.

Septimus looked morose at the news. "Centurion Ursus is cleaning house, and for that matter I expect he's been wanting to, but you just had ours going on nicely. It seems a pity."

"You're coming with me," Faustus told him, "because I'm going to bust their optio down to latrine orderly. I told Ursus I wanted you. Until he gets a replacement, Aculeo can hold them together. There's not much of the campaign season left," he added. Fortunately.

He paraded them in the morning while they were still shaken by their near disaster.

"Do you understand why Ocella and Caninus are dead, ten more are in hospital, and your centurion is invalided out?" he demanded and no one had the nerve to answer him. "No ideas? Not even a glimmer?" They shuffled their feet.

Cornutus, their lately demoted optio, glowered at him. Faustus fixed him with a returning stare.

"I will tell you. Because you are despicable oath-breakers whose stupidity has cheated the Empire of three of its soldiers. Your flea-bitten bodies belong to Rome for the duration of your enlistment and any death through your own foolishness deprives Rome of her rightful property. Therefore you will forfeit three months' pay for the trouble you have caused, and I'll dock you again every time you annoy me."

There was a howl of protest at that, and he glared at them. "There are worse punishments," he suggested.

Shortly thereafter the column pushed east through the territory of the Venicones to the edge of Caledone lands. The Venicones, who had been receptive to Roman overtures in the past, made no effort to attack them and Agricola no effort to engage, instead sending an envoy with good wishes and the present of a gold cauldron for the Venicone chieftain. It was late in the season and a better idea to keep matters diplomatic. The point was to show the Caledones that Rome could reach their territory if Rome so chose.

VIII

Lughnasa Fair

Summer

It had rained all morning but now the mountains shook off their sodden cloak and the meadow thronged with the clans gathered for Lughnasa Fair. It was a Seventh Year and even more people than on ordinary years poured into the high meadow, crowding it with their wagons and the chariots of the Caledone lords. A ring of girls in daisy crowns were dancing the sun out from behind its veil of cloud while traders pulled the covers off their goods. Lorn was there, and many other traders including a stranger from the Iceni lands who had brought a load of Gaulish glassware and was hoping to buy northern woolens and fox furs to take south again. A tumble of young hounds, both human and canine, careened into the canopy of a trader's cart after a ball and were driven out again with curses. Wives of the scattered holdings, who rarely saw each other, gathered on blankets spread on the wet grass and shared their news, presenting marriageable daughters to prospective mothers-in-law.

At the far end of the meadow the horse fair was in progress around a ring staked out to show the paces of the stock for sale. Calgacos's orders that no ponies be sold out of his clan was a matter for argument, some agreeing that the Roman advance in the south argued for keeping the numbers of the horse herds high and some scoffing at the notion that Romans could find their way to the mountain holdings, much less lay siege to them.

The trader from the south was disappointed to find that Dai, owner of the pair of chariot ponies he had been eyeing, wouldn't sell to him. "It's a shame," he said regretfully. "These would do nicely in the races at Colonia." The Roman passion for chariot racing as a sport and the British use of chariots as a transport of war had combined happily in the south into races that would shred the nerves even of a professional from Rome.

"Can't," Dai said. "Headman's orders."

Emrys watched a dappled filly being trotted up and down by one of his own men and considered the matter. Many of the men whose wisdom he respected had come to buy rather than sell this year, but he had given no such order himself, as yet.

"Emrys."

He turned to find Calgacos unexpectedly at his shoulder. Calgacos was alone and unarmed but for his belt knife, as all went at Lughnasa Fair. Emrys's scarred face twisted in a half smile. "You will have my Kindred down upon us in a moment. Or yours."

"I will chance that for the sake of talk between us alone," Calgacos said flatly. "The Romans are camped along the river that flows between our hunting runs, yours and mine, and those of the Venicones. The Venicones have let them through for the price of a gold cauldron."

The semblance of a smile disappeared. "I have heard. I have spies as well as you. Ossuticos of the Venicones may regret that when he finds himself drowned in that cauldron."

"That will not turn the Romans back."

"No."

"Also the Romans have promised the Damnonii protection from Caledone clans in exchange for peace and hostages."

Emrys snorted. "They buy their way north with gold cauldrons and promises. Are you inclined to sell your holding for a cauldron?"

"They take the easy road when it opens," Calgacos said. "If a tribe will bow to them, they will put garrisons of their Eagle soldiers across their land and then move on to the next. They only waste their spears on those who will fight them. We must fight them. It will come to that, Emrys."

"With you as war leader?"

"Someone must be. If we don't unite in this, we will go under. How much is pride worth?"

"Would you bring your holders under *my* command?" Emrys asked.

"No," Calgacos said flatly. "You are not ready to make an alliance with teeth in it. When you are, I will ask the Druids. I am willing to let them choose."

"I still smell a trick," Emrys said.

Calgacos shrugged. "Are you willing at least to stop any of your holders' ponies being sold south to come into Venicone and Damnonii hands?"

"I will think on that," Emrys said, "but my ponies are not your business." He walked away toward the men gathered around the dappled filly.

Past the horse fair, a row of new chariots, bright with blue and scarlet paint and silver fittings, were drawn up on the grass and the trader from the south was inspecting them instead. Calgacos gave him a long, thoughtful look.

The sacrifice of a white horse to Lugh Bright Spear, made by the Druids in the pool of sunlight beside the sacred stone, marked the midday. Afterward, the human business of the day, of horse sales and bargains and matchmaking, resumed until the light faded to deep summer twilight. Then the meadow was dotted with fires and torches and the erratically moving gleams of lanterns flickering like glowworms.

"You are wanted." Coran Harper touched Calgacos's shoulder.

Calgacos stood, knowing without being told what Coran meant. The Druids summoned whom they chose by consultation with the stars. The choice came every seven years and had not come to him since he had been headman, but there was always meaning in it and there was no refusing. He followed Coran Harper.

Aelwen, stirring their supper in a pot over the fire, watched him go, knowing where he was bound by the fact that it was Coran Harper who had fetched him. The skin on the back of her neck prickled and she slapped at it, irritated with herself. Whispers from other women said that their men came back to them changed, but Aelwen told herself he would still be Calgacos, still be her husband, even afterward.

Within the grove on the meadow's edge, Calgacos stood shivering in the deepening chill while Vellaunos and the younger Druids stripped him of his shirt and breeches and marked his chest and belly with handprints of wet clay over the tattooed markings of his clan. It was said that the Seven Year King had been a ritual ending in death in the long-ago days before the Sun Lord had mastered the Mother's people and given his own the lordship of the land. Now as the Sun Lord's day slipped into night, the Mother was still owed her due and the headman of a clan was chosen to pay it. Calgacos had known that it would fall on him eventually, but now with the Romans baying at their heels, he felt somewhat more like sacrifice than prayer.

Vellaunos held a bronze cup to his lips and Calgacos drank and gagged at the bitter taste. Whatever it was ran through his veins like a murmur of bees and the trees in the grove seemed to move toward him and then retreat.

Vellaunos lifted the antlered head, the skull of a great stag with the hide still on it, toward him. Calgacos bent his neck to let them settle it on his own head and the life still in the thing made his skin crawl. The smell was musty and rank and he could see only peripherally through the stag's eyes, slewing his own left or right. When they had knotted the strips of leather that held it in place, Vellaunos – or someone, he couldn't tell – took him by the arm and led him from the grove into the meadow. All around the stone nine fires burned in a circle and he felt their heat as he passed between two of them. He could hear the thin sound of bone pipes and a path opened for them through the crowd to the sacred stone and the great spotted bull that waited beside it.

Aelwen watched the Horned God walk through the firelit crowd, her husband's presence in him recognizable to her only by the familiar contours of his naked body beneath the paint. His face was invisible under the stag's head, its great antlers spread above him like trees. Some old magic deeper than even the Druids' memory rode on the music of the pipes and the crowd drew in its breath as he passed.

Vellaunos led him to the stone and put a bronze knife in his hand. The bull's horns were painted red, twined with freshly cut barley, comfrey and clover, and it stood quietly waiting on ground already soaked with the horse's blood. Aelwen realized that it must have been fed some drug, and wondered if her husband had as well. His steps were slow, like someone moving through water.

Vellaunos lifted his arms to the now dark sky and the stars that were splashed across it, looking to Aelwen like some great white bird. He touched the bull's head between the horns, and the stag-headed god felt for the vein in the throat and drew the bronze knife across it. The bull fell, thudding into a pool of blood.

Aelwen turned away when Vellaunos began to paint the bull's blood over the clay handprints on the Horned God's chest and thighs. The smell of it was overwhelming and her stomach rebelled. She took small Ceridwen by the hand. Bleddin she had seen on the edge of the crowd with Rhion's other hounds. He would know who was under the stag's mask, but Ceridwen didn't need to. Ceridwen's knowledge of the Mother was in the baby birds fledging from their nests, and the corn ripening under the summer sun. Now she had seen the Goddess's darker visage in the bull's blood, and before that the white horse's. She did not need to see it riding on her father's shoulders.

It was very late, almost morning, with the sky paling over the eastern mountains when Calgacos climbed into the wagon bed and lay down beside Aelwen. His skin felt icy and his hair was still wet from the river where they had taken him to wash away the god and come back into himself.

"Hush," he whispered when she started to sit up. "Lie down and let me under the blankets with you. I am cold."

"Was it…?" She didn't know what word to use. Fearful? Dreadful? Holy?

"It was… well enough," he said, burrowing deeper into the furs. "It will give Emrys something to think on."

"Do you think the Druids meant to speak for you in that by choosing you last night?" she asked.

"Maybe. They won't admit it. The Horned One tells them who is to wear his face, that is all they will say. How he tells them is secret."

"There was a handfasting last night," she told him. "Idris and Maldwyn's other daughter. They should have come to you first but they made the excuse that you were with Vellaunos. I didn't like it."

"Idris would avoid coming to me any way he can, but his hold borders Maldwyn's. That is not a bad alliance."

"She looked unhappy. I think Maldwyn is forcing her. Her sister ran away with Emrys's man to get away from Idris, I am almost certain."

"He can't force her."

"Of course he can!" Aelwen looked at him as if he were a fool. "She could come to you and complain and you could forbid it, and then he would make her life a burden thereafter and Idris would spread lies about her. Unless there is another man to marry her, she will take Idris."

"Is there?"

"I don't think so. I would take her into our household if it wouldn't start a feud between you and Maldwyn and Idris."

"It would," Calgacos said flatly. He lay down and pulled the furs over his ears. "I need to sleep before I can think. My head aches like Gofannon's hammer."

Later in the morning they came to ask Calgacos's blessing – even Idris wouldn't forego that. The smell of the roasting carcass of last night's sacrifice saturated the air and a black circle of birds rose and settled around their own feast, the bones and offal piled at the meadow's edge.

The girl, Goewyn, looked blank-faced and Calgacos bent to speak to her. She was dressed in a new gown and a heavy gold and enamel necklace, plainly a bride gift, sat on her thin shoulders.

"Are you willing to make this match?" he asked her.

She nodded silently.

"Of course she is," her mother said. The mother was a small round woman like a robin.

On the face of it there was no reason that the girl should not be. Idris was a handsome man to look at, tall, with even features and a fall of pale corn-colored hair. He was master of a good smallhold and wealthy enough to give a wife some luxuries.

"Speak then," Calgacos told her. "You must tell me yourself."

"I am willing," she said in a small voice.

"Then the headman blesses the match," Calgacos said. "May you have sons and daughters in your house, cattle in your pastures, and corn in your granary."

"None of which are enough," Aelwen said irritably later as the household packed their wagons for the homeward journey, "if the husband has the morals of an adder."

"I can't forbid it," Calgacos said again. "She gave her agreement in front of witnesses. The Druids would overrule me."

"The Druids have their heads in the stars. Or under the water, watching fish!" Aelwen said. "They hardly ever wed except for harpers like Coran. What do they know of marriage?"

"Enough to stay away from it?" Calgacos suggested and she smacked his arm, hard. "Ow!"

"I warn you, if he mistreats her, I will bring her to us."

"*If* he does, and it's proven. Otherwise you let them be. Idris doesn't need a grievance, Aelwen."

"Not when he finds them so easily."

They left it at that, but when the wagons were loaded, she put Ceridwen in with the women of the household and rode with Calgacos in his chariot, tucked into the crook of his arm, something they had not done since before the children came.

–

In the Orcades Islands where the traders went after Lughnasa to sell the last of their goods before migrating south for the winter, the man with the Gaulish glass laid out his wares on tables in the harbor quarter meeting hall. The ship was a squat craft roughly refitted from whatever its previous purpose had been to a merchant vessel with brightly painted eyes on either side of the prow and a yellow sternpost that gleamed brightly through the falling rain. While the women admired the glass and the polished silver and bronze mirrors, he spoke casually with their men about the population of the islands and their government.

Eirian looked wistfully at a silver mirror with waves embossed around the rim. When she put her finger to its surface a face looked back at her. She pulled the finger away and looked again, sideways so it wouldn't notice her. The face, which had not been hers, was gone. There had been a flash of scarlet over it, and something bright like polished metal, brighter than the mirror's surface.

The trader was chatting with her father Faelan. "…None so bad," he was saying. "Where they have come now there is peace and clean water, and goods coming in from Gaul, like this glass, many fine things."

Eirian looked at the mirror again. The waves around the edge rippled like living water and she could see the seals, far out in the firth, dark eyes solemn.

"When Romans come somewhere these days, they stay," Faelan said. "Whether they are wanted or not."

The seals said, "Will never stay." Or "Ever stay." Eirian couldn't tell which.

The trader looked amused. "Rome would bring a central government, better markets for your trade goods, bring these islands into the civilized world."

Faelan snorted. "For which reason we keep ourselves to ourselves, with water between us and those things."

"Goods like that mirror your girl is coveting," the trader suggested, eyeing Eirian.

Eirian put the mirror down. "Not that one. No." She pushed it away from her with her fingertip.

In the evening the trader gave his small crew shore leave and they spent it drinking beer in the tavern room at Madoc's brewery. Eirian, sent to fetch a keg for Faelan's household, dawdled as long as she could, watching them and listening to their voices, foreign as a flock of overwintering birds. Their speech, she thought, came from the mainland south, overlaid perhaps with something else. Traders were always odd, but who wouldn't be, spending their lives on the road or the sea, never roosting anywhere more than a few days. Maybe that was the life her mother had come from, and gone back to, and certainly that was better than the village speculation that she had been one of the selkie folk. The last time one of the old aunts had snatched at her hands to inspect them for webbing between her fingers, Eirian had slapped her and earned a beating, but they hadn't done it again.

She ought to feel guilty for that, she supposed, because both aunts had died last winter, and she had never doubted that they loved her. Now there were just her father and brothers, who no doubt loved her too in their way, but also regarded her as a convenience. She was reminded of that when Madoc prodded her gently and said, "Faelan will be wanting his beer, child."

In the morning she went to see Catumanus. The two of them walked to the sea cliffs and stood looking out over the firth toward the mainland in the south. She told him about the mirror.

Catumanus considered that. "What did you think of the men?" he asked her finally.

"I thought they were odd," she said.

"Bring them into your mind's eye now, like eggs in front of a lamp. See what you see inside the shell."

She did and they shimmered in her vision, one layer, one man, over another. The trader had a mustache and then he didn't. He wore a gold torque at his throat and then a red scarf. Eirian opened her eyes and squinted at the brightness of the sun on the water where the trader's ship was disappearing into it.

"I thought so," Catumanus said.

–

Calgacos's household heard no more of Idris and his bride or how they fared until the autumn cattle drive when Idris brought her with him to the headman's hold to consult Vellaunos Chief Druid because she was unwell.

"Vellaunos can find nothing wrong with her, but she is skin and bones," Aelwen said. "I asked her if he mistreats her and she just bit her lip. You are going to have to do something, Calgacos."

"Not if she won't talk. And Idris is doing enough of that for everyone," Calgacos said.

Unexpectedly, at the end of summer the Romans had pulled back south of the Venicone lands again, and Idris was in a foul temper over the matter of the horse herds.

"They are gone south to their lackeys the Votadini and the Damnonii. The headman has made a fool of me and cost me the price of a dozen yearlings!" he began again as soon as the rest sat to their meal. He stood and paced back and forth on the hearth, scattering ash and tinder with his passing.

"You will set your boots on fire, Idris," Calgacos said, "or the floor straw. Sit down, you are not giving a battle speech."

Idris glared at him and turned to the council lords at the table. "The so great Romans, the most fearsome Romans, against whom we must needs hoard all our horse herds, have gone south again into the lowlands along the Clota and they are making new camps there."

"That is a fine thing, then," Celyn said. "If they have gone away from our borders. And whose war band drove them back?"

"None," Idris said. "Plainly they saw they could not make their way through our mountains, as any fool could have known, and so they have given up."

"The Romans don't give up," Coran Harper murmured. He drew his fingers along his harp strings in a little biting tune before he settled it in its bag. "Not as a rule."

"Where are they then? And it was the headman's business to have known this," Idris added. He gave a long look toward Calgacos.

Aelwen rose. "While you are shouting at us all, Idris, I will go and have a care to your wife and see that she is fed. You would be better served giving your attention to her!"

"Laziness is the only thing that ails her," Idris said to her retreating back. "Vellaunos could find nothing amiss."

"Nothing in the body," Vellaunos said. "A disturbance in the life force or a curse perhaps. We must consult the stars. And you, Idris, must make an offering to the Three."

Idris gave him an evil look as well but he held his tongue.

–

"Tell me what the matter is, child." Aelwen put her hand on Goewyn's. The girl lay on a bed in the room where the unmarried among Aelwen's household women slept. The wrists that rested on the coverlet were skeletal and her hair was dull. "You are stick thin. Can you not eat?"

"I can eat. Vellaunos Chief Druid fed me to prove it," Goewyn whispered. "I can but I don't."

"Why not?"

"To spite him."

"You'll starve yourself to spite your husband?"

"He has no care for me. He wants the land I'll have when my father dies. If I die first, he won't have it." She sounded very practical about the matter and Aelwen was horrified.

"Why did you agree to take him then? I would have stood up for you if you refused."

"There was no one else to marry me," she said, echoing Calgacos's assessment. She closed her eyes. "I didn't want to marry anyone else. I didn't want a man at all."

Aelwen smiled. "What else are we to do but find a man? You just needed a better one than Idris. It isn't too late. Ask the Druids for a divorce. I will speak for you."

"He hasn't broken the marriage contract," she whispered. "I just can't bear him. When he comes to me in bed I think I will vomit. I did once and it made him so angry I thought he would kill me then."

"Ohhh." Aelwen was silent. She knew some women like Goewyn. They married of course but they found their hearts in other women, and the husbands generally never knew. Or did not care, what women did among themselves not being important. There was no great shame in it. But married to Idris... to a man to whom she was just a claim on some land... "Let me talk to Calgacos," she said. "Let me think."

Aelwen returned to the great table in the council hall to find Celyn and Dai speculating over where the Romans would push north again, *if* they did, with the use of cups and the salt jar to stand for mountains and the passes between them, and Idris sulking. Calgacos watched them all silently, letting them talk it over and get the idea in their heads, Aelwen thought. When she was yawning, she signaled to her women to come away and they left the men to their beer and argument. Goewyn was asleep and Aelwen smoothed the coverlet over her. Drifting into sleep in her own bed she heard the men's voices and Coran's harp song and then finally Calgacos climbing in beside her. He reached an arm out to pull her to him.

A scream jolted her from sleep at first light. Aelwen sat up heart pounding, and Calgacos dove from the bed into his breeches. No one screamed again but there came a confusion of voices and wailing from the women's room and the youngest of them appeared in the door in her nightshift.

"Oh, oh, she's dead, lady!"

"Who is dead?"

"The poor lady! She's hanged herself from the rooftree without waking any of us." She burst into sobs.

Calgacos pushed his way through the women into their chamber while Aelwen took the weeping girl in her arms.

"Hush, child." Oh poor, desperate Goewyn. Aelwen cursed herself for not having seen what was in her mind, how close to the cliff she stood, poised to dive.

Calgacos and the women took Goewyn down and laid her out on the bed again. Her face was terrible to see and Aelwen wanted to bring Idris and make him look at it. Calgacos pulled her away.

When Idris came from the guest house he was clearly shaken. How could she do a thing like that? he asked people at random, while Vellaunos drove the women from the room and set about purification and Calgacos wrapped the frail body in a blanket and put it on Idris's wagon. No one spoke the thought that everyone was thinking, which was that Idris had driven his new wife to her death and now he was touched with an ill luck that wouldn't wear away. No one wanted to be near him.

They buried Goewyn where her father's village laid their dead, at her sister's demand. The sister came with her husband and a guard of Emrys's spearmen and threatened to call the

Druids down on everyone if Idris kept her. Goewyn's mother had dissolved into a guilty, weeping puddle and her father was grim-faced and silent. The sister took charge, eyes flaming, and ordered her laid to rest with proper grave goods, including her bride gift.

Aelwen and Calgacos made part of the sad little procession under a rainy sky. Idris followed the casket, protesting to anyone who would listen that he had done nothing ill to her. The mourners gave him a wide berth as they halted at the open grave and lowered the wicker casket down into the muddy earth where her bronze cookpots and her jewelry were already arranged. Finally, having had enough, Aelwen spun around and shook a finger in his face.

"Hold your tongue! This was your doing, Idris. If you show yourself again in my house or around any woman of my house, I will see that you regret it."

"*You* will see?" Idris glared at her. "The headman's wife carries his sword for him now? Am I not a free man?"

"One more word, Idris," Calgacos said clearly, "and you will find out. My wife speaks for me and for the clan. You are on the edge of dispossession. Still your tongue and go home before I do it."

There was a sharp intake of breath and Celyn and Dai both put their hands on their knives, but Idris stared at him for a long moment and then turned away, stalking over the sodden ground to his chariot.

—

"So you come to me because Calgacos has threatened dispossession?" Emrys looked amused. He gave his attention to the blade he was fitting onto the shaft of a new hunting spear and waited to see what else Idris had to tell him.

"Calgacos is not fit to lead, if the Romans come," Idris said.

Emrys caught the eye of the slave hesitating in the doorway and shook his head. Idris could get a drink from the well if he

140

was thirsty. Hospitality carried some later obligations and Emrys did not intend to entangle himself in them. "You were of the opinion that they will *not* come," Emrys commented.

"That is true, lord." Idris shifted from one foot to the other and waited to be asked to sit.

Emrys did not ask. He fastened a heron's feather onto the spear's collar with a red thong and admired the effect. "Then why is it that you have come to me?"

"The Votadini and Damnonii made treaty with the Romans. The Venicones let them loose on the borders of our hunting runs, and Calgacos did nothing," Idris said vengefully. "He grows weak."

"It may be that the Damnonii will find that treaty dangerous," Emrys said. The Caledone clans made regular forays to the south for cattle and any other loot that could be ridden off with. Now the Damnonii would have given up much of their weapons store in their agreement with the Romans.

Idris glowered at him. "Calgacos has given orders that no one should raid south this year."

"Indeed?" Emrys considered. "Sit down, Idris." He would go that far to see where he might stick a spear up Calgacos's nose. "Was there disagreement over that?"

"It was said that the Damnonii should be punished for making treaty with the Romans," Idris said carefully.

"They will no doubt receive a just reward for it," Emrys said. "Do Calgacos's clan lords follow him in this?" Calgacos's holders wouldn't like it if Emrys's clan gathered in spoils they had missed a chance at.

"Calgacos goes lordlywise in any matter, doing as he pleases," Idris said sulkily.

"Well then, if there is disagreement, perhaps someone will gather the courage to challenge him." Even the prospect of a challenge would weaken any claim to leadership. "I might well consider alliance under a different headman, despite old griev-ances." Emrys refrained from suggesting under whose headship such an alliance might rest.

"I will think on that," Idris said. He hesitated. "I would not like it known that I came here. My wife's sister is a vengeful woman and will spread tales. You should have a care to her."

"Certainly. And my condolences on your loss. Perhaps you would not care to have Calgacos know either."

Idris flushed. "I was careful in my travels. I am not a fool."

Yes, you are, Emrys thought. *I don't trust you and I expect Calgacos doesn't either, but you are useful.*

IX

Constantia and Tribune Lartius

Spring, 834 ab urbe condita

My dear sister,

I am glad to hear of Manlius's continued success and
that you liked the gifts. I do miss you, you know, and
I hope my nephew is thriving. Please give my congratulations to Sulpicia on her marriage. And stop suggesting
other girls to me. I can't marry on my pay, you twit, and
I don't want to anyway.

We are remaining where we settled into winter quarters last autumn, at a place known locally as Camelon,
building something more solid here than tents, as the
governor plans for this to be a permanent fort. My men
have been on duty cutting and routing out timber drain
pipe and making roof tiles. Pandora chased a field mouse
through the tile field and left great pawprints and we are
not in good odor with the camp prefect just now.

I have been promoted up three centuries, largely
because of someone else's incompetence, and have inherited his incompetent underlings, including one Cornutus
who, if you want someone to tangle a formation or drop
a crucial tool in the latrine, is the man for the job.

We will probably spend the next season securing the
land we have brought under Rome's banner and fostering
an appreciation for Roman ways in the tribal nobility.

The natives are being encouraged, occasionally forcibly, to move out of their hill forts and into villages where they can be better governed. The local building style consists of round houses made of stone or wattle-and-daub with a thatched roof. A village full of them looks like an assembly of enormous mushrooms, dotted with the occasional rectangular house built in Roman style by those with modern inclinations.

The most high born of their young men are being sent south to Londinium for an education, and we are building schools here in the north for the tribal population to learn Latin and Roman history, as well as Greek and the arts. Demetrius of Tarsus is in his element, holding forth to a captive audience on rhetoric and poetry and the works of Euripides, and forcing the poor brats to memorize great chunks of Homer. Cornelius Tacitus, who is the governor's son-in-law, is finishing his assignment here as tribune and spends all his time madly making notes for the history he intends to write. He plans to return to Rome to stand for quaestor there. And lest you think that I am an amicus of the governor's family, I get most of my information from Paullus. He and the other officers' personal slaves have an informal dice and gossip club and if there is any news to be known, or disreputable secret to be enjoyed, they know it.

"Hoy! Faustus! You're wanted!"

Faustus laid his pen down with all the wariness that such a greeting deserved. Galerius stuck his nose around the tent flaps, which were rolled back to catch an evening breeze.

"Surgeon Silanus wants you!"

"Which one of my malingerers has annoyed him now?" Faustus rolled up the letter to Silvia and stuck it in his desk.

"Worse," Galerius said. "He's lost his daughter."

"Lost her?"

"Literally. He's scouted the camp for her and found not a sandal print, and worse, she left him a letter."

"Oh, Mercury." The god of mischief seemed the proper invocation. "Why does he want me? He should go ask Tribune Lartius."

"He has. That isn't going well. Go and see him. He knows you're friendly with her."

"Not *that* friendly if that's what he means."

"I don't think so. He's looking for Tuathal too. Anyone she might confide in."

Faustus groaned. He straightened his tunic, looked at his lorica on its rack, and decided that armor probably wasn't necessary as long as Silanus didn't think he was responsible.

He found the surgeon in a fury and his juniors hiding in the dispensary with the apprentices. The orderlies had fled, and Aunt Popillia, sitting miserably in a chair, looked as if she wanted to as well. Tribune Lartius was still there.

"I assure you, Surgeon, I had no idea she would do anything so foolish," Lartius was saying. "I thoroughly disapprove, I must tell you." He looked at Aunt Popillia. "She should have had better supervision."

"She said she was just going to the market," Aunt Popillia said. "But her horse is gone and half her clothes."

"Precisely my point," Lartius said. "Lax supervision. I have felt that for some time. Allowing her to ride a horse was unseemly."

"Lartius, get out of my surgery," Silanus said. "If you don't know where she is, then go away. The little ninny says she'll come back when I allow her to marry you and that will not be on this side of the Styx. If then."

Lartius sniffed. "I fear my family may no longer approve."

"Excellent. Now get out."

When Lartius had departed, Aunt Popillia put her head in her hands and burst into tears.

"It isn't your fault, Popillia," Silanus said. "Not even Juno could control Constantia when she gets the bit in her teeth." He looked at Faustus. "Do *you* know where she's gone?"

"I don't," Faustus said. "She wouldn't tell me, sir, because I would have ratted on her. She knows I don't like the tribune."

Silanus narrowed his eyes at him. "He doesn't like you, Centurion. In fact he suggested that she had run off with you."

Faustus was outraged. "Tribune Lartius is a weasel. I told her so. She'll be miserable if she marries him."

"You had best be telling the truth, Centurion," Silanus said, "because if you aren't, I will see that you spend the rest of your days shoveling out drains."

"Yes, sir. It's not that it doesn't worry me," Faustus added. "We've been friends. Didn't she give any hint of where she was going?"

"No," Aunt Popillia said weepily. "All she said was that she was going somewhere safe and that I wasn't to blame, but she had to force her father's hand because the tribune is about to be posted back to Rome." She burst into tears again.

The disappearance of the senior surgeon's daughter was the talk of the legion, and the legate sent out a search party to no avail. Even Governor Agricola when he rode through on his rounds of inspection passed word to the border scouts to keep their eyes open. Constantia did not reappear.

Faustus consulted Paullus, whose cronies among what Faustus termed the Dice and Rumor Society knew nothing.

"They all say anyone who would run away to marry Lartius must be mad anyway," Paullus volunteered.

So that bit of news was out. Faustus knew that Silanus – and probably Lartius – had been hoping to keep Constantia's reasons to themselves. "Well, keep your ears open. She's too young for a fool stunt like that." He felt like a man watching a duckling set out on some African stream full of crocodiles.

"She's bound to be in some village or other," was Tuathal's assessment when he, Faustus and Galerius settled around a table at Ingenuus's tavern, now reincarnated in the vicus growing around the new fort. "Lying low with someone she met at a market day. She's like your cursed dog," he added as Pandora laid a gray head across his thigh and looked soulfully at the bread and cheese in his hand. "She chats up everyone. Silanus had me up in front of him for questioning but I said she wouldn't have told me either. I have important matters to put forward with the governor. I'm not going to risk it by playing the fool like that for her."

"Did he believe you?"

"He was stamping about the place frightening the patients and shouting that the dispensary was a mess and missing half his supplies because no one ever keeps the stock properly cataloged, so it was hard to tell. But I think he did."

"How is your matter with the governor going?" Galerius asked him. "And bring us more wine," he added to the girl who passed by with a tray of someone's dinner.

Tuathal leaned back in his chair and stretched his booted feet out in front of him. Pandora promptly sat on them. Faustus hadn't seen much of Tuathal while they had been on campaign and he was startled by how much the boy had grown. He would be seventeen now and his chin and cheekbones were beginning to settle into the face he would wear as a man. He had the same lordly way about him but it was tempered with a certain practicality now. "The governor has yet to be convinced," Tuathal said. "He wishes to subdue the island first. And yes, it is an island, my mother's people know that and so do the Old Ones. But he wants to prove it to the Senate for some reason."

"He wants to conquer it all," Faustus said. "How can he know he's got all of it if he doesn't prove it's an island?"

"I do not understand the Roman passion for conquest of other lands," Tuathal said. "I am serious. Do you belong here? No. Does the land call to your blood? No."

"Maybe," Faustus said.

"You perhaps," Tuathal admitted. "But that's not why you came. And you?" He poked a finger at Galerius.

"Like the governor, I am in it for fame and money," Galerius said. "Less than the governor's, no doubt, but not inconsiderable if I rise to a high command. And anyway, my family have always followed the Eagles."

"Faustus, why did you join up? It wasn't to conquer your mother's people. I won't buy that dubious pig if you're selling it."

"I'm not," Faustus said. "I wanted out from under my family's accursed, debt-ridden farm. Let us say that the idea of embodying the land did not hold the enticement for me that it does for you."

"It was in your family's holding for a long time?"

"Two hundred years," Faustus said dismally. "Ever since Quintus Fabius Maximus defeated the Allobroges. My ancestor came from Umbria to invest in land there."

"Have you any family left in the province?"

"My sister Silvia, who is respectably married to the quaestor of Narbo Martius and thinks an army career is low."

"Tell her how many roof tiles you stamped out today," Galerius said. "Impress her."

"It is in the governing, not the conquest, that Rome solidifies the Empire," Faustus said, raising one finger in a rhetorical pose and quoting Centurion Ursus. There had been grumbling about spending a fallow year cutting drain pipe. Faustus had used the time to knock the third century into a better state, supplementing the workday with extra full-pack marches and pilum drills. Now his feet hurt and his arms were sore because the only way to do it properly was to do whatever he ordered them to do, faster and better. All of which had made little impression on Cornutus, who had left all his gear out in the rain to rust and was now cleaning it under Septimus's instruction. The new junior centurion assigned to his old century was a man promoted up from the ranks, with ten years behind him, who had bumped Aculeo up to optio and had them well in hand. Faustus thought about them wistfully as he walked back to his quarters, now part of a timber-framed barracks row, with Pandora padding at his heel through the late summer light.

Paullus was oiling Faustus's leather shield cover, an empty dinner bowl at his feet, and Pandora flopped down beside him to inspect the bowl. In his own chamber, Faustus found Silvius Valerianus sitting on his clothes chest. He wondered if his conversation with Tuathal had summoned him. He never knew what did.

"The duty of a Roman son is to his family," his father's shade announced. He was a silvery opalescent form on the clothes chest.

"I need clean underwear," Faustus said. He was reasonably sure that the form wasn't solid, but he was reluctant to put his hand through it all the same.

The shade didn't move. He looked as if he was wearing a toga this time, a formal attire generally not worn except for appearances in the law court or sacrifice to the gods. Or possibly for haunting undutiful children. Faustus wondered if he should have taken the Lemuria ritual seriously. If it really did date to Romulus and his twin at the founding of the City, then it was old and powerful. "Why are you here?" he asked desperately.

"Why are you?" his father retorted. "Why are you not tending to the land that you inherited, that is no doubt going to ruin without us?"

"Because I don't want what you wanted. Or what my brother wanted. Leave me be!"

"And what did you want? That drove you to betray your responsibilities?"

"My own life!" Faustus snapped. "An army career. The thing you scorned as not fit for families like ours. Provincial farmers who were too proud to carry a pilum or take up a shield."

"In the old days the army was not a career. In the old days a man left the plow to take up a sword when his country called, and laid it down again afterward."

149

"The old days were well before you were born. I told you when I was nine that I wanted to go in the army."

"You were a child, you did not know what you wanted."

But he had. The Tenth Gemina had marched through Gallia Narbonensis on their way back to Hispania from Carnuntum and the whole countryside had turned out to see them go by. That was at the start of the civil war, but Faustus hadn't known that, only that they filled the road for as far as he could see, and he yearned after their scarlet uniforms and shining steel plate, their uncovered shields gleaming with crossed lightning bolts and the bull insignia of the Tenth. They shone. Silly really, but that had been the start of it. He had watched the great gilded Eagle of the legion swaying above their heads until it was only a small gold speck in the distance.

There was a set of toy soldiers in the toy box that Faustus had paid little attention to before. Now he lined them up on the edge of the atrium pool with a small bronze dog and two wooden horses for the baggage train, and marched them from Pannonia to Hispania.

"I knew," Faustus said now. "I still know."

"That was before your brother died," his father said, as if that settled matters. Marcus's death had left a fault line across the family, one of those places where the ground is prone to shift, dividing the before from the after where nothing is now stable. Their mother had grown sadder and their father more determined that his plan for the family should not change, that Faustus should move into his brother's place, and his wife should leave off weeping.

"Do you think you can get me to resign?" Faustus asked him. "Is that why you are here?"

His father's shade was silent.

"Because the farm is sold. I can't buy it back even if I wanted to. You can't change that, so why are you here?"

"I…" His father's translucent face looked momentarily puzzled. "I don't know."

150

He was gone. Faustus lifted the lid of the chest, took out clean clothes and an oil flask, and went to bathe. The bath house, its water supply and furnace had been among the first matters attended to. Despite the fact that most couldn't swim, and were wary of running water, a Roman soldier regarded proper baths as an essential equal to his sword and regular meals. It was a seductive luxury with which Rome tempted its newly conquered. Faustus found Tuathal soaking in the warm pool.

"When I am king in my own land, I will have a bath house," Tuathal said when he saw him. He floated contentedly, his black hair spread out around him like a seaweed curtain. The clan marks of his mother's people showed on his chest and belly.

"And your lords who bathe once a month in the river will sneer at you for a decadent Roman," Faustus said. He oiled his skin and scraped off the day's grime before settling gratefully into the water.

"No doubt. I am corrupted by my association with you. Nevertheless." Tuathal dove under the surface and came up again shaking the water from his hair.

"Will you be a client king of Rome then, or will you bite the hand that put you there once you have it?" Faustus asked him when he surfaced.

Tuathal smiled sweetly. "Do not think that I am not aware of what I bargain for," he said. "Rome and your General Agricola have taught me a great deal. Rome should remember that."

"Fortunately I am not Rome, but only a lowly servant thereof. With troubles of my own."

"We are all dispossessed in some way," Tuathal said. "By our own will or others'. Even Constantia is howling for what she hasn't got, and in her case shouldn't have. And you have something about your ears that you don't want and do have."

Why not? Faustus thought. Like the Old Ones, Tuathal seemed to see farther into the next realm than most, and if Tuathal thought he was mad, it didn't matter. "I keep seeing my dead father's shade," he said. "He berates me for denying my duty, and I don't even know if he's real."

"I suspect there is no difference," Tuathal said, "if he is real or not. How real is a spirit anyway? I have found that I see them sometimes. And my old aunt, my mother's sister, practically swept them out of her way when she walked. She said they were just memories of themselves and they clung to things they had wanted when they were alive."

"If I saw them all the time, I might not be bothered by this one," Faustus said. "It's the particularity of it that troubles me."

"I shouldn't let it." Tuathal heaved himself out of the water. "There are plenty more of them. There's an old man with a beard in the corner there right now, and a little girl who plays with a doll where the wash house drain runs to the river." He began to dry himself. "She gave me a flower once. A buttercup, out of season."

"You're making that up."

Tuathal pulled his shirt over his head and stepped into his breeches. "Certainly not. I'll show you the buttercup."

Faustus, staring after his retreating back, had no idea whether he was serious or was intending in his way to be reassuring. With Tuathal it was hard to tell. He glanced at the corners but no old men appeared from them.

In the morning news came that drove all consideration of spirits out of his mind. The new emperor Titus Caesar Vespasianus, barely two years into his reign, was ill. He had dedicated a new public bath in Rome and the great amphitheater begun by his father, and then set out for a stay in the country, only to sicken so badly that it was feared he would die. Or might already be dead, given the time that news took to travel, even by military post.

The work of the occupation paused, as if listening to its own heartbeat, and then resumed uneasily. No one knew what would happen if Titus died. His presumed heir was his younger brother Domitian, about whom little was known, and who had been given little previous authority, military or otherwise, by either his father or his brother.

"It looks shady to me," Galerius said. "Clio says a tribune told her that Domitian had him poisoned."

"Do you get all your news from Abudia's whores?" Faustus asked.

"A lot of it." Galerius grinned. "They see more of the top ranks than we do."

"I suspect that Governor Agricola isn't telling important secrets to officers he knows will spill it all to some girl in bed."

"Well no, not that one. And that tribune probably should have kept quiet. If it's true that won't be a good secret to know."

–

Governor Agricola noted each packet arriving by military post with a watchful eye and met again with his legates and other commanders, summoned from their various camps. Upheaval in Rome could spread ripples across the Empire. Agricola gave orders that in the event of the emperor's death no attempt among his command to raise any candidate to the Principate but Domitian would be tolerated. Tribune Tacitus was dispatched to Rome to see what was happening and to bring news of the governor's absolute loyalty to both the ailing emperor Titus and his brother. Agricola was well loved. It was entirely possible that his legions, and he had four of them in Britain, might have backed him had he encouraged it. Any sniff of that occurring and half his troops would be recalled to stop it.

"I have no desire to wear the purple," he said to his wife, watching her make ready for bed. "I should sooner slit my throat. And if I tried it, someone would shortly do that for me."

She put down her comb and regarded him fondly. "That, my dear, is one of the reasons I consented to marry you. I was warned, of course. You were held to have an unhealthy interest in philosophy which might affect your ambition. I think that was what decided me."

"We lost my mother to the civil war," Agricola said. "And two of your cousins, innocents all. I would not see another one, much less be the cause of it."

"No." She held out her hands to him in the firelight. "You will govern Britain, and that is all the fame I require."

In another week the news came. The Emperor Titus was dead, and his brother had assumed the purple, acclaimed by the Praetorian Guard as Caesar Domitianus Augustus. There were rumors that Titus had not yet been dead when Domitian had set out for the Praetorian Guard barracks in Rome, but nevertheless the Senate confirmed his succession, granting him tribunician power, the office of Pontifex Maximus and the titles of Augustus and Pater Patriae, Father of the Country.

News came to Britain on the day of the autumn equinox, which many considered to be another omen of some sort, although no one knew exactly what. The patrons of The Capricorn espoused theories that grew more fantastic toward the bottom of each wine cup.

"Don't they think?" Faustus inquired irritably of Galerius. "That's not when he died, just when the courier got here."

"Not often," Galerius said. "And not deeply. Still, there's likely to be another *donativum*, and that will make him popular. For a while at least."

"The gods grant him a long reign," Faustus said, and tipped a bit of his own wine on the ground for them and for the old emperor, recently deified by the new one and the Senate. Who would succeed Domitian was unclear. If he died too there might well be a war.

The new emperor appeared to have excellent health, however. He sent his soldiers a *donativum* to ensure that he kept it, and set about curtailing the powers of the Senate ever further, possibly for the same reasons. No new rumors surfaced and the Roman occupation of Britain went back to solidifying its hold on the native residents with schools, bath houses and regular patrols.

Agricola oversaw the same oath of loyalty that his troops had sworn to Titus only two years before. He sent congratulatory messages to Domitian, with a report on the progress of the campaign so far, stressing the devotion of the army in Britain to their new Caesar.

The senior surgeon of the Augusta gave his attention to ferreting out his daughter. He suspected that Tuathal's assessment of a lair somewhere among the native villages was accurate, and was also aware that any Roman patrol searching such a village would have found most of its legitimate residents in hiding, much less any runaways whose presence would mean a beating for someone.

This time the surgeon came to Faustus. "She's been gone a ten-day, and her horse hasn't come back, which I take to mean she isn't lying dead somewhere." Silanus looked grim nonetheless. "Also she's taken a store of things from the dispensary. It dawns on me that there's too much missing to be sloppy record keeping. She knows enough medicine to set up as a country physician."

"Do you think that's what she's done?" Faustus had to admire her nerve.

"I don't know." Silanus ran his hands through his hair. "But it's possible. You took her to see the hill people, Valerianus. She talked of them afterward. Is it possible they would know something? That she has gone to them?"

That hadn't occurred to Faustus. "I doubt it. They don't welcome outsiders. But they might well know where she has gone, since you mention it. They see more of us than we see of them."

"I don't see them at all," Silanus said. "I didn't use to believe they existed. Would they talk to me? How do I find them?"

"I don't think you can," Faustus said. He considered. "Any of them who may be around here are not the same people as the ones I met. Although I think they communicate, the gods know how."

"Could *you* find them?"

Faustus considered further. "Maybe. If you square it with Centurion Ursus. It's likely to take a while, even if I'm successful."

Consequently he found himself sitting in an oak grove, weaponless and servantless, his armor and sword tied to Arion's saddle, and Arion tethered at a distance. It had taken him the better part of a day to find a likely grove, one that looked tended in some way, with a spring or other shrine at its heart. This one had a smooth round stone at the center, with a little hollow at the top. In the hollow lay one bird's egg, a piece of polished malachite, and the seed head of a poppy. Faustus added a silver coin. He settled down at its base and took out a handful of dried meat and a boiled egg. He had brought enough food for three days. If that didn't turn someone up, then they didn't want to talk to him.

He was ready to give up after two nights of sleeping on the ground when he sat up from his blankets and saw the man squatting on his heels next to him. This one, dressed in a wolfskin kilt and woolen cloak, looked much like Salmon, but older. His black hair had a streak of gray.

"Why are you sleeping in our grove, Eagle soldier?" the man inquired softly. He carried a small bow and a quiver of bronze-tipped arrows on his back. Faustus suspected that there was at least one more of his kin in the trees, probably with his own bow drawn.

"I have been told by an Old One in the south that I bear your blood," Faustus said carefully.

The man considered him. He leaned forward as if to smell him, and then sat back on his heels. "That may be, but there is considerable blood of the Sun People on top of it."

"That is true."

"What do you want of us that a drop of blood will buy?"

"Only information," Faustus said. "Your people know much, and watch closely, perhaps just now especially our own movements."

"We watch," he admitted. "But what is it that you think we have seen? Besides that your Eagle army has driven the Sun People down as they drove us, which is only a small satisfaction."

"A girl from our camp in the valley has run away from her father after a quarrel."

The little man stiffened, expressionless. "The affairs of the Eagle soldiers are none of our concern," he said carefully.

They do know where she is, and don't want to be blamed. "I doubt your people had a hand in it," Faustus said. "But I think you may know where she has gone. I am called Faustus," he added. "The Old One of the Sidhe of Llanmelin would vouch for me." *Probably.*

"Do you think we converse by magic? It would take days to send a runner south and back. Why should I help you?"

"For the reason that until she is found there will be soldiers looking for her under every rock and maybe finding things they were not seeking."

"They will not find us."

"Perhaps. But they will be a very great nuisance."

The man was silent a moment, thinking. "We worried when we saw you in the grove, for the reason that you knew to look for us here," he said.

"That I have told to no one," Faustus said. "The girl's father is our healer, not the commander. He doesn't care where your people live, only to find his daughter."

"What will you give me?"

Faustus pulled his pack from under the blankets, relieved. He suspected that it was better to pay for what the little dark people could tell him. Owing them some price undisclosed at the time might not be wise. "Three lengths of good cloth, a set of bronze bowls, and a fine mortarium," he said, a selection chosen with regard to what he had observed in Grandmother's house.

The man inspected them and ran his fingers along the inner surface of the mortarium. It was hard fired pottery, bright blue,

157

and studded with sharp grits of quartz. The edge had a lip for pouring. It was a far better tool than any stone quern. He smiled. "The village by the ford that is upwater from your camp."

Faustus waited while the village headman recited all the reasons that he had never seen the Eagle surgeon's daughter. A crowd had gathered behind him and a pair of small children leading a goat cart stopped to stare at the Romans.

Faustus leaned from the saddle. "The girl is the new emperor's niece," he informed the headman. "Her mother is distraught," he added for embellishment. "And has written to her brother."

"Your soldiers have been here before, looking for her," the headman protested.

"Not as thoroughly as they will," Faustus assured him. "I am certain that your chieftain would not like to have one of his villages responsible for breaking the entire treaty he has made with Rome."

The headman spoke to a woman beside him and she seemed to argue.

"We can take your houses apart stick by stick, Mother," Faustus said. "Whether we find her or not, it will be a great unpleasantness."

The headman snapped something at the woman and she seemed to give up. She stumped across the yard to a cluster of round dwellings that sat along the stream's edge. Smoke filtered from their thatched roofs. In a few minutes she was back with Constantia by the arm. A small boy led her horse, hastily packed bags tied around the saddle horns.

Constantia wore an air of outraged dignity but it was obvious that she wasn't going to win and she let Septimus boost her into the saddle. She wore a pair of native breeches and her blond hair hung down her back in two braids in the tribal style.

"I suppose I'm lucky you didn't get a tattoo," Silanus growled at her. "You idiot! Have you been playing physician? You'll be fortunate if you didn't poison someone."

"*You* taught me!" Constantia snapped back. "That would be your fault."

Faustus turned Arion back down the track along the river, and let them argue as they rode.

"I don't suppose it occurred to you," Silanus said, "while you were trying to blackmail me into letting you marry that ass, that if I changed my mind I had no way to tell you?"

"Have you?"

"Of course not."

"And you!" Constantia snapped her head around to glare at Faustus. "You have no business in my affairs. And lying into the bargain. I wish I *was* the emperor's niece, I'd have you condemned to the mines."

"Fortunately you're not," Faustus said. "And if you were, you'd marry the man *he* picked. Possibly your uncle. Being in the imperial family is no picnic."

"You are horrible and I hate you."

"You are spoiled and you're lucky we didn't leave you there. You could have married Urg the Headman. Cooked his gruel over a peat fire. Borne his hideous children."

Her temper had not cooled by the time they rode through the camp gates and Faustus gratefully gave his attention to the further reformation of the third century. The next day was the Meditrinalia, the ancient festival of new vintages, which was a traditional event so old that no one knew quite what the name meant and thus was a matter of settled ritual practice even in the provinces. Libations were offered to Jupiter and to Bacchus, and a good deal of wine was consumed by the celebrants in the process. Faustus decided that the third century had made sufficient progress that they might be given the afternoon and evening free to sacrifice, and took the opportunity to settle himself in Ingenuus's ever-expanding establishment to do the same.

Ingenuus did a healthy business in wine and native beer, as well as hot stew and Rutupiae oysters shipped upriver from the coast, and the upper ranks as well as the lowly patronized his tavern. Faustus observed Tribune Lartius consuming oysters and wondered how his reunion with Constantia had gone. Septimus and the third's watch commander were eating stew at another table, and Galerius, in a fit of foolhardiness, was playing latrunculi for money with Tuathal.

A narrow-stripe tribune sitting with Lartius said something to him and laughed, and Lartius leaned across the table, his face in the other man's. "Watch your tongue, Gratius. Don't link my name with hers. She's not fit to marry. She was just a provincial diversion."

Tuathal gave Lartius a long stare. "She's lucky he feels that way," he said to Galerius, loudly enough for Lartius to hear. "Otherwise her father might have given in and let her marry the pig."

"You watch your mouth too, you Hibernian brat," Lartius told him.

"Did you tell her so, Lartius?" someone asked. "That's beastly. I saw her when I went to get some salve for my blisters. She was crying. I thought it was because old Silanus dragged her home."

"We barely spoke," Lartius said. "The girl spent half a month in some filthy native shack. She couldn't have expected me to actually marry her."

Faustus stood up. He knew he had had a skinful of wine, but it only served to pinpoint his anger. Lartius was drunker than he was and wasn't going to shut up unless someone shut him up. "Keep your mouth closed, Tribune," Faustus said. "Before someone knocks the teeth out of it."

Lartius stood and staggered toward him and everyone else hastily got out of their way, holding food and drink over their heads. The tribune who had been sitting with Lartius tried to catch his arm but Lartius pulled away from him.

"Outside!" Ingenuus said. "Outside! Not in here!"

Lartius ignored him and swung a fist at Faustus. It connected with Faustus's ear and Faustus drew his own fist back.

"Outside!" Ingenuus shouted.

Lartius slipped in a puddle of spilled wine and Faustus jumped him as he stumbled. They struggled together on the packed dirt of the tavern floor. Neither was wearing armor, and they fought to find a grip on tunic front or collar. Faustus felt Lartius reach for his belt knife and grabbed it first and flung it away from them. Lartius reached for Faustus's knife then, and Faustus fought him as he clenched his fingers around it. "No knives, you fool!" he gasped.

They rolled into a row of clay wine jars standing on their ends along the wall and two came down on top of them, cracking Faustus across the forehead and sending a flood of wine over both. Lartius's grip on the knife hilt loosened and Faustus wrenched it free and threw it across the room.

They lurched away from the wine jars and Lartius felt on the floor for where his own knife had fallen. Someone else had the presence of mind to kick it away again and they rolled under a table still fighting. Ingenuus picked up the table and kicked them both in the ribs with the same mailed sandals he had worn in the legion. Faustus drove his fist into Lartius's nose and Lartius kneed him in the belly, driving his breath out. He was trying to get it back when Gratius and another tribune pulled Lartius off and held him.

"You're drunk," Gratius told them both. "Go home to bed."

Lartius's nose was pouring blood. He looked at Faustus crouching on the floor. "I'll have your commission. I'll have you discharged!"

"You started it, Lartius," Gratius said, "and with a man who's so far your junior that you ought to be ashamed. You're about to sail for home and if you're planning to stand for quaestor, you'd best leave off if you don't want your love affairs all over the Senate." Broad-stripe tribunes were on a political path and served only a few years. Narrow-stripe tribunes were career military men. They were not always fond of each other.

"Come along," the other tribune said. He pointed at Faustus. "Someone get him to bed too."

"Someone owes me for the wine." Ingenuus folded his arms and stood in the doorway.

Gratius slipped him a handful of coins. "It was almost worth it." Lartius glowered at him, but he was weaving on his feet and he let them escort him out. Gratius picked up Lartius's knife on the way out and stuck it in his own belt.

Faustus got to his feet somewhat unsteadily himself, and the other patrons began to reassemble their meals and their dice games. Galerius and Tuathal towed him toward a table where Septimus inspected his head.

"You've got a big gash there and it's bleeding like a sacrificial pig," he said. "I expect it ought to be cleaned."

Faustus could feel it running down his ear.

Galerius peered at his scalp. "I'd say all that wine's washed it out nicely."

Faustus's hair was dripping with Ingenuus's second-best vintage. "It's just as well," he muttered, "because I'm not going to the surgery. She'd probably hit me with something else. My head hurts enough already."

"Not like it's going to in the morning," Galerius said cheerfully. "Come along."

Faustus lined up at parade that next morning with a black eye that showed clearly under his helmet rim. The third century apparently considered that a badge of honor, and raised a shout of "Ave Valerianus!"

Centurion Ursus hefted his vine stick and they subsided, but Faustus thought he was laughing.

Centurion Ursus then took them on a forest infiltration practice that took the better part of the day. To send an entire cohort through dense woods and have them come out the other side in formation is not an easy maneuver. By the time they had done it to Ursus's satisfaction on the fourth try, and retrieved the hapless legionary who had ended up a mile to the west, it was dusk, and Faustus was too tired to think about either Tribune Lartius or Constantia.

Silanus, however, had made up his mind and ordered his daughter south to Aquae Sulis where she could be properly chaperoned. Faustus emerged from his quarters in the early morning to see Silanus's carriage harnessed and standing outside the surgeon's house on a side street near the hospital. Silanus's slave and Aunt Popillia's maid were loading boxes and bags onto the roof. Constantia was still furiously and indiscriminately angry with her father, Faustus and Tribune Lartius, and only gave him an evil look, but Aunt Popillia patted his hand and tutted over his black eye.

"The silly girl ought to be thanking you," she said, "so I shall do it."

They were going to live with Publia Livilla, an old friend of hers, Aunt Popillia confided. Publia Livilla often took on the task, for a suitable recompense, of giving country girls a town polish. Between them Aunt Popillia and Publia were supposed to polish Constantia, or attempt it. Faustus thought he wouldn't bet on it, watching Constantia's vengeful profile through the carriage window. He could understand Silanus's hurry in getting her on the road, however. Tribune Lartius was due to sail for Rome in only a few more days, but there wasn't anyone in the camp who didn't feel that it would be better if Constantia didn't encounter him in the meantime.

Tribune Lartius duly departed, after an angry interview with the legate Domitius Longinus, who held Lartius to blame for everything that had happened and said as much. For form's sake, Longinus called Faustus into his office and gave him a short irritable lecture on the dangers inherent in punching tribunes, and then went back to more pressing affairs, which included dispatches that described increasing border problems on the Rhenus frontier in Germany. There was, the legate considered, a very good possibility of detachments being sent from Britain to deal with it. He began to note the excellent reasons that these detachments should not come from his own legion.

X

Several Moves on the Governor's Gameboard

Autumn

Constantia followed Aunt Popillia and Aunt Publia through the market streets of Aquae Sulis, refusing to be intrigued by either a blue silk gown or a cloak of gray wool with a border embroidered in colored silks. She thought of the two as the dragon aunts, although they weren't really very dragonish. Aunt Publia was small with an imposing tower of gray curls capping her head like a small, overflowing flower pot. She had been sympathetic at the same time as she had told Constantia firmly that she had indulged in enough nonsense and there would be no more of that. Her little house in the Street of Lilies was luxurious after an army camp, and just now the aunts were attempting to further divert her with shopping. Trailed by Aunt Publia's maid with a market basket, they had examined silver bangles set with carnelian, enameled hair pins, and ear drops hung with amethysts and pearls. Constantia had shrugged.

"I know what you need," Aunt Publia said as they made their way through streets crowded with soldiers on leave and invalids visiting the temple and the healing baths. She paused to glare at a man in a litter until he told his bearers to make way for them. "Tell me," she said briskly to Constantia. "What do you really want?"

"I want Lartius's cock to fall off," Constantia said. "Infested with maggots."

"Constantia!" Aunt Popillia looked horrified.

"Leave her be, Popillia," Aunt Publia said. "I imagine that's a popular sentiment. Although you are not to say so again, please," she added to Constantia. "Not that frankly."

"Yes, Aunt."

"Now then. Let's see if we can arrange that. It's in the hands of the gods, of course," she added. "But we'll try, and it will make you feel better, I promise."

They were approaching the Temple of Sulis Minerva and Aunt Publia turned to the row of shops on either side of the great courtyard and the immense gilt bronze statue of the goddess. Here one could buy various votive offerings to the goddess, whose sacred spring had been a site of healing and petitions since before the Romans had come. Aunt Publia passed by a stall selling silver charms representing various body parts and another offering bronze bowls and vases. A woman with hennaed hair and an elaborate gold lunula at her throat sat at a counter in the third stall. Behind her on a shelf were baskets with thin lead tablets rolled as smooth as wax.

"Here we are, dear," Aunt Publia said. "We'll give your complaint to the goddess and ask for her help. I know several people who have purchased curses here and found them effective."

Constantia began to look interested.

"Certainly," the woman behind the counter said. "I have a number ready-made, or we can do you a special. Have you had something stolen?"

"That's the usual," Aunt Publia said to Aunt Popillia. "The thievery at the baths is something dreadful. You can't turn your back on anything." She said to the woman at the counter, "It's a man who has behaved very badly."

"Ah!" The woman reached for a basket on the shelf behind her. "Let's see what we have."

"It won't fit your ready-made ones," Constantia said.

"Suppose you tell me what has happened then, dear," the woman said sympathetically.

Constantia thought of Lartius saying to her in her father's surgery that she couldn't really have expected him to actually marry her and take her home to Rome. She was a provincial diversion, surely she had realized that? She blurted that out to the woman at the counter and the woman sighed.

"Oh my dear, that's one of the most common. A Number Six will do nicely." She picked a tablet from the basket. "We'll fill in his name now, to make certain the goddess recognizes him. I do feel that sometimes the deities get distracted. It's as well to be specific. And what would you like to have happen to him?"

Constantia opened her mouth to answer and Aunt Publia said firmly, "It would be very satisfactory if his nether parts should wither, along with the rest of him, of course."

"A most common and understandable wish." The woman picked up a sharp stylus and began to fill in the blank spaces on the tablet. When she had finished she handed it to Constantia for her inspection.

Constantia laughed. Something about the little lead tablet in her hand lifted part of the humiliation that had sat around her like a cloud. "Oh that's lovely. I hadn't thought of cursing him, except in my head of course. Do these work?"

"Very often," the woman said. "Sometimes in their own way. The gods can be capricious, but I have found that if we give them time, they often arrange things." She took the tablet back and began to roll it up. "Take this to the Sacred Spring and say a prayer to Sulis Minerva before you throw it in." She picked up a small hammer and an iron nail and pounded the nail through the rolled tablet.

Constantia took the tablet, with its curse nailed inside, and they made their way to the spring. Its hot mineral water fed the bath complex beyond the temple, and the edges of the pool were crowded with visitors making their offerings to the goddess before visiting the healing baths. She looked at the rolled curse in her hand and grinned at it suddenly, then flung it into the pool and watched it sink. It was satisfying to say the things that she had been crying too hard to say to Lartius himself. That he had reduced her to abject tears had been a burning part of her misery. Even if the curse didn't work, the little lead tablet had relieved that.

Spring—Summer, 835 ab urbe condita

> *My dear friend Faustus,*
> *You were right about Lartius and I am sorry that I*
> *was a pig when you came and got me from that village.*
> *I have asked my uncle the emperor to promote you to*
> *governor.*
> *Apologetically,*
> *Your friend Constantia*

By some nefarious process, probably flirting with a courier, Faustus thought, Constantia had wangled her letter into the military post, but it made its way slowly and chased the Second Augusta about most of the province. He read it finally in the spring when a supply train caught up to them in Novantae territory. The new Emperor Domitian had ordered that conquest in Britain should stop below the Bodotria–Clota line, and the entire campaign had been flipped on its head.

Ignoring the emperor's wishes would have been dangerously imprudent, and Agricola obeyed, however reluctantly. The emperor himself was campaigning in Germany and it was clear now that his focus was on a victory there under his own banner. Agricola sent a tactful message of compliance to Domitian, and continued to lay down a series of forts along the neck between the Clota and the Bodotria, reinforcing the ground gained. Balked of any northward movement, he began an operation designed to remind the Selgovae and the Novantae of their obligations, using detachments of the Augusta, the Adiutrix and the Valeria Victrix. Domitius Longinus had proved prescient: a sizable vexillation of the Ninth Hispana had recently shipped out for the Rhenus frontier in Germany.

"Still, better them than your men," Agricola said to Longinus over maps and dinner.

Both men regarded the Ninth as possibly unstable, and perhaps better split than left as a whole. The legion had been badly mauled in the Iceni rebellion twenty years ago and had nearly mutinied during Julius Frontinus's campaign. And in the meantime, Agricola had three full legions and more than half of a fourth, and it was going to be necessary to justify their presence to Domitian. He ordered the Fleet and the Augusta detachment to raid the coastal Novantae villages, where their obligations appeared to have been forgotten to such an extent that they were harboring pirates. The proximity of the Novantae peninsula to the shores of Hibernia suggested an expedition of frontier scouts and surveyors to reconnoiter the possibilities there.

Tuathal, having been told to attach himself to the Augusta and stay there, demanded to go with them.

"Certainly not." Agricola pointed a finger at him. "Sit down."

Tuathal sat, angrily. "I should be in the vanguard. This is my right."

"The frontier scouts are scouts, not an invading army. They are quiet about their business. You are not a quiet person. Nor have you had any training at being one. You will go when the intention is to invade." Agricola gave him a long look. "Do I make myself clear?"

Tuathal was silent.

"I could treat you as a hostage, you know," Agricola pointed out.

-

"He could," Faustus said that night when Tuathal slung himself into a chair in Faustus's tent in a high state of indignation.

"I am the rightful king," Tuathal said stubbornly. "It is my place to lead, not to sit at my ease while your scouts go first."

The Seventh Cohort had spent the day chasing pirates driven inland by the bottlenecks of the Fleet across their harbors. This had also required laying down wooden road over large areas of bog, driving pilings into the water until they hit firm ground. They were footsore and weary, and Faustus wanted to point out that conquest involved duller and dirtier jobs than galloping in and waving your father's sword. Tuathal's impatience was a live thing, crackling like lightning around him, so he just said, "If this is your notion of ease, you may come and build bog road with me tomorrow. The surveyors will give us a map and an idea of distance, and the availability of forage, and every other thing an army on the march needs. Be patient or you will burst something."

"Elim mac Conrach sits in my father's hall on my father's throne. I cannot be patient." Lantern light glowed on the gold eyes in the pommel of his father's blade.

"Have some wine then." Faustus passed him a cup and the pot that Paullus had been heating over a brazier. "It makes my head hurt to look at you. You're like a walking volcano. What will you do if he decides not to do it?"

"He will do it," Tuathal said. "It is my destiny. I have been told this by my dreams, and also by the Druids in my mother's village."

Tuathal's mother's kin, the Epidii, inhabited the western islands of Britain and were kin to the clans of Hibernia. They generally kept to themselves, allying with neither of their closest British neighbors, the Caledones or Damnonii. Thus Rome had left them, for the moment, to themselves.

"I should not," Faustus said, "care to believe everything I see in my dreams."

"That is because you are a Roman," Tuathal said. "You have clogged the pathways whereby dreams may speak to you with maps and surveyors."

The Druids of the Epidii and Tuathal's dreams, however, seemed to prove themselves prophetic when the scouts returned to tell the governor that the thing was doable.

"With the Fleet and two legions, maybe less," the senior of the scouts said. He held a prefect's rank under the red and green checkered cloak and the flowing mustache.

Agricola thought. "And what force to hold it if we do?"

"You'd have to leave most of them there, I'd say. For a while at least. Unbroken ponies doesn't begin to describe that lot."

"According to our guest, Tara's king is the heart of their society," Agricola said. "The other kings are subservient to him?"

"Insofar as any Hibernian is subservient." The prefect poked a finger at the map spread on the governor's camp desk. "Here, this promontory they call Drumanagh is already a trading port with the British. We took the rest of the Gaulish glassware – it always sells well, we ought to get a cut from the factory for all the glass we've peddled – and two of us set up at the Beltane markets along the way from there to the king's hall at Tara. The sub-kings were all riding in for the Beltane fires and there is always talk at markets. They give away more gossip than they sell hides."

"And the talk?"

"It appears that the high kingship is a slippery throne to sit on. Elim mac Conrach usurped the title from young Tuathal's father, who also killed the king before him. Not what you'd call a stable dynasty. There may be some regretting now over the hand that some had in putting this one on the throne."

"Enough to welcome young Tuathal?"

"Very likely. Not enough, you understand, Governor, to welcome you and your legions."

"No." Agricola smiled. "They so seldom do, despite all the benefits we bring."

The prefect looked uncertain as to whether the governor was joking. "Prophecies and portents and such carry weight with them," he said. "We did our best to seed a few of those. Just the idea that someone or other saw it in the stars or the soup bones or whatever." Beltane was a sacred gathering, one of the four great festivals of the year, and a time when magic and power saturated the air. Unlike Samhain, its opposite across the wheel of months when the doors were open to the dead, Beltane was the time of beginnings, of new crops and new lambs, and marriages, and the setting out for adventure. It was entirely likely, given the right omens, that substituting a battle over the kingship of Tara for the spring cattle raids would seem a fine idea.

"Very well." Agricola rolled up his map. "We will let those rumors cook for a while, and concentrate on settling the coast here so that it stays stable. Next season we will sail." Domitian after all had not said anything about expeditions to Hibernia, only that they were to go no farther north than the Clota–Bodotria line. Hibernia was well south of that and could be taken and held with far fewer legions than the north of Britain. Agricola was aware that the vexillation of the Ninth was not the only force he was in danger of losing if the Rhenus didn't settle down. Or if Domitian found him too ambitious. He would have to go carefully but he had no intention of forgetting the north.

—

Celyn and Dai stood stubbornly in the doorway of Calgacos's hold, where the headman sat mending a pony harness. In his light, Calgacos noted irritably. It was a task he could have given a slave but a wise man mended his own harness.

Dai folded his arms across his chest. "Dispossess him. Now."

"That slinking ferret Idris has been in Emrys's hall," Celyn said. "Dai and I followed him. He's been running loose in Emrys's lands all year, it looks like."

"He has. I am not without observation," Calgacos said.

"And you have let him be?" Dai was indignant.

"I would prefer to know what he is doing."

"Morrigan! *I* know what he's doing! Conspiring with Emrys!"

Calgacos tugged on the mend to see if the stitching was going to hold. He picked up the awl to set another stitch and be certain. "He is angry at my orders not to raid south the past summers," he said.

"He was slinking about all autumn, chattering away to anyone who would listen," Celyn said. "'The Romans have pulled back and left the Damnonii undefended. It's time they were taught a lesson about running tame to the Romans' hand. Calgacos is too weak to do it.' Pah!"

"And who was listening?"

"None of our holders," Celyn admitted. "They will if Emrys raids Damnonii villages and brings back cattle and spoils."

Calgacos set the harness aside. "Come into the hall." He stood and shouted for a slave to bring them beer. It was dim and smoky inside, but there were fewer ears. "I have spoken with Emrys," Calgacos said when the slave had brought three cups of beer and gone about her business again.

"At Lughnasa two summers back!"

"Since then. Through the Druids or Coran Harper. We have met twice. It was not anyone's business to know."

Dai gaped at him.

"Do not look at me as if a fish had begun to speak. To raid clan against clan, for no better reason than some ill that someone's grandfather five times over once did that no one can now remember, will mark the end of us if the Romans come. Emrys knows this."

"Then why does he let Idris run tame about his hold?"

"For the reason that there is still enmity between us, and still a difference of opinion as to who should lead the clans against the Romans, and in what manner. I have warned Emrys to let the Damnonii be, but that is a matter of pride. We are a people who do not swallow pride easily."

"May the Morrigan swallow Idris," Dai muttered. "I do not understand why you will not dispossess him. You have reason enough, and proof now."

"And who to put in his place?"

"Anyone!" Dai said.

"To go outside his line would make a grievance," Celyn said. "That is how he came to the hold in the first place. Calgacos is right. Take the hold into your own lands, for now," he told Calgacos.

"And leave Idris as tenant to me?" Calgacos asked. "Or send him out of the clan landless? He will go to the Druids over either."

"Vellaunos would rule for you," Dai said with certainty.

"Probably," Calgacos admitted. "There is also the matter of loyalty from smallholders who would fear they might be next."

"We come back to where we started," Dai said. "Do something about Idris, headman, or we will do it for you."

"No! If it must be done, then it will come to me when there is no other way. I've had this out with Rhion already. Do I need to put a curse on the man who disobeys or will you listen to me in this?"

"We will listen," Celyn said, and he gripped Dai by the arm to make him agree. A headman's curse was a dark thing, and often came back to kill the man who had set it as well as the man who bore it. They would not push Calgacos to that.

"It will come in some way," Dai said. "He is a walking ill fortune. It will light somewhere."

–

In the two years since the treaty with Rome, the Damnonii hill forts had begun the same deterioration by which the wild lands were eating Llanmelin in the south. At the same time the Damnonii villages built on their lower slopes had prospered.

In the largest of these, a few rectangular Roman-style buildings were beginning to appear in place of round houses of mud and thatch. There were earthworks around the perimeter, and wooden gates that could be closed at night, but with the patronage of Rome to shield them there was no need for more. Nor would Rome have allowed more. The crannog dwellers in their stilt houses in the lakes were vulnerable too to anything more than a handful of raiders, without the lords' hill forts to keep watch.

The raiders from the north were more than a handful and they came without warning except for the deep vibration of hooves and chariot wheels in the ground. Those minding the herds or bringing in the first cutting of grain left their animals and their tools and fled for the gates or the crannog causeways, slamming defenses shut behind them. They lowered bags of valuables into the village wells or the lakes in the hope of hiding them, and stood ready to hold off the northern men as long as they could.

Emrys's raiders knew where the new villages were as well as the old crannog dwellings. They swept through them one after the other, the lords' chariots followed by men who could run as fast as the ponies, and all hungry to teach the Damnonii a lesson at spearpoint. They broke the gates open, and swarmed across the crannog causeways, throwing the defenders into the water. They pulled the bags of jewelry and silver dishes up again, knowing where they would be, and set fire afterward to anything that would burn.

Emrys allowed them to loot what they would, and take women if they could catch them. He had also allowed Idris to ride with them, despite the fact that Calgacos would hear of it, or maybe because of that. It would solve a problem of Emrys's own if Calgacos killed Idris or even dispossessed him. If Calgacos dispossessed Idris, Idris would be a man with ill luck riding his shoulders and Emrys would have an excuse not to allow Idris into his own clan. Idris was a hound that would bite any master eventually.

Emrys saw him in the light of flaming roof thatch dragging a Damnonii girl through the smoke. An older woman clung to his arm and he slashed her across the throat with his knife. She fell in a spray of blood and Idris took the struggling girl by the hair and one wrist. He threw her into his chariot and held her while his driver tied her hands behind her. Idris went back into the burning house and came out again with a wooden chest that he shoved in beside the girl, kicking her to make her move. Few of the others had chased down women, concentrating instead on gold and anything else with value. Married men were less likely to bring a woman home as it angered their wives. Idris would have done it anyway, Emrys thought, seeing the girl weeping on the chariot floor.

Emrys swept his chariot around the village in a circle, driving his own men ahead of him. The houses were in flames. A raid was ordinarily a matter of cattle-stealing and little else, but this time they took care to destroy. The Damnonii chieftain's head was to be taken if they could catch him, to make an example of him for the next chief who thought to treat with Rome. Failing to find him, they rode for the next village, where a warning had no doubt gone out already in the black smoke that rose in the air. It didn't matter. The Damnonii had not only slighted their defenses according to the Roman governor's orders, they had handed over the best of their weapons, war spears, shields and swords, allowed to keep only heavy hunting spears and bows, and the slings which were not worth confiscating since they were so easily reproduced. None were of use at close quarters against the swords of the northerners.

The Romans came boiling out of their garrisons as soon as their watchtowers saw the smoke, but Emrys's raiders knew when to withdraw. By the time they did, a third of the Damnonii villages were ruined, even their wells fouled for good measure, although the Damnonii chieftain had escaped to send an angry message to Governor Agricola.

As the raiders left they made a point of detouring through the fields, riding down the grain crop and even the kitchen garden beds. The warriors on foot drove the Damnonii cattle before them, and as many of their sheep and goats as could be herded into the moving mass.

Goewyn's sister Aregwydd watched them ride home, splashing through the mud puddles of the morning's rain with the village children and dogs dancing about the ponies' hooves to see what they had brought back. The gold necklace that her husband put around her neck did not entirely take away her anger at seeing Idris pull the Damnonii girl from his chariot. Aregwydd made the sign of horns at him and called down a blessing from the Mother on the girl. It wouldn't matter whether the girl set herself to please him or not. He would mistreat her because he could.

"Leave it, Aregwydd," her husband said. "He isn't your business any longer."

"His holding borders my father's and I see his viper's face every time I want to visit my mother. My father was a fool and I haven't forgiven him either."

"Your father has to live next to him. Do you want me to come with you the next time?"

"No. You stay off of Calgacos's territory. There is bad blood enough between this clan and his. This raid will make more when Calgacos hears of it."

Autumn–Winter

To the south Governor Agricola contemplated the dispatches from Damnonii territory with satisfaction. The attack provided the opportunity required to return to plans for a northern campaign. Now there was a plausible necessity to take the north, as the Damnonii had been promised the protection of Rome. Even the emperor must agree with that. Agricola crafted a careful message to that effect, laying stress on the honor of the Empire, its responsibilities to its client allies. The Hibernian campaign was abandoned before it began.

"You won't change his mind, you know," Faustus told Tuathal when he came to Faustus's camp in the evening to list his grievances. "We are very small pieces on his gameboard, even you."

Tuathal's anger and desperation radiated from him like the heat shimmer around a lamp flame. Paullus handed him a cup of wine without asking and Pandora put a sympathetic head in his lap. He scratched her ears. "I begin to think I must make my own gameboard," he said after a long moment. "I will, you know. I never knew my father. This is all the inheritance I have of him."

"Is that what drives you?" Faustus asked. "Not having known him? If you had, would it be different?"

"No doubt. If Elim mac Conrach had overthrown him when I was of an age to remember, no doubt I would be maimed and thus the matter decided for me. I might still kill Elim mac Conrach but only to put another man on the throne, for vengeance."

Faustus felt a certain wistful jealousy toward a man who had never known his father and decided that might not be wise to say. He wondered if Tuathal's father ever appeared to him, to urge him on with his quest. Tuathal had never said so. Perhaps there was no need. Only disobedient sons with no appreciation for their inheritance needed such visitations.

Marcus Silvius Valerianus had died unexpectedly, to the surprise of everyone including himself, of a fever that spread to the lungs. Faustus and Silvia had taken it in turns to sit by his bedside when the physician's prognosis became gloomy, while their father listed over and over the steps that were to be taken to borrow money for Silvia's dowry, to stabilize the farm's finances, and to make the proper sacrifices for his shade after his passing. Faustus had fulfilled only the last one.

Marcus Silvius's face had been greenish and pale under its sheen of sweat, and the room had begun to smell of death. "Aemelianus in Narbo Martius will lend the money, I have already spoken to him. He will give you a ten-year note."

Ten years.

"When that is settled, you must go to Sulpicius immediately and speak for his daughter."

Sulpicia.

"I know that you will do your duty, my son."

Duty.

Silvia came in with a basin and a cool cloth for her father's head. "Go and rest, I will sit with him for a while." Faustus had fled, sobbing for his father and for ten years' servitude to the farm and a lifetime with Sulpicia. Marcus Silvius died in the night, with Silvia sitting by his side.

If his duty had been to a kingdom instead of a country farm, Faustus wondered now, watching Tuathal's dark, brooding face in the firelight, would he have felt any differently about it?

His watch commander came with the night's password. "It's 'north', sir," he said, and Faustus had his answer. Word had gone round already that they would be on the march into the wilds of the Caledone lands, finally, even though it wouldn't be possible to launch a campaign until spring. Just now the weather might clear and then the next day hurl a blizzard at anyone hapless enough to be on the march. But this was what he had signed up for, the excitement of an unknown frontier, the satisfaction of being part of that shining tide he had watched march by when he was nine. He could wait for spring, just barely.

In the meantime, he had a long-accumulated leave due him. He had promised Silvia to use it to visit Narbo Martius, and admire his nephew, and Manlius's thoughts on drains and provincial government.

–

Faustus stood in the Street of Lilies looking for the house with the blue door. He hadn't meant to be in Aquae Sulis, but the water in the Channel had been rough, as it often was in winter, and he had somehow detoured inland.

He found what looked like the right door and pulled at the bell. A slave in a blue tunic and a silver armband opened it promptly and inspected him.

"I'm Centurion Valerianus," Faustus said, hoping he would do. The slave looked very particular. "I have come to call on your mistress and her guests."

"Wait here," the slave said dubiously. But when he came back Faustus could hear a cheerful chatter of voices behind him and Constantia appeared as the slave led him through the atrium to an elegant sitting room.

"Faustus! What are you doing here?"

"I, er, have leave, and…"

"And you came to visit us!" Aunt Popillia said, appearing behind Constantia. "Publia Livilla, my dear, this is the young officer who was so gallant."

"If you mean he started a tavern brawl over me," Constantia said. "But it was gallant, Faustus, truly it was. Did you get my letter?"

"I did."

"Then you must stay and dine with us," Publia Livilla said. She nodded to the slave who had answered the door. "Tell Cook one more for dinner, please. And the Chian wine. I find that gentlemen enjoy that."

"That's very kind of you." Faustus hadn't known what to expect, hadn't thought about it really, just seized on a direction that had turned him away from the harbor.

"In the meantime, you may take Constantia for a walk, if you wish," she added.

"Oh, let's," Constantia said. "Now, while it's not actually raining. The aunts won't let me ride and I'm beginning to feel like that poor man." She gestured at the mosaic of Sisyphus on the sitting room floor, endlessly pushing his rock uphill.

"He's very depressing," Aunt Publia admitted. "But he came with the house and mosaic work is expensive. I simply regard him as a reminder not to attempt things that I know are impossible. One of which is you on a horse."

"Yes, Aunt." Constantia took her cloak from its hook in the atrium, murmured a quick devotion to the household gods in their niche in the wall, and waited impatiently by the door.

"I expect you drive them mad," Faustus observed as she tucked her arm through his and towed him briskly down the cobbled street past the temple and baths toward the open country along the river.

"I do," she admitted. "They dawdle so when we walk. Aunt Publia inspects each lamp in the market when she wants to buy a new one, and then changes her mind halfway home and goes back for a different one. And Aunt Popillia stops in every single shop no matter what they're selling. It doesn't matter if it's slop pots or talking parrots."

"How long did she follow the army around with you and your father?" Faustus asked. "I expect she's been deprived of shopping."

Constantia sighed theatrically. "I expect she has. She's in clover here."

"And you?"

"I want to go home," she said.

"Wherever that is at the moment? We'll be going north in the spring."

"I know it's my fault but Father has to let me come back sometime. I don't suppose you could convince him?"

"The fact that your aunts trust me to take you for a walk is probably the limit of my influence," Faustus said.

"But will you talk to him? I wasn't nice to him when I left, and I've written to him to apologize and he says he misses me but he still won't let me come back."

"We're starting a major campaign as soon as the thaw comes," Faustus said. "He may be worried about having you with the column."

They stopped where the path ran out into farmland and a bull in a field lifted its head to watch them. Constantia climbed the fence rail and sat down on it. "I am weary of people doing things I don't like for my own good," she observed.

"I have some sympathy for you over that," Faustus admitted. "I was supposed to spend my leave in Gaul with my sister," he added.

"And you came to see me instead?" Constantia looked suspicious.

"I don't think so, not really. I... just didn't get on the ship. The weather was bad in the Channel and... I just didn't."

"And just happened to find yourself in Aquae Sulis?"

"Something like that." He propped his elbow on the fence beside her.

"What have you done with Paullus?"

"He's at the inn where we're staying. Did you think I'd sent him off to Gaul by himself?"

"You might have. 'My master sends greetings but he found that the water in the Channel was wet and so could not come after all.'"

"He's got Pandora with him. We can take her out for a walk tomorrow if you'd like. She never stops for anything." Faustus had wondered if Paullus was disappointed by the change of plans, whether he missed Gaul and his companions from the old household, mostly now with Silvia, but he hadn't seemed to be. Paullus appeared bent on the same process of self-reinvention as his master. Faustus had let him arrange a match between Pandora and Galerius's hound at a time convenient for puppies and to keep half the money when they were sold. Pandora had proved to be an excellent hunting dog and Paullus had customers on his books for the next two litters.

"Did you get in trouble for hitting Lartius?" Constantia asked him. "I've been hoping that you did something permanent to his face."

"I think I broke his nose," Faustus said. "And spoiled his Adonis-like features."

"Oh, don't," Constantia said. "I'm mortified enough. I know it was partly that he was so good-looking. But truly it was mostly that he said he loved me, the lying swine."

"Did you love him?"

"I must have." Constantia looked thoughtful.

"Maybe you just wanted to be sure that he loved you," Faustus suggested.

"Well, that is what Aunt Publia said. It's the only power a wife has to make sure she's well treated."

It occurred to Faustus that his father had loved his mother. Certainly he had treated her well according to his own lights. Why hadn't that been enough? Because Faustus was fairly certain now that it hadn't been.

"You'll find someone to marry that you love," he said, floundering for some reassurance that the whole thing wasn't just an accidental knot in whatever thread the Fates were spinning.

"Just now I'd rather go back to that village and live with the Damnonii than marry anyone," Constantia said rebelliously.

Faustus grew solemn. "No, you wouldn't. The Caledones raided the Damnonii in revenge for making peace with us, and a third of their villages went up in flames. You'd be dead, or a hostage of some Caledone lord if they found out who you were." *And the governor wouldn't bargain to get you back either.* He didn't say that part. He suspected she knew it. She had followed the army long enough.

"Oh. They were kind to me. I'm sorry."

"The British spend more time fighting each other than they do fighting us. They don't learn either. By the way, that bull's looking at your backside on the fence with a sort of calculating expression."

Constantia slid down from the fence rail. "When I was little and found out girls couldn't join the army, I gave my gold lunula to Diana to make me into a boy."

Faustus gave her an appraising look. She really was beautiful, in an ethereal way that belied her personality utterly. "Apparently that didn't work," he said.

"Obviously," Constantia snapped. "Once I was older I didn't want to be a boy anymore, I just wanted to do what men could do."

Faustus smiled at her. "A modern Amazon?"

"I would be an army surgeon like Father, and if you condescend to me anymore I will tell Aunt not to feed you tonight."

"I'm sorry," Faustus said penitently. "To be honest, I think you'd make a fine soldier."

"I think I would too," she said, "but I'd rather put people back together. It's our only chance to see what's inside them, after your sort have cut them open. We aren't allowed to. I helped Father with a dreadful belly wound last season. A sword had gone in and been pulled sideways somehow and cut him nearly to the spine. The poor man died anyway, but we tried. I took notes afterward about where things were inside him, and made a drawing."

"If you don't want to marry," Faustus suggested, "just trot that out over the wine and cakes and you'll drive off any suitors that come calling."

"That's what Aunt Publia says. Just take a letter to Father for me, please? There are plenty of other families still following the column, there's no reason I shouldn't come back."

"There are any number of reasons," Silanus said some weeks later when Faustus had presented him with the letter and Constantia's plea. He had spent the rest of his leave going to see the White Horse for himself and in various whorehouses, and it was the tag end of March when he caught up with his legion, which had settled for the winter south of the Clota estuary. Silanus was supervising the packing of the hospital carts in preparation for the northern campaign. He inspected a tray of forceps and gave them back to the orderly. "These need to be cleaned properly. Scrub them, don't just wave them around in the vinegar." He eyed Faustus again. "Am I to understand you spent your leave in Aquae Sulis visiting my daughter?"

"Purely in a friendly way," Faustus said hastily. "Just a few days. I was supposed to go to Gaul and see my sister, but I didn't."

Silanus nodded. "That happens when you try to go home, unless you come from an army family."

"I haven't been home since I finished my training," Faustus said. "My sister already considered me a bloodthirsty savage. I'll have to go eventually," he added gloomily.

"Your sister no doubt leads a sheltered life," Silanus commented. "And I expect Constantia's willfulness is my fault for letting her run tame in an army camp and in my surgery all these years."

"Did you know she made drawings of someone's insides?" Faustus asked, diverted.

"Yes. Another thing I shouldn't have permitted. Very well, Centurion, thank you for the letter. I will think on it."

XI

The Horned God and the King Horse

Spring–Summer, 836 ab urbe condita

This is it, Faustus thought, as the third century merged seamlessly into its place in the Seventh Cohort, and the Seventh Cohort into the column of the legion. Septimus had drilled them relentlessly over the winter, to the point that they had looked relieved to see Faustus again.

At the outset of the march, Agricola extracted further hostages and grain supplies from the Venicone chieftain, his price for the protection that the treaty with Rome had promised. That was a matter of practicality as much as distrust of leaving the Venicones at his back, since ten days' rations were the most that could be carried on the march. Beyond that the column relied on forage, and resupply by ship at the river mouths.

Eight thousand legionaries from the Ninth, the Twentieth, and the Second Augusta marched north. The remainder of the Ninth was in Germany, and the balance of the Augusta and the Twentieth, along with the Second Adiutrix, had been left to hold the peace of the southern province and the newly conquered territory. Centurion Ursus had been stewing for fear that the Seventh Cohort would be one of those left behind, and had made a generous sacrifice to both Mithras and Mars Ultor to ensure its place in the column. Tuathal Techtmar accompanied them, largely because Agricola did not want to turn his back on him either, but Demetrius of Tarsus was firmly ordered to Selgovae territory to establish a school for the heirs of Selgovae nobles at Trimontium and stay out of the governor's hair on campaign.

Accompanying the legionary cohorts and their civilian followers were eight thousand auxiliary infantry and five thousand cavalry, all laden with weapons, helmet, shield, and the rations, foraging basket, tools, cook pot and dinner tin that hung from carrying poles or were tied to the saddle of each troop horse. Thus loaded, a soldier could still march twenty miles in a day, but the mules and oxen that pulled the baggage carts supplied the brakes that slowed the column. To leave hospital equipment, tents, spare weapons and the great siege engines in the rear unguarded was not a possibility in hostile territory. The larger the army, the larger and slower grew the baggage train, so that on the march the column might stretch from the previous night's camp to the new one. Once settled they most often spent three nights in a camp, time enough to use up the local graze and firewood, and for the water supply to be fouled by men and horses. Part of the destruction and subjection of a hostile territory was achieved simply by the army's passage through it.

By midsummer they had skirted the friendly settlements of the Venicones and moved northeastward into the edges of Caledone territory. The marines and the Fleet were raiding the coastal settlements of the northern clans to terrify them into compliance before the arrival of the main army.

-

There was no one among the Caledone clans who did not now take notice. Calgacos spoke furiously to Emrys when he prodded him out of his camp at Lughnasa Fair, and Emrys laid his ears back and shouted at Calgacos until the Druids intervened.

"This is your doing, Emrys!" Calgacos kept his voice barely level. "You must needs raid the Damnonii and stick your spear in a wasps' nest."

"The Damnonii were taught a lesson," Emrys said icily, while the clan lords on both sides put their hands on their sword hilts. "A lesson which you were unwilling, or too lazy, to teach them. It is a lesson that Ossuticos of the Venicones will heed despite having been bought for a gold cauldron."

"Ossuticos is a craven fool," Calgacos said. "But no doubt he will thank you who gave the Romans reason to come north again!"

"When have the Romans needed a reason for anything? You are the one who first said that they would come, and bade me listen."

"Nor did you!" Calgacos snapped. "And when they turned toward Hibernia, and sent scouts across the water thinking to put that princeling of the Epidii into the king's hall there, and we saw we had breathing space to prepare for when they turned our way again, you must needs provoke them into it now!"

"It may be, Calgacos, that some among your holders feel differently about it. How sure are you of your position?"

"If you mean the dog from my hold that has been slinking about your table, you should have a care that you are not bitten, Emrys. For the little he is worth, you may keep him."

Celyn and Dai swung their heads around to look at Idris, who edged back.

Vellaunos looked toward Nemausos, the Druid from Emrys's hall, and some agreement passed between them. Druids were not bound to a clan or a holding but to their craft. They stepped between Calgacos and Emrys.

Vellaunos spoke. "By the Spear of Lugh I put peace upon you, Calgacos, and on you, Emrys. Let be now, lest you bring the darkness on yourselves."

On the far side of the rainy meadow the traders had laid out their goods and the horse fair was going on. The women of all the gathered clans, less inclined to enmity than their men, sat on rugs in the rain shades of their wagons and gossiped while a thin drizzle fell. Vellaunos thumped his staff on the grass and the drizzle lessened and stopped as if the weather heeded his word. His white beard was beaded with the wet mist and caught the pale sun as it crept through the cloud cover. The women and the horse sellers turned toward him as his voice rolled across the meadow. He was no longer an old man half-asleep at the council table. He seemed to shimmer in front of them, grow larger, white gown blazing like the sunrise.

Calgacos and Emrys listened in angry silence. Vellaunos's threat of darkness was literal and the darkness that a Druid could conjure was terrible.

"By the waters of the sea I bind you. By the land beneath your feet I bind you. By the fire I bind you and by the air in your lungs I bind you."

Calgacos could feel Vellaunos's words settle on him like invisible threads. A man who broke such a ban would find the natural world turned against him, swallowing him down, sucking the breath from his throat.

"There will be no war between your two clans," Vellaunos said, "until the Romans have gone." He looked from one to the other. "After that, you are released."

There was no point in arguing. They turned their backs on each other and even that did little good. After the white horse had been offered to Lugh Bright Spear, the Druids decreed an off-year sacrifice to the Mother in her form as the Morrigan of Battles. In the evening, not entirely to his surprise, Calgacos saw Coran Harper come through the dusk to fetch him, but when he followed Coran to the grove he found Emrys there ahead of him, the antlered skull already on his head and the handprints of wet clay overlying the clan marks on his chest. Emrys swayed a little on his feet and Calgacos thought that he had already been given the bitter drink that he remembered from three years past.

As Calgacos paused, questioning, Vellaunos came forward with the bronze cup and then the white head of the horse sacrifice. It was still wet and bloody and Calgacos gagged as

Vellaunos stripped his clothing from him and set the head over Calgacos's. He could barely breathe for the rank stench of blood; the eyeholes had been newly cut and were ragged with flesh. He felt the Druids putting their hands on him, marking him with the clay of the earth which belonged to the Mother and to which all men came at the end. The thin sound of pipes shimmered around him, echoing in the white horse's skull.

Because it was not the year for the Seven Year King, only four fires were lit, at the quarter-points around the stone. No bull had been brought, but it was the intent that mattered, and after much consideration the Druids had chosen an ox from a holder's wagon, selected for an unblemished hide and the span of its horns. It waited stolidly by the sacred stone, decked with meadow flowers. Vellaunos, or someone – he couldn't see out of the horse's head – put the bronze knife in Calgacos's hand and closed the fingers of Emrys's hand over it.

"Make the cut together," Nemausos whispered, and they did, cleanly, feeling the hot blood spill on their bare feet as the ox went down. They stood side by side, weaving a little from the drink, as the Druids painted them with the ox's blood, overlaying the clay, warm and sticky and rank.

Afterward, they were taken to wash in the river, and to let the Horned God and the King Horse leave them. It was dawn when Calgacos finally felt the drug leaving him as well, and began to shiver. Standing beside him in the cold running water was Emrys. The Druids were not to be seen, not even Coran Harper who had stayed with Calgacos the last time. There were only the two of them, naked in the river. Their clothes sat in piles on the bank and they began to dress wordlessly.

Their belt knives were there, and the knife that Calgacos kept in his boot. With the Druids' ban hanging over them there was no chance that they might be used. Calgacos looked at his belt knife before he slid it into its sheath. It was of fine workmanship, with a hilt of horn capped with gold. He eyed Emrys and then held out the knife.

"I will trade you," he said. "And seal the peace."

Emrys considered and then took out his own knife, with a hilt wrapped in gold wire. He smiled a little. "Until the Romans have gone."

"Until the Romans have gone."

"But if I were you," Emrys said, pulling on his breeches, "I would rid myself of Idris."

—

Ossuticos of the Venicones was not best pleased to find the Caledone lords in his hall, green branch or not. There were half a dozen holders of each clan behind them, but it was the fact that they had appeared together that most troubled Ossuticos. He welcomed them into his hall because he had to, and offered them beer because he had to.

When they had drunk and he had ceremonially bid them welcome, he sat back in his chair and waited to see what they would say.

"The Romans have trampled through the Damnonii lands to skirt around yours, Ossuticos," Calgacos said. "Are you thinking that they will not be back to rectify that omission?"

Ossuticos sat silent for a moment, and thought on the odds. "We have seen the Romans come and go for a generation," he said finally. "There has been no trampling of our fields."

"When they have dug themselves in here in the north, there will be stone roads through your fields," Emrys said. "And tax collectors in your holds. And Roman judges to decide matters for you at your councils."

"We have taken no side in your wars as yet because we looked to defend ourselves," Ossuticos snapped. His glance went angrily between Emrys and Calgacos. "Your own clans have been more trouble to us than the Romans."

"The time for clan to raid clan and tribe to fight tribe has ceased," Emrys said.

"As it did when you raided the Damnonii and burned their villages?" Ossuticos asked. He was older than the Caledone lords, his hair growing white enough that he no longer bleached it, but he was not so old that he was willing to assent just because Emrys came lordlywise out of his mountains to tell him so.

"The Damnonii earned that for treating with Rome," Calgacos said. "I was against the raiding, but the Damnonii should not have been surprised. Nor should you be when your alliance with their governor doesn't save you."

"Save us from the Romans? Or from your raiders?" Ossuticos glared at them both.

"It is your choice, Ossuticos," Emrys said. "You can fight us and afterward the Romans, or you can band with us and fight the Romans now while you still have the chance. Strike at them now while you are at their backs."

"And if I do not?"

"The Romans won't need to burn your villages."

Ossuticos looked from one clan chief to the other. The inference was plain, and his tribe was small and no match for the combined forces of Calgacos and Emrys. Nor for the Romans, which was what had kept the Venicones receptive to Roman overtures. But with the force of the Caledone clans behind them, it might be different. Certainly it would be a fine thing to drive the Romans into the sea. In any case, he had no choice.

—

As the Romans marched north they had left behind them a string of camps and watchtowers in the borderland, along a ridge that looked both north to the Caledone mountains and south to the highlands of the Venicones' hunting runs. Ossuticos's warriors came howling over the wooden ramparts of those camps late in the day and they caught the Romans at their supper. The Romans, pulling on their mail and helmets, met them on the walls while the warriors behind them battered the camp gates with felled trees.

At the camp above Alauna Water, the Venicones came with torches as well as spears, and once through the gates they flung the fire into anything burnable, from tents to the stores in the granary. By the time the garrison fought them off, the camp was in flames.

Eastward, they overran the barracks of a cavalry camp and let the horses loose, mounting them bridleless and driving the rest before them down the ridge. They came upriver from ships beached at Tavus Mouth, slipping past the Roman river patrols to strike the camp at Tamia.

Afterward, having thrown the dice that could not be called back, Ossuticos gathered his war band and pulled his people into the highland fortresses that had gone unused for a generation.

–

An attack had been expected to come from the Caledones in the north, through whose territory Governor Agricola was driving his column, and the frontier scouts had all pointed their noses in that direction. By the time the border wolves had begun to scent that Calgacos and Emrys had made a pact with each other and gone by their own ways through the Roman lines to make Ossuticos regret his compact with the Romans, Alauna Camp was in flames.

Couriers with the news came into Agricola's camp on sweating horses, reporting the damage but also that it was now contained. Nowhere had the Venicones stayed long enough for the main army to come to the camps' defenses, retreating when they saw the watchtower beacons flower into flame along the ridge. The damage done and the suddenness of an enemy that came screaming from the trees and river and vanished again the same way was the point, as Agricola well knew. Small bands whose leaders knew the landscape with an intimacy that not even the Roman scouts could achieve would make the Romans' army look always over their shoulders.

"Are you feeling that this is your fault?" asked his wife, who knew him well, when she found him sitting amid a litter of dispatch tablets, cursing.

"It is," he said grimly. "I have been distracted. And that is not *your* fault, but under the circumstances I want you out of danger."

Domitia sighed. "We have been married a very long time and I have followed you for most of it, including to the wilds of Britain once before."

"Not with an infant coming."

"Julia was six."

"That is not an infant. A baby has broken our hearts before now." He reached out his hands to her. "Domitia, do this for me or I will order you to. I have never given you a direct order in our entire lives, but I will now."

"Very well." She kissed his hands. "I shall take Theodosius and his kitchen underlings with me and let you pay for my banishment with burned porridge."

By morning, Agricola had called his legates to a council and met them as they appeared at dawn. He was freshly shaved and in his cuirass, his purple woolen cloak about his shoulders. No one had slept that night. They were mildly surprised to find Domitia sitting with him. She kissed him on the cheek and left as they came in, pulling her mantle over her head against the morning drizzle.

"I am sending her south," he said, and elaborated with a half smile, "I have only just found out that she is pregnant."

They murmured congratulations and kept their thoughts to themselves, which were that Domitia Decidiana was forty at least. She had not had a child since the birth of Julia and a son who hadn't lived, some twenty years before.

"It is not the most propitious timing," Agricola said, "but one takes what the gods give in cases like this and one is grateful."

194

"Indeed, sir." It was clear that he was hoping for a son again, a late-in-life heir after all this time. "We will pray for a successful outcome."

"Thank you." He sent a slave for watered wine, olives and bread, and spread a map with the scouts' latest information across a folding table. "Perhaps I have been distracted these past two days since I learned of my wife's condition, and that has had an ill effect. There must be no more of that. I take responsibility to myself for not looking to our rear. Therefore I intend to ease my conscience by making the Venicones thoroughly regret their treachery at the same time that we discourage any further attack from other quarters. First, I wish to hear your thoughts on the matter."

"The Caledone tribes are scattered across a great deal of ground," the legate of the Valeria Victrix said, "which gives them the advantage. *And* they'll be at-our backs while we go after the Venicones."

"Can they be lured into coming together?" the new legate of the Augusta asked. In the way of things, Domitius Longinus had been promoted to a minor provincial governorship the year before and Arrius Laenas was his replacement.

"That seems preferable," the legate of the Ninth Hispana said. "Strike-and-run attacks by a widely dispersed enemy wear the men's nerves down."

Agricola nodded, but he was wondering again if he should have taken the Adiutrix and left the Ninth to garrison the south. He had been wary of leaving them away from his eye. The legate of the Ninth was a good man and was new to his command since the near-mutiny in Julius Frontinus's governorship, but he had his hands full. Just now a rumor was circulating that the Hispana was cursed, a legacy of Boudicca's mauling of it. That tale had been quashed before, but it had an unholy ability to rise up again any time they were unsettled.

All the same, provoking the Caledone tribes into coalescing into one army that could then be defeated with the tactics that

Rome employed most efficiently was likely the best plan. He pulled the map toward him and they bent their heads over it.

—

"What we ought to do," Galerius pronounced, "is squash the Venicones like bugs and then go north with a settled rear behind us."

"And what are the Caledones doing while we're squashing their allies? Playing rota?" Faustus asked.

"Dropping out of the trees on us most like," the centurion of the second century said.

Centurion Ursus, inspecting his cohort preliminary to the expected order to march, paused to recommend that they leave the strategy to the governor. "Your business is to follow my orders and my business is to follow the legate's orders, and his business is to follow the governor's. Thus we achieve a discipline and cohesion lacking in the enemy."

"Yes, sir," Faustus said. "But isn't the Caledones' lack of cohesion also our problem just now? It's like swatting flies in a midden to go after them all at the same time."

"It is the governor's problem, certainly," Ursus said. "Your problem is the man of your century I just observed writing scurrilous verse about you on a tent wall."

Faustus, who knew exactly the poet he was looking for, stood and stalked purposefully toward his century's barracks tents. Ursus grinned. The verse had been flattering, if filthy, and was actually a mark of Centurion Valerianus's solidity with his century. Ursus thought him likely to be promoted again soon, and would regret losing him, but Centurion Valerianus was due for a cohort command. He began to consider where he might poach a replacement who would suit his standards. As the campaign headed toward a pitched battle for the north, promotions from the ranks would become more common. A season in the field had a way of thinning out unsuitable officers and identifying the rank and file who were capable of command.

That eventuality became considerably more likely when Governor Agricola launched his attack. He split the army into three columns, one legion to each with attendant cavalry and auxiliaries, and launched them in rapid succession against tribal holdings throughout the lowlands and up the glens that ran northwestward into the mountains. The Fleet and marines raided every coastal settlement north to Taexalorum Head and then westward. The intent was both devastation and provocation, succeeding in the former but not the latter. Rather than a pitched battle, Agricola found his army slogging through the same sort of dale-by-dale fighting that had gone on for the better part of a decade during the conquest of the Brigantian Hills when he had been legate of the Twentieth. The northern tribes fought back more like bandits than a disciplined army, and while Rome might sneer at that tactic, it made them impossible to completely control.

"We burn them out of a village, they disappear into the hills, and next thing they're dropping out of the trees on you," Septimus groused. The century had lost a man in the last skirmish and Septimus took it personally.

"If the optio has a better strategy, I am sure the governor would appreciate it," Faustus said. "Short of sending a message saying 'Please stand still and fight.'"

"They can't keep it up forever," Septimus said hopefully.

Faustus thought that perhaps they could, if they were willing to, but it wasn't likely. Aside from the villages torn open and burned, the army was gradually eating the countryside bare. At some point it would come to a battle. The question was whether the Roman army could supply its own needs and keep its nerve for long enough. A soldier wanted certainty. A battle was a certainty, live or die. Chasing a faceless enemy was wearing them down.

By now the rumor about the Ninth had filtered out of its camp and into the Second's. When the Dead List came in with another of their own on it, Faustus paraded the third century, praised their discipline and their courage, and made a public sacrifice for the shade of the dead man. It helped somewhat.

XII

The Cave of the Horned God

Summer–Autumn

Ossuticos and the Venicone fighting men went north to the Caledone lands when the Romans drove in the walls of their hill fort with siege engines. They took their women and children and as many of their cattle as were left and joined the stream of refugees flowing from the burned villages into the farther glens where the Romans had not yet ventured.

There Ossuticos furiously claimed his place in council with Calgacos and Emrys and the lesser Caledone chiefs and headmen. The clans who inhabited the lands from the Venicone and Damnonii territory north to the great triangle of sea that divided the northern coast, and cut the eastern highlands from the clans of the west, were loosely related, and all considered themselves Caledones. Most spread along the coastal lowlands, some in the mountain glens, and a few in the wild uplands that no one else besides the birds could find. For centuries they had married each other, raided each other, and known no other particular enemies. It had taken them years to listen to Calgacos on the subject of Romans. Now they met at the ancient site where Lughnasa Fair was held, holy ground and thus not conducive to quarrels, and a place from which the northern lords could see the Roman advance and be converted, those that still needed it. The Cornovii of the western mainland were less closely related, more kin to the islanders of the

Orcades than to the Caledones, but they too had seen, and the burned villages and the fields stripped of anything edible were conversion enough. Refugees from the lowland villages had fled up the glens into the mountains and now every highland clan had anywhere from a few households to a thousand or more to feed and clothe. That it was now a matter of either war or conquest was clear. Each chief had called up his lords and the other holders under his command to send them against the Roman advance. But no alliance had been made under a central commander and none was likely, as both Emrys and Calgacos knew, until the Druids enforced it. There were too many old enmities, too much posturing and pride and rivalry.

Only the islanders stayed aloof, insulated by the waters of the firth. Eirian had been with the new pig girl, feeding the sow and her piglets, when her father and her uncle took their shouting match out of the house and into the yard, arguing all the way to the shore where her uncle had beached his boat. Three men from the mainland waited beside it. He was not actually her uncle, Eirian knew, and she had never seen him before, but he was kin of some kind through an island cousin's marriage to a mainlander of the Cornovii and so the title was a courtesy, the only one he had been accorded in Faelan's household.

"You leave others to defend you!" he shouted furiously at Faelan.

"No!" Faelan shouted. "We keep to ourselves and do not meddle in the affairs of the mainland and we have thrived thereby."

The sow lifted her head and snorted angrily at the noise.

"Are Romans really coming?" the pig girl asked.

"Hush," Eirian said to both of them. "I don't know, but not today."

"When your chieftain sends for aid, that is the answer you send him?" the man demanded.

"Nall of the mainland is no chieftain of ours," Faelan said. "We have none."

"You are Cornovii."

"We are free men, and only because we are Cornovii have I listened to you this long," Faelan snapped. "You come here lordlywise demanding fighting men to go south with you and my answer to that and to Nall is no." He turned away and had slammed the house door before the visitor reached the boat that waited for him.

Eirian watched them set out into the threatening currents offshore, making their way toward the firth that divided the islands from the mainland. "Watch," she told the pig girl. "See how they know these waters. No one who does not ever gets here undrowned. That is what will keep the Romans away. Father says," she added.

"Maybe they are not all that bad," the pig girl said hopefully. Almost anything would be more interesting than pigs.

"Maybe you should see to clean straw for the sow," Eirian said.

—

"The headman is short-sighted," Idris said, watching Maldwyn to see his reaction. "I have brought you a house gift, such as the headman could give if he had not forbidden you from raiding over the last summers." Gifts cemented the relationship between chief and holder, and holder to those under him.

"It is very fine," Maldwyn said, admiring the enameled pony bridle that Idris had presented, with the uneasy knowledge that such a gift required some form of reciprocation, even from a son-in-law, and also could not be refused.

"It may be that Calgacos is too weak to lead us in war with the Romans. If the command goes to Emrys that would shame our clan."

"That must be thought on," Maldwyn said carefully. Idris had gained a following among some of the younger holders, and his distribution of the loot from the Damnonii raid, as well as judicious other offerings from his personal wealth, had begun to be convincing. On the other hand, Calgacos was dangerous and to put a foot wrong would prove it. Maldwyn was saved from further commitment by his daughter Aregwydd, who came from her mother's rooms, saw Idris, and looked furiously at them both.

Aregwydd made a gesture with her fingers that might have been a curse or might have been merely rude, but it made Idris's neck itch. The girl wasn't a priestess or a headman's wife who should have held such a power, but since her sister's death just having her in the same room seemed to suck the breath from Idris's lungs. He settled his cloak around his shoulders and pulled the hood up against the rain that had started up again. "We will speak again, Maldwyn. These are important matters for the clan in these dangerous times."

Aregwydd turned a venomous eye on her father as Idris left. "Keep him out of your hall!"

"He is a neighbor," Maldwyn said. Aregwydd still barely spoke to him when she came to visit her mother, besides to berate him for a coward.

Aregwydd caught sight of the pony bridle and snatched it up. "He buys you with costly trash! You should wear it yourself and let him drive you!" She threw it at him and it fell against the firedogs in the hearth and chipped the face piece.

Idris took his next gift to Celyn's hold and was given no better welcome.

"Take yourself out of my hall, Idris!" Celyn glared at him, while Dai, who had been lounging by Celyn's hearth, rose lazily with a menacing eye. Celyn's fosterling, his sister's son who was just turned twelve, looked from one to the next and then to Celyn's spear leaning by the door.

Dai shook his head at him. "It won't come to that, lad. This one has an adder's tongue and little tooth."

Idris stood his ground. "I have brought a house gift," he said pointedly.

"Take it away again," Celyn said. "I won't be entangled by you."

202

"That is an insult," Idris said.

"It is," Dai said. "Get back on your horse with your poisoned gift before you get a greater one."

Idris snickered. "Dai speaks for Celyn now. Perhaps Celyn should marry him."

"The last person to marry you, Idris, hung herself." Dai looked disgusted. "Go before we set the dogs on you."

Idris glared from one to the other, calculating what might have been the extent of his mistake. "You will regret this." He turned on his heel.

"All the same," Celyn said, as his pony's hoofbeats faded down the track, "Calgacos will have to do something now."

Rhion found Calgacos in the courtyard of his hold, where a pair of young hounds were rolling a barrel of sand between them to clean the rust from his mail. Calgacos had bought more mail from Lorn in the spring, and given it as his own pointed gifts at Lughnasa. There was little body armor among the Caledone lords and the Romans were plated like tortoises. The smithy at every holding had become an armory.

"Celyn and Dai are right," Rhion said, "hotheads that they are. Idris has been courting your young holders, impressing them with his defiance of your orders. And house gifts of Damnonii gold."

Calgacos watched Aelwen's women hanging clothes on a line between the trees that overhung the cow byre. The life of the hold went on despite looming war and it was wash day. "I have sent cattle to every hold, including Idris's, to feed those fleeing the lowlands," he said irritably.

"And at every hold Idris then comes with his gifts, and telling a long tale of his bravery and his spoils from the raid that the headman forbade them," Rhion said. "They are beginning to listen to him, despite your cattle."

203

Calgacos was quiet a moment, while the boys tumbled his mail in their barrel and the women hung out the wash. "Call a council so Idris may see what else I will give him," he said finally.

"You are going to fight him, aren't you?" Aelwen laid her mirror down and faced her husband as he dressed for council.

"Maybe," Calgacos said. He pulled his shirt over his head and fastened his belt. Emrys's knife rested in the sheath that hung at his hip.

"He's brought that Damnonii girl with him," Aelwen said. "To throw his defiance in your face before the council." She fastened her ear drops and necklace and slid three gold bangles up each arm, her lips compressed. "What are you going to do?"

"I am not sure yet. I think he hopes not to fight me and depose me by election of the council, and I think also that he hasn't the backing yet. That's why I called it now. Whatever happens, you are to stay out of it. Understood?"

Aelwen nodded. She watched him take out his torque of twisted gold and put it about his neck. He picked up the gold armbands by habit and then put them back.

The council hall was crowded with the clan's holders, even those who might ordinarily plead age or distance. Idris sat slouched on a bench with two of the younger smallholders on either side. Maldwyn sat three places down, picking at a thread in the hem of his shirtsleeve with unconvincing concentration. Aelwen took her place as the headman's wife and looked them over. Most looked uncomfortable, Celyn and Dai furious, and Rhion grave. Vellaunos Chief Druid was expressionless. A challenge to the headman by one of his holders was not a matter for Druids unless some law or ban was broken. She thought angrily that if the Druids took their heads out of the stars it might be better for everyone.

The smell of roasting meat came from the kitchen but there was no food on the table that was still pushed against the wall. Nor did a slave come with cups and beer, although the council lords looked expectant.

Calgacos did not sit, but stood before them. "We have now made alliance against the Romans with those clans with whom we have otherwise warred from beyond common memory. Now we war against the Romans and the outcome will spell whether we live as free men or under the Romans' yoke like cattle." Calgacos took his sword from its place on the wall, drew it from its sheath and laid it on the hearth where the blade flickered in the firelight. There was a collective indrawn breath. "If there is one who wishes to contest with me for leadership, let him speak now." He turned his head, hawk-like, from one to the next.

The youngest of the smallholders stood, his eyes bright with excitement. Idris made a move to stop him but it came too late. "The headman made alliance. We did not."

"I remember you at your spear-taking, Selisoc," Calgacos said. "Also when you took your holding and swore to me as headman. Do you forget that?"

"If the headman is inadequate, another may challenge him," Selisoc said stubbornly. His eyes slid to Idris, sitting motionless.

"Do you challenge me?" Calgacos asked.

"No! Not I." Selisoc looked at Idris again.

Calgacos grinned. "You put forth Idris, when Idris has not put himself forth?"

There was a snicker from Dai. Idris snapped his head around toward him. "There is reason for discontent," he said.

"And you hoped to use it to depose me without having to fight me for it?" Calgacos suggested.

"If the council votes—"

"And does it?" Calgacos's gaze swept the council. He could count as well as Idris. Idris had not been ready to make his move. Calgacos would force him to it. He looked to the man on Idris's other side, who looked away now.

"You, Ula? No? You, Maldwyn?" No one wished to vote when they were still outnumbered. To lose would leave them open to whatever vengeance Calgacos chose to take. "What of the rest of you who follow Idris for his leavings?" Calgacos inquired contemptuously. "Silver harness fittings and gold bangles. Did you bring that girl with you to bargain her to the next man who will back your claim, Idris?"

Idris stiffened. He wore a gold torque that was thicker than Calgacos's. Gold armbands from some Damnonii lord's hoard snaked up both wrists. "My claim is a match for yours, in blood. Our grandmothers were sisters' daughters to each other. You know this. The Druids know this. Ask Coran Harper."

Coran Harper nodded. "That is true."

Dai opened his mouth to speak and Celyn put his hand on his arm. "Let be," he whispered.

"Indeed," Calgacos said. "Then here is my word, *cousin*. Prostrate yourself and re-swear fealty to me now, or challenge me. If not, you are dispossessed."

There was another sharp breath from the council.

"Prostrate myself?" To force a holder to flatten himself to the ground before his lord was an insult that was reserved as the last punishment before dispossession, a humiliation worse than the loss of cattle or gold. Idris's hand went to his sword.

"Prostrate yourself."

"The Morrigan take your house and everything in it!" Idris spat.

Calgacos felt a wave of relief. He had been half-afraid that Idris would bow to him. "Do you challenge me, or do you only caw like her crows?"

"I challenge you!" Idris drew his sword, his face flaming with fury. The council lords stood and pushed their benches toward the wall.

"Hold until the space is cleared," Rhion said.

Calgacos turned to Vellaunos. "Is it true that I am under ban solely not to fight with Emrys? Not with this ferret?"

"It is true," Vellaunos said. "The ban applies only to Emrys." He looked as if he might say something more, but then closed his lips together and sat at the far end of the room, his staff in his hand, watching.

Calgacos lifted his sword from the hearth and took his shield down from its hook on the wall, testing the grip. He waited while Selisoc brought Idris's shield from where it hung on the side of his chariot. Idris took it and drew his own sword.

They circled each other warily at first, feeling out their footing on the packed earthen floor and the herbs strewn across it.

"This should be fought outside on open ground," Idris said. "And better light."

"Fight me here, Idris, where you challenged me," Calgacos said. "You know the rule."

"Then the floor must be swept," Idris said.

"Will you sweep the battlefield when you lead my Kindred against the Romans?" Calgacos snapped.

Idris lunged furiously at him. Calgacos blocked it and struck back, a glancing blow that Idris caught on the rim of his own shield. They backed away, circled again, closed, hammering at each other, pulling back again. A long, heavy sword could not be wielded at close quarters. Calgacos kept his attention on Idris's eyes as well as his sword arm. *He will look the way he intends to strike.* He remembered the weapons master of his boyhood saying that to the small hounds sparring with each other in his uncle's courtyard.

Aelwen watched them with her fists clenched in her lap. The noise of iron blade on bronze shield made her head ring. The light was dim, only the daylight from the doorway and the flickering light of the hearth and the lamps hung from the roof beams. They moved in and out of it like the figures the ancients had left in the holy cave above the lake, where the dance of torchlight could bring their carved gods alive. In a whisper she promised the Mother and the Morrigan, the forces of life and death, her gold ear drops and a cow each year of her remaining life if the death that ended this dance was not Calgacos's.

The space between benches and table and the great iron firedogs in the hearth at the hall's center was not large and they fought each other the length of it, the council lords scrambling out of their way. Calgacos stumbled against the stacked benches. Idris pushed the advantage and Calgacos shoved his shield at him hard, righting himself. Idris raised his sword arm to strike at Calgacos's legs. The weapons master's voice whispered in his ear. *A man who doesn't shift his feet to the next blow does not intend that blow.* Calgacos brought his shield up to cover his ribs instead and Idris's blow nearly shattered it. While Idris was off guard he closed with his own sword but it bit into the edge of Idris's shield. Calgacos felt it catch in the oak beneath the bronze facing and he yanked hard, twisting the blade to get it loose. The shield came forward with it, pulling Idris off balance.

Idris had been angry at being pushed to the challenge and now he let the anger sweep over him, too angry to watch Calgacos's eyes. Calgacos aimed his next blow at Idris's shoulder and saw the red blood blossom in the fabric of his shirt. Idris staggered and his shield slid sideways, the grip caught in the spiral armband on his wrist. He crouched, wrenching both free, and Calgacos kicked the shield away from him, the gold coils still twisted in the grip.

"You should have known your plunder would come back to bite you when you disobeyed my orders," Calgacos told him, and a murmur went around the room. Such things were portents.

Idris stood, blood dripping from his shoulder. He held his sword with both hands now. Calgacos threw his own shield onto the table that should have been set for the council's dinner. "I will not take advantage, even of a traitorous fool," he told Idris. "But this is the last mercy I have for you."

They began to circle each other again, shieldless, each looking for any advantage. Calgacos was aware of the heat from the hearth and the bulk of the iron firedogs at his back and began to edge sideways. Idris moved to push him closer to the flames and Calgacos struck, aiming for the neck. Idris parried, breathing hard now, Calgacos's blade sliding down his own, and then Idris pulled away and swung a downward blow. Calgacos felt it bite into his ribs. He could see the blood from Idris's shoulder running down Idris's arm, wet and slick on the hands that clenched his sword hilt. Calgacos aimed another blow, hammering at Idris's blade this time, and it spun from his hands. Calgacos kicked it away.

Idris faced him with only a belt knife now, his eyes glittering in malign fury. Calgacos kept his sword in front of him, pushing Idris's back to the fire. He could feel his own blood dripping from his ribcage, soaking his shirt and breeches. He couldn't tell how deep the wound was. He swung the sword in a low arc, dodging past Idris's knife, seeking for the hamstring at the back of the thigh. The blade sank into the heavy wool of Idris's breeches and through its folds and Calgacos felt it bite flesh. Idris's leg went out from under him. He fell, and as he went he wrapped an arm around Calgacos's legs, toppling him as well. They thrashed in the ashes on the hearth.

Idris fought viciously, with little left to lose. Aelwen watched with her hands to her mouth until Rhion reached out and pulled them gently back into her lap. Idris was more dangerous than ever with an injury that would likely not heal enough for him to walk without a limp. The headman must be whole. He would have challenged Calgacos for nothing, except his own fury and pride. He pinned Calgacos to the hearth, and Calgacos's sword clattered on the hearthstones. Calgacos struggled to push Idris's knife away from his throat and Idris sank his teeth into Calgacos's hand.

Calgacos writhed from under Idris's weight, put his left hand around Idris's throat and drove Idris's head back into the iron frame of the firedogs. Idris's knife slid past Calgacos's cheek and Calgacos, gasping, straddled him and drove Emrys's knife into his throat.

There was blood in the ashes of the hearth and spattered in the herbs on the floor and the smell of death overcame the scent of mint and thyme. Calgacos sat, still breathing hard, while

Aelwen stripped his shirt off and washed the cut on his ribs with vinegar and rubbed salve into it. He saw with relief that it was not deep, only bloody. When she had wrapped clean linen around his chest, Vellaunos Chief Druid stumped across the hall to stand before him.

"There must be purification," Vellaunos said.

"You said there was no ban to my fighting him," Calgacos protested. "He challenged me, Vellaunos. I did not begin it."

"Nevertheless, for a headman to kill one of his holders requires purification. You should have known this."

"And you could have told him!" Aelwen snapped.

"It wouldn't have mattered," Calgacos said. "It had to be done." He stood, looking angrily at the Druid. Such purifications were rarely pleasant. "I will go with you, Vellaunos, when I have settled what is to be done with Idris, and with his holding." Celyn and Dai had dragged the body from the hall into the courtyard. Even for Idris, it was not right to leave it for the carrion birds and the rain outside his door.

"No," Vellaunos said. "Now."

"Go," Rhion said. There was no arguing with Vellaunos. He looked at Aelwen and back to Calgacos. "She and I will see to feeding these lords and to the body. His tenants can keep the hold until you name another to it."

The floor was washed and the roasting ox was carved and served to a subdued council. Maldwyn stayed to himself, with Selisoc and Ula. A handful of other young holders who had followed Idris, and now did not care to have that known, gave them a wide berth. Idris's body was sent home with his driver for such burial as his tenants might feel obliged to give him. The Damnonii girl stayed.

Aelwen faced Rhion down over that.

"She belongs to the hold," Rhion said. "To the next holder."

"She belongs to me," Aelwen said, "because I have decided so. I would send her home to her village if Emrys's men had left anything of it standing. She has bruises all up and down every finger's width of skin that shows. Touch her and I will make a woman's magic that will shrivel every man's cock for ten days' ride from here."

"Believe her," Dai said, laughing with relief because the fight had gone the right way and he could let loose the knot that had gripped his insides.

"Leave the girl with Aelwen," Celyn said seriously, "so that she doesn't take the road that Goewyn did."

"*That* is a debt that is insufficiently paid," Dai said. "Calgacos should keep that holding for Goewyn's sister's son when he's of age."

"The sister's husband is Emrys's man," Rhion protested.

"That may not matter," Celyn said. "After."

–

Calgacos followed Vellaunos through the pine forest. After a while their way veered into cleared pasture and then scraps of open grassland studded with mountain sorrel and meadow rue, and then as the sun sank, to forest again. He did not ask where they were going because by now he knew. There was nothing else here on this slope above the lake but the cave. It was the old gods who extracted penance for ancient sins like murder. Calgacos had made his respects there when he was chosen as headman, and again when he had married Aelwen. That had been in daylight, although no daylight actually reached the cold depths of the cave. But still, he had known that Lugh Bright Spear waited outside and that had eased the crawling sensation that ran down his neck when he held up his torch and saw the Horned God dancing on the wall, carved into the living rock, his round staring eyes, antlers and erect penis painted red with ochre.

Now he had worn the Horned God's mask at Lughnasa and he found that that did not reduce the crawling sensation in the least. "What am I to do?" he asked Vellaunos as they made their way through the outer passages into the dark of the final chamber.

"Wait."

"For what?"

"For what comes," Vellaunos said. "I cannot tell you what that will be."

"Cannot or will not?" Calgacos asked rebelliously. The horned figure on the wall above them seemed to take a step toward them as the flame from Vellaunos's torch wavered with the draft in the chamber.

"Cannot. That is up to the gods. In the morning you may return. I will come for you." Vellaunos stumped away down the dark passage and took the torch with him.

In the deep blackness, Calgacos felt the walls begin to close in on him, and the edge of panic. He bit his lip to still it with the taste of his own blood, still running through his body, still human and alive. The god forever dancing in the blackness on the wall above him made no sound.

He tried to sleep, the swiftest way to pass the time. Whatever was to come to him would presumably wake him up. Or he would dream its presence into being.

He didn't sleep. And nothing came to him, not the god, not the Morrigan, not Idris's ghost. Only a long wakefulness in which a man might contemplate every mistake made over a lifetime, every fear of future error at a time when everything in the familiar world seemed to depend on him for its continued existence.

There was no way to tell the hour, and he was bone cold. He wrapped his cloak more tightly about him against the dank chill inside the mountain. And then he thought he must have slept because there was suddenly a small rushlight beside him and a figure crouching there on its heels. The rushlight was barely enough to show him that it was not Vellaunos, and not a god, only a small man with black hair and a heavily tattooed face, dressed in wolfskins.

212

"Why are you here, Sun Man?" the figure asked him.

"For penance," Calgacos said. He sat up.

"We heard," the little man said.

Calgacos looked at him with interest. He knew the little dark people of the hills still lived in these mountains, the few of them that were left, but they generally made their presence felt in missing chickens and ripe grain harvested the day before its owner planned to cut it. "And why are you here?" he asked him. The light was a relief and he wanted to keep it there.

"This is our cave. It was a holy place long before our people came to it, but it is ours now. We know that your people also come here, at certain times, and we make it holy again when you have gone."

Calgacos smiled. "Are you annoyed that you will have to purify it again now that I have sullied it with my own purific-ation?"

"That, yes, but also when we saw the old priest bringing you here, it was thought to be a sign. My brothers and I have seen the Eagle soldiers coming from the south. We have spoken to our Old Ones and decided that we must help you. I am called Otter," he added.

"I am Calgacos," he said for politeness's sake, although it was clear that Otter already knew that. "How can you help, against the Romans?"

"If we are not looking over our shoulders always for your kind to come hunting us, then you will see," Otter said.

Calgacos paused, thinking, looking out into the darkness of the cave, while Otter watched him silently. "Any alliance is valuable now," he said carefully. "It may be that this is one we should have made before."

"The Sun People have hunted us like hares since they came over water," Otter said. "Why would you have?"

"It may be that the Romans' coming has changed my thinking somewhat," Calgacos said.

"It is different being the hunted, from the hunters." Otter picked up the rushlight in its clay cup and stood, the tiny flame flickering his shadow dimly against the wall, elongated and graceful. "You will not see us, most like."

When Vellaunos came at last and fetched him home, Calgacos wolfed meat from last night's meal and huddled in a blanket by his own hearth, still not warm. "If you come on the little Old Ones, leave them be," he told Rhion and a somber council.

"Leave them be? The little thieves climbed my apple tree and stripped it bare just a seven-day ago!"

"And milked my cow," Maldwyn grumbled.

"If your cow's gone dry, Maldwyn, talk to the Goddess about it, and think on your mistakes maybe!" Dai snapped.

"Stop!" Calgacos glared at all of them. "I have not slept the last night and you may thank your good fortune that it was me and not you. The Old Ones see much, including where the Romans are, when we may not. If we rarely see them come and go, nor will the Romans unless they wish it. Leave them be. I have struck a bargain and some apples are a small price."

–

The Second Augusta detachment pushed north, prodding its nose into the glens above the ridge between the coastal mountains and the northern highlands, with the Hispana parallel to it within a day's march, and the Adiutrix south of them on a punitive sweep through the Venicone lands. They left a landscape of burned villages behind them, but the Caledones had fled from them and fought the advance up each glen. An unnerving eruption of ambushes and downed trees followed them.

Water was fouled before a camp could be set up, and a flaming arrow, shot more for nuisance value than anything else, made a lucky hit in a cohort banner and was seen as a portent, despite the officers' lectures on the dangers of being fanciful. Vengeful troops boiled out of the camp at any sign of these events and the Caledones melted into the trees again.

As they cut a trail that would eventually be a road northwest through the Tavus valley, Faustus set a guard of half his century while the other half worked, and still he saw a man drop silently into the muddy roadbed. The guard poured into the trees in pursuit.

The fallen man lay across his shovel with a small arrow in the narrow gap between his back plates and his helmet's neck guard. Septimus turned him over, supporting his shoulders, but there was no breath or pulse, and so he pulled the arrow.

"Centurion!"

Faustus came to see the little bronze-tipped arrow that Septimus held across his palm, and called the guard back because they weren't going to find anything except perhaps more little bronze arrows in their necks. "When we get back, send this to Ursus," he said.

He was wearily soaking blistered feet in a pan of hot water when the primus pilus sent for him. Paullus brought him dry socks and laced his boots while Faustus reluctantly put his helmet back on his head. The padded lining was damp and sweat-soaked and stank. If only they would stop building road in the mud long enough to wash anything.

Aulus Carus too had been promoted elsewhere over the course of the campaign and Tarpeius Naso now held his position. Naso was in his tent outside the First Cohort barracks, and when Faustus entered and saluted, the primus pilus held out a trio of arrows like the one that Centurion Ursus had sent him that afternoon. "Yours isn't the first one of these we've seen," he said. "I'm told you've had some congress with the little hobgoblins or whatever they are that live in the hills to the south. Are these the same people?"

"Very likely," Faustus said. "They seem to be all related."

"Bronze tips." Naso prodded the arrowheads with a finger. "Like something out of antiquity."

"They don't use iron. They call it a Wrong Thing."

"So they have chosen to take sides," Tarpeius Naso said. "I always understood that they were the enemies of the Britons."

Faustus watched as Naso set the little bronze-tipped arrows in a map box on his desk. "From the extent of my knowledge, they know how to live with the Britons," he offered. "They have done so for centuries and there is a balance between them. We can overset that balance if we choose to, and they fear we will choose to."

"We could dig them out of their hills and open their burrows like an egg," Tarpeius Naso said. "Why provoke us?"

"For fear that we will do it anyway, I expect, sir," Faustus said. He hesitated. Questioning the primus pilus was somewhere on the border between impertinence and insubordination. "But is it worth it?" he asked finally, thinking of Curlew and the Old One. "In time and men?"

"That is for the legate to decide," Tarpeius Naso said. "To my mind, yes, for the lesson of it. Thank you, Centurion."

The shade of Silvius Valerianus appeared in the middle of the Via Praetoria as Faustus returned to his tent in the summer dusk. "They are not a people for you to concern yourself with." His father's face wore the disapproving look it had always shown when Faustus consorted with the slaves or played with the tinker's children when their wagon stopped at the farm to mend broken pots.

"Pluto! Will you go away!" Faustus made the sign of horns at him.

"How can I? I'm in *your* head."

"Then you aren't real." Faustus could see the legion's standards through the folds of his father's toga.

"How can I know?" the shade asked.

"Why are you here?"

"I don't know that either." He faded into the dusk.

Faustus ground his teeth. If anyone should have followed him to Britain it should have been his mother. Maybe she had, flying straight to the land where she had been born, as the local people thought that exiles did. The low road, they called it, through the earth. He wondered if his father was actually chasing her instead and didn't know it. He had been a possessive man and inclined to think his possessions should all think as he did. It must have galled him when they didn't.

"You father wishes the best for us," his mother had told him once, adding, "by his lights."

It was the day he had learned that he was to inherit not only his dead brother's position as heir, but also his future wife. Faustus was ten and Sulpicia nine, so they were too young to marry, as Marcus had been, but a childhood betrothal was common.

"She and her parents will dine with us tonight," his mother said. "So you may get to know each other." She had found him sulking in the kitchen garden, and stood over him exasperated, hands on her hips. "Please wash before then, and put on a clean tunic."

"I know her already," Faustus protested. "When she and Marcus were betrothed. I don't want her."

His mother put down the basket she was carrying. She was always carrying something somewhere. The mistress was expected to supervise the slaves on the farm and to know how their work should be done. Faustus had sometimes wondered if his father had chosen to marry her because she had been one of them. She sat beside him on the garden bench. "Faustus, do not fight this. You will only anger your father. Sulpicia is a nice girl, and even pretty. You are fortunate."

"Just because he didn't betroth me to someone with spots and a bottom like a hippopotamus? I don't want to marry her."

"There are things about which we have no choice," his mother told him. Her profile was backlit by the sun, like a cameo, dark hair pulled into an elaborate knot, with short curls framing her forehead. She had a small hidden tattoo like a flower between her breasts. Faustus remembered it from when he was still young enough to bathe with her. It had always seemed exotic to him, some small part of her that refused to be Roman.

"Did you want to marry Father?" he asked abruptly.

"No," she said. "But I did not want to be a slave either." She put the basket back over her arm and stood. "Faustus, don't fight him on this."

He hadn't, simply because there was no way to, and his mother's answer had faded into the back of his mind, faced with the prospect of marrying Sulpicia. She was, as his mother had said, a perfectly nice girl. She followed him about the farm and gardens when they were sent out to get acquainted, and whenever he said anything, she replied, "Oh, yes, I think so too," clearly coached by her mother.

He wondered now what she had thought of him. Had she been relieved too when her father broke the betrothal? There was no knowing.

The summer dusk deepened into darkness and glowworms began to show in the meadow outside the camp, little spots of ghostly fire. The world seemed entirely too full of unanswered questions. His watch commander came around with the password, and the lanterns of the night patrol bobbed past along the camp walls, momentarily illuminating helmet and spear point. His mother had been a Silure, no kin to the tall, blond Caledones. But if she had indeed had sidhe blood, then his tie to this land went deeper into the bone. It wouldn't keep one of those little bronze arrows out of a chink in his armor, though. He thought he had best remind himself of that occasionally.

XIII

The Bog

The attack on the Ninth Hispana came well after the mid-hour of the night, when the watch had finished their sleepy rounds and were dreaming on the turf walls of their marching camp. By ill chance, or by some arcane knowledge, or by spies who should have been caught but weren't, they struck the most vulnerable of Agricola's three columns, and they struck in force, after Agricola had concluded that they could not be provoked into forming a war band large enough for Roman tactics to be useful.

They flowed out of the forest that covered the slope below the camp, moving noiselessly from the trees into the cleared land around the walls, and they came on foot, more than three thousand, with ladders to bridge the ditches and scale the walls, rams to break the gates, and hot coals in boxes slung on their backs to set fire to whatever would burn.

The first man to see them moving silently upward among the stumps of the cleared land shouted a warning and the camp shook itself awake to find them pouring over the walls. The legate of the Ninth flung himself from his bed and took up his sword without waiting to put on his cuirass. His optio grabbed him by the shoulder and thrust it at him.

"The primus pilus has them forming up. We can't have you killed, put this on!"

The legate fidgeted while his optio buckled the plates together. He jammed his helmet with its identifiable eagle feather crest on his head and went out into the night.

The Ninth was fighting hand to hand with the shrieking warriors, no longer silent now but howling like demons as they swarmed over the walls, war-painted and half-naked, wild white hair standing in spikes above tattooed faces. A beacon was already burning on the tower that surmounted the eastern corner of the rampart and the legate squinted into the night to see if an answering flame came yet from the next watchtower in the line.

"Where are the scouts?" he snapped.

"Here, sir." One of the frontier scouts appeared at his elbow. "We never had a sniff of them, sir, I swear it!" He looked furious and ashamed.

"That much is obvious. Get to the governor's camp. Three of you, one at a time, out by the dexter gate." There the fighting was lightest, and the border wolves had the best chance of getting through the enemy to the governor. If the governor wasn't also fighting off a horde of Caledones.

The scout disappeared and the legate waded into the melee. Commanders usually commanded from a suitable distance, but there was no distance here, and the bedraggled cohorts of his legion needed to see him. They had been driven back from their own walls and now the legionaries and their auxiliaries were massing at the center of the camp, surrounding the Principia and barracks tents and the baggage wagons where a cluster of terrified civilians huddled. The invaders cut the cavalry horses loose from their pickets and they thundered frantically through the chaos. The leather tents didn't burn well but they managed to set a catapult frame ablaze and its column of flame lit the darkness around it, picking out wild, painted faces and the hastily donned armor of the defenders.

"Hold them! Circle a shield wall and hold them!" the legate shouted and the trumpeter at his side blew the call, again and again. *Hold*. Hold until you can't. He could see the pinpoints of beacons burning farther down the ridge now. Mithras send that they carried only his own alarm, and not word of a simultaneous attack.

Governor Agricola, camped with the Augusta, had also seen the beacons. He called the legion out of bed and sent a courier to the legate of the Twentieth even before a scout rode in on a lathered horse. The legate of the Ninth had been right to send three, because only one made it through the besieging Caledone army. That it was an army, and not a band of marauders, was clear in the scout's report.

The *Form Up* call that had shaken everyone out of their tents changed to *Prepare to March*, and Faustus trotted up and down the line, inspecting his sleepy, unnerved century and saying, "No kit, just weapons, armor and shield, that's the order," and "I don't know, but you can see the beacons so use your head."

There was only half a moon, just risen, in the sky to show their way. The cavalry rode out first under its uncertain light. The infantry's vanguard, marching at quick step behind them, bore lanterns along the half-dug road, and a substantial rear guard watched their backs, aware always of the possibility of ambush. An auxiliary cohort was left behind to guard the baggage train and everything else they were abandoning in camp to make speed. The scout's word as to the numbers that had hit the Hispana assuaged Agricola's suspicion that it might be a trick to catch his own column defenseless, but there was always that possibility.

"The Ninth," Septimus said, stumbling at forced march pace in the near dark. "It would be."

"Shut it!" Faustus snapped. They had been told nothing official but it was clear they were heading for the Hispana's camp and rumors were circulating like a flock of crows.

"I never believed that story about curses," Septimus said stubbornly, "but you have to think there's something."

"I'll bust you to flat pay if you do any more rumor-mongering, that's what I think," Faustus said. The woods on either side of them were ink dark. His neck itched with wondering what was in them.

The cavalry had already engaged with the Caledone attackers when the auxiliary infantry and the cohorts of the Augusta caught up to them. The sky was paling to the east and the gold Eagle and the silver cohort standards gleamed in the dim light. As they converged on the battle Faustus saw a second Eagle in the distance – the Twentieth at the end of a forced march from the west.

The besiegers turned to face the relief column with blood-soaked spears and long swords and Roman heads tied to their belts by the helmet straps. The blood that dripped from them shone blackish in the murky light.

Faustus shouted "To me! Stay with your standard!" knowing the effect those heads would have on his men. "Keep formation!" If they broke to pursue individual vengeance the Caledones would plow right through them.

"To your standard!" Septimus shouted. The signifer held it high above their heads and they closed back into formation around it.

The Caledones, faced with Agricola's relief column on one side and the defending Ninth Legion on the other, began to fight their way out. They carried whatever plunder had struck their fancy, armor stripped from the dead, bronze cook pots, silver plates from officers' baggage, and sacks of coin from the legion's pay chest. They rode freed cavalry mounts and drove others before them while the cavalry from the relief column tried to turn them.

Faustus rolled out from under the hooves of a cavalry horse with a Caledone warrior on its back, bridleless and bareback and snorting at the unaccustomed scent of its rider. He came up as the horse reared and he put his pilum into the Caledone's ribs. Its barbed point caught in the ribcage, and he abandoned it and drew his short sword, shield in his other hand. The Britons had lost the cohesion they had maintained during the attack and now fought as they always had, howling and throwing themselves like rabid wolves at the enemy. The Augusta cohorts tucked their shields over their heads against the spears and slingstones raining down on them and pushed forward up the slope. One of Faustus's men went down with the shards of his shield driven through the bent plates of his lorica behind a heavy Caledone war spear. More Caledones poured through the open gap as his fellows pulled him away and struggled to close up the line. Faustus moved into the open spot, his signifer beside him, and they followed the standard and the blood-red crosswise crest toward the camp gate.

The cohorts of the Ninth made a sortie from their defensive ring at the camp's center as the relieving column drew off the invaders. They pushed the Caledones toward the Praetorian gate where the Augusta was closing on them, and the sinister gate, outside which the Twentieth waited. Caught between them, the Caledones broke. They poured out of the camp through the dexter gate in the dawn light, while those caught in the other two gates hacked their way free, leaving both Roman and British dead behind in a grisly path.

Faustus felt his shield clawed away by the edge of a Caledone one and pulled it free just before a sword swung into the gap. He closed with the man, where his short sword would have the advantage, slammed his shield at the painted face and slid his sword up under the Caledone's shield as he brought it up in defense. The man dropped, head downward on the slope, blood pouring from his neck, bright against the bleached white spikes of his hair.

Faustus stepped over him, pushing the last besiegers back into the camp and onto the swords of the defenders. Then a trumpet sounded the *Pursuit* and the relief column turned to reform and chase down the attackers who had fled.

It was full light now and in the camp it shone on a devastation of trampled tents and half-burned furniture strewn among corpses and moaning wounded. The center shield wall had broken and the Caledones had pushed through to ransack the military baggage and the wagons of terrified camp followers. Now as the last attackers were being hunted down, the civilians began to creep out of this perilous refuge, futilely collecting the shards of their belongings. An innkeeper sat weeping among his broken wine jars but the women of a brightly painted brothel wagon with a smashed-in carriage surveyed it grimly, shrugged, and set about helping the legion's surgeons in the wreckage of the hospital tent.

The relief column swung around the walls to join the Twentieth in pursuit of the enemy that had fled through the dexter gate. The cavalry rode down the stragglers and a Batavian cavalry prefect signaled to his trumpeter to sound *To Stables*. The loose horses turned in their flight, scrambling back up the slope through the fleeing Caledones. The trumpeter blew the call again and the prefect watched with satisfaction as other stolen, saddleless, bridleless and hungry mounts responded, turning stubbornly around for their morning feed until most of the Caledone riders gave up and slid from their backs.

The Caledones fled through a wooded slope thick with pine and scrub and the way grew rougher as the Roman column pursued them. Mindful of ambush, they kept formation even when it slowed their way. At the wood's edge the land flattened and the pursuers gained ground, overtaking the rear of the Caledone retreat. Those in the rear turned and fought, went down or were taken prisoner at spearpoint. The ground was rough, wet, tussocky clumps of grass interspersed with moss and sundew.

"Bog," the Augusta legate, on the slope above, said suddenly.

"The Caledones are navigating it all right," his staff aide said, watching the retreating horde stream across it.

"I don't—" the legate said, and then "Halt them!"

The trumpet sounded *Halt Pursuit* and then again. The Caledones fled across the watery landscape on paths the Romans couldn't see and man after man pursuing them went down in the muck, scrabbling at the grass as he sank.

The pursuit slowed, halted, bumping into the ranks of those in front struggling backward from the reaching maw of the bog. Faustus felt the edge of it shiver under his boots.

"Stand still!" He put out a hand to the men of his century on either side of him. "Wait until the ranks behind us get clear and then back up slowly." He prodded his vine staff at the ground and the ground heaved. "Is everyone accounted for?"

"Cornutus!" someone shouted. "He's in!"

"Where?"

"Someone grab his hand!"

"Careful, it'll get you too!"

Faustus edged carefully along the line. Cornutus. It would be. Cornutus had been busted from optio for failing to follow orders when Faustus had first taken command of the third century. He had not improved, and routinely "didn't hear that order, sir," when the order didn't suit him. Faustus surveyed the heaving bog and the panicked Cornutus thrashing in its grip.

"Be still! You'll go in deeper."

Cornutus kept thrashing, and sank lower. It was up to his chest now.

Faustus laid his shield on the quaking surface and someone handed him another one. He put it down, shed his lorica and stretched out along them, praying. He held out his hands to Cornutus. They were still an arm's length from reaching and Cornutus was sinking.

"Stop heaving about, you fool!" Faustus told him. "Stay *still*!" He wondered how long the shields would float on the gelatinous surface of the bog before it sucked them down too. Slimy water bubbled unpleasantly close to his nose, covering and uncovering the floating moss and the sticky hairs of sundew. "Give me my staff." He put his hand up behind him and felt someone gingerly place his vine stick in it. He pushed the staff across the surface of the bog to Cornutus and gripped one end tightly. "Hold onto this until we can get a rope."

"Optio's gone for one!" someone said.

The stick was sliding from his grasp, slimy with bog water. Faustus let go of it and Cornutus wailed. Faustus unbuckled his belt and edged it gingerly out from under him. He rebuckled it and pushed the ring of leather toward Cornutus. "Grab that, it's easier to hold onto." Cornutus's fingers clenched around it and he tried to pull himself toward Faustus.

"Don't do that! Wait for the rope!" The edge of Faustus's shield tipped under the surface of the bog and he screamed at Cornutus, "Move again and when I get you out I'll crucify you!" His nose was level with the sundew now, which he noted had dissolved a butterfly. The wings fluttered a little with the movement of the quagmire.

"Rope's here." A circle landed in the muck beside him and Faustus snatched it. The right side of his shield was dipping dangerously. He felt hands close around his ankles behind him.

"Get the rope around him," Septimus grunted. "We've got you."

Faustus heaved the rope at Cornutus and it missed, sliding down his shoulder into the muck.

"Get it around you," Faustus shouted, and Cornutus dragged it free, sinking lower as he did, and drew it around his chest. Faustus saw it tighten as the men behind him pulled on it.

Nothing moved. Cornutus wailed again and the rope dug into the plates of his lorica.

"Heave!"

"Get back yourself, sir!"

"I can't let go of him," Faustus gasped. "I'm afraid he'll go under." The belt was cutting into his fingers and the bog rose around them in stinking burbles and murmurs like something smacking its lips.

Cornutus floundered and the bog heaved around him, higher.

"You can't have him!" Faustus told it, gasping. "He's *mine*!"

"He's coming," Septimus shouted. "You get back now so we can pull him in!"

Faustus felt the hands on his ankles tug at him and saw Cornutus rise a hand's breadth out of the muck. He crawled backward along the shields as the bog gave up Cornutus with a hideous sucking noise and Cornutus flopped onto Faustus's shield. They towed him backward with the shields until they both lay gagging on the grass at the bog's edge. The bog clung to them like some kind of thick, revolting soup and its stench was appalling. Faustus's stomach heaved.

A little blue-painted stick driven into the ground in front of his nose caught Faustus's eye. He sat up, coughing and dripping bog slime, and squinted his eyes out across the deceptively grassy surface of the bog. Another stood farther out and he thought he could see a handful more scattered across the tufts of grass and moss that covered its surface. He prodded the little stick with his fingertip and then pulled it up.

Faustus staggered to his feet as the pursuit was called back. Cornutus was up too, shivering and wild-eyed still and dripping with slime. Faustus expected the bog would trouble Cornutus's dreams. He thought it might his own.

He tucked the small marker into his boot with the sensation that it might turn suddenly to an adder. He could think of but one source for guideposts that only a native people could plant, to aid a war band of clans from other hills.

–

The relief column dug in their own fortifications beside the Hispana's camp, and settled there for the time it took to assess the damage and burn the dead. Most of the casualties came from the besieged Hispana, with a few among the relief column and, hideously, several dozen lost to the bog, too far in to save. Faustus had passed the little blue stick to Centurion Ursus, who sent it up the command chain to the primus pilus, the legate, and finally the governor, where it confirmed what everyone already suspected.

The Caledones had looted the camp with a thoroughness that was professional. Much of what had been taken would now have to be requisitioned and the missing pay chests accounted for to the Senate in Rome. Neither the Senate nor the emperor was likely to be pleased, especially given the order that they were not to go above the Clota–Bodotria line. That had been ignored after the attack on the Damnonii, and now they had come very close to disaster. No one cared to indulge the unwelcome thought that things came in threes, but there was a grim sense of inevitability when, with the pyres of the dead still burning, a dispatch rider from Eburacum came north with a story that made the governor's face pale. It was disastrous, ill-omened and dangerous, and there was no hiding it, much as Agricola would have liked to.

A cohort recruited from among the German Usipii and still in training south of Eburacum had mutinied and murdered their officers.

"Six centurions and a military tribune," Galerius said, horrified. Mutiny was the thing that every commander feared, and it spread like leprosy.

The mutinous cohort had headed for the nearest harbor, killed the crews of three ships there, and forced their helmsmen to take them out to sea. It was thought that news that the emperor had begun campaigning in the Usipii homeland north of the Rhenus had been the provocation. Every commander paraded his men, spoke of loyalty to Rome and to each other, and held prayers for the murdered officers.

Tuathal Techtmar, who had been relegated to the baggage train and arrived indignantly with the supply wagons when the fighting had ceased, had been in Agricola's tent complaining about that when the news had come. He came to the Seventh Cohort's camp after evening prayers to share what he knew with Faustus and Galerius.

"The only reason to chase them now would be to get your ships back before they sink them," Tuathal said. "Three boatloads of cavalry on ships with no sailors. I'm thinking Agricola will let the sea do it for him."

"Likely it will if they're trying to sail back to Germany," Faustus said. The German Ocean between Britain and the

Rhenus was as unpredictable as a cat and would be particularly so now as the year edged into autumn. He said a quick prayer to Neptune that they should drown as unpleasantly as possible as an example to anyone else with mutinous ideas.

"They were raiding the coast villages north of the head at Oceli," Tuathal said. "The prefect in Eburacum sent troops to drive them out to sea again. As you say, likely they won't come back." Tuathal was less horrified than the Romans by the mutiny, which seemed to him a perfectly reasonable thing to have done when Rome marched into the Usipii's homeland. He was nineteen now, taller than he had been a year ago, lanky and beginning to be muscular. His face had hardened into an adult aspect, tightening to the chin and cheekbones. He was clean-shaven in the Roman style, his dark hair trimmed to the top of his shoulders. He sat idly scratching Pandora's head while Paullus, who had arrived with the baggage carts, heated wine and handed cups around.

"This is very good," Faustus said, distracted. "It can't be mine. Where did you get it?"

"It was reissued," Paullus said. "Someone didn't need it anymore." He didn't elaborate. *Reissued* generally meant *don't ask where it came from*.

"Well, have some yourself, since you stole it," Faustus said. "It's an evil night. If I don't dream about that bog I'm going to dream about Usipii mutineers sailing up the river into the camp."

"Thank you." Paullus poured himself a cup of wine. "I threw your tunic on the midden," he added. "The one you went into the bog in."

"I did not want it back," Faustus said. "Not even the rag-pickers would." His belt and boots and shield had been cleaned and he really couldn't blame Paullus for the tunic. It had stunk of bog water, a smell of decay that no amount of washing was going to take away. The faint whiff of it from his other gear was bad enough. He had wondered, between meeting the Old One

229

at Llanmelin and the little blue trail markers in the bog, whether this province that had bred his mother was going to take him in or spit him out. The bog had offered an unpleasant third possibility, a gruesome combination of both. He shuddered and tipped another measure of warmed wine into his cup, with a drop on the ground for the souls of the Usipii cohort's dead officers.

The mutineers were on the governor's mind as well, along with the status of the province's other auxiliary cohorts.

"Are there any that are unstable, by your best assessment?" Agricola looked around his field tent where the legates of the three legions had gathered.

"By my best assessment, no." Arrius Laenas, the legate of the Augusta, said. "But the Batavians are also Germans, and the Batavi staged a costly rebellion during the civil war. They've been dependable in Britain," he added.

"So far," the legate of the Twentieth said.

"A bad idea often spreads more swiftly than a good one," the Ninth Hispana's legate murmured. "They fought well, though, I must give them that credit."

"Did you see them call their horses out from under the Britons, at the end?" Laenas asked. "Battlefield poetry."

"Indeed," Agricola said. He motioned to an optio. "When we are through here, send the Batavian prefects to me. I want to shore up any weak spots. And we will intermix them over the autumn with a solid draft of recruits from the southern tribes."

The young men of the southeast of Britain had come of age under Roman rule and took Roman ways and Roman luxuries for granted. Their opinion of the untamed tribes of the northern highlands was somewhat akin to a Roman's idea of wild apes or the dog-headed men of Libya. They were far more willing to fight them than they were their nearer kin in the midlands.

"Nor will I waste the Fleet to catch a pack of murderous fools who will no doubt bring their own punishment on themselves," Agricola added, confirming Tuathal's suspicion. "We have better use for the Fleet here to patrol the coast and the marines to drive the Caledones farther into the mountains before they can get what is left of their harvest in."

The legates nodded. Many of the highland tribes relied on the flatter coastal lands for grain-growing. If the already meager autumn harvest went to Rome or even if it was simply destroyed, it would mean a winter of bone-deep hunger. The coming spring would now bring the all-out war that had been brewing for years. If the Caledones went into it hungry it would be greatly to Rome's benefit.

"With luck, they will fight each other over it," Arrius Laenas said.

"*Or* we will drive them to choose a war leader to bring all the clans under one command," the Hispana's legate said. "That is the other possibility."

"That is probably an inevitability now," the legate of the Twentieth said. "The attack on your camp was carefully coordinated. They may have done so already."

"I don't think so." The Hispana's legate looked somber. "They would have won if they had. They came close."

Agricola pulled a map from its case on his desk, deliberately ignoring that fact, which already troubled his sleep. "According to the Damnonii, if they are not lying – and I can't see a reason to lie over this – Calgacos and Emrys are the great chiefs among the highland clans, and they are old enemies. It was Emrys's men who attacked the Damnonii, and likely it will be one or the other."

"Can we bring either of them under our influence?" Laenas asked.

"Considering that Calgacos, according to our scouts, has been calling for war against us for several years, and the state in which Emrys left the Damnonii villages, no." Agricola spread the map out and prodded his forefinger at the places where the Caledones' harbors were known or thought to be. The map was the latest iteration of the Fleet's surveyors' attempts to chart the coastline. "The Fleet can stop traffic by ship through their waters. By that we may keep them from moving men by boat, and cut off trade."

And put a stone in the shoe of any chieftain who was given sole command. In the governor's experience, only supernatural intervention could prevent Britons from fighting each other when they would have done better to fight Rome. This was his last chance at taking the north. A letter from the emperor had made it plain that it would require only the stroke of a pen to recall him if he did not produce a victory.

XIV

Winter Quarters

"The wars of men are not the province of the Druids!" Emrys spat. "How often have you said that?"

Nemausos stared at him unblinkingly until he subsided. Nemausos was younger than Emrys, but he was a Druid. He did not require Vellaunos Chief Druid, standing stolidly beside him, or any of the other Druids assembled in the meadow to speak for him. Around them the headmen of the highland clans had gathered finally to make a pact against the Romans under a single standard. When a vote had come to no conclusion, Vellaunos had called the Druids away with him into the grove. There they read the patterns that the fish made in the river, the skeins of starlings wheeling above the tree canopy, and as the sky darkened and the assembled holders fidgeted and drew their cloaks around themselves against the dank air, the stars that came and went behind the clouds. All in all, they conferred for the better part of a day and night while no one dared to disturb them. Then they returned with the dawn and spoke for Calgacos.

"Everything is the province of the Druids," Nemausos said now to Emrys. "The grain in the fields, the cattle on the hillside, when you are born and when you die. The reason we do not ordain these things is because they are small and unimportant, not because we cannot."

"Now a great weight hangs in the world's balance," Vellaunos said. "And so we speak."

With the exception of Emrys, the assembled holders bent their heads toward the Druids in submission. The Druids rarely gave an outright order, but when they did, it was binding. In its way it was a relief to have the thing decided for them. Emrys stood for a long moment silhouetted against the rising sun, his white hair limned with an otherworldly light, radiating fury, but finally he too bowed his head.

"I will look to Calgacos as warlord," he said grimly, "but I will command my own men."

"Agreed," Calgacos said. "Every man follows best his own lord." He looked them over, holders of his own and Emrys's, and the lords of smaller, scattered clans from the far north. "We will have one chance and one only, I am thinking," he told them. "Best we spend the winter preparing. If ships can be got through their blockade, we must buy grain and all the arms we can send the gold for. And make what we can from our own forges. School this season's yearlings to saddle rather than to drive."

There were protests at that and even Celyn and Dai began to argue with him. Calgacos cut them off.

"In every battle, the Romans throw up a shield wall against our chariot line and wait for us to break. Our war chariots are good only for frightening the front ranks. Thus we will keep enough for that purpose and send mounted fighters instead against their cavalry. We cannot fight the Romans as we have fought each other."

"That is not our way!" someone shouted.

"I'll send a message to the Romans for you then," Rhion snapped back, "and ask them please to fight us honorably."

Bleddin, who had taken his spear just that season, the warrior patterns new and bright on his face and chest, stepped forward. "We will fight as my father the warlord tells us to fight, my spear brothers and I!"

"We will need you," Calgacos said, fighting down the wish that Bleddin were two years younger, too young for the battle line. "You and even those who will take their spears in the spring." He looked to the older lords. "Before the weather turns any worse you must send your women and children to the holds farthest north and inland, for safety. When we lure the Romans to where we can best entrap and finish them, we cannot leave our weak ones in their path."

"I will not go," Aelwen said flatly when he told her. "Nor will Aregwydd and my brother's wife and any number of other women I could name for you. This is our land. If, as you say, we have one chance, then we will fight beside you as we have been taught. We were trained with the hounds until they took their spears." She stood glaring at him in the kitchen doorway, a ladle in one hand and an apron over her green gown, while her kitchen women bustled about the hearth and pretended not to hear their mistress fight with the headman. Her red hair, tied up away from the fire's heat, made a tangled cloud around her face.

"And when the hounds were given their spears you went to husbands and households," Calgacos said. "You are not warriors."

"Is there any man of yours who will face me down when I am angry?" Aelwen asked him.

"That is not the same. And no. But we do not put our mares into the chariot line."

"I am not a horse!" Aelwen snapped. "And I heard you tell Rhion that it may come to the mares. It will come down to numbers, Calgacos. Let me ride with you."

"And let every man with a wife in the war band be distracted by fear for her? Myself included. No."

"Other men manage their fears!" Aelwen said. "Celyn does not ask Dai to stay at home."

"Celyn and Dai are both warrior trained. That comes before whatever love they have between them. That is different."

"It is not. Furthermore, I can drive as well as any man. You have seen me. Put us in the chariot line to drive then, and give you that many more fighting men."

235

"And who will care for Ceridwen when you are killed?"

Aelwen was silent. Then she said, "And who will care for me when you are dead?"

There was no answer to either question and they came to no resolution. They had the winter to sort it out, Calgacos thought, taking her in his arms.

They had the winter to make him believe that she meant it, Aelwen thought, leaning her head against his shoulder, burying her face in his hair.

–

Julius Agricola sat with the Batavian cohort prefects and shuffled enlistment rosters, fit-for-duty rosters, officers' postings new and old, and various other lists. Following that, a series of orders went out through the ranks of his assembled army.

Faustus considered his with interest. The imperial cypher, which all military orders bore, gave it an air of portent. The governor's seal was appended as well. Centurion of the second century of the First Batavian Cohort of auxiliaries. A fairly substantial promotion, amounting to second-in-command of the cohort, and a milliary double cohort at that. Ursus wasn't going to be happy, he thought, and wondered what had happened to the man he was replacing. He thought of the bog again and hoped it wasn't that. Now that he had seen the bog first-hand the image of his original predecessor going down in it was the stuff of nightmares.

"A lateral transfer to the Asturians in Pannonia," Aulus Atticus, prefect of the First Batavians, told him when he reported and asked hesitantly about the man whose place he was taking. Atticus was young and cheerful with a crop of wavy brown hair and a lanky frame. "It really amounts to the governor pulling a few officers who might possibly be doubtful in the wake of the Usipii debacle, and sticking in ones known to be sound. I heard about your adventure in the bog by the way. Nothing wrong with the last man, specifically," he added. "Certainly not mutinous. None of the officers are German anyway. Just not as sound as we'd like, to be second-in-command. We'll leave it at that."

"Yes, sir."

"Do you speak German?"

"Not really."

"Well, most of them speak Latin, and you'll pick it up. Just don't ask them how to say something. They'll tell you something filthy and then stand back and watch you say it to the governor."

Faustus saluted and went off to take a look at his new charges. If the previous commander wasn't "as sound as we'd like", Faustus wondered how he had progressed to second-in-command of a milliary cohort of ten centuries.

The Batavians paraded smartly for their new commander, touched fists to chests in salute, and stood at attention while Faustus inspected them. The First was an infantry cohort, equipped with heavy and light throwing spears, short swords similar to the legions', oval shields painted a dark emerald and overlaid with saffron sun rays, and hauberks of mail, their helmets topped with fox-fur caps. His optio and signifer were friendly and respectful, and fluent in Latin. If their previous commander had done them any damage, it wasn't evident. Relieved, Faustus dismissed them and went to see what Paullus had nosed out about Aulus Atticus.

"His man speaks highly of him," Paullus said. "I always think that's a good sign. He's from an army family, he'll be working his way up to a legionary command most likely."

Paullus had also been to the armorer to requisition a hauberk of mail and the horsetail helmet crest favored by auxiliary officers. The speed with which he had produced them lent Faustus to think that they might also have been reissued.

"What was wrong with the man before me?" Faustus asked, inspecting the hauberk. "'Not quite sound' isn't very informative. Mithras, this thing is heavy."

"Aulus Atticus thought he was too timid," Paullus said. "Hesitant. Might not act fast enough if anything boiled up."

"Mmm." Faustus could see Atticus's point. An incipient mutiny wasn't an occasion to stop and think for a while.

"The mail is easier to keep clean," Paullus said, "if I may be allowed to favor it." Polishing the plates of Faustus's lorica had been a daily chore. Mail, worn regularly, practically polished itself.

Galerius, who was newly promoted to Ursus's second century, came by to congratulate him, and see if there was any more of the reissued wine. "We're posted down to Brigante country for the winter," he said. "Someone else will have the honor of holding the frontier, and welcome to it because the blasted country gets colder the farther north we go, and it's cold enough to freeze the balls off a bronze god already." The sky was leaden and a bitter wind whipped between the tents, prying its fingers into every opening. The army would be glad to be within walls before the capricious winter weather hit them. Galerius raised his cup. "To the spring, when we'll finish the job."

–

The Cornovii of the northern islands were reputed to have been seals once, and Calgacos, observing the man across the table from him, could almost believe it. Faelan was muscular and thick-necked, with dark eyes in a round face behind a bristly mustache. He inspected the gold jewelry and fittings that Calgacos had emptied into a glittering pile on his kitchen table.

"Bad weather for getting boats across, and under the Romans' noses," he said.

"And yet, we are here," Nall observed. He was chieftain of the mainland Cornovii and had come with Calgacos to bargain with his kin, to Calgacos's relief. The islanders were strange people and kept to themselves, marrying occasionally with their relatives on the mainland but otherwise isolated.

"We keep the Romans from your own door," Calgacos said. "Surely that is worth the risk, for a sea people who know the tides and currents."

"A war host must be fed and we have not the grain to do it," Nall said. "The Romans have not been through *your* fields," he added pointedly.

The Caledone villages had emptied themselves out in a migration that had taken them to the farthest northern coast, across the great triangle of water that separated the western highlands from Caledone lands and from which there was little place else to go except the islands. The western lords had been slow to ally, but when Calgacos had shown them how the Romans had flowed like an incoming tide across the lower part of Britain and never drawn back again, they were persuaded that the tide would reach their own feet if they did not. Now his holders and Emrys's and every other clan from as far south as the Venicones were crowded into halls like Nall's, too small to hold them, and eating their hosts' granaries bare. The Roman Fleet's blockade made crossing north to the islands dangerous but any other trade impossible, and the grain he was here to buy with the last of everyone's gold would be only such as the islanders were willing to spare.

"The Romans make it a dangerous passage, across the firth," Faelan said, eyeing the gold.

"Nor have you sent us men to fight them as we asked," Nall said.

"Nor will we," Faelan said. "The Romans were here once, in my grandfather's time. They left again. We will sell what we can." He turned to a girl stirring a pot on the hearth. "Eirian! Bring our guests beer and meat! And tell your brothers that they should be at milking and not sitting about lordlywise as if there was nothing else to do."

"They are mending nets," she said, "but I will tell them." She dipped three bowls from the pot, and brought them with three clay jars of beer. "I will send some to your men too," she told Calgacos. "What are Romans like?"

239

He looked at her curiously. She was slight, with pale brown hair tucked under a kerchief and an apron over her gown, but he supposed her to be a daughter of the house and not a slave.

"A trader from the south told me that they heat their houses with fires under the floor," she told him, "and another said that some of them have tails." She looked dubious at that, but anything was possible.

"I have seen no tails," Calgacos said. "They appear as men like any others, but they *want*. They keep on *wanting*, more and more. When they have one thing they want another," he added pointedly, with a glance at her father.

"Mind your manners!" Faelan said. "The lords are not here to speak with you."

Eirian filled a small pot with stew and dipped a jug of beer from the barrel that sat in the kitchen. She took them to the crew of the boat that was pulled up on the shore beside the fishing currachs, and went to give Boduoc and Eogan their father's message, for what it would be worth. They would do the milking when the cows came to the gate and bellowed. She looked at the sun. It was early for them to be coming in from the pasture. Her father simply liked to give orders, to her, to Boduoc and Eogan, to anyone.

"Father says to start the milking," she said, sitting down beside them and picking up a section of net to mend.

"Tell him thank you for teaching us to suck an egg," Boduoc said.

"He is talking with the warlord from the mainland," Eirian said. "What do you suppose the place the Romans live is like?"

"Like ours, I suppose," Eogan said. He looked at their house, a solid, substantial round stone house with several outbuildings, and the green pastures and stubble of the winter harvest beyond it.

"The traders say their cities are made out of marble," Eirian said wistfully. "With water inside the houses. I would like to see that."

"Well that's just foolishness. Who would want water in the house?" Boduoc looked at her suspiciously. "Why do you want to know? What would anyone want that we don't have here?"

"Whatever her mother wanted," Eogan muttered.

Eirian flung the net down. "Mend your own nets, beast!" Her mother had left when she was a baby and no one knew where she had gone, including Eirian's father, or so he said. The rumors said she had walked into the sea, either in a selkie skin or to drown herself, but the seals never told Eirian when she asked.

Their father came out of the house with Nall and the warlord from the south, and her brothers rose when he shouted at them. Eirian glared at their backs. They would take the grain across the firth at night most likely, when it would be easier to skirt the Roman patrols. She knew they wouldn't let her go with them, although she could manage a boat as well as any of them. There would be a great battle, so the seals said, between the mainland clans and the mysterious Romans and she wouldn't see any of it.

–

Agricola spread his army out into winter quarters. The Second Augusta went into the legionary base at Eburacum with the Hispana. Auxiliary units were posted in Selgovae territory and to the ridge garrisons between Alauna and the newly built fortress of Castra Pinnata, where the Twentieth was to winter and make certain that no ground was lost before spring. A series of watchtowers between them served as warning of any attack and dispatch riders went regularly along the line despite the weather.

The First Batavians went to Trimontium, which sat below the old fortress of the Selgovae and the three hills that gave it its name, and Faustus set himself to learning German, most of which he suspected he would not be able to use in any polite company.

Aulus Atticus was a restless commander, inclined to order drill and marches whenever there was not an actual blizzard. However, he was open-handed, generous with allowed holidays, and his cohort clearly liked him. At Saturnalia he produced a feast and good-naturedly allowed the Saturnalia princeps, drawer of the lucky bean, to order him about with impunity. When the next dispatch rider came in, an extra measure of wine went around to celebrate the news that the governor now had a son.

Besides the First Batavians, an ala of Asturian cavalry was in residence, and both prefects jointly sponsored the building of a temple to Mithras outside the fortress walls. Each of Agricola's new forts had begun to develop its own vicus, a mix of locals and camp followers who attached themselves to one cohort or another. Atticus found a professional stone carver among them and Faustus watched the twin torchbearers emerge from a block of limestone with some fascination. For the statue of the god himself, Atticus paid for a block of Luna marble to be shipped from Rome.

The temple was completed toward the end of winter and Faustus went with Atticus and a few other officers to pray at the dedication and ask the intercession of the god for the coming campaign.

"Take our pleas before the Lord of Boundless Time…"

Faustus's father had thought the worship of foreign gods an insult to Jupiter and Juno and the state gods of Rome, another instance of the unsuitableness of an army career for a man who valued tradition. Aulus Atticus, on the other hand, came from a family whose men had served the Eagles for seven generations. There were more traditions than one, and in this one Faustus found at least part of his place. Coming out into the sun from the darkness where only the oculus had lit the main chamber, he stood blinking for a moment until Atticus clapped him on the shoulder.

"We'll have guests tomorrow. The governor's sent his chief surgeon on an inspection tour of all the hospitals and he's lighting with us next if the weather holds clear. You came from the Second Augusta, didn't you? You'll know Constantius Silanus."

An assignment as chief surgeon for an army was a posting that only came with a major campaign. "From what I know of him," Faustus said, "that's an excellent choice."

"My surgeon is shaking in his boots. But he can't be too fierce. He has his family with him. His daughter and an old aunt. You're to come dine with us."

Faustus laughed. "So he's let her come back."

Atticus grinned. "I did hear that story. What's she like?"

Faustus thought. "Beautiful. Intelligent." He found he was looking forward to seeing her again.

Atticus raised his eyebrows.

"And obstinate as an army mule," Faustus added.

Constantia seemed glad to see him when he arrived for Atticus's dinner party. Aunt Popillia was with her.

"I am here on sufferance," Constantia whispered to Faustus when he greeted her. "I have promised not to dally with soldiers or fraternize with the natives."

She looked older than he remembered, in a gown of fine blue wool and a saffron colored overtunic pinned at the sleeves with pearl pins. Her corn-colored hair was dressed in an elaborate arrangement on her head and pearl drops dangled from her ears. Her cheeks were lightly rouged and her lips reddened. Publia Livilla's "polish".

The Asturian ala's prefect and both the ala and cohort surgeons were there as well, not exactly shaking but displaying a healthy respect for Silanus's seniority and rank, while surreptitiously eyeing his daughter. Atticus ordered the dinner served in formal fashion, with four couches set around a central table, and Faustus found himself sharing one with the cohort surgeon, next to Constantia and her aunt. The prefect set an excellent table and possessed an excellent cook. A first course of oysters sent in snow from the coast was greeted with enthusiasm, as was a particularly good Falernian wine.

243

The evening otherwise began on a somber note. Silanus had brought with him from Eburacum the grisly news of the fate of the Usipii mutineers and that dominated the early dinner conversation, a second-hand horror that no one could quite let go of.

"Two of the helmsmen apparently tried to turn their ships back," Silanus said. "The Usipii killed them and threw them overboard and they washed up on the beach. I can't think that lot got very far with one helmsman between three ships. They tried raiding the coast again and were driven off and by that point they must have been starving."

"We think some of them did get across the ocean," Constantia said. "Neptune knows how, but Father got a letter from a friend in Germany who says the Suevi picked up a shipful of them and sold them as slaves. Father's friend recognized the insignia on one man's belt."

"They resorted to cannibalism at the last," Silanus said.

Aunt Popillia shuddered. "Silanus, please."

Constantia appeared more interested than horrified. "I keep wondering what I would have done if I were them," she said thoughtfully.

"I know exactly what you would have done," Faustus said. "I can't think why your father feels the army has a chance to coarsen you."

"Very amusing. Oddly, he doesn't want me in harm's way because he's fond of me. I've had to give in." She sighed. "Aunt and I are to stay in Eburacum until sent for."

"Are you disappointed?"

"I'm used to it. And Demetrius of Tarsus has landed there for the duration, which will make Aunt happy."

"You won't go back to Aquae Sulis?"

She smiled at him over her wine cup now. "Aunt Publia despairs of me. We were paying guests, you understand, and Father doesn't feel like paying any further for a reformation that hasn't happened. Eburacum is less expensive."

"In other words, Publia Livilla failed to find you a suitable husband," Faustus suggested.

"She found several. I frightened them away," Constantia said with satisfaction.

Aunt Popillia sighed. "One of them was a tribune."

"I'm through with tribunes. Besides, I don't *want* to get married."

"Stick to your resolve," Faustus said. "Let me be your model."

Aunt Popillia looked as angry as he had ever seen her. "That is a more difficult position for a woman, Centurion," she informed him.

He regretted the comment immediately. "I wasn't thinking," he whispered, and Aunt Popillia appeared mollified.

When the last course had been served, Silanus nodded to the two surgeons. "I want a final look at your supply lists. You're garrisoned together here but there's no saying how the governor will order the march. You both need to be prepared to be your own field hospital at the same time that you're feeding cases and possibly staff up the line to the central surgery."

They departed for the fortress hospital and Faustus escorted Constantia and her aunt back to the quarters allotted them near the Principia. There was a full moon riding in a clear sky, and its light was reflected by the fort's newly whitewashed walls, leaving the shadows in sharp contrast. Something in one of them caught Faustus's eye and he stopped. Constantia started to speak and he laid a hand on her arm.

Two officers of the Watch went by along the perimeter, and after they passed the Praetorian Gate a figure emerged from the shadows behind them and beckoned. Something indistinguishable came through the gate, a dark jumble of legs and heads, like an ungainly elephant, staggering slightly, the light glinting on mail.

"Right, we're in. Now get him to barracks."

"I can walk." The middle of the elephant sagged and arms on both sides heaved it upright.

"No, you can't," another voice hissed. "You're sloshing. Shut up before someone sees us."

"Can't see me. Invishable. Gotta cap of invishability."

"That's a cook pot. You took it from the tavern and it still has soup in it. Shut *up*!"

Constantia started to laugh. "Are those your men?"

"Yes." Faustus sighed.

"Cap of invishibility. Jus' like Pluto. Can't see me."

"Well everyone can see *us*. Keep quiet or we'll throw you in the bath."

"Are you going to do something?" Constantia asked.

Faustus shook his head. "That's Indus. He's only trouble when he's bored. He'll straighten right up when we march."

"You're going to let him get away with coming in drunk after hours?"

"It won't serve any purpose to put him on report," Faustus said. "I'd have to charge his mates with him, and that's four men out of the line when we drill. Sometimes the most effective thing a commander can do is look the other way. And then give him latrine shoveling duty tomorrow and let him wonder how I knew."

"Very wise," Aunt Popillia said. "I tell Constantia that you can judge a man by how he commands those under him. That would have told her what was the matter with Tribune Lartius."

It was light enough for Faustus to see Constantia glare at her. He was beginning to think that Aunt Popillia approved of him despite his glib remark about marriage. When he left them at the door of the guest house, she pressed his hand warmly and said they hoped to see him the next day before they went south.

He stood in the crystalline moonlight a moment after they had gone inside, listening to the fading steps and shushing noises coming from his miscreants. A splash and a howl told him that they had indeed thrown Indus in the bath.

He turned toward his own quarters, flattered that Aunt Popillia found him eligible and relieved that Constantia didn't seem to. He couldn't afford a wife, didn't want a wife, and remembered his last meeting with Sulpicia with the sense of having escaped a burning building.

She had come to visit Silvia and commiserate with her on the family's misfortunes, and she had asked Faustus to walk in the garden with her, with the earnest face of someone about to do an unpleasant duty.

"Father is very sympathetic, of course," she began. Sulpicia was a pretty girl, with dark glossy hair and big eyes, like the starlings that were settling to roost in the trees overhead. She twisted the ends of her mantle in her hands, and then smoothed them out as if ordering herself to be dignified. "And of course all the preparations for the wedding have begun already."

Faustus's heart sank. They weren't going to call it off. His father had talked old Sulpicius around. The starlings' nattering overhead made him want to throw rocks at them.

Sulpicia sighed. "I have grown very fond of you, Faustus, of course. That is natural. We were planning to marry."

Were? Faustus held his breath.

"But I know my duty."

The birdsong seemed suddenly mellifluous. "Of course." Faustus tried to sound encouraging, a man prepared to be jilted in the name of duty.

"Silvia has tried to persuade me not to abide by Father's decision," Sulpicia said.

"That was kind of her," Faustus said, teeth gritted.

"She's a lovely girl, and kind-hearted, and so worried about her own betrothal. But I cannot defy Father."

"Of course not."

"It's kind of you to be so understanding." Sulpicia's face was grave, although with what Faustus thought was a certain air of enjoying the role. "But it will be best if we do not see each other again." She pulled the small gold ring from her finger and put it in his hand.

"Of course." He closed his fist tightly around the ring in terror that it would somehow leap back onto her finger.

247

"I would not want you to hold onto hope. That would be cruel."

"If it will make you feel any better," Faustus said, "I will promise not to do that. And I'll have a word with Silvia."

Their mother had died shortly after that, followed by their father. Faustus had sold the farm and had a talk with Manlius just in time to keep Manlius from breaking it off with Silvia, who did want to get married. Sulpicius had found another husband for his daughter with little trouble, according to Silvia. She was now the mother of two promising children, and, Silvia noted, quite fat. Faustus assumed that that was supposed to assuage the longing for her which both women assumed he cherished. Sulpicia was both romantic and practical and the notion that she had broken his heart was possibly a small pleasure to her.

Faustus lay awake until the last protests from Indus and the last "*Will* you be quiet!" from his caretakers subsided, superseded by the normal night noises of a camp, the steady tramp of the mailed boots of the Watch, and the yip of a fox somewhere on the hillside; Paullus snoring on the pallet at his bedside and the stamp and snuffle of the horses in their stall. As he closed his eyes Faustus made a mental note to be sure the tavern got its cook pot back before the owner went to the prefect.

Eirian lay on her belly at the edge of the sea cliffs, in the spot where she came to watch the water and the gray-brown shapes of the seals basking or their round, dark-eyed faces staring back at her from the waves. Today she was watching the Roman warships pass by in the firth. They looked like bugs to her, sails reefed against the wind and sprouting oars in two banks, with dark staring eyes at the prow. They were painted blue to disappear into the sea but the winter sun flashed on the steel plates that their crew wore. They were terrifying and enticing in their strangeness and they made her stomach clench with a sensation that was both fear and some kind of yearning. In his

248

grandfather's day, Faelan said, the chief of the islands had met with a Roman chief and they had exchanged presents and then the Roman chief had gone away again. When the Caledones and their allies had beaten them back, Faelan said, these would leave too.

Farther down the coast, past the seal rocks where the land sloped to the harbor, the fishing boats sat loaded with the grain that the mainlanders had bought, waiting for the tide and the nearly moonless night to slip across the water to the mainland. They had paid little enough, Faelan had grumbled to Eirian and her brothers, but they had paid what they had.

Eirian watched until the Roman patrol craft were out of sight, and then made her way back down to the village before her brothers came to fetch her and remind her that she was supposed to be making cheese. It made them uneasy when they caught her staring out to sea. They should marry and find someone else to lord it over, Eirian thought. With both her mother and her brothers' mother gone, they and her father treated her as a universal wife to keep the house and see to their clothes and supper. No one was likely to marry her, her brothers pointed out when their father couldn't hear them. He had beaten the boys for tormenting her with that when they were children, although she knew he thought so too. If the Romans came, she thought rebelliously, what would it be like to go away with them in one of those blue ships, and then she made the sign of horns against ill thought. Anyone going away on one of those ships would likely be doing it in chains.

-

The grain was barely enough to keep everyone alive until spring came, but until then there were still things to be done and in the doing some forgetfulness of their hunger: mend spear points and hauberks, and set the coals going at all the forges. Every smith apprenticed hounds and fighting men alike and taught them to pump the bellows that fed the fire, and carry buckets from the well for tempering. At night they drank, and sang, and exhibited their burned hands as badges of honor.

Calgacos stood outside Nall's overcrowded guest house and listened with mixed exasperation and amusement to shouts of laughter punctuated with drunken threats. He had promised to put a curse on any man who actually fought another and so they made do with insults and boasting. Coran Harper was singing just now and the rest were howling along with him, drunkenly out of tune. There was beer enough, brewed from grain that was baked into bread afterward.

While Calgacos watched, Rhion staggered from the door and stuck his head in a snowbank. He shook the snow from his hair, pissed against a tree, and staggered back inside. In a moment Celyn and Dai came out, laughing, taking great gulps of the clear, cold air. Dai scooped up a handful of snow and jumped on Celyn's back, pushing it down his shirt collar. Celyn roared and threw Dai off him, packing up a great ball of snow in both hands. He chased Dai around the guest house with it.

Aelwen came and stood beside Calgacos. Her neck and arms were bare of the jewelry she had once worn and she had twisted thin bronze wires into her ears to keep the holes from closing up. She watched Celyn and Dai roll in the snow. "They are like half-grown wolves," she said. "Or locusts. Nall's wife is fretting for ways to feed us all. She will be glad when we have gone south again."

"Aelwen, you must stay here."

"I will not. She has said she will keep Ceridwen safe. And Efa is staying." Efa was her brother Rhion's wife and heavily pregnant. "I am going with you."

"I cannot lead a war band if it has you in it! You will jeopardize everything because my mind will be in two places."

"Very well. I will not fight. But I *will go*."

"Aelwen—"

"I can help the Druids with the wounded. I will be useful. If you forbid me, Calgacos, I will follow you anyway."

The night was clear and cold. He watched the stars glowing in Lugh's Chain across the black sky. If he were a Druid, he might read the future in them, as they claimed. Or not. Vellaunos only foretold the future when it was already evident to any fool.

"I will tell you something hopeful," Aelwen said, reading his thoughts as she often could. "That child Hafren that Idris stole from the Damnonii has left off weeping into every pot while she stirs the stew. Selisoc is courting her. Life goes on."

"Selisoc is fortunate to have his own life go on as it has," Calgacos said grimly. "He came close to being dispossessed."

"Hafren gave him her opinion of that and showed him the scars of what Idris did to her. Selisoc is thinking differently now."

"When we have driven Rome into the sea," Calgacos said, "we will give them a fine wedding."

"Is that what it will take?" Aelwen asked. "For them to leave us in peace? To drive them out of Britain entirely?"

"Heart, I do not know. We haven't the power to do that, even in alliance. But we must make our northern land not worth their while. Their masters in Rome consider defeat a disgrace, and they punish the defeated. They will call this ambitious governor home if he loses an army to us."

XV

The March North

Spring–Summer, 837 ab urbe condita

Tuathal inspected himself in the silver mirror that was Clio's prize possession, while she watched him with amusement from the mattress.

"You look very fine," she told him. "Like a peacock fanning out his tail."

He ran her comb through his black hair and settled the gold fillet around it.

"Remember me when you are king in Hibernia," she suggested as he pushed an enameled pin through the dark folds of his cloak.

"When I am king you shall have a husband from among my household."

"I don't want one," Clio said. "I want a wagon of my own, better than this one of Abudia's, and a house in the city with lions on the floor."

Tuathal grinned. "No husband?"

Clio made a snorting noise. "Aifa got married. She was pining for some centurion and when he left she married another one who had just retired, because she missed the first one I suppose. She's had two babies that died and her husband thinks it was her fault they weren't healthy, and she wishes she hadn't done it."

"Noted. No husband. A house with lions on the floor."

Clio smiled. He wouldn't do it of course, but he always left her a handsome present beyond what Abudia charged him. He was just killing time in her bed that afternoon until the governor agreed to see him. It was the start of May, the smell of spring was in the air even in an army marching camp where it had to fight with the smell of burning bread and inadequate drainage, and the whole cumbrous machinery of the Roman army had begun its march north. She thought that Tuathal had grown into a man who needed more to do than trail after Governor Agricola like a tame duck, but he was probably going to have to remind the governor of it.

–

Tuathal stood looming over Agricola's desk, reminding him of exactly that. He was tall now too, and his father's sword hung easily from his belt. The gold eyes in the hilt stared out at the governor.

"I am older than some of your officers. I want to be given a command. I have been over five years in your camps waiting for your promised aid when I could have been leading a war band to take back my father's kingship."

Agricola looked up from the dispatches on his desk, grim-faced. "If you wish to raise a war band in Hibernia, Rome will not stop you."

"Give me a command in your own army and I will fight for Rome so that Rome may be willing to fight for me afterward."

"You give me a headache, Tuathal, and I already have one." The governor looked exasperated, or possibly only tired. "I can't just give you a commission in the Centuriate. There are channels to go through and you aren't a citizen." Only Roman citizens could join the legions, or the command chain.

Tuathal was unmoved. "The governor, who is a consular legate, has broad authority for irregular assignments. Give me some command. I am not a pet, nor a child any longer."

Agricola looked him over, seeing him newly, and concluded that he was in some sense right. And he would be trouble if he had no employment. He pulled a tablet and stylus from the recesses of his camp desk. "Very well. I shall send you to Aulus Atticus with the First Batavians as staff aide. Valerianus is his second and I imagine he will vouch for your abilities, and Atticus is a good man. He has the freedom to give you what responsibility he sees fit. This is the best I can do." He pressed his ring into the wax.

Tuathal took the tablet and balanced it in his palm, looking out at the wild blue-green landscape rising steadily higher to the north. The flaps of the governor's tent were pinned open to catch the spring air and the sense of promise that floated on it, and their scarlet leather made a martial splash against the green and the dun-colored barracks tents. A skein of starlings swung overhead like a veil twisting and unfolding, tracing an unreadable pattern across the sky. He nodded to the governor. "Very well. You will not regret this. May your gods and mine give favor to our endeavors."

"I have made sacrifice for our success," the governor murmured. "They do not always listen." When Tuathal had left, he bent his head again to the letter on his desk. He had opened it eagerly, looking for news of his son, held and named by proxy in his absence, a sign of the gods' favor. Instead it held only grief. His wife's hand was ragged, the characters sloping down the tablet in despair.

> *My dearest husband,*
> *It is with great sorrow that I tell you that our son, so recently given to us, has been taken from us again. He died four days since after a short illness and only today can I bring myself to write to you...*

The campaign was all he had left, he thought.

The ascent into the highlands was slow. The Caledones had fled north but something had stayed behind and that something felled trees in their path and taunted them into reckless pursuit in bogs and woods. They found the water fouled ahead of them, and little bronze-tipped arrows from the trees sometimes hit their mark. Even when they did not they unnerved everyone. Except for the trampled fields around native villages the land was thickly wooded anywhere the Romans had not already cleared it. Everyone was put to cutting a way through the forests that would not leave cover for the invisible enemy that flitted around their ears like midges.

As a result their progress north amounted to more hard labor than actual fighting, punctuated only by an occasional skirmish with the few natives who still stubbornly inhabited the villages in their path. Mostly those hid as the Roman column swept by like a scythe in a field.

Aulus Atticus rode cheerfully up and down the line, encouraging the tree-cutting and praising their progress, but Faustus found himself reiterating endlessly to his men that there was not something supernatural in the woods, despite the fact that the woods made the back of his neck itch. The whole army was afflicted with the same conviction. The forest made noises that no one could identify, shadows moved unexpectedly, the branches looked like the Wild Hunt riding overhead, and altogether the trees inspired the old fear of wild places that was named for the great god Pan whose realm it was. Romans were people of the cities, where streets ran in orderly lines and trees grew in gardens and pots.

At nightfall Galerius made his way across the camp from his cohort's tents to visit and complain. He brought a wineskin with him and settled by Faustus's fire. "The whole cohort's having hysterics about invisible hobgoblins in the forest. That Egyptian who follows us around selling amulets is practically out of stock.

Every one of my men has three or four hung around his neck and horns painted on the inside of his shield."

"Maybe they are right," Tuathal said, "that there is something in the forest."

Faustus snorted and reached for Galerius's wineskin. "You know perfectly well who's in the forest and it isn't elves. Don't encourage them. They're flighty enough already."

—

They spent at least three days, sometimes five, in each camp, clearing the land ahead before moving on. Scouts reported a Caledone war host, the size of which could not be determined, to the north, but always more than five days' march away. As the Roman army moved north, the Caledone war host retreated, staying just out of reach. Agricola studied his maps with grim purpose. There was only so far the Caledones could go before they had to turn and fight, but the farther north they went, the more of Agricola's men had to be left to hold what was behind them. Where the Caledones might be intending to halt was uncertain. Even with the information provided by surveyors and the scouts, maps were never accurate, only rough approximations, and more often guesses.

As they moved slowly northward and found no one to fight except the intangible presences in the forest, the energy that should have gone into battle began to erupt elsewhere, with a higher number than usual on report for various transgressions. Abudia acquired a large dog and an even larger henchman to keep order around her wagon. Ingenuus took to keeping a cudgel on the counter of his rolling tavern. Agricola considered banishing all civilians from the column but decided that might just make matters worse. The pent-up energy and uneasiness had to manifest itself somewhere.

Nor were the officers immune. Two of Ursus's junior centurions got in a fight with each other and one of them broke his arm to Ursus's fury. Gambling was constant, with some dice games more or less permanent, and bets otherwise placed on anything with an element of chance. Tuathal found Faustus and Galerius, both very drunk and propped on their elbows in the grass, watching a pair of snails make their silvery way down a rock and cheering them on. Faustus was trying to entice his with a daisy leaf while Galerius prodded his in the tail with a stalk of grass.

"Come on, Incitatus!" Faustus waved the daisy leaf ahead of his snail. The snail appeared uninterested in it, although it continued its slow progress.

Galerius poked his snail with the grass stalk again and it withdrew into its shell.

"See?" Faustus said. "An apple is always better than the crop. No wonder your horse bit you."

Galerius was indignant. "The vet was looking at his hocks. He wanted to bite the vet. I was just at the wrong end."

"Your snail's gone tortoise."

Galerius craned his neck to peer at it. "C'mon out, damn you."

"If you pick it up, you forfeit," Faustus warned him.

Tuathal glared down at them both. "This is what senior officers do on campaign?"

Galerius gave up on his snail and rolled over on his back. "Young Tuathal, you lack experience. What else is there to do just now?"

"Incitatus has crossed the finish line," Faustus said. "Pay up."

Galerius produced a coin from the pouch at his belt. "You should let me keep it for you. You'll just spend it on beer and women."

"So will you if you keep it." Faustus held out his hand. "Tuathal, when you are king in Hibernia, remember this lesson." He dropped the coin down the front of his tunic.

"You're drunk," Tuathal said. "What lesson?"

"Um. There was one... Oh, now I remember. War is serious."

Tuathal looked at Galerius, who appeared to have gone to sleep. "You do not seem to think so."

"When you lead an army, young Tuathal, what do you think your soldiers will do when they are not fighting? Stand at attention in rows and think deep thoughts about your cause?"

Galerius opened his eyes. "They will brawl and drink and bet on snails and you will have to stand for a certain amount of it or they will not be fit for battle." He closed his eyes again. "The trick is in knowing how much."

"Governor Agricola was wise to send you to us," Faustus said. "You are young and green. But you show promise." He stood and kicked Galerius. "We have trees to fell in the misty dawn, so we'd better go to bed."

They staggered off, leaving Tuathal looking thoughtful. He watched the snails until they had completed their journey and disappeared into a tuft of scrub grass, bound for wherever instinct drove them.

-

As Agricola's assembled army made its way through the summer, slowly but with the inevitability of the tide, northward up the glens of the Caledone holds, the Caledones continued to retreat. Furiously, the army despoiled anything in its path and left behind its own snail trail devoid of forage, fuel and clean water. North of the new fortress at Castra Pinnata they increased the patrols that went ahead of the main column. Aulus Atticus, at Tuathal's insistence, gave him a vexillation from the cohort to lead on patrol every so often, at first with Faustus to keep an eye on things, and then on his own. Tuathal began to watch the prefect and his junior officers closely, with Faustus's words in his head, and to learn when to bend a little and when absolutely not to. The Caledone war host now let itself be seen occasionally in ambushes that lay in wait for unwary patrols. After his detail had fought their way out of the first of these, Tuathal changed their formation, lectured each man on what to look for in the countryside around them, and the next patrol resulted in an ambush of the Caledones who had thought they were waiting for the Romans, and whose armor and weapons they dragged triumphantly back to camp.

Faustus reported that Tuathal was a born commander, and an extremely quick study.

He was also half British, Atticus noted uneasily.

"So am I," Faustus said. "Tuathal was raised by the Epidii and they're only tangentially connected to the Caledones, and furthermore not involved in this war. He doesn't want to bollocks up our campaign, he wants to get it finished and go invade Hibernia. Preferably with Roman help. He's the least of your worries."

"Mmm. Very well, Centurion. I trust that you are right." Like everyone else, Atticus was antsy with wanting to fight the enemy that kept receding north as they approached. It made everyone restless, he told Faustus. "When we actually engage, then I'll feel as if I can breathe."

–

"Why are we playing catch-me like a bunch of girls at a fair?" Emrys demanded. He balanced back and forth from heel to toe as if he wanted to spring on something.

"For the reasons that I have given you," Calgacos snapped. He took a deep breath. He couldn't afford to antagonize Emrys beyond a certain point. "We cannot fight them in the way that we have always fought each other."

"We have half again their numbers," Emrys said.

Celyn and Dai, patrolling the camp in the dusk, watched his face, uplit by the lantern in his hand, with some unease. The truce between their headman and Emrys had lasted longer than anyone but the Druids could have enforced and it was like a live wild thing tied with a fraying rope.

Calgacos sat on a stone watching the small lights of fires and lanterns springing up across the meadow. "The Romans have been outnumbered before and won. This is our one chance and very likely theirs. We must draw them north as far as we can, past easy resupply for their men and inland from their warships, onto ground that will favor us, if we are to be sure of them. Therefore we keep them chasing us for now."

Emrys stood thinking. Calgacos was right but it went against the grain. Their scattered hosts were waiting for the word to come together, and if it did not come soon they might well take matters into their own hands and break the delicate alliance. He said so to Calgacos.

Calgacos rubbed his thumb along his sword hilt, feeling the metal, summer warm, fit to his hand. "I have spoken to the Druids and the clan lords of the northern hills, and to the Old Ones, and the time is close, Emrys, I promise you."

"When?"

"I do not wish to give the Romans warning. You must keep your men leashed a little longer."

"And I am to be kept blind and leashed as well?" Emrys spat.

Calgacos hesitated. "It is your right to be consulted. It is only that I do not want word of our hosting to go ahead of us. In a ten-day I will send word to gather on Pap of the Mother atop the Old Ones' mountain."

Emrys considered that, mollified. "It will give us the advantage of the terrain," he conceded. "And the Old Ones? That was their king's hall once, despite there is nothing there now but ruins."

"For that reason, I have spoken to them." Calgacos smiled a little. "I am told that they will have to purify it afterward."

Emrys snorted. "The little beasts find us unclean?"

"Extremely so. And carrying iron, which they do not like." He stood. "I will send word to the allied chieftains when the time has come."

"Remember," Emrys said, "there is a limit to any tether."

When Emrys had gone, Calgacos sat staring into the growing dark at the youngest of the fighting men, boys really, only just come to their spear-taking, gathered about their fire. Despite what he had told Aelwen, more than half their mares were in the chariot line or under saddle. He heard Bleddin's voice and a ripple of laughter. Behind him in their tent Aelwen was mending Bleddin's boots by firelight. She had agreed not to take up a spear when it came to battle, but would not leave him. He found her presence a comfort he could not admit.

One last chance to preserve their world. One chance to go on being themselves and not Rome's tame tribesmen. He looked into the dark, toward the mountain that was held to be the breast of the Goddess herself.

–

Something was up. Faustus watched the camp slowly boil up like a cauldron on the fire, or an anthill prodded open. Just a few stirrings out of the ordinary at first, a courier vaulting into the saddle and the chief quartermaster coming out of the governor's tent at a trot. Then a string of barked commands, a curse from someone rousted unceremoniously from sleep, the rumble of wagons being hitched and put in line. The smoke of doused fires hung in the air and the engineers snapped orders to break down the defenses and refill the ditches.

Tuathal appeared at Faustus's elbow. "The prefect's compliments and we're to set out *expeditus*."

Faustus raised his eyebrows. That meant marching light, at quick step and without baggage. To do so indicated an emergency and also required a very precise idea of where the enemy was and that it was not behind you. He scrambled into his boots and Paullus came up with his hauberk and helmet. Faustus held out his arms while Paullus dropped the mail over his head and handed him his sword and belt. "Mount up and stay with the column," Faustus told him. "We aren't waiting for the baggage to roll."

"What is happening?" Paullus watched wide-eyed as the camp rippled like bedclothes being shaken out.

"I expect we've found the Caledones," Faustus said.

"That we have." Aulus Atticus was knotting his helmet strap. "The scouts just slid in with word that they're massing at last and the governor wants to hit them before they're ready. We've got the place of honor this time – auxiliaries first, legions to the rear until called for." He grinned.

–

Agricola watched the column form up, shaking itself loose of the civilians and the baggage, including the heavy catapult wagons. The border wolves who had come in overnight reported that the Caledones were being very quiet about their movements. Two of their number had been hunted down and killed when a dog had barked at them. Those now reporting had climbed trees and spent the night there.

The war host, the scouts said, were massing their numbers, which looked close to being thirty thousand, along the top of a mountain called Pap of the Mother. They had the high ground there and the Roman army would have to come at them from below or wait for them to come down, in a contest to see who could starve whom first. But they were still disorganized, sorting out their forces, making camp, very likely not all of them there yet, and no doubt fussing among themselves for the best ground, the scouts said. One of them shook his head. "I wouldn't be in charge of that lot. They've got numbers but no discipline."

"They have enough discipline to bind themselves in alliance against us," Agricola said. "I do not intend to underestimate them."

Pap of the Mother lay roughly twenty miles from the coast, the scouts said, and was instantly recognizable. "Looks like a giant tit. A great giant tit. If the old girl was to stand up she'd have her chin on the moon."

"Thank you. We shall hope she doesn't." The Mother who presides over death as well as birth should have had her fill of him by now, he thought sadly, and then shook the thought away because that was an appetite never sated, only part of the music that all things danced to.

He was taking a terrible risk, shedding the baggage train for speed. If they lost, there would be no defending the slow-moving wagons, and the way south again was long and dangerous without them. If they lost they would not get back.

-

They hugged the coast to keep at least within reach of the Fleet until they had to turn inland. The rain had begun to sheet down at dawn and now the round shape of Pap of the Mother rose up dimly ahead of them in the storm, still half a day's quick march away.

"Why bother fighting them," Faustus grumbled, as Arion sloshed through the rivulets of mud that ran down the rise they were climbing. "We could just wait until they drown."

"They are on the higher ground, Centurion," Atticus pointed out.

"Turn into frogs then," Faustus said, water dripping from his helmet. Atticus seemed oblivious to it and whistled a marching tune under his breath.

A crack of lightning overhead made Arion jump and the rain sheeted down harder.

"Actually," Tuathal said, "it doesn't look as if it's raining on the mountain. Druids are said to have power over the weather."

Atticus snorted. "Druids are said to have six kinds of magic and seven shields of power or whatever it is. So was my aunt's cook who was supposed to be a witch. All she ever managed was to chase the mice out of the granary and she had a cat to help with that. A fearsome cat, I grant you. I'll take the business end of a sword."

Tuathal smiled. "No gods at all?"

"Of course," Atticus said. "I'm not a heathen. But absolutely no Druids. They give me the horrors."

"That in itself should be some evidence of their powers," Tuathal suggested.

It was obvious by late afternoon, when they came at last to the northeastern slope of the mountain, that it had not rained on its height but only on the Romans' path. The sky cleared as the column approached the flat plain below, in the wake of the surveyors who had already marked out the borders of a camp along the bank of a small, fordable river. The column was put to building defenses, leveling the ground, and setting up the barracks and officers' tents in orderly rows with the usual routine efficiency, in clear view of the Caledones encamped on the crest of the mountain.

"Give them something to think about," Atticus said with satisfaction, watching what amounted to a portable city rise from the bare plain. "Let's see *them* do this."

Faustus nodded. "And then take it all down and do it again at the next camp. If the Druids have magic, we have engineers."

"Engineers are magic, as far as I'm concerned," Atticus said. "They drop a plumb line and peer along a level and say, 'Dig here, just this far, put the dirt over there,' and the ground lies down and behaves, flat as a table, and all the corners are square."

Governor Agricola arrived with his commanders and observed the progress, and then rode out in the twilight with the surveyors to inspect the ground at the foot of the mountain. Pap of the Mother was one of four peaks making a ridge that curved inward like an amphitheater facing the plain below. Agricola splashed across the river where the engineers had cleared its banks, and again across a small tributary. He looked south to the mountain, trailed by his aides and the legionaries assigned to the governor's guard. At this distance it was hard to see what might be happening at the peak but there was movement and the scouts had reported the massing of a great host, still collecting along the ridge and the southern slope. The country to either side of the ridge was wooded, with clumps of trees and scrub dotting the rocky plain at its foot between waves of purple heather. Plenty of cover there, one of the governor's aides noted uneasily, for a man with a bow.

"He would have to be a better marksman than any we possess," Agricola said, and continued his inspection of the landscape.

"No doubt," the aide said, thinking of the little bronze-tipped arrows that had dogged their path. The governor was wearing cuirass and helmet but was bare-armed and bare-legged and any injury would be considered ill luck on the eve of a battle. And the arrow poisoned as like as not. He edged his horse closer to the governor's.

Agricola spent the better part of two hours, trailed by surveyors, aides and guard, considering every foot of ground for the length of the ridge, noting slope and hillocks, wet spots along the river banks, tree cover on the eastern and western flanks, and the path of the small tributary that ran through the plain from the west. The Caledones no doubt watched him from their mountain.

When he was satisfied, he sent one of his guard to cut a rowan branch, large enough to be seen from above. He took it in his own hand, waved it over his head and then sat on his horse, waiting.

—

"You will go down to him?" Emrys demanded. His scarred face was furious. "To talk treaty before we have fought?"

"No. To see him. I want to see him," Calgacos said. "No doubt he wants to see me," he added.

"And why should he? And like as not he will have you killed."

"Like as not he won't. Not under a green branch. But if there is some chance I might convince him that we will be too much trouble for him, I will take it. I want the whole of the war band brought up to the ridges where he can see them."

"You would call a great hosting like this one and then not fight?" Emrys was incredulous.

"I would do what it takes to leave this land in peace!" Calgacos snapped. He knew there was very little chance. It was possible that he was doing it because Emrys didn't want him to.

He rode down the old track that ran from the ancient stone ruins at the crest to the plain below, with Rhion and a dozen spearmen, their number matched to those he counted with the Roman general.

An optio found Faustus in his tent about to strip his hauberk off. "You're wanted. And I'd wear that if I were you. The governor wants you to translate for the enemy."

Faustus made himself as presentable as possible after a day of forced march and ditch digging, and brushed the dirt out of his helmet crest while Paullus saddled Arion again. He followed the optio curiously across the river to the little group waiting on the plain.

The Caledone warlord was tall, his pale hair loose down his back under a helmet with a bronze sun wheel for a crest, his bare chest tattooed with tribal markings. He wore a long sword in a red leather scabbard belted at his hip over a ring mail hauberk. He reined his horse in opposite Agricola, his men behind him and another lord on horseback at his right. Faustus blinked. He had seen that one before and in a moment it came back to him. He saw Rhion's eyes open wider as well.

"Rome offers a chance to make peace," Agricola began and nodded to Faustus to translate. Rhion listened carefully and added a word or two, possibly for clarity, or possibly an opinion as to the governor's intent. Calgacos listened to both before he spoke.

"These are free lands." The Caledones' leader glared at Agricola. "What right does Rome have to make war here in the first place?"

Faustus translated that into Latin, and added that the man translating for Calgacos was a spy. "He was traveling in our territory as long ago as four seasons back. I bought a dog from him in Brocavum."

"Rome stands by her allies," Agricola said blandly to Calgacos. "Your clans invaded the Damnonii holds who were under our protection. And then fomented rebellion among the Venicones."

"Rome's 'protection' is suspect," Calgacos said. "And the price for it is high. The Damnonii and the Venicones should have known better." His expression was disdainful.

"If you accept our peace, we will consider those matters settled," Agricola suggested. "Lay down your weapons now and we will take no more prisoners, other than hostages for good behavior. We will also send grain to feed your people until you can replant your fields. In return you must agree to pay taxes and build and maintain roads under our supervision. Our garrisons will oversee peace between the clans but otherwise defer to each clan in tribal matters. You will acknowledge and sacrifice to the gods of Rome and the Emperor Caesar Domitianus Augustus but otherwise retain leadership of your tribes. That is Rome's offer."

Faustus translated all that with care, although by his expression he suspected that Calgacos understood some Latin.

All that the Caledone warlord said was, "Have you looked up, commander of the Eagles?"

Agricola noted the host spread along the ridges to either side of the Mother. "I have. Do you reject Rome's offer?"

Calgacos didn't answer. He nodded to Rhion and they turned and rode away up the slope, the spearmen trotting behind.

It was clear that the governor's aides wondered why he had bothered, and Agricola seemed to be aware of that. "That was for form's sake," he said. "When there is a peaceful path to annexation, Rome must take it. But mainly now he will have something to think on if the battle does not go well and perhaps it will undermine his confidence. The outcome of many battles has been decided inside some commander's head."

When he rode back to camp he called his legates and the auxiliary prefects to a council.

While Aulus Atticus was in conference behind the red leather walls of the governor's tent, Faustus paraded the Batavians, gave them a speech that praised their bravery, and announced their promised spot in the middle of the front lines.

"We're to do the work, because the legions aren't up to this one," he told them, and they shouted back their opinion of the legions.

"Who's afraid of water and can't swim? The legions!"

"Who's too delicate for battle? The legions!"

"Who gets ambushed in the night? The legions!"

"And who gets you through? The auxiliaries, that's who!"

He grinned at them. "Make me proud," he called out, and they cheered him in response.

As night fell it was obvious that the excitement of the coming battle ran high. Months of slogging through marsh and forest, skirmishing with a largely unseen enemy that had to be swatted away over and over like midges and then came back again, had left them as tightly strung as so many catapults. Faustus, eating army bread baked in a camp oven and washing it down with the skin of wine Paullus had slung over his saddle as they scrambled into line, could feel the tension as if the torsion springs ran down his own spine. Along the barracks rows, a voice rose into the night.

The Hispana are all afraid of the dark
And the Twentieth cannot cross water,
Their catapults always shoot short of the mark
And Augusta are lambs to the slaughter

So who saves your ass when the natives get unruly?
Who gets the center when the battle line gets hot?
The Batavians, First Cohort of Batavians!
Batavians, the best of the lot!

Faustus grinned in the dark. Indus, he thought, elaborating on his commander's motivational speech in a variation of one of the songs that the army marched to along the Empire's length.

"Shut up!" A shout came from the Valeria Victrix camp, indicating that the song had hit its mark.

"Blow it up your tunic!" a Batavian shouted back.

Faustus let the song go on for a few more increasingly scurrilous verses and then sent the second century signifer to squelch Indus before someone started a fight.

He knew he ought to sleep. And should be tired enough to, after the forced march, but the things that sit at the back of the hearth when a man is focused on the immediate began to raise their heads and crawl out of their pots, his father mainly, who had forbidden him the army when the army was all he wanted. He had not seen Silvius Valerianus in a year, and in that time had become convinced, not unreasonably, that his shade emanated entirely from Faustus's own head. Now as if in answer, his father appeared, wraith-like against the black sky, more insubstantial than before, like smoke against the spangle of stars overhead, but recognizable in his peevishness.

"Go away!"

"You thought about me," the shade said.

"Does thinking pull the dead out of their graves?" Faustus felt annoyed.

"Possibly." The shade itself looked thoughtful. "If you are killed tomorrow is there someone who can think of you and test that?"

"Now I know you're my hallucination," Faustus said. "My father didn't have that much imagination."

"Imagination puts a child at odds with its duty."

Faustus had been lounging by his fire. Now he sat up and stared furiously at his father. "You did your best to beat it out of me," he said between his teeth.

He had been fourteen, hiding in the hayloft after dinner and reading Petronius when he should have been with his father's actuary, learning to manage the accounts for the farm. Silvius Valerianus had found him, dragged him down the ladder, and beaten him with a rake until his mother had heard the shouting, come from the dairy in a fury, and brandished a pitchfork at her husband.

"Where did you get this filthy thing?" Silvius demanded, dropping the rake to snatch up the scroll.

"It isn't filthy!" Faustus protested. "It's very funny. And educational," he added, grasping at anything to prevent his father from burning it. He was only halfway through. He got to his feet, bleeding. "Let me have it. I'll only read it when I have free time."

"Free time contributes to delinquency and a habit of indulging in vulgar entertainment." Silvius Valerianus tucked the scroll under his arm. "No son of mine is going to read this."

"No wonder Marcus dove into shallow water!" Faustus shouted. "I should have too!" He ran blindly through the farmyard, dodging chickens and a litter of piglets to hide in the shed where Paullus slept with the dogs. Neither of them said anything. Paullus silently got a bucket of water and washed Faustus's back and then gave him the blanket off his pallet and watched him while he slept. Later, when he had sold the farm and everything else on it, Faustus had made a private vow that he would never sell Paullus to anyone but Paullus.

The Watch made their rounds and one by one the fires died down. His father's shade said nothing more but lingered like a wisp of smoke until a breeze came up and blew him into the night. Arion and Paullus's horse stamped and whuffled, tethered to the tent pegs, their saddles piled out of the rain that was as likely as not to come again. In the morning, Faustus thought, he would send Paullus well to the rear and order him to stay there. If it all went bad, Paullus could pass for a Briton now. He might make it out.

XVI

Battle

Vellaunos stood amid the tumbled ruins of the ancient fortress atop the promontory that was the Breast of the Mother. Around and behind him on the scattered lichen-covered stones the assembled Druids of the highland clans had gathered, their gold sun disks catching the early light, reminding the gods of their petition. They ranged from a pale boy whose beard was only beginning to grow into his office to an aged Druid who walked with two sticks and a nervous companion steadying him on the rough ground. It didn't matter. A Druid of any age was a conduit for the power of the gods and an interpreter of their will. The business of Druids was beyond the everyday affairs of men unless they were called to render some judgment when no other agreement could be reached. They possessed the power, although rarely exercised, to start or stop a war between clans. Individual chieftains and headmen might rise and fall while the Druids studied the secrets of the earth and sky. That they had given their attention and concurrence to this war made clear that the way of their world stood in the balance.

Vellaunos stretched his arms to the sky and opened his hands. A pair of blackbirds took flight, wheeling in the air overhead. The Druids shaded their eyes, watching the pattern of their flight.

Aelwen held her breath. The Druids were capable, if they saw the wrong omens, of ordering the entire war host home again and Calgacos would not obey. There was no other way now, Druids or no Druids. She had left off her gown and put on shirt and breeches, and a shield and spear hung from her pony's saddle. There were other women, Aregwydd among them, who had stubbornly demanded their place in this last great battle. She and they would obey Calgacos until they couldn't.

Calgacos stood with Emrys and the other clan lords outside the ruins and waited for the Druids' signal. A full third of the war host had arrived only the afternoon before and were still trail-weary. They spread along the ridgetop in a dark mass behind him, a grim reminder of what was at stake. Where they should have glinted with the gold trappings that marked every man's worth and standing, there was only the ashen gleam of steel and ring mail. The gold helmet fittings and shield bosses, scabbard tips, gold torques and armbands, belt buckles and enameled pony harness, all had gone to pay for the grain that had fed them through the last year. The only golden things left of all the clans' wealth were the Druids' sun disks lifted to their gods.

Vellaunos turned and raised a hand in signal to an apprentice to bring the sacrifice forward, and Calgacos watched as he did so, relieved. A pair of red cows, their horns laced with mistletoe and oak leaves, were brought up and when they had been given to the gods, Vellaunos cut them open and knelt to examine the entrails. It was still possible that he would see some ill omen there, but after a long inspection he stood and raised his staff to the sky again.

Calgacos wondered what the Romans below were saying to their own gods.

"Now," Emrys said beside him. "Now we do this thing." His forehead and cheeks were daubed with blue woad, his helmet crested with the raven symbol of his clan.

"Now we wait," Calgacos said and Emrys bristled. "Look you, Emrys, let them venture out of their hole and come to us a little and it will serve us. Let them fight us uphill." He inspected his lines while Emrys glowered. The chariots were poised to take the front rank on the plain below, with the foot soldiers and the mounted riders behind them to meet the Romans when the chariots withdrew, and more horsemen on both wings to come around the Roman flanks. He had fought the various clan chiefs, Emrys included, to position a reserve of one third of the war band on the slope above and hold them there.

"That is not how a chieftain fights," Nall of the Cornovii had shouted furiously. "A chieftain takes his war band to the front line!" He was crimson in the face and looked ready to fight Calgacos if he was held back from the first charge.

"Who will follow a lord who stays at the rear like a cowardly Roman?" Ossuticos of the Venicones spat.

"Ossuticos is most fierce and scornful of the Romans," Calgacos said. "Now that he has left their protection. Nevertheless, you shall have what you request."

They were positioned now as he had ordered, but they twitched at the leash. They must be loosed at the right time. Once loosed he would not be able to call them back, nor even control them.

–

Agricola and his generals stood solemnly to observe their own omens, fidgeting while the military haruspex, stripped to the waist, removed the liver from a sacrificed sheep and inspected it before the standards. Battles had been postponed for days over such things and Agricola did not have days. The haruspex announced that the signs so far favored Rome but the sacred chickens were yet to be consulted. Their cage was brought out and the keeper produced a bag of feed, supplemented by a handful of dried berries from the larder of a commander who was taking no chances. The chickens hurled themselves at their breakfast in a flurry of feathers and a cheer went up.

Agricola let his breath out. Ill omens were a serious matter, whether he personally believed in them or not. A bad omen could set the entire army on edge and become a prophecy that fatally fulfilled itself. After a brief final conference with his generals, he returned to his tent and changed his purple governor's cloak for one of army scarlet. The red vexillum of battle rose over the tent as Agricola emerged, and orders snapped down the line.

Faustus gave a last inspection to his century, proudly paraded in their fox-fur caps, their shields uncovered and gleaming with the cohort's sun-ray insignia. He dismounted and sent Arion to the rear with Paullus. The prefect remained mounted in order to be seen, but the rest of the Batavian officers would fight beside their men.

Six cohorts crossed the river in formation, with the rest of the auxiliaries awaiting orders and the cavalry on either flank, the legions in reserve behind them. The Caledones had begun to pour down the hill and their chariots thundered past the front ranks and came around again, raining spears on the Batavians and shrieking battle cries. Bronze war trumpets bellowed through brazen mouths until Faustus's ears rang.

"Shields up and push them," Atticus shouted. "They've got nothing but noise."

The Roman ranks moved steadily forward through the din. Couriers came from Agricola, watching not far from the front lines, and the line paused and readjusted, spreading into a wider arc. They moved forward again, halted and readjusted once more, and each time spread a little farther around the ends of the Caledones' chariot line, while the auxiliary cavalry had begun to engage with the Caledone horsemen, pulling them off the Roman flanks. The day was turning hot and a cloud of dust churned up by their hooves rose over the battlefield.

"Almost," Faustus said to Tuathal beside him, in the shadow of the cohort standard. "Almost. He'll call for it in a minute, mark you. This is what you do with chariots. Remember this when you get to Inis Fáil."

As he spoke the Roman trumpets called *Encircle* and then *Engage* and the ends of the auxiliary line closed around the chariots. The Batavians pushed their way into the tangle, opening ranks to the careening chariots and then blocking their paths, downing horses. Each chariot had a driver, nearly naked and painted for battle with blue woad, and a warrior in ring mail and helmet, armed with a heavy battle spear. The throwing spears had all been cast and the Caledones thrust down from their perches with the iron-bladed spears that could go through a shield into the man behind it. Their wheels were fitted at the axles with blades that cut the shins of anyone in their path, but the Romans had learned about those, and fended both rider and horse off with their own spears. In a melee the chariots could not turn easily and they began to go down while loose horses careened over the trampled heather, trailing broken wheels and chariots and entangling others in their traces. The Romans began aiming for the horses that still had drivers and horse after horse went down shrieking, piling wreckage in the path of the rest.

The Caledone foot fighters had moved up now through the chariot ranks, and the chariots became embroiled in the infantry battle. Those that could maneuver began to pull away, their riders leaping down to fight on foot.

The front six cohorts fought their way hand to hand up the slope now as a shower of spears rained down on them from higher ground. The bellowing of the Caledone war horns never stopped, battering at Faustus's ears. He gritted his teeth and shut it out, pushing steadily up the hill. They beat at the Caledone foot fighters with their heavy shields, stabbing upward or hacking at legs and feet, while the second rank lunged with their spears at those off balance or downed. With smaller shields and heavy long swords, the Caledones were at a disadvantage at close quarters, the circumstances in which Romans fought best. Slowly they forced their way up the slope.

A Caledone warrior, bare-chested in checkered breeches and blue war paint, swung his sword at Faustus's head and Faustus raised his shield to block the blow. The heavy blade drove the shield down into Faustus's ribs and stuck there, weighing it down. Faustus pushed his own sword into the gap between the Caledone's shield and the man's bare ribcage while he struggled to pull the sword loose. The blow drew blood but the blade came out of the shield and Faustus staggered backward as it did, stumbling over the body of a dead horse in the wreckage of a chariot. He fell and the Caledone came after him. Pale eyes glittered from a blue-painted face and his wild red hair swung around him, already matted with someone's blood. Another sword slid past the Caledone's wavering shield and Faustus saw Tuathal pull back and strike again, this time into the man's neck. He scrabbled for his footing on the stony hillside and Tuathal reached down and pulled him up.

They were past the wreckage of the chariots now and the century and cohort pulled back into formation with the ease of long drill. Aulus Atticus was at their head, sword raised in signal to follow him. "Batavians! The best of the lot!" he shouted over his shoulder to them.

—

On both flanks, the Roman cavalry had engaged with the Caledone horsemen. Cavalry drilled with the same relentless energy as the infantry and could maintain any formation at a dead gallop. On either flank they drove a wedge into the front lines of the Caledone horsemen until they scattered.

Emrys, watching with Calgacos from the ridgetop, cursed as the Roman cavalry routed the highland horsemen, who fought as the Caledone foot warriors did, in a mad charge without formation, an onslaught that relied on sheer numbers and fero-city. The Caledones began to retreat into the trees that clothed the western slope below the mountain. In the distance they could see the other mounted flank streaming across the plain with the Roman cavalry in pursuit.

"You have wasted horseflesh and fighters who could have gone in the chariot line!" Emrys shouted over the din.

"They have drawn off the Roman cavalry," Calgacos said, "which was the intent."

"Now we will fight as men should!" Emrys raised his hand in signal to his clan, held impatiently in reserve.

"Wait!" Calgacos laid a hand on his arm. "Not yet. Let them come a bit more up the slope to us."

"No!" Emrys shook his arm free. "I do not hold back while Ossuticos of the Venicones claims the place of honor!"

"Ossuticos and the Venicones are expendable!" Calgacos snapped. "You are not!"

It had been an offense to Emrys to hold his own men back while Ossuticos and Nall of the Cornovii were in the front ranks. Now he ignored Calgacos and started down the rocky hillside, his warriors streaming behind him. The raven standard of their clan rose above them. With them loosed on the Roman lines, Calgacos's own clan began to follow despite his furious orders.

"You won't hold them now," Dai said.

"Nor should you," Rhion said.

Calgacos surveyed the boiling mass on the slope below. The Romans were slowing under the onslaught. It would do, he decided. He couldn't hold them more than a moment longer anyway. He raised his arm, sword in hand. "To me!"

They hurled themselves down the hill, racing to outpace Emrys's men, the Kindred lords of the clan in the front beside their leader.

From his vantage point, Governor Agricola saw a bright flash of light from the sun wheel crest of the Caledone warlord's helmet. He smiled with a certain grim satisfaction. The Britons considered it a matter of honor to put their high lords in the forefront of any charge, to give heart and example to the rest. Pride would allow nothing else but it had never served them. He spoke to an aide and couriers fanned out to the auxiliaries in reserve. Nine cohorts moved up into the line and the reserves of the cavalry rode in on the flanks.

The raven standard swung wildly over Emrys's head and the lord who bore it went down in a spray of blood. Someone else snatched it up but another holder fell and those behind saw him go down. The men from the dead lord's village wavered, uncertain, and Emrys shouted at them to follow him instead, but each man, used to following his own lord, did not come easily to another's command. Along the line two more of his holders fell to the Roman advance and their leaderless ranks began to falter. Calgacos, under his own sun wheel standard, sent Dai staggering through the melee to Emrys, with orders to pull back and regroup, but Emrys was past listening. He shoved Dai away with a snarl and hurled himself at the Romans pushing steadily forward behind their shield wall.

The Cornovii were holding the eastern flank with Nall, red-faced and urging them on, at their head. Calgacos saw Nall's standard go down too, and from his own ranks Selisoc and Ula were both somewhere on the field dead or wounded, while their men stumbled in ragged lines to Calgacos's standard. *The Morrigan take Emrys and every other prideful fool!* The Caledone line began to crumble with the loss of so many lords. The oncoming wave of Roman infantry pushed up the slope more easily now, while his men went down before it.

Calgacos looked for Dai again and saw him standing over Celyn. Celyn's helmet had come off and his straw-colored hair was matted with blood that was already congealing. Dai straddled his still form to beat the oncoming Romans away from it and something on his face was making them part to go around him.

"Leave him!" Calgacos said and Dai shook his head. His eyes looked through Calgacos to the next world.

"Leave him!" Calgacos gripped Dai by the arm and dragged him up the slope through the chaos. "Bring up the chariot line again," he said to Dai's blank stare. "Drive it into the Romans to slow them until we can push them back down!" He still had the reserves left on the ridgetop but superior numbers would not save them if they couldn't slow the Roman advance first. He took a deep breath and spoke the orders he had sworn he would not utter. "The women. Put the women in the line to drive."

The chariots swept down the hill again, their drivers furiously maneuvering the lightweight wicker carriages and the deadly scythed wheel hubs through the oncoming Roman lines, breaking their formation, clogging the upward slope. The Roman cavalry in pursuit added to the confusion and the advance began to slow.

Faustus saw that there were women at the reins, painted and marked as the men were, and apparently as fearless. One driver lost her warrior to a Roman spear and as he went over its side she wheeled the chariot and came around again to slam the horses into the Roman shields before they could balk. An opening crumbled in the shield line and the Caledones beat the Batavians back through it before they could close up, driving them down the slope. They recovered, following Atticus as he rallied them, and pushed upward again, through and over ground littered with dead men and horses. Most of the dead were Caledones but they came on anyway in wave after endless wave, the chariots and the dust making it impossible to see anything more than a few feet in any direction. "Keep your shield up and keep moving!" Faustus shouted and they closed in around him and kept going, climbing over broken chariots and the bodies of the dead. Faustus saw Indus, bleeding from a blow to his forehead that had also dented his helmet like a broken melon, roll out of the way of a chariot's wheel and come up to wrestle the warrior off its platform, pinning him to the ground with his own spear before he staggered back into the line. His right hand hung by his side now and he dropped his shield and took his sword in his left. Tuathal leaped onto an overturned chariot, his father's sword raised above his head.

A Caledone warrior climbed the wheel and Tuathal drove his sword down and the man fell back.

They were moving more slowly now, and then not at all, fighting just to hold the ground they had taken as the Caledones reserves poured down from the ridgetop. What was left of the Caledones' chariot line drew off and the fresh reserves, loosed at last, took up the battle, spreading out to engulf the Roman lines.

"Batavians!" Aulus Atticus took his horse through an opening in the melee, jumping the wreckage of a Caledone chariot to push into the advancing enemy. Faustus and the standard bearer followed on his heels but he was too far ahead of them, his horse outpacing the men behind him, sword raised to rally them to follow, but too far out, too far...

The horse went down before they could reach him and by the time they did he lay still, a gaping spear wound in his throat. The cohort began to falter. "To me!" Faustus shouted. "To me, to your standard, for Aulus Atticus! Blood for blood but keep formation, damn you!"

With Tuathal on one side and the cohort signifer on the other, they tried to hold their ground. The Caledone reserves fought furiously, the slight to their honor at being kept back from the first advance driving them on. Many of them were young, Faustus saw, boys come to their spear no longer ago than the spring. And now there were women among them too, barely recognizable in shirts and breeches, their faces painted like the men's, and fighting like men, spear-trained. This was the Caledones' last chance, just as it was Agricola's. There would not be another one for the side that lost.

Faustus gave his optio command of the second century, and now in command of the cohort, he held them in tight formation, listening for the trumpet call that would signal any new order, shields up against the howling enemy that descended on them. It was like fighting through marshland or the desperate inability to move within a dream. He blocked a spear thrust and pushed his shield into the adversary, driving his sword up under the Caledone's shield, saw that it was a woman as she fell, and had no time to think about that before the next warrior came at him.

He sent Tuathal to the other end of the cohort's line and between them they began to pull men who were flagging or wounded, sending them back through the ranks while the shield wall opened up just enough to bring up men from the next row. Two of them carried Aulus Atticus between them. Faustus was grimly certain that he was dead, but the gods occasionally sent miracles. In any case, his body must be recovered and his ashes sent to Rome.

While neither side could advance, the Caledones, many without armor and each following their own lord and no other, were taking the worst of the casualties. But despite the slain they kept coming.

No couriers could have ridden through the confusion of the dead men, downed chariots, and hand-to-hand fighting of the front lines now. The trumpet call that Faustus had listened for cut through the din: *Hold in Place*. And then the *Advance* call of the cavalry, and they held as the last four alae of cavalry reserves swept out against the Caledones. They cut off the attempt to outflank the Roman lines and the Caledones' advance began to shatter. Cavalry horses shy from a solid wall of men but if the line crumbles then their weight will push them through any gap. The cavalry drove the Caledones downward with the Roman lines at their backs, and the clan lords at the forefront were the first to fall. With any central command long abandoned, each clan and village had only their own lord to look to, and without him, they disintegrated.

The pressure on the line released like a taut string snapping. The Batavians and the rest of the auxiliary cohorts moved forward again with the Caledones fleeing ahead of them east and west along the slopes of the hillside. With the efficiency born of those endless drills, the infantry line pulled into notched formation and opened room between the cohorts for the cavalry to pass in pursuit.

While the cavalry hunted down the sundered war bands, the infantry made their way up the hillside to the top where the Caledones' camp lay beside the moss- and grass-covered ruins of what must have been an ancient fortress, older even than the people of the hills. It was deserted again now, as it must have been deserted once before, strewn with the detritus of a place left in haste, overturned pots and rags of clothing, and the carcasses of the morning sacrifice. The Druids and any other civilian camp followers had fled as well, down the other side of the mountain. Faustus stood a long while looking at the barren stones. Tuathal came to stand beside him. He was bleeding from a gash down his shin, tied up with a strip torn from his tunic.

"Go and get that seen to," Faustus said reflexively as he would to any man of his command and Tuathal smiled wearily and gave him a sketchy Roman salute, fist to chest.

"What I have seen today I shall remember in Inis Fáil," he said.

Faustus was staring at a shoe on the ground, too small to be a man's. "The desperation of a war band that has had to put its women into the line?" he asked.

"No. I have seen how Rome conquers people like mine, even against a war band with greater numbers. And never even calling out half its strength," he added, looking now at the orderly ranks of the legionary cohorts still arrayed along the riverbank below. "When I take a Roman army to Inis Fáil, it will be thus."

A rider came up the hill along the old road and halted to confer with the infantry commanders. "The governor's compliments, and please attend to any stragglers that the cavalry miss. I'm thinking there won't be many prisoners."

Faustus nodded. He doubted any of them would surrender. It made the task simpler but grimmer.

"Governor says if you stumble on their warlord, get him alive though, if you can. We haven't found him yet." He mounted and moved down the line.

Faustus nodded to the signifer and formed up the cohort to follow him. Until there was a new prefect they were his, although he grieved for Aulus Atticus, whom he had liked.

They hunted the Caledones who had fled into the woods and underbrush through the afternoon. A few bands who still had commanders and had managed an orderly retreat waited in ambush for the pursuing Romans rather than be taken. After the first patrol had been jumped and had to fight its way out, the hunting parties spread out to encircle each stand of trees or scrub and work their way in, driving any hiding there onto the spears of dismounted cavalry troopers. As Faustus had predicted, few were willing to surrender, perhaps finding the idea of death preferable to the slave market. Faustus thought he might well have felt the same. But by the time dusk was falling it was beginning to make Faustus want to weep. So many of these last ones were heartbreakingly young, and no doubt had itched to join their spear bands as he had itched to join the army. To his relief they didn't find any women, although there were dead women on the battlefield among the wreckage of the chariots. There was no sign of Calgacos.

The dead on the field were being stripped of anything valuable. There was little enough to loot but weapons and the armor that only the lords had worn. The wealth that Britons prided themselves on and displayed on arms and neck and on horses was missing. It was plain by the state of their bodies that it had gone to buy what food they had had over the past year.

For the thousands of Caledone dead, lying naked under the darkening sky and the circling carrion birds, there were few of the Roman dead to carry back to the camp. No more than five hundred on the Dead List, Atticus's watch commander told Faustus, and perhaps twice that many wounded to be treated in the hospitals that by now had caught up with the column.

Besides Aulus Atticus, there were two more dead from the cohort's ranks. When Faustus had found Paullus and assured him that he was not dead too, he signed the list, putting his name below that of the Batavians' surgeon. He bent over to let Paullus pull his hauberk over his head and then stripped off his sweat-soaked tunic. His chest was stippled with the marks of his own ring mail, driven into the skin by a blow from a Caledone shield. Paullus brought him a clean tunic and he splashed his face with water and washed his bloody hands and went to the Batavian medical tent to see the wounded, now also his responsibility.

The medical corps had marched with only the implements they could carry, and now were engaged in setting up hospitals proper around the casualties being treated. Constantius Silanus came through the Batavian hospital tent, dodging orderlies unpacking the dispensary chests, and nodded at Faustus when he saw him.

"A good afternoon's work, Centurion."

"Thank you, sir. We've lost our prefect though."

"Have you? A sad business. I liked that young man." He looked as if he might say something more and Faustus wondered if Constantia had liked him too. Silanus was thinner than Faustus remembered from the winter and his face looked ragged somehow. He felt ragged himself. The culmination of so many years' campaign felt not triumphant but weary, laid out on cots in the medical tent and on the pyres stacked outside the camp walls.

Silanus didn't say anything more and Faustus gave his attention to his men, passing along the lines of wounded with praise and congratulations, making mental notes of those who should be recommended for awards. There were nearly as many broken bones from the weight of the heavy highland swords as actual wounds. He was relieved when the Batavians' surgeon told him that it didn't look as if there were any who would have to be invalided out. Indus, with stitches in his forehead and his arm in a sling, gave him a cheeky grin and said that he supposed that this would get him off latrine duty now.

"And a silver *phalera* if my recommendation goes through," Faustus said. "I saw you out there. I'd recommend you for promotion if you could keep your head out of a beer barrel."

Indus looked thoughtful. "I might think on that, sir."

They gathered in the early morning for prayers for the slain and to light the pyres. The governor made a victory speech. Awards were announced and Faustus found himself decorated with a *corona aurea* for having held his ground and the cohort in the face of his commander's death. Galerius came to the Batavians' camp afterward to congratulate him and they stood together to watch the dark smoke of the pyres rise into the sky.

"You'll get a promotion out of this," Galerius prophesied. "There always are, after a campaign, and you earned it."

"They won't let me keep the Batavians," Faustus said wistfully. "Not a double cohort."

"Probably not, but something. Old Ursus has recommended me for promotion to cohort rank and I happen to know he sent your name in too, despite your not actually being in his command anymore. Ursus considers things like that a mere detail. Come along and I'll buy you a drink on the strength of our prospects and we can look up Clio."

With the baggage train had come the rest of the civilian camp followers and Abudia and other madams were doing business, charging double because they could.

"Amazing how the possibility of death inspires a man to want to spread his seed," Galerius said. "There's something innate to human nature in that, I think."

"I admire your ability to philosophize on any subject."

"Oh no, Clio says so too. There's always extra business after a fight."

Faustus considered that. It actually seemed unpleasantly likely. "Drink, and then Abudia," he said. "I want to get that notion out of my mind first."

Anyone of the auxiliaries not indulging in Abudia's offerings was drinking in Ingenuus's tent or similar rolling taverns, wearing bits of heather on their helmets and bragging that they had done the job while the legions sat in camp. When the legions began to get surly about that, their commanders squelched them and pointed out that, as Galerius said, the auxiliaries had done the job for free because there was no loot to speak of. Faustus and Galerius set an example of amiable coexistence over a pitcher of wine, and then went to see Clio.

–

The governor's aide laid a list on Agricola's desk and saluted. "The enemy dead have all been stripped now, sir."

"Any sign of Calgacos?" Agricola asked.

"No, sir. There are thousands but we've been over them all, with the staff who were there when you met with him. We took Centurion Valerianus with us for a second look at any faintly possible ones since he got closest to him, barring yourself."

"No doubt he loved that," Agricola said.

"He did not. We found him in Abudia's."

"And hauled him off to look at naked corpses."

"Yes, sir." He paused. "Do you wish to burn them now, or leave them for the crows?"

"There are too many," Agricola said. "Since they are not unpleasantly near any of our permanent camps, leave them. It will be a useful reminder. But pull out any that are in the water. Water flows elsewhere eventually, often to some place you want to drink it."

He sat silent then, thinking. They had done the thing. They would plant sufficient forts to hold the north and present Domitian with a newly expanded province, eventually extending its reach to take in Hibernia. Any man should be satisfied with that. He would send for his wife now, he thought. She should not have to mourn their son alone. Had it been the uncertainty of the campaign that had robbed them of this late child? Or just the whim of the gods? It was impossible to tell.

His aide coughed gently and Agricola realized that he was still there. "The scouts report followers trailing the war host at a distance. Women mostly."

Agricola looked past the open tent flap to the rain that had begun again, churning the camp to mud. "This country is Jupiter's own watering pot. We might as well be fish." He gestured to a slave who was lighting a brazier. "Bring me some hot wine. If the women come for the bodies, let them have any they can carry off."

XVII

The Sidhe of Bryn Dan

They looked like wraiths in the morning mist, silent figures under the gray rain that had been sheeting down all night. The Romans in the camp across the river watched them but did not interfere. The women walked among the dead, peering at faces and stopping when they found a familiar one. These they loaded onto wagons that trailed their progress through the dead.

Aregwydd, with her husband's body on a cart, thought it sad that some would have none to come for them. He had been stripped of his ring mail and weapons and his eyes had been open. She had closed them forcibly so that he might not see what had come about. The gash in his throat that had killed him gaped white, blood and battle paint washed out by the rain, and the clan marks were stark against his pale flesh.

Because village and hold had fought each under their own lord, their slain lay mostly together. The searchers took their own and left the rest to the other women or to the crows. They would bury who could be found, and let the Mother take back the rest, absorbing them into the clay and the beaks of her birds.

The women made their slow way across the plain with the wagons rumbling behind them, and vanished again into the rain.

–

Aelwen walked beside the litter, her cloak over her head, dogged, one foot in front of the next. Her right arm throbbed under the bandage torn from her shirt. The two men carrying the litter were no larger than children but strong enough to bear it on their shoulders. They had appeared out of the trees as she had struggled to drag a chariot over the rocky ground, the ponies that had pulled it dead on the battlefield, their traces cut with her belt knife.

Now they went by some path she could not see, through unfamiliar glens, stopping once to hide as something that she could not see either went by.

The body on the litter groaned and she put her hand over his. She had thought Calgacos dead and had been still grimly determined that the Romans should not have him. When he had stirred she had redoubled her efforts, dragging at the chariot pole while her injured arm dizzied her at each pull and the Roman cavalry hunted them through the underbrush.

A dismounted cavalry trooper had come at them and she had braced her spear for a last stand. Then he had dropped almost at her spearpoint, a little dark-fletched arrow protruding between his neck and hauberk collar.

"Come, lady."

The little men had taken Calgacos off the chariot and disappeared into the trees while she ran after them. Sometime in the dusk they had stopped and fashioned the litter. Otter, the elder of them, she thought – it was hard to tell their age – had examined her injured arm and dressed the wound with something from a skin pouch he wore at his belt, and he and Kite had worked with Aelwen to pull the ring mail hauberk over Calgacos's head and clean the deep bloody wound that had driven the iron mail into his flesh and split his right shoulder open. They dressed it with the same salve and she tore most of the rest of her shirt off to make a bandage.

Kite set Calgacos's sword and belt knife aside with the mail. Otter pointed his finger at Aelwen's.

Of course. Iron. She drew her knife from its sheath and laid the blade with the rest. Otter nodded.

Aelwen had seen the little dark people of the hills before, but not often and mostly while driving them from her hen house. These were clad in wolfskins and belts of fox tails, their faces thickly tattooed. Glass beads decorated the strands of black hair that hung past their shoulders.

"Time to move on, lady," Kite said. "They will be hunting you still." Their voices were musical and oddly accented.

Aelwen nodded and stood, weaving a little on her feet. Otter pulled a flask from his pouch.

"Drink."

Aelwen drank. It was odd tasting but not vile, just odd. She could feel it in her veins after a moment and felt less weak. *Never you take what the Old Ones give you to eat*, her grandmother had told her once, but she didn't have a choice. She wiped her lips with the back of her hand. "Thank you."

Otter and Kite picked up the litter.

"Will he live?" she whispered to them.

"That is for the Great Mother," Otter said. "But we will take him to her."

Aelwen followed behind them into the darkness. Sometimes they stopped and hid again, and sometimes there were whistles and bird calls in the night, or the noises of frogs where there was no water. Those she guessed to be Otter's brothers, traveling with them unseen. She knew that the Mother meant both the Goddess and also the Old One of their house, mother and grandmother to the generations after her and residence of the Goddess in her earthly form.

She was not entirely sure how long they traveled. The rain stopped and began again and she lost track of time. They mostly hid by day, although sometimes they went cautiously in the light. Calgacos's forehead was hot to the touch and she knew he was delirious with fever when he asked her in a whisper for the count of new foals from the spring, and then if Rhion had come back from the south yet. Was he reliving all the years since then? Then he was silent and twice she put her hand to his chest to be sure he was still breathing.

They saw one Roman patrol that went by their hiding place without stopping, drawn past them in pursuit of what she thought must be men of Otter's house. No sounds of fighting followed and after a while a nightjar's chattering trill came from the north and they went on.

By the time they stopped beside a heather-covered hillside dotted with scrub trees and brush, she had no idea where they were. A circling of birds high in the distance might have been the battlefield, or only the carcass of some animal's kill. A stone set into the hillside slowly became a doorway as she looked at it carefully. Otter and Kite slid into the gap below it and in a moment they came out again and picked up the litter, beckoning her to follow.

The passage into the hill looked like the entrance of the Horned God's cave, but it opened instead into a round low chamber with corridors branching from it into dim light beyond. In the chamber, flickering rushlights sat in niches in the stone walls. Kite and Otter carried Calgacos through the outer room and down one of the corridors and she followed, feeling herself drawn deeper into the earth as they went. A shaft overhead let in a pale beam of light but the air grew colder and she shivered. They halted in a small room where an ancient woman waited in a chair, bundled under a rug beside an empty bed. The bed was wood, elaborately and intricately carved, and piled with wolf and fox skins and woolen blankets.

The woman looked at Aelwen. "I am the Old One of the sidhe of Bryn Dan." Her skin looked like ancient dark leaves, her face marked with faded loops and spirals tattooed in her long-ago youth, and her hair hung in fine gray plaits down her shoulders. Sitting, they reached nearly to the earthen floor. Her hands were twig-like, thin-fingered as if the skeleton had already come through the skin.

Aelwen said, "I am Aelwen, wife of Calgacos," although she suspected the Old One knew that.

Kite and Otter laid Calgacos on the blankets and the old woman bent forward to look at him closely, pulling the bandage away from his shoulder and sniffing it. She spoke in her own tongue and they left and came back with a basin and cloths, pots and jars of herbs and salve, and a pitcher of something.

Aelwen watched them nervously, but surely they had not brought him here to poison him, and the Old Ones were said to be as knowledgeable as the Druids, even consulted by them on occasion.

Calgacos lay still while the Old One washed out the wound and smeared it with salve but Aelwen could tell he was awake and gritting his teeth. The woman bound it up again with a fresh bandage, murmuring as she did.

"Sit him up," she commanded.

Otter and Kite pulled Calgacos carefully to a half-sitting position and she put a cup of liquid from the pitcher to his lips. He swallowed obediently and then gagged and she pushed it against his mouth insistently.

"Drink, lord of the Sun Men, if you wish to live."

He swallowed again.

They laid him back down. He looked at Aelwen as if startled to see her, and then closed his eyes again.

"He will sleep now," the Old One said. She wiped what was left of the paint from his face with a cloth and put more blankets over him.

"Thank you," Aelwen said. It seemed insufficient. "We are grateful for—"

"It was not done out of kindness," the Old One said frankly, "but because your man is part of the balance of things. The world may need him in some way that I cannot be certain of."

"To keep your people from being hunted by the Romans as ours have been perhaps," Aelwen said.

"Perhaps. But if so, he will not be the one to do it. If he lives he will have no more use of that arm again, ever."

Aelwen was silent. Then he would be no more the headman either. The headman must be whole, or the clan suffered the same ill luck as its lord. She had not wept yet, for the defeat or the dead, but now the tears came unbidden.

293

The Old One watched her unmoved. "Everything has a price, lady, the Druids will tell you that. Your man has bought what was needed and his arm was the price."

"What has he bought if he has not held the Romans back?"

"You will see. Our people and yours were here before the Romans came over water and we will both be here when they leave. This Roman governor has won what he cannot hold. You will see. Now, let me look at your own arm, and I will send for clean clothes for you." She gestured at Kite and Otter to leave them.

Aelwen held out her arm obediently and the Old One stripped the bandage and the remnants of her shirt from her and inspected the wound.

"This will heal," she said, washing it briskly while Aelwen gritted her own teeth. "How did you come by it?"

"A Roman sword. He called in the women at the last, to drive the chariots against their line and slow them. We did so, but it was not enough."

The Old One traced the wound gently where it cut across the blue patterns of Aelwen's house. "And now it is written in your clan marks that you are also a warrior."

A girl came in with an armful of cloth. "This is Wren," the Old One said. "My granddaughter's daughter."

Wren smiled at Aelwen and put her bundle down. She spoke to her grandmother and held up a tunic of pale checkered wool. It would have made a gown for Wren and come only to Aelwen's knees.

"You may stay with him until he wakes," the Old One said, "and then we will see how he fares. I will send you some food."

They left her then, Wren giving her arm to the Old One to lean on. Aelwen put on the checkered gown over her breeches and washed her face and hands with the water that the Old One had used. Wren came back with bread and a clay bowl of stew that smelled of meat seasoned with herbs. Hare, she thought, gulping it down ravenously. She wiped the bowl with the bread.

There was a cup of some drink and she emptied that too, and then sat down in the chair the Old One had occupied.

Aelwen slept. A long time perhaps. She woke groggily to find Calgacos awake as well. He was very pale, his barley-colored hair matted and dark with sweat, but he seemed to have come back into the present.

"The little dark people came for you and brought us here," she told him.

He thought that over. "Who is left of us?"

"I don't know."

"Bleddin?"

She shook her head. "He stood and fought with his spear brothers at the last to let me bring you away." The tears came again.

Calgacos closed his eyes for a moment. "Celyn too," he said after she thought he was asleep again. Celyn had been his hound when he was young.

"The Old One says you have done what was necessary," Aelwen said. "That we will still be here when the Romans have gone. I don't know how she knows that."

"I have thought on this while I slept," Calgacos said. "Or dreamed it, I don't know. You must go to Emrys if he has survived, and tell him to take the command, and my clans and any others that will come to him."

"There will be time for that when you have healed."

"No," Calgacos said insistently. "If we are to outwait the Romans we must have one leader now, someone who can get terms from them that will keep them from hunting the rest down."

"I will think about that when you can travel."

"No." He had tried to sit up and now he lay back wearily. "My sword arm is useless. I heard the Old One say so, and in any case I knew it already. You must go to Emrys, or if not him, to whatever lord may be best in your mind. There must be no possibility for our people to argue against him, and so I cannot go."

295

Otter came back with a pot to let him piss, and after Otter the Old One, leaning on a stick. She sniffed the wound again and nodded. Then she turned to Aelwen.

"We will keep him here until he is healed but you cannot stay."

Aelwen started to protest, and Calgacos said, "They have done much against their customs just to bring me here. Every one of them that traveled with us must have had to purify himself, and the ones who touched my mail will have had a worse time of it. Their prohibition against iron goes deep."

"Iron is a Wrong Thing and Sun People smell of it," the Old One agreed. "To have brought you into our house is a matter of honor but it is not such a one as we wish to extend."

"Go and find Emrys," Calgacos said again. He hesitated and then told her abruptly, "If you wish, if it serves you to marry again, you have my leave."

"What?" Aelwen stared at him. "The wound, or whatever it was *she* gave you" – she glared at the Old One – "has affected your mind."

"No," Calgacos said. "I have thought on this while we slept. Or dreamed it. I told you. I cannot go with you. If it comes to that, go to the Druids." He smiled wryly. "When you can find one. They will release you."

"The Druids have no doubt gone to roost in Inis Fáil. And you have gone mad." The people of the hills would have guided Vellaunos and the rest by paths that only they knew, because despite being Sun People, Druids were holy.

"Aelwen, you do not understand. You are my heart. But I cannot go with you. Not now and not later. That is the rest of the price. Take my belt knife and sword to Emrys. He will know the knife since it is his."

"We left them on the trail," Aelwen said. "They did not like handling them."

Calgacos turned to the Old One. "Send someone for them." She hesitated and he said, "That is your share of the price."

After a moment she spoke to Otter and he nodded.

Calgacos closed his eyes again and Aelwen stood rooted to the stone of the chamber floor while every excuse and argument floated through her head and left again. Calgacos was right. The Old One was right. There was nothing to do but what he asked of her. She wanted to fling herself onto the bed with him and howl… but she did not.

They brought her a horse from somewhere, gingerly because of the iron in the bit. It had been loosed on the battlefield perhaps, saddleless but with a bridle and snapped-off reins dangling. She found a stone from which she could mount without using her injured arm and took the reins in her left hand. Calgacos's sword belt was buckled about her waist with the dagger in its sheath, its hilt scored with the grooves where gold wire had wrapped it once. Kite and Otter went with her as before, walking ahead of the horse purposefully. They said their brothers had "gone to see" and come back with word that Emrys was camped with such other lords as had survived. She didn't ask them where they were bound. She would know soon enough.

—

agricola's army began a slow, ostentatious march north, making a show of power to the scattered remnants of the Caledones and their allies who they knew were watching, foraging what little was left and plundering what the retreating Caledones had not set on fire to spite them. The prisoners who had surrendered were marched with them, on full view to anyone interested. The baggage train and all the civilian followers who had caught up with the column trailed behind them again in a ragtag wake like gulls behind a fishing fleet. They halted for three or four days at each camp to dig in another reminder to the Caledones of what Rome could accomplish. When they moved on, they left the walls and ditch intact, and a century or two to hold it. Some camp prefects adjusted the angle of the walls to the contour of the ground; others simply marked out the regulation rectangle despite any obstacles and dug until the ground matched it.

"Is he planning permanent garrisons?" Faustus asked. "This far north? Or is this just for show?"

"A little of both, I expect," Galerius said. "It looks good in the governor's report to the emperor, and makes a point to the enemy, and he can decide which ones to make permanent when he sees the response from both directions."

In the meantime, as Galerius had predicted, a spate of promotions and transfers came through. Centurion Ursus was posted to Germany to command the Fifth Cohort in the First Adiutrix, and Galerius had been given Ursus's command of the Seventh in the Augusta. Faustus too had his promotion: commander of the Ninth Cohort of the Augusta, whose centurion had also been transferred upward elsewhere.

Paullus got out Faustus's old lorica and helmet and polished them to a shine befitting a cohort commander, and Faustus discovered to his pleasure that there was nothing actually wrong with the Ninth Cohort, a welcome change. They paraded smartly and exhibited a befitting restraint when taunted by the auxiliaries over having sat out the great battle. They were suitably impressed by the *corona aurea* and there appeared to be no malingerers. The only one skipping parade and drill had an actual case of food poisoning from eating dubious oysters in one of the traveling taverns, and apologized abjectly while throwing up in a basin. The first century optio was a time-expired retiring veteran who was going to "find a nice girl and a bit of land" in the south, and Faustus immediately went to the legate and poached Septimus from the Seventh Cohort before Galerius could object.

The column marched on, in parade gear and with shields uncovered for a more impressive display. Tuathal was given temporary command of the First Batavians until a new prefect could be appointed, in a gesture clearly meant to provide him with command experience before the coming invasion of Hibernia. Agricola intended to spend the winter in the camps along the ridge between Alauna and Castra Pinnata. The ridge camps were being expanded and reinforced as permanent forts and a great deal of speculation was expended on which cohorts would be left to garrison them in the spring and which would go to Hibernia with the governor.

"And there's your trouble with taking in new territory," Galerius said when Faustus began making small offerings to Mars Ultor for the promise of being sent to Hibernia. "Once you have it, you have to govern it. It's not nearly as interesting a job."

"That's for civilians," Faustus grumbled.

Galerius swept his gaze over the jagged teeth of rocky uplands and the wild blue-green swells falling away in the other direction. "Civilians aren't up to this place."

"Well, not yet." Faustus tried to envision his brother-in-law Manlius discussing municipal finances and sanitary drains with the Caledones.

"Not ever," Galerius said. "Mark my words."

–

They had got as far as the estuary mouth of one of the rivers that flowed from the highlands into the northern ocean when the delegation that Agricola had been expecting rode down from the mountains under a green branch. None had a face that Faustus knew: a tall man with a scarred cheekbone and lime-bleached hair cut short, and a woman with fox-red hair and a healing wound on her right arm. A slight, sandy-haired man with them proved to be an interpreter. All bore clan markings pricked into their skin in blue woad.

Agricola met them in the Principia tent with solemn formality. "Greetings in the name of the Emperor Caesar Domitianus Augustus. I am his consular legate in Britain."

Faustus translated that and Agricola's invitation to take the chairs set out for them. The Caledone envoys settled themselves with the interpreter standing behind them. The scarred man wore a bronze torque about his throat and bronze armbands where his gold ones had been, but his hair and mustache were freshly bleached to near white and his shirt was of a fine deep blue wool. The woman wore breeches and leather boots under a gown tied up at the sides for riding. Her flame-colored hair hung down her back.

"So," Agricola said, testing the waters. "You are sent by Calgacos to ask for terms."

"I am Emrys, chieftain of the allied clans of the Caledones," the white-haired man said. "Coran will translate your words for me, and confirm that your translator does not change mine."

The sandy-haired man spoke after him in heavily accented Latin, and Faustus repeated it for the governor's less well-trained ear.

"Where is Calgacos?" Agricola asked.

"I am Aelwen, wife of Calgacos," the woman said. "Calgacos is dead."

"Indeed?" Agricola looked as if he was thinking. "And you are the warlord elected in his stead?" He looked at Emrys.

"I am chieftain," Emrys said. "We are come to arrange peace. Therefore there is no need for a new warlord."

"Indeed," Agricola said again. "I was not aware that one chieftain ruled over all the clans of these mountains. Quite the contrary." He ruffled his fingers through the feathered crest of his helmet, which sat on the desk before him. "How have you managed this?"

"Matters change," Aelwen said. "Of necessity."

Agricola allowed himself to look amused. "Quite so. And the terms we offered when Calgacos turned them down are no longer on offer."

"We can still fight you, Commander of Eagles," Emrys said.

Agricola glanced at Aelwen. His eyes rested on the angry scar that ran down her arm. "I understand that Calgacos put the women into the line at the last. What do you have left to fight us with?"

"We can still trouble your camps until every stick that cracks in the dark makes them fearful," Emrys said. "You know that."

"Do you discount what women can do?" Aelwen asked him softly. "You should not."

"I would not be so foolish," Agricola said. "Nor will I reward your kind for turning down peace when you could have had it. From each clan you will now send us ten hostages, male and female under the age of twenty-five, and ten cows and sheep. You will provide our garrisons with grain for the winter up to a half portion of what you can still reap. In return we will give you seed for the spring planting. After you have taken your hides and wool to market in the spring, you will pay taxes in proportion to the adult population of each clan. You will supply labor to build roads where we wish them. You will acknowledge and sacrifice to the gods of Rome and the Emperor Caesar Domitianus Augustus. Your tribal councils will be overseen by judiciary magistrates from our garrisons in your territories. And you will hand over the Druids among you." Agricola sat back and folded his hands on his desk.

"The Druids have flown," Emrys said. "There are none to hand over. You may send your men to search for them," he added. As Aelwen had said, the Druids had no doubt gone to roost in Inis Fáil and would return when it suited them. The Caledones had lost wounded to the lack of their healing knowledge and he was inclined to wish the Romans on them anyway.

"What will you do with the hostages?" Aelwen asked.

"Educate them as Romans in the hope of bringing civilization to your country," Agricola said.

Emrys opened his mouth to say something that was bound to be furiously ill advised and she forestalled him. "And what of the prisoners you have taken and have been parading through our countryside to make sure that we see them?" she asked, sliding the conversation past the governor's insult.

"Do you want them back?" Agricola inquired.

"No." They spoke together.

"No? *They* surrendered peacefully."

"Exactly," Emrys said. "They are therefore of no use."

Faustus supposed that if Emrys took back the prisoners who had surrendered it would weaken his stature as chieftain. That might matter greatly just now if he wished to keep this new and unwieldy alliance intact. Faustus murmured a suggestion to Agricola, who nodded.

Faustus said to Emrys, "Don't you want to at least look them over, to see who might be among them?"

"No." Worse than taking them all back would be pulling one or two of his own clan from the lot. Emrys knew it too. He wouldn't chance seeing someone he cared for.

Aelwen said, "Hostages are a different matter. We all make the choices that we must. But they will have no choice when they are selected. So you are warned: if they are mistreated, there will be war again."

"Consider, lady, that they may have better lives among us than they have had heretofore," Agricola said.

"You think highly of yourselves, Commander of Eagles," Emrys said, retrieving his temper and translating it into scorn.

"What is a 'better life'?" Aelwen asked. "You will not succeed in raising a wolf cub as a lapdog."

Agricola considered that with elaborate politeness. "I imagine wolves might experience a certain wistfulness for the hearthside," he said. "Assuming that dogs think about these things."

"The question is whether you can make one into the other!" she snapped.

"Or back again. Do you accept my terms *this time*?"

"We accept," Emrys said. "But do not think that you can hold these mountains, Commander of Eagles. For our lifetimes perhaps, but not longer."

"Then you may tell me so in the Underworld… chieftain of the Caledones."

The emperor was pleased. Orders arrived awarding Agricola "triumphal ornaments", the nearest that anyone but an emperor could come to an actual triumph, and construction of a commemorative arch adorned with statues of both the governor and the emperor at the Port of Rutupiae, the official entrance to the Province of Britain.

The hostages were also delivered, most of them frightened youngsters, and some young enough to need the care of the older ones.

"He thinks he's pulled a sleight of hand," the legate of the Second Augusta said, watching their tearful arrival. "We didn't give him a minimum age, did we?"

"No," Agricola agreed. "I didn't. These will do nicely. I wasn't lying about our purpose. They will be entirely Roman by the time they are grown. Their mothers are no doubt angry at the chieftain too," he added. "That's useful."

The hostages were sent south to Eburacum with a cohort of native nursemaids, to the charge of the garrison there. Their military escort returned to Agricola, bringing Demetrius of Tarsus and a mule loaded with the scholar's belongings.

"Did I ask you to bring him?" Agricola inquired.

"No, governor, he attached himself," the escort's decurion said. "The commander at Eburacum said to take him."

"Yes, I wager he did. Tell him not to unpack."

-

"Centurion Valerianus, how do you find your new command?"

"They are an excellent cohort, Governor." Faustus waited uneasily to find out why he had been summoned. The cohort hadn't done anything that he could think of that would earn the governor's personal ire. They had, in fact, remained exemplary and he blessed his predecessor.

"I'm delighted to hear it." Agricola produced a tablet sealed with the imperial cypher and handed it to Faustus.

Faustus held it gingerly as if it might have bees in it. Maybe the cohort was too well behaved and they had a troop of rabid apes who needed direction instead.

"I am sending ships of the Fleet to circumnavigate the entire province of Britain," the governor said. "Thus proving that it is an island, and in the process to make diplomatic niceties with the archipelago of smaller islands to the north, which are called the Orcades. They will take a cohort of the Second Augusta aboard, and your legate and I agree that you are the man for the command."

Faustus winced. It was not advisable to say to the governor, *Thank you, sir, but I'd rather take them to Hibernia.* Agricola seemed to read his mind, however.

"You will winter in the Orcades. As soon as the spring weather permits, you will rejoin us for the campaign in Hibernia, if that eases your mind, Centurion. And that is more explanation than any officer of mine should expect from his commander." He paused. "This is an important mission, Valerianus. The people of the Orcades did not take part in the recent war and I wish to make it clear to them what an excellent choice that was. You will pay for anything that you requisition, give their village headman a nice present, and keep your men from abusing the civilians. We are not invading them; this is a voyage of exploration and diplomacy only."

"I expect they will appreciate that, sir."

"Yes, no doubt. One other thing, Centurion. Demetrius of Tarsus will accompany you. He wishes to conduct scientific observations of the natives."

-

"And then he told me that I had demonstrated 'an understanding of native thinking and a level head in a crisis,'" Faustus said. "So I suppose he thinks there is going to be one."

"And Demetrius!" Galerius hooted. "A bonus!"

"He's right," Tuathal said lazily, helping himself to more of Galerius's wine. "You're a good choice to make overtures to the islanders. Just beware the finwomen."

"The what?"

"Any strange woman on the beach really. If she's a selkie, she'll just break your heart, but the finwomen kidnap human mates and drag them under the water to live there."

"He should send you. How do you know all this?" Faustus demanded.

"The hostage children, poor mites. They were terrified you were going to eat them so I told them how I grew up among you, and how I'll go back to my own people as king, and they felt better about things."

"Well, I don't feel better about the finwomen."

"Just stay off the beach."

"How do I keep Demetrius off the beach, or out of anywhere really? And if the finwomen get him, how do I put that in a report?"

"He's not a bad old boy," Galerius said.

"I suppose not," Faustus said. "He brought me a letter from Constantia, by the way. You will appreciate it."

> *My dear friend Faustus,*
>
> *It is miserably hot in Eburacum and we are afflicted with a plague of blackflies. Aunt sends her regards and hopes that you are not drinking too much as it affects the bowels. Demetrius is writing a short treatise on the goddess Epona, contrasting her British cult with that of the Gauls. There is nothing to do here except play with the granary cat's new kittens and wish that I was with the column with Father. Tell Galerius that the changing room girl at the public bath is still pining for him. I can understand why because she told me all about their activities and his efforts compare favorably to Jupiter's in her estimation.*

"Let me see that!"

Faustus snatched the letter away from Galerius and kept reading.

> *Tell Tuathal that that Moesian scout he threw dice with is complaining because his dice were weighted but Tuathal beat him anyway and he thinks it must have been sorcery. I think his dice weren't very good. Or Tuathal swapped them when he wasn't looking. Probably that.*

Faustus looked at Tuathal, who smiled modestly.

"Which was it?"

"Sorcery," Tuathal said. "Spread it about, please. It won't hurt when we go to Inis Fáil."

Faustus folded up the letter and stood. The cursed ship was supposed to sail in the morning. And instead of consorting with Clio in winter quarters, he was going to spend it being diplomatic with islanders who would probably turn out to be murderous fish people. He would go back to his tent and dream about Inis Fáil and the spring.

XVIII

The Seals

Autumn

It was dark of the moon and the only light in the house came from the banked embers on the hearth in the main hall, but Eirian felt more than saw the rustle in the darkness. Not mice, a sound she knew, or the cat after the mice, or the hounds asleep by the hearth in midnight dream pursuit of hares. A soft footstep, unmistakably her father's but trying to be quiet.

Eirian sat up in bed, holding herself still to listen. After a moment she heard the faint sound of the door latch. She pulled her cloak around her nightshift and padded into the hall. A hound lifted its head and lay back down again. Nothing that signified danger then. Her brothers were snoring in their shared room, loudly enough that only a pause in their breathing had let her hear the quiet footstep.

Eirian eased the door open and slipped out barefoot. What would her father be doing out in the night? Whatever it was, he didn't want anyone to know, and therefore Eirian wanted to. Down the path that led to the shore she saw a flicker of light and followed it: her father with a half-closed lantern.

Faelan was not ordinarily a secretive man, other than about Eirian's mother, and she had a brief yearning thought that somehow he was going to meet her mother on the shore, that the rumors were true, however unlikely that anyone would wait seventeen years to come back from the sea if she had any love for her husband or for the child who wouldn't remember her. Eirian pushed that thought aside because now she could see a boat drawn up on the shore, just the hull of it, lit by her father's lantern. She hid in the lee of Eogan's currach and watched as they went past, her father and three others. They were only shadows in the dark: one was tall and the others nearly as small as children. She tiptoed after them, barefoot and soundless in the wet gravelly sand that crunched under her father's boots.

"We will go no farther than this, Faelan," one of them said as they came to the boat shed. "The place smells of iron." The voice was odd, musical and slightly accented, only partly with the speech of the mainland.

Eirian heard her father grumble and a second voice said, "He has kept the Romans from your doorstep. This is your share of the price for that. Did you think there was no price for sitting out this war?"

"There were Roman ships in the firth this morning!" Faelan snapped.

"They are coming with treaty agreements and not with spears. That is what he bought you."

"Take him in, Faelan, or we may extract another price." The second voice was still mellifluous but quietly menacing.

The tall man had not spoken and now Faelan lifted the lantern toward him and Eirian put her hand over her mouth. His face was thin, the bones seemingly barely covered by the skin, and the eyes hollow, but she knew him anyway: the warlord who had come the past winter to buy their grain. The warlord who had led a great host against the Romans and lost.

Eirian backed away. This was something dangerous to know with the Romans supposedly sending envoys to the islands. She slipped back into the house, heart pounding. After a while she heard the sound of the wagon coming out of the hay barn and then the faint rattle as it pulled away from the yard. When she slipped out again before dawn, down to the shore, there was

308

no sign of any boat but their own. The wagon was still gone. Faelan came home at first light while Eirian was stirring up the fire, just as if he had been out to see to the cows, but there was slick mud and dried eel grass on his boots.

Faelan shouted Eirian's brothers out of bed and they in turn shook the herd boy and the pig girl out of their pallets in the cow byre. The cows were milked and turned into the pasture. Eirian fed the chickens and collected eggs from the various places the hens hid them. She stirred up porridge and salt cod for their breakfast and ignored Boduoc's demand for eggs.

"I'm saving them for a cake. Go away. You'll miss the tide."

When they had gone, she looked her father in the eye. "Give me your boots to clean before someone wonders about them."

He handed them over silently, finishing the last of his breakfast while she brushed them clean. Except for the boots, last night's visitors seemed not to have been there at all. They were a piece of knowledge at the back of her mind that rested as uneasily as a strung bow.

What might come by daylight? Roman ships in the firth. She had seen them too the day before, not patrol craft but liburnians in military scarlet, sails bearing the eagle ensign of Rome billowing in the wind. The painted eyes on their prows were bright and watchful and she had seen the bronze-tipped rams just under the water. Enveloped in their iron shells, the men aboard might as well have had tails or horns or the bluish skins of finmen.

–

Faustus stood in the stern of the *Victoria*, flagship of the three vessels of the exploratory fleet, and hoped the helmsman knew his business. The currents around the Orcades were erratic and dangerous for anyone but a local. The helmsman had been recruited by the frontier scouts who had also provided information on the residents of the islands. The border wolves said that except in great emergencies there was no central authority among the islands, their people being inclined to suspect that such an authority would meddle in their personal affairs, or want taxes. If there was a dispute that blood money or negotiation could not solve, the priests would rule, the border wolves said. It didn't often come to that. They were less inclined than the mainlanders to raid each other for amusement and generally gave their attention to lovingly cared-for farms and fishing the cod and herring that abounded in their waters. Messages exchanged via the scouts had suggested that the inhabitants of High Isle, the southernmost of them, would receive a peaceful diplomatic delegation with equanimity if it brought sufficient presents.

The morning was fair, the sky empty except for the black-and-white flight of a lapwing overhead. The sails were furled and the oars slid out of their oar locks in three banks. As the ships nosed into the harbor one after the other, the crowd of villagers on the wharf grew greater, and Faustus saw small children set on their fathers' shoulders to watch the show. That was probably a good sign. They drew back warily, however, when his cohort began to disembark.

"We'll stay in harbor a few days," *Victoria's* squadron commander said. "Just in case, as you might say."

What he meant was "Just in case they decide to murder you in your sleep and you need to leave." After that they would be on their own until the ships came back from their explorations to haul out for the winter.

On the dock, a small muscular man with a bristly mustache came forward to meet them. His shirt was rough wool but he wore a gold torque at his throat and a gold spiral ending in beasts' heads on his right forearm.

Faustus saluted him, fist to chest, for politeness's sake. "I am Centurion Faustus Silvius Valerianus, representative of Governor Gnaeus Julius Agricola and the Emperor Caesar Domitianus Augustus."

Faelan looked unimpressed. "I am Faelan," he announced. "Keep your men on the dock for the now." His speech was an understandable variant of the southern dialects and Faustus set himself to tune his ear to it.

Faustus noted that beyond the throng of watchers was another array of villagers, these armed with spears. "We might hold a council," he suggested.

"Aye," Faelan said. He stumped away toward a series of taller buildings that rose above the low sheds along the wharf. Faustus followed, beckoning Septimus and two of his cohort to come with them. The harbor quarter consisted of circular stone-built structures of two and three stories thatched with straw and seaweed, and was a warren of chandlers, ropemakers, and storehouses. Gulls squabbled over scraps among the salting pans farther down the wharf, and a granary cat sunning in the street stood and stretched as they approached before stalking away.

Faelan pushed open a door and nodded at two men waiting inside what appeared to be a meeting hall. "I've brought the Roman," he informed them. They grunted an ambiguous greeting and inspected Faustus and his men dubiously.

Despite this unprepossessing beginning, two hours later a grudging agreement had been reached on a suitable site for a camp; on supplies; on guides and an introduction to the villages of the farther islands. The process had been sweetened by the emperor's gifts of gold spice boxes, silver ewers, and sets of delicate glass drinking cups decorated with an African menagerie, the transportation of which by sea had given Faustus a permanent headache.

Inquiring about a space to serve as a civil headquarters for his delegation, he was told that the village had no inns as such but there was a brewery with a spare room. Faustus agreed to an exorbitant price for the room, negotiated by Faelan who was probably going to pocket half of it.

On Demetrius's behalf, Faustus was promised introduction to the local priest who doubled as village harper and blacksmith and was plainly, to Faustus's relief, not a Druid.

Septimus had been sent to direct the surveyors to the site chosen for the camp, an empty field near the shore too rocky to cultivate and too salty for graze, and by the time Faustus and Faelan had settled other matters it was nearly built. Faustus noted Faelan's startled observation of walls that seemed to have heaved themselves out of the ground by magic, leaving neatly cut ditches in their wake.

Faustus paraded his cohort on the newly laid out drill field, and promised them retribution for any misbehavior involving the natives. When he had turned them over to Septimus for a brisk evening drill just to keep them busy, Septimus elaborated on the possible punishments for disobedience, including crucifixion, decimation, or simply having their livers cut out by Faustus personally. The shift from a wartime footing when practically anything was permissible when dealing with the enemy to a peacetime diplomatic mission when a foot put wrong could spoil the whole effort was notoriously difficult. Faustus began to have a healthy appreciation for Governor Agricola, who had been negotiating those waters for his entire career. It wasn't even full dark when a farmer came to his makeshift office in the brewery to complain of a missing pig. Faustus was more interested in the dinner that Paullus and Pandora were negotiating in the kitchen, and paid for the pig without question. A mistake, probably.

"Now they'll all have pigs go missing," his landlord said.

The brewer, whose name was Madoc, was glad of the fees for his room and inclined to be chatty once he learned that Faustus spoke his language, albeit awkwardly. The archipelago had some seventy islands, he said, more or less. He didn't suppose anyone had counted them rightly, "and then there'll be some that aren't there at high tide, you understand, which throws off the count." Only about twenty were inhabited, by farmers and fisherfolk. It was fine farming land, he said, unlike the rugged islands that lay two days' sailing north of their own, where there was nothing but fish and roosts for gulls.

"Do you hunt the seals?" Faustus asked. "I saw great crowds of them on the rocks as we came in."

"Bad luck follows the man that kills a seal," Madoc said. "On the northern islands, if the seals grow too numerous and the fishing suffers, they will, but if you ask me that's why their land is so poor. It's said that when the world was young all the people here were seals and only some grew legs and came ashore."

"Give me another beer," Faustus told Madoc, intrigued, "and have one yourself." The beer was reasonably good, but it would have been politic to drink it even if it wasn't.

"I will then, thank you. It happens sometimes that one of them goes back to the water, and so you don't kill them because he might be your kin, you see."

That seemed reasonable to Faustus, and something he had best warn his men of. "Are those the selkies?" he asked, thinking of Tuathal's tales.

"Aye. Maybe. Those come out of the water and leave their skins on shore and look just like human women, mind you, only more beautiful. But she'll always go back to her skin unless someone hides it. Many's the man that's married a selkie and lost her again."

\-

The villagers proved warier than Madoc, who had spent a lifetime serving drink to the foreign sailors who docked their merchant ships in the harbor. They were less inclined to conversation and maintained the air of people observing a large dog which may or may not be rabid. The squadron commander of the exploratory fleet sailed three days later with a cheerful promise to be back when the weather turned, and Faustus worked out several defensive strategies in his head in case things went bad, but so far there had been no problems other than disappointment at the lack of payment for further imaginary pigs.

Demetrius formed a friendship with the priestly blacksmith, studying the language and recording the – Faustus suspected – often fabulous history of the islands. It was an old country, probably older even than the firelight stories of seals. Standing stones and stone rings dotted it and there were barrows near them usually, the graves of the forgotten kings of antiquity. The scholar spent the balance of his time with scrollcase and pen, nose to the ground or to the air, noting each insect and bird and producing the conviction in the village that he was mad, but likely harmless. Patrols went out regularly, only to keep them fit through the winter, Faustus assured Faelan.

The village was the only one of any size on High Isle since the rest of its land was mountainous. Faelan had promised a guide to the mountains and to the largest of the sister islands, and while he waited for that to be settled Faustus set the cohort to digging drains and channels to bring water to the camp and its newly built bath house. That edifice was the source of much astonishment among the islanders, the Roman predilection for bathing never failing to perplex everyone else. The engineers attached to the cohort diverted some of the water to a trough in the public square, a gift intended to emphasize the benefits to being a client of Rome.

Once you had pacified a country, or bribed it into acquiescence, as Galerius had said, you had to run it. The Orcades were not at that stage yet, but Faustus knew he was supposed to be laying the groundwork for a gradual integration of the islands into the province. It was pretty country, he decided, and the weather was mild, even if it did rain almost constantly. His cohort was less enthusiastic.

"There's no decent wine," Septimus informed him, listing their grievances. "And no whorehouses either."

"Then they will have to learn to like beer and get better acquainted with themselves," Faustus said. "This is a diplomatic mission."

The first diplomatic crisis arrived shortly. It took the form of a girl who appeared at the brewery in search of the Roman commander. She was little, with pale brown hair like a sandpiper, eyes the color of seawater, and what might be a deceptive delicacy to her bones – she looked as if she could be stubborn.

"One of your men is courting my pig girl," she announced.

"Your pig girl?" Faustus had a moment's uncertainty, thinking of the seal people.

"From our farm. She sees to the pigs and her father is in a rage and has tried to kill him."

Faustus blanched. "What happened?"

"He laid the soldier's arm open and then ran when he saw more of them coming. He's hiding somewhere."

"Has my man harmed the girl? And what is your name? I'm Centurion Valerianus," he added.

"I'm Eirian and I know who you are, that's why I've come to you. He hasn't raped her if that's what you mean, he told her he wants to marry her."

"Well, he can't marry her," Faustus said. "They aren't allowed to marry while they're enlisted." At least technically. There were plenty of unofficial marriages, made legal on retirement. Faustus had no intention of letting his men acquire brides just because they were bored and there were no whorehouses. He would tire of her, most likely, and then where would the girl be? "Where is my man now?"

"He's gone chasing after her father. You have to stop them."

She looked frightened at the idea. They would only tie him up and drag him back to Faustus, if they knew what was good for them, but she didn't know that. "I'll do what I can. Where's the girl? Find her and bring her along."

At the camp gate he found seven of his cohort returning furiously breathless but empty-handed and Septimus ordering them back to quarters.

"What did I tell you—" Faustus roared at them "—about going after native women?"

"To be fair, sir," Septimus said, "you didn't say don't marry them."

Faustus glared at the legionary with his scarf tied around a bloody arm. "Varus, isn't it? Stick to your hand, curse you."

Varus saluted. "Sir, my enlistment is up this fall. Sir, I've been planning to buy a bit of land around Isca to retire on and find a wife."

"And what does the girl think about it?"

"Sir, she wants to come with me, sir. Just ask her."

Eirian had appeared at the gate with the pig girl in tow. She was a short plump child with a head of bushy brown hair coming out of its combs. She trotted over to Varus and put her hand in his.

"Do you want to marry this man?" Faustus demanded. "And leave your island with him?"

She nodded happily.

Faustus felt the headache coming back. It was obvious that Varus hadn't needed to force her and also that she was possibly already with child.

She looked repentantly up at Faustus. "I am sorry about Father. I told him but he never listens." She hesitated and then said, to Faustus and Varus both, "Please don't hurt him."

"If he keeps off me," Varus grunted. "Old fool."

"I'm not going to hurt him," Faustus assured her, "if he will listen to reason and not try to kill me too. Varus, you'll be docked a month's pay for your wife's keep on the voyage south. And you can't have her in camp, so find her some place in the village or leave her on the farm." He turned to Eirian. "You go find the old man and bring him to me. No doubt he'll be happy if he's paid a bride price. Varus, you're docked for that too." He glared around him at all of them, hefted his vine staff meaningfully, and stalked into the camp as the Watch sounded the call for evening prayers.

—

"You are a fool!" Eirian told the old man, her eyes flaming. "You are lucky I did not let the Romans have you!" The Romans were everywhere, poking their noses into everything with the curiosity of otters. If they had gone looking for the old man, who knew what they might have found?

"You should have come to me," she said when he looked at her stubbornly. "It isn't your affair, you bound her out to us for the year. Now you will have to take his bride price."

"How much?" he said.

"Whatever they offer!" she snapped.

The pig girl's father was duly bought off, and there was peace for three days until Septimus brought another miscreant up before the commander. This time it was a young legionary, Bassus, newly recruited to the fourth century in the spring. His centurion, after the Varus incident, had bumped him up the chain to Septimus for discipline, and Septimus to Faustus.

"What's he done?"

"We were just hunting hares," Bassus said, aggrieved.

"On the beach," Septimus said. "Where they look just like seals."

"Oh, no."

"Yes, and the whole village is up in arms. There's a delegation waiting for you there. They won't come here for fear of bad luck or something that's come back with him."

Faustus, his temper rapidly heading southward, hefted his vine staff and struck Bassus across the back, hard. "Get to quarters! I don't know what kind of restitution they may want, but you'll do it. You were told not to kill seals."

"Didn't think you meant it," Bassus muttered, teeth gritted.

"Well, now you know I did."

Faustus threw his heavy cloak over his armor – it was raining again – and strode through the puddles along the shore to the harbor quarter and then to his makeshift office. Madoc's brewery was full. He saw Faelan and Eirian, who he had learned was Faelan's daughter, and a number of village elders, including the priest. Demetrius was there too, earnestly taking notes while everyone else argued noisily.

Faustus held up his hand. "Quiet!"

They glared at him.

"I understand that one of my men has done something to offend you."

They began to shout at him all at the same time, and the priest Catumanus stumped forward to hold up his own hand. Him they obeyed. "They have brought ill fortune on us," he said to Faustus. He wore a leather apron over shirt and breeches and the smuts on his face said he had come straight from the forge. He looked both less priestly and more powerful than other priests that Faustus had seen, except perhaps for the holy mother on Mona.

"They?" Faustus asked.

"Just one, but there were two more with him."

"I see. And what penance may be made for this?"

"You would impose that?" the priest asked.

"Anything short of death, yes. He knew better."

"Then strip him and leave him on the beach for the seals. If they do not take him, he may return at dawn."

That might be only marginally short of death. A fully grown seal was capable of killing an unarmed naked man, and of outrunning him on the sand. Faustus thought hard. He had warned them. The whole winter's success might turn on this. "Very well," he said.

–

Eirian watched the man being marched down to the shore, not quite to the seal rocks but close enough for the seals to see and smell him. Only once before had she seen someone left for the seals. Ordinarily it was considered that the man who killed a seal would bear the ill luck alone. It was only when a man had done something wicked besides that the others feared the luck might be contagious. This time it was because he was Roman, an interloper, who might bring the gods knew what in his tainted wake.

It was cold and the wind that nearly always blew across the island whipped over the sand, carrying a spitting rain with it. She could see the man shivering, curling himself into a ball on the shore. The tide was coming in. It would drive him farther up the beach as the night wore on, leaving him standing in waist-high water before dawn.

They left him there, with two of his fellows sitting higher up the shore on watch. They were weaponless, there not to save him if the seals came for him but to see that he didn't run.

The commander had surprised her. She had not thought he would be willing to offer up one of his own that way. The seals had come for the other man she had seen left for them. She thought maybe he hadn't known that.

The Romans were a disruption, an ill wind in themselves, she thought, marching lordlywise along the roads and seducing pig girls. What would happen if they had found the man her father had hidden? Perhaps it was foolish to have thought they might stumble on him hunting for the pig girl's father. But when you knew a thing like that, you couldn't rest easy and nor could you ask questions, not even of Father, who had after all taken the Romans' gifts. He had taken to pouring his beer from the silver ewer, and the glass cups sat on a shelf where no one was allowed to touch them.

—

Despite his anger, Faustus found it difficult to sleep. Being eaten by seals was a grisly fate and an image all too easily imagined. He was awake before first light and woke the junior surgeon assigned to the cohort. He found Septimus waiting for them at the gate.

"He's still there," Septimus said. "Presumably alive."

"All right, let's get him." It was important that the cohort see that their commander, who had condemned him, was also the one to come for him.

The tide had gone out again and they found Bassus on the cold sand, freezing to the touch and shivering uncontrollably. The surgeon wrapped him in blankets and ordered the two watchers to carry him. "If he doesn't succumb to an ague he'll survive."

"The seals came," Septimus said. "I went out with a lantern just at high tide. He was backed against the cliff and they were in the water in a circle around him. If he's gibbering mad now, that will be why."

Faustus eyed the seal rocks, which were empty now. "And they just went away again?"

"Something called to them, or I thought so. They stuck their heads up out of the water like they were listening and then they dove and swam off."

"Mithras, what a country. The isolation is getting to you," Faustus said, although here on the northern edge of the world he didn't find it entirely unbelievable.

–

His guide appeared the following day. Faustus was surprised to find that it was the girl Eirian, and when she saw his expression she informed him briskly that she could handle a boat as well as any of the island men and better than he, so he asked no questions. He took Paullus and Demetrius and ten of the first century and left Septimus in charge of the camp.

"No girls," he told Septimus. "No seals. Is there anything else I should be forbidding?"

Septimus considered. "I have no doubt they will think of it."

"See that they don't."

They set out at first on horseback, to ride north across the wild emptiness of High Isle. Eirian, in shirt and breeches and mounted on one of the shaggy little island ponies, observed Faustus and his entourage with amusement. Demetrius had hired a mount in the village and rode beside Paullus with Pandora trotting at their heels. "Your slave rides while your men walk?" she asked Faustus, laughing. Such an affront to their dignity would have stirred a furious protest in free men of the Orcades.

"They are trained to march," Faustus said, "and make bad cavalrymen. You put an infantryman on a horse at your peril."

Eirian tucked that information away as possibly useful. Any information was useful. Her father had made that clear, and also, obliquely, why he had chosen her.

"Stay away from the Calf," he had said as they were setting out. "That place is holy and not to be polluted by foreigners."

There were any number of holy islands, sacred for the springs and small lakes where the gods of the Orcades made their homes. Eirian had been to the one called the Calf with her aunts and Catumanus when she was thirteen and her blood began, to make her respects to the Goddess at the spring. It was a lonely windswept place but no more holy than the others that he had not warned her away from. She tucked that bit of knowledge away too.

"Why did you send your man to the seals?" Eirian asked Faustus now as they rode. "You could have let him do as he pleased and it would have angered the village but there would have been little we could do against it."

"Except perhaps to make us look forever over our shoulders," Faustus said, "which is not Rome's wish. When Rome has promised peace, we keep our word." *Mostly*, he admitted to himself. "To let our soldiers do as they please is bad for discipline and dishonors Rome."

"What if the seals had taken him?" she asked.

Faustus hesitated. That had been a risk. "It would have been bad," he admitted. "I am the commander. I could have kept them from retaliation but it would have soured matters between the cohort and the village, and the cohort and myself. I took a chance."

So he was such a one as would risk something to keep his word. Still, it was as well that the man had lived. She took a good look at the commander now, with his helmet slung by its strap from his saddle. He had a fine-boned face, clean-shaven, and a cap of short dark hair. He wore the same iron plates that his men did, over a scarlet tunic and tight breeches that met his leather boots at the knee. His cloak was scarlet too, as was the crosswise crest on his helmet. The color of fresh blood. She thought of the fleeting image she had seen in the trader's mirror, four years ago. When Demetrius pointed across the water at the Calf rising humpbacked from the sea, she said abruptly that it was nothing, deserted, and distracted him with a barrow grave rising like a mirror image inland.

They skirted the coast until, before dusk, she turned them westward. "Tomorrow we will cross to Great Island," she told Faustus and Demetrius. "And tonight I will show you the Stone Ship."

They followed her through a steep-sided valley, a nearly treeless landscape where the wind blew constantly, until they came to an ancient tomb rising like a great vessel frozen in mid-voyage across the desolate peat. Cut from a single rock thirty feet long, the entrance was closed with a block taller than a man. The Roman soldiers made the sign of horns and stood well back from it.

Demetrius walked around all four sides, making notes. "Most unusual. Extraordinary. Ordinarily these are built up from smaller stones and covered with earth. This is cut into a single great stone. Oh, marvelous." He circled it again and pushed at the block that sealed the entrance.

"Demetrius…" Faustus said.

"Catumanus tried once, he told me, but it does not budge," Eirian said. "Likely it is only bones now, but if it wouldn't let Catumanus in, Demetrius should not."

"There's more than bones in a place like that," one of the men muttered.

"Who built it?" Faustus asked.

"Maybe the Old Ones," Eirian said. "The little dark people who were here before us."

322

"I've met them," Faustus said. "Are they here in the islands too?"

"Oh, yes. They say it was not them. Sometimes they say it was their ancestors. Long ago when they were kings in the land."

"In any case, you have made Demetrius very happy," Faustus said. "This is a prize addition to his studies."

"Catumanus said that I would like him," Eirian said. "I find that I do. He is not a soldier, is he?"

"No, he is a scholar, a man whose job it is to study things and think about them."

"Among us, that is the job of priests," Eirian said, while Demetrius took measurements of the tomb with a string. "What do your priests do then?"

"They read the omens," Faustus said.

"Like the Druids," Eirian said.

"You do not have Druids here?"

"No," Eirian said. "They speak to the Sun Lord. Our gods are born of the water."

They camped for the night at some distance from the tomb, their escort having protested forcibly at sleeping near it. A little stream ran down the valley, musty with peat but drinkable, and they saw deer tracks in the boggy ground. There was enough dry scrub to coax a fire to flower in the lee of the tents, and the small deer that Paullus and Pandora tracked supplemented provisions of bread, dried meat and military grade wine. When Pandora had gnawed the carcass to her satisfaction, Faustus thought to drag it away so as not to attract wolves, until Eirian said there were none.

It was a strange place, Faustus thought, devoid of most threats other than man. They lingered by the little fire, cloak-wrapped, as the stars came out to wash across the sky. Eirian sat cross-legged beside him and Pandora came and laid a greasy muzzle across her legs. Eirian scratched her head.

"You study us like curiosities at a fair," she observed. "Who studies you? Demetrius has written down all our old tales. Tell me yours."

"I will tell you a story," Faustus said, before Demetrius could begin on the complete works of Euripides. "I will tell you about the founding of Rome, over eight hundred years ago." A tale no doubt as fabulous as those of Catumanus, but no matter. "It begins with twin babies named Romulus and Remus. And because they were the grandsons of the king's brother, from whom this king had stolen his throne, they were ordered left on the bank of the Tiber to die. The Tiber is the great river that flows through the City and its god is Tiberinus, Father of the River. Tiberinus rescued the twins and had them nursed by a she-wolf, who is the patroness of Rome to this day. There is a great statue of her in the Forum. Then they were adopted by a shepherd named Faustulus, which is very like my own name, because my father was a traditionalist. They were raised as shepherd boys until their true identity became known."

"What happened then?" Eirian asked.

"They put their grandfather back on the throne, with fatal results for his brother, and founded their own city on the banks of the Tiber where the god had rescued them as infants."

Eirian considered that and spotted the obvious discrepancy. "Why is Rome named for only one of them?"

"Well, then it got awkward." Faustus poked up the fire. "They got into a fight over where to build their city and Romulus killed Remus."

"Kingship has always been bought thus," Eirian said. "It is why we have no kings in these days. A king brings more ill luck than fair. No wonder your people are constantly at war."

"There was a time after that that we had no kings," Faustus told her. "Only the Senate to govern the City. Now we have emperors."

"That is the same thing," Eirian said.

"Not exactly." Faustus supposed it was but the Principate was notoriously sensitive about it. There was an elaborate pretense at the emperor being elected.

"Our last king went away to the Old Ones when he grew old, and he left no heir," Eirian said. "And so no one ever set a king on the throne afterward when they saw how well they got on without one."

"When we came to these islands last there was a king," Faustus protested. "He met with Claudius Caesar's envoys."

"That was a village elder," Eirian said. "Ask Catumanus. They chose him to represent the islands and tell the Roman envoy what he wished to hear so he would go away again."

Faustus laughed. He found that entirely too possible. He suspected that they were simply waiting for him to go away again too.

Nevertheless, in the morning when they came to the coast and the great inner harbor that the islanders called the Bowl, he could not help noting how well such a harbor might accommodate the Fleet.

XIX

Solstice Night

Winter

Apparently he was not going to die. Miraculously he found now that he did not want to. The angry tangle of scar tissue that was his right shoulder made the arm almost immovable. He could pick things up – his fingers worked – but not reach above his waist nor behind his back. He took the staff that had been brought him at his insistence and swung it with his left hand – up, out, across, block, all the movements he had learned as a boy from a long-dead weapons master, translated to a mirror image that fought with muscle memory.

Calgacos could see the shores of larger islands from anywhere on this windswept, treeless bit of land floating in the outer rim of the Bowl. To the south was the coast of High Isle where he had bought grain to stave off hunger for one last winter until they could push the Romans back. Or so he had thought. He leaned on the staff and looked across the water. Nothing pushed the Romans back. The Old Ones said they would leave eventually when the land itself, the waters and the mountains, pushed them out. He only half believed that, when he lay wakeful at night counting the things he had no doubt done wrong, but it was no matter, if he looked the thing in the eye. He himself could not go back, not now while Emrys was trying to hold the scattered remnants of their people together and must be allowed to do so without ghosts in the council hall. Not now while Aelwen was the glue that bound his own clans to Emrys. Not now while the Romans were sending their "envoys" to these islands, and if they found him it would start a war here among the people who had taken him in.

Calgacos filled his ewer at the spring that bubbled up from the peaty ground. The hut beside the spring had been built by some long-ago priest to sit in and speak to the gods of the water. It provided shelter enough to build a fire and stay out of the wind. The men that Faelan had taken him to had rowed him to this place and left him with food, and brought him the staff and a belt knife when he asked for one. They never stayed for long. He thought they were as afraid of him as they were of the Romans. Maybe more so. He was marked now, touched by some kind of ancient bane, a maimed king in all but name who had lost the kingship but couldn't die. When the Romans went he knew he must go too. He didn't know where, but he must leave before the islanders decided to abandon him here.

–

The harbor called the Bowl was cupped in the fingers of High Isle, Great Island and a scattering of smaller islands, some only dots in the open water. Access was guarded by three sounds, all notorious for currents that could fling the unwary and unskillful against hidden shoals, Eirian told Faustus.

She brought them to a small farm that hugged the coast, with fishing boats tied up at a jetty, and negotiated for one of these and permission for eight of their escort to make camp along the shore for two nights with Paullus and the horses.

"I'll not take you to every village on the islands like a traveling fair," Eirian said. "We won't be welcome at some. Nor will I trust your men away from your sight for long. If you want more than this you must hire a boat yourself. Agreed?"

"Agreed." Poking their nose into too many isolated settlements was probably a misguided idea. Demetrius and diplomacy would have to settle for this much.

The two legionaries chosen to accompany them suggested they draw lots for the assignment. Like most of the legions, they couldn't swim and they disliked boats, and in particular small boats. Faustus refused to reconsider and with mournful expressions they climbed aboard.

With a skill that impressed Faustus as much as it unnerved him she took them across the windy waters of the Bowl and up a smaller bay to a beach where a village sat on the headland of Great Island. This too was stone-built, with thatched roofs topping round towers of two and sometimes three stories. Faustus assumed there to have been considerable communication between High Isle and the rest of the archipelago because they were plainly expected, if not entirely welcome. Eirian spoke quietly to an elder of the village and then presented them as "the ambassadors of Rome". Faustus was aware of how alien they must look to the villagers gathered warily to stare at them. People from another world across the sea. Merchants from the Mediterranean had had some trade with the islands since before Claudius Caesar's time but it was dubious whether anyone north of the Bowl had ever seen an actual Roman. Eirian negotiated for quarters in the village council hall, and Faustus presented the old man with a hearth gift of a gold spice box. It was obvious that it was hoped that they would be gone by morning.

The next day Eirian cut the expedition short. "There is bad weather coming. I want to be back across the Bowl before it does or we may be here for days."

It began to blow harder and to rain when they were halfway back, proving her right. The sky darkened and jagged forks of lightning shot down from it to the water.

"Get down!" Eirian snapped to Demetrius and the terrified legionaries. "Centurion! Help me get the sail down." She put the end of a rope in his hand. "Take this and pull when I tell you!"

The boat was taking on water, sloshing around their ankles. Eirian gave Demetrius a wooden scoop and he began to bail frantically. She shouted orders to Faustus which he obeyed with alacrity, pulling on the ropes, staggering against the waves that rolled the boat from side to side while Eirian wrestled, cursing, with the sail and the steering oar. The waves lifted the boat and dropped it again with tooth-jarring force while the wind roared and the waters of the Bowl roared back.

"Take the oars!" Eirian shouted over the storm at Faustus as the sail came down.

He found the oars and lifted one into the oarlock. He had done a day's training six years ago on calm water, to know what it was like in case he ever commanded marines, he had been told. He struggled with the oar in the heaving sea and bellowed at his men, "Brocchus! Can you handle an oar?" He hoped so. The other, Priscus, was vomiting into the seawater under the oar bench.

Brocchus got up and took the second oar. "My father had a fishing boat," he shouted between ragged strokes. "I joined the army so I wouldn't have to row the cursed thing."

Eirian kept the bow angled into the waves as much as possible, hauling on the steering oar against the boat's determination to turn broadside and swamp. Her hair had come loose from its plait and was plastered against her face in the driving rain and she had shed her cloak to free her arms. She looked to Faustus like one of the old sea gods of the islanders' worship. He hoped she had some of their powers.

They struggled through the howling wind, teeth clenched, wrestling with unwieldy and unfamiliar oars, guided by the tenuous control of the steering oar, and came to the coast of High Isle, almost invisible in the rain, as the storm howled itself into a frenzy.

Eirian ran the boat onto the shore without risking battering it against the dock. Faustus, leaning over the side and gasping as the rain pelted down, muttered a thank you to Neptune Seafather, although it was unclear to him whether the god had been trying to save him or drown him.

Paullus and the escort left behind came down to meet them and helped drag the boat up the shore where the rest of the farm's craft were already secured against the storm.

Faustus declared the expedition at an end. He could tell the governor that he had negotiated with the villagers of the Great Island, and report first-hand on the possibilities of using the Bowl as anchorage for a fleet assigned to garrison the islands. Demetrius too, dripping and white-faced, would have a tale to tell and seemed eager now not to venture out onto the water again.

The farmwife took pity on them and let them all come into the dairy. Paullus made a fire and they concocted a stew of dried meat and foraged greens and a hare that Pandora had caught earlier in the day.

Eirian cast a sideways look at Faustus. His dark hair was still dripping with the rain but the energy that had filled him as he fought the storm with her had stilled.

Faustus caught her watching him. "Is it always like this? To go from calm to storm so quickly?" He yawned. The warmth and the stew and the last of the wine were making him sleepy, relieved just to be on land.

"Often enough," she said. "Are you worried for your great warships?"

"If they are caught in something like this unawares, yes. But I was thinking that it is like some other world here, not just the storm, but the feeling that everything shifts when I am not watching it. I'm sorry, that doesn't make much sense." He had had the feeling all day, before they had even left Great Island, that they were sailing into some place other than the one they had left.

"The islands are like that," Eirian said. "There was a great battle fought near here, in the long ago, maybe by the Old Ones against our people, I don't know. But there was a woman on one side who was a priestess of the Mother and who called on her when all her people's warriors lay dying, to bring them back to life. The Mother did so, but the other side as well because there is a price for everything. And so they fought the battle again and died once more. But when the sun rose the next day they came alive again to fight. And they fight it still, every day, and die each night."

"Have you seen them?" Paullus asked.

"No, and nor do I want to," Eirian said. "And it may be only a tale." She looked at Faustus. "Now you tell me one."

It was warm and homely around the fire and the chill was beginning to leave his bones. The farmwife's cheeses were arrayed on shelves above her worktable and milk crocks caught the glint of firelight. A barn cat inspected them for drips and then settled itself on the shelf among the cheeses, out of Pandora's reach.

The rain was a steady pounding on the thatch now. "I'll tell you the story of how winter came," Faustus said. "And why it goes away again."

"Because the sun moves to the south and then moves back," Eirian said.

"That's the boring version. It all started because a man – a god – wanted a woman and didn't wait to be asked."

"That is not new either," Eirian said.

"The girl was named Proserpina," Faustus said, ignoring that. "Her mother was Ceres, the goddess of all growing things. It was always spring and summer in the world then, and the god of the Underworld, Pluto, saw Proserpina picking flowers in a meadow one day and wanted her, so he drove out with his black stallions hitched to his black chariot and carried her off to his black palace in the Underworld. Her mother was furious and went to the great god Jupiter to intervene. Jupiter wouldn't do anything so Ceres clothed the world in ice and said that it would stay that way until she had her daughter back."

Eirian looked at him approvingly. "Then what happened?"

"All the people began petitioning Jupiter to help them because there were no crops growing and they were starving.

And in the Underworld, Proserpina refused to eat, to spite Pluto."

"Wise," Eirian said. "If you eat in someone's house you braid a tie between you."

"Exactly. But finally she got so hungry that she ate six pomegranate seeds."

"What are those?"

"Tiny little red seeds from a fruit that grows in the east. Very pretty but there isn't much to them. But that was enough. When Jupiter finally had had enough of people petitioning him and Ceres badgering him, he sent a messenger to the Underworld to fetch Proserpina back. But because she had eaten those six seeds, he ruled that she must go back to Pluto for six months of the year, and live with her mother on the upper surface the other six. So we have winter while Proserpina is underground because Ceres is still angry."

"I like that story," Eirian said. "What does Pluto do in the summer when she's gone?"

"Sulks, I suppose," Faustus said. "He has a terrible three-headed dog named Cerberus. Maybe they walk along the River Styx together and bite people." He almost said *I'll ask my father* and thought better of it, although Paullus looked like he was thinking the same thing. He hadn't seen his father's shade since before the great battle, and he thought that if he were to appear anywhere it would be on these islands that were already half in another world. And that Eirian might be among the people who would not think he was mad if he told her.

"We will leave for home when the weather clears," Eirian said.

Faustus, for some reason, now felt wistfully reluctant. It would be pleasant, he thought vaguely, growing sleepier, to stay and live in this dairy with Eirian and Pandora and a cat. And Paullus, although Paullus was looking at him uneasily.

"What will you do among us until your ships can sail again?" Eirian asked, startling him awake.

"Try to keep my men out of trouble," Faustus said, unnerved now. "We'll have parade drills and other exercises to keep them sharp and remind them they are Romans and not bog trolls. Would you like to come and watch?" he asked impulsively. "They are quite impressive."

"I would." She smiled at him. "Thank you."

Septimus reported on their return that nothing untoward had happened in his absence, but the men were restless with the twitchy boredom that winter quarters engendered. Faustus decreed an exhibition drill of the sort staged for visiting dignitaries. The preparations would keep them busy for a while, and he put up a prize of some good wine he had been hoarding for the officers' use to award the century with the best performance. He would invite the whole village and surrounding farms to come and watch because, certainly, he was not showing off merely for Eirian.

The weather obliged with a sunny day and the village trooped through the camp gates with curiosity rather than fear. He saw Faelan and his sons, and Catumanus. He had done the right thing about the seals, Faustus thought, and Bassus had recovered, to his relief.

Faustus had ordered a reviewing stand built and seats enough for the village audience and there was a festival atmosphere. On impulse he invited Eirian up on the reviewing stand. Surely that was appropriate for someone who had been their guide and saved them all from drowning. She was dressed in what Faustus took to be her best, a blue woolen gown the color of seawater, black boots and a brown cloak fastened with a gold pin. She wore gold drops in her ears and like many British women a leather belt at her waist, carved and colored with fanciful animal shapes, sinuous as water. A serviceable dagger hung from it along with a ring of keys.

The cohort formed up before the reviewing stand and saluted to the sound of trumpets. "They are very fine," Eirian whispered. They were resplendent in newly polished armor, shields uncovered, and crimson parade crests affixed to their helmets. The trumpets sounded again and they formed a square, a flanking formation, double and triple lines, and flowed back into a square again. "Is this how you fight?" she asked Faustus. "In lines and squares?"

"Not entirely," Faustus said. "This is how we train to fight so that when it comes to battle, no man loses his place and the line keeps in formation."

Eirian was silent as the square divided, opened into a crescent and came together again in a "pig's head" wedge. "I am thinking," she said at last, "that the Caledones did not understand this."

"No," Faustus said. "The legions like this one were never even called into the line. The auxiliaries won the battle before the regular legions were needed."

"You did not fight in it?" Eirian asked.

"I did," Faustus said. He touched the *corona aurea* that hung across his parade cuirass. "I was a commander of auxiliaries then. Officers move about, you see, if we get promoted."

The exhibition finished with a trumpet fanfare and a final salute to the commander, and Faustus helped Eirian down from the reviewing stand. The villagers gathered around for a closer look, curiously inspecting the cohort and century standards, the shields freshly painted with the winged lightning and Capricorn badge of the Second Augusta.

Eirian's brothers passed them in the crowd and one of them muttered under his breath as they went by. "Have you looked at her fingers, man?" The other brother snickered.

Eirian flew at him and gripped his shirt with both fists. She stood on her toes to put her face into his. "Mind your tongue, Boduoc, or I will see to it for you!"

"Aye, Boduoc," the other brother said, laughing. "Best you keep off the shore or they'll come for you."

"And you, Eogan!" Eirian let Boduoc go and spun around. "You are not funny!" She hit him hard on the ear with her fist and Eogan staggered and shoved her away. They walked off laughing.

Eirian stood, fists still clenched, squeezing her eyelids shut to stop furious tears.

"What was that?" Faustus asked her.

A small knot of people had stopped to stare at them. "Boduoc thinks he is funny," Eirian said between her teeth. "Come away before I go after him with a knife."

She stalked through the camp gates, pushing into the crowd clogging them, and Faustus followed. She took the path that led out of the village toward the sea cliffs, wordless and fuming. Faustus thought she looked like a kettle on the boil that would scald any careless hand. When she sat down at the top of the cliff, he sat beside her.

She was silent a long while. Finally, she said, "My mother came from the water, so the village thinks, and went back to it again the year after I was born."

From the water? "What does your father say?" Faustus asked her.

"My father does not say." She spread her fingers out on the rock beside him. "Seal children are supposed to have webbed hands. That was what Boduoc meant."

"I don't see any." They were strong, long-fingered hands. He had watched them yanking on the rigging in the storm.

"No. Boduoc just likes to remind me that I don't belong. He's angry because Father sent me with you instead of one of them."

"I'm glad he did," Faustus said tentatively. It was hard to know what to think. Here in the sunlight on the sea cliffs the stories of seal women seemed far-fetched, nursery tales to entertain children. "What do you think about it?" he asked.

"I don't know. My brothers weren't old enough to really remember her, no matter what they claim. And Father won't say, but like as not that's because she left him. Mostly I think she was some seafarer's woman who sickened of the water and came ashore and found she didn't like it. Or didn't like my father. A woman needn't be a selkie to want to leave my father."

"Who else is there to ask?"

"She kept to the farm while she was here. Catumanus saw her once. He says it doesn't matter. The seals won't say either."

"The seals?"

"Anyone can listen to the seals," Eirian said, as if she had tried to explain this many times before. "Sometimes I know what they're saying. It's just a matter of listening."

Faustus thought that sounded unlikely. That it was a matter of listening, and that she could understand them, both. On the other hand, Septimus had said it sounded as if someone had called to the seals in the water and drawn them off Bassus. The hair on the back of his neck rose just a little, but Eirian was sitting solidly landbound in the sun on the edge of the cliff, carelessly swinging her feet above the jagged rocks below in a way that was more reminiscent of goats than seals.

"Is it only the females who can change their skins for human?" he asked her, curious now.

"Males too," Eirian said. "But selkie men don't bide. They will give a woman a babe and leave."

"The unearthly are known for siring babes on mortal women and taking their leave," Faustus said, smiling. "I expect it's often a better tale to tell her father than that it was a handsome tinker who passed that way. There was a girl on our farm who said the father was Jupiter. I don't suppose it matters."

"It matters to the child," Eirian said. "This is my home and I never quite belong to it. Or to the water." She watched a flurry of gulls pecking at the leavings of the tide below them. "At least my mother had a place to go back to."

Faustus thought of a sleek woman with the look of Eirian about her, rooting through the rafters of their house, prying open trunks, finally lifting out the skin. Putting it around her shoulders, transforming. Would his own mother have done that if she could? Would she have left him and Marcus and Silvia, swum back to the Sabrina? He imagined her that way, dark hair as slick as seaweed. Fanciful that, but the thought of a selkie woman trapped in a landward house hit a bit too close to home.

"My mother was Silure," he said abruptly. "From the south of Britain. My father bought her in a Gaulish slave market."

"Does it trouble you, to fight against her people?" Eirian asked him.

"She was Roman in all but blood by the time I was born. My father freed her and married her."

"And she never wanted to go back?"

Faustus was silent now. He had never thought she did. Never thought of it at all. "I was sent to Britain because I speak her language," he said. He knew it wasn't an answer.

"Did it feel like home in some fashion then, to come to Britain?"

"My home is the army. Britain is – I don't know. There is a piece of me in the Silure Hills, certainly. Even a bit of the little dark people's blood, or at least the Old One at Llanmelin said there was." Why had he told her that?

Eirian's eyes widened. "Where is Llanmelin?" she asked cautiously.

"It's an abandoned fortress of the Silures. The Old Ones don't live in it, but their place takes its name from there."

Far to the south then, Eirian thought. But the little dark people spoke to each other, one sidhe to another. Would the Old One at Llanmelin know the two who had brought the Caledone warlord across the firth? This legion's home fortress was in Silure territory, he had said so.

"What will your army do in the spring?" she asked tentatively.

"We'll leave a garrison in the forts in the new territory. Auxiliaries most likely. My legion will go back to Isca Silurum."

"We heard…" she felt her way "…that the Caledones' warlord was killed in the battle."

"So said his wife and the man who leads them now. We never found his body, and we looked, before we let the Caledones take their dead." He grimaced. "I was one of the people who knew him by sight and so I was detailed to search through the bodies. It is not an assignment I would choose again."

"Perhaps he was carried away beforehand," Eirian suggested.

"Perhaps. And perhaps there would have been a great funeral for him, and our scouts saw none."

And now, Eirian thought, the price for the islands having sat out the war was to sit on the edge of a knifeblade waiting for the Romans to come looking there.

"I must go back," Eirian said abruptly. "I am sorry for my brothers' behavior. They are pigs." She stood, pulling her cloak around her.

"They are. I should go back too or my optio will be wondering if I have fallen in the sea. Please don't let your brothers spoil our acquaintance."

"No. I like you better than I like them."

"I would be flattered," Faustus said, "if they were not so dreadful. That's like being better than rats, or a fever."

Eirian laughed and they walked companionably back down the path in the rapidly falling dusk. She turned off toward her farm before they reached the village and wished him a pleasant evening. But something about Calgacos had made her wary.

—

He didn't have time to wonder about it further because the Fleet ships came into harbor as he was walking home, bringing more bored men to pack into a winter camp. And then his father, whose ability to appear when Faustus was up to his helmet crest in other matters, came to sit on his bed.

"She wasn't a seal," the shade said.

"She might as well have been. Did you ever ask her if she wanted to go home?"

"Of course not." Faustus thought his father's translucent face was uncomfortable. "The farm was her home."

"What does Pluto do in the summer while his wife's gone?" Faustus asked on impulse.

His father looked irritated. "Is that a joke?"

"I thought you would know."

"The Otherworld isn't what you think. And I gave your mother a better life than she would have had in some wattle-and-mud house in Britain. She had slaves and good clothes and I bought her a piece of gold jewelry every year at Saturnalia."

"What woman could resist?" Faustus murmured.

"Most women would think themselves lucky," his father said. "You are disrespectful."

"And you are imaginary."

"Don't make the mistake I did." The shade vanished.

Faustus sat trying to decipher that until he heard the Watch call midnight. He buried his head in the blankets and willed himself to sleep.

–

The Fleet anchored in the harbor overnight and the next day they built a boat shed of cut turf, stone and sail canvas. The ships were hauled out of the water on rollers and propped up under its roof. The crews began scraping the hulls while Rutilius, the squadron commander, inspected them for damage. Once repairs had been made they would be left to dry out before they were recoated with wax and pitch.

"How was the voyage?" Faustus asked him. "I began to worry about you with the last storm." It was raining again, steadily, and difficult to see where the water ended and the sky began.

"Afraid you'd have to swim home?" Rutilius grinned. "I worried about us too. Nastiest set of currents I ever sailed through. We sighted some more islands that lie north of these that must be Thule that your scholar spoke of, so that should

339

please the governor. We just sighted the coast, mind you, and went ashore for a day. No one looked pleased to see us so we upped anchor with some speed. Then we skirted the western coast to within sight of Hibernia before we turned back. Have you tamed the locals yet?"

"They are not entirely eating from my hand," Faustus said. "But we have made a beginning. It's precarious, anything could overset it, so keep your men on a short leash. I've already had to make amends for one who killed a seal. They think they're half human, warn your crew."

"I never saw a people with so many superstitions," Rutilius said, "barring maybe the Germans. I served two years in the Rhenus Fleet and every boatyard was hung about with charms against elves and wights. In any case, they won't be interested in seals unless they think they can fuck them."

"I don't recommend it," Faustus said. "Or anything else in the village. I mean it. Keep them on a leash."

Rutilius took note, but it was getting harder as the winter went on to keep some seven hundred restless soldiers and sailors from trouble. Dice games erupted in fistfights, the scouts attached to Faustus's cohort and Rutilius's crew took turns trying to cheat each other at latrunculi and fleeced everyone else, who then came and complained to their commanders. Madoc threw four of Faustus's cohort out of his brewery and banned them, and punched a crewman who had fondled his wife's buttocks. Faustus increased drills and patrols; Rutilius found defects in the work done on the liburnians' hulls and ordered it done again. As Saturnalia approached they conferred on exactly how much license to allow.

At the same time the village made ready for the solstice, when the winter sun died and then rose up again to drag daylight back over the horizon. This far north darkness fell at mid-afternoon and the sun would be coaxed back with bonfires on every hilltop. Because wood was scarce, for weeks the children had been gathering armfuls of heather and peat and piling it to dry on the sea cliffs where the fire would be lit. There would be barrels of Madoc's beer and roast mutton.

Faustus debated trying to keep the celebrations separate. On the other hand, Rutilius argued, there would be a certain amount of goodwill generated by observing the native holiday. Faustus settled on ordering up a substantial Saturnalia feast for the camp and assigning the first century, who were under his direct command, to keep order, with the promise of a month's release from latrine duty if they stayed sober.

The solstice fell on the last of the five days of Saturnalia. The cohort had behaved itself insofar as anyone behaved at Saturnalia, but had not misbehaved in the village. Thus they were allowed to visit the bonfire on the promise of continued rectitude. Rutilius too let his crews loose for the festival, to Faustus's unease. The Fleet men were less well disciplined, or at any rate Rutilius's standards differed from Faustus's. Faustus sought him out before the fires were lit to remind him that this was a diplomatic mission. The Fleet crews were getting daily more free with the village women. It didn't help that some of the women were willing to sell their services. A man who was full of Madoc's beer was less likely to distinguish the willing from the unwilling.

—

The night sky was ink black and clear, lit only by the sweep of the stars. The fire was a bright, warm beacon in the cold, and in the distance here and there could be seen the glow of bonfires on distant farms and the small islands scattered off High Isle. On the Calf, Calgacos saw them ringing the Bowl and knew that it must be the solstice, the longest night of the year, and yearned toward those fires, toward the gathering of humans about them singing to call the sun back to the sky, soaking up the warmth of the fire and of each other against the dark and cold.

On High Isle, Faustus watched cautiously as the village gathered about the flames, muffled in hooded cloaks and fur boots, drinking beer from Madoc's barrels. The air was full of the smell of roasting meat from the spits set above smaller fires in pits to either side of the great one. Catumanus had said the prayers that would bring the sun back to the northern skies and an offering had been made to what Faustus took to be Lugh Bright Spear's northern incarnation, who lived in the waters to the east of the island. Now the village turned to celebration, shaking off the dark of winter in the firelight, token of spring to come.

A trio of men from the Fleet crews, distinguished from the cohort soldiers by their blue naval tunics, stumbled through the crowd shouting for someone unseen and staggering nearly into the fire. When one grabbed a woman by the breasts, Faustus's watch commander caught his shoulders and threw him against his fellows. He got to his feet and was about to launch himself at the watch commander when a Fleet centurion stepped in and stuck his vine staff in the sailor's face. The watch commander backed off.

Faustus saw Rutilius in the crowd and observed with some relief that he was taking note. Faustus was disinclined to discipline Rutilius's men as long as Rutilius or his officers did it. His cohort, with the example of Bassus, had confined themselves to minor mischief so far, knowing that their commander would enforce his restrictions in ways that no one would like. The Fleet crews were plainly used to more license.

Faustus saw Eirian standing on the edge of the crowd, alone, watching the flames. He took a cup of beer and went to stand beside her.

She looked up at him from the fox-fur ruff of her hood, eyes reflecting the flames like little gold dots on seawater. "Are you enjoying yourself, Centurion?"

"You might call me Faustus. I have dealt with enough people tonight who call me Centurion."

"When being ordered back to their camp for being drunk and singing rude songs?" Eirian asked.

"I really did hope no one had enough Latin to follow that one," Faustus said.

"Unfortunately all the Latin I have learned has come from your soldiers," Eirian said, "and so I knew a number of the words. They will have a fat head in the morning from Madoc's beer, though."

"They will. If that is the worst they get up to I'll consider it sufficient punishment."

"These new ones will make trouble soon," Eirian said, watching the Fleet centurion and his drunken charges. "They walk through the market lordlywise and order people about and don't pay for half of what they take."

Faustus gritted his teeth. He would have to make certain things clear to Rutilius, who technically outranked him.

"When do you sail south again?" Eirian asked.

No wonder she wants to get rid of us, Faustus thought. "In three months, more or less, depending on weather."

"Will you remember us?"

"Of course," he said, startled. The fire was warm on their faces. She turned a little toward him, and its light made an aureole of the fox fur around her face. "I will remember you," he said, smiling, "especially." He fished in the pouch at his waist. It had been an impulse, buying the little carved dog from his cohort surgeon who made a hobby of whittling small creatures. It was as long as his thumb, lying regally, head up like a sphinx, but it wore a comically expectant look. "We have a habit at Saturnalia of giving small things like this to friends," he said to Eirian, balancing the dog on his palm. "This one reminded me of Pandora, who likes you, so I thought I would give it to you."

She took it and examined it in the firelight, smiling. "Thank you, Faustus." She tucked it in the leather pouch that hung from her belt. "I wish I had something to give you."

"You could tell me a story," he suggested. "We could walk a bit."

"All right."

And why had he done that? he thought as they walked up the path along the sea cliffs. This was dangerous. He wasn't Tribune Lartius having a provincial fling.

"I will tell you about the Great Selkie," Eirian said, "who lives in the waters off the western islands and the time he came ashore." She halted where they had sat on the sea cliffs after the parade drill, and he spread his cloak out on the cold stone.

"You will freeze without that," she said as they sat down on it. "Here." She put her own cloak about them both and they sat looking out onto the dark waters of the firth and the tide rolling in.

For a mad moment he wanted to put his arm around her, but the steel plates of his lorica reminded him what a bad idea that would be.

"This happened long ago," Eirian said, "as all stories do. There was a woman who lived on the cliffs above the sea on an island to the west. One day, as she was walking on the shore a man came out of the waves. He was very beautiful, more beautiful than any man she had ever seen, and she lay with him in one of the sea caves. They stayed there from one full moon to the next and he brought her gifts of shells and stones polished by the seafoam and bits of gold jewelry from shipwrecks under the waves."

Sounds of merrymaking and song drifted toward them from the bonfire. Septimus and the Watch had things in hand. "Then what happened?" he asked.

"One day," Eirian said, "he went back to the sea. She saw him change as he slipped into the breakers and when she looked again there was only a great seal far out in the water. It looked back toward shore and then dove under the waves. Not much later she found that she was with child. The baby was a boy and every autumn at the time when his father had come ashore she went to the sea and called for him, taking the child with her. But no one came. Then when the child was seven she took him as she always had to walk along the shore. She heard the

344

seals crying far out in the water and as she watched, the child became a young seal and slipped from her into the waves where she could see his father waiting. She called to them both but there was no answer. This was long ago, but people still see her each autumn when she goes down to the sea and the sea caves, crying for them. Only the seals cry back."

"Why did you choose that story to tell me?" Faustus asked.

"I don't know. It came into my head that if I was indeed a selkie, you might be one too, coming in the autumn and going again in spring. A stupid fancy, no more than that. We tell these tales to explain the things in the heart that have no explanation."

They sat for a long while on the cliff top, silent, and then Faustus heard Septimus shout his name. The songs and laughter changed to angry voices. He stood, unwrapping them from Eirian's cloak. "That doesn't sound good." He set off at a trot, with Eirian running behind him.

XX

Eirian

A woman was shouting furiously at Septimus, while Rutilius stood watching, apparently amused. "You must slow down," Septimus said helplessly. "I cannot understand you."

"What is the matter?" Faustus demanded.

"My daughter!" the woman screamed, turning to him. "My *daughter! My Adaryn!*" A girl who looked to be about ten clung to her skirts.

"What is it, child?" Faustus bent down to her.

"Not her, it's her sister," Septimus said. "I think she's gone off with one of his crew." He jerked a thumb at Rutilius.

"She went to dance," the woman said, "and he took her away. Cari saw them."

"He told me not to tell," the girl whispered. She started to cry. "She didn't want to go. He said he would come back and kill me if I told."

Faustus turned to Rutilius. "This is what I warned you of!"

Rutilius looked unconcerned. "They'll come back when they're finished." He looked around him. "There's a lot of that going on tonight."

"Not with an unwilling girl!" Faustus snapped. "I want them back now!"

"Then find them," Rutilius said.

Faustus turned to Septimus. "Go find me Paullus and tell him to bring Pandora and a lantern." To the mother, in her own tongue, "Have you anything of hers with her scent on it?"

"Her cloak. She gave it to me to hold while she danced."

"That is *my* man!" Rutilius said. "You are not going to hunt him down with dogs. He'll come back and I'll speak to him."

"I'll speak to him now," Faustus said, "before he hurts that girl."

"He is my man and I outrank you!" Rutilius said.

"I outrank you on shore," Faustus informed him. He was fairly sure he did.

"Look you, Valerianus, it's just a girl. My men have need for amusement after a hard season at sea."

Paullus appeared with Pandora, and Faustus said to Rutilius, "This is my camp and I command here." He didn't wait for Rutilius's answer. He took the cloak from Adaryn's mother. "Which direction did they go?" he asked the child.

She pointed.

Eirian had been silent, picking out what she could understand of the talk between Faustus and the other Romans. Now she said, "I will go with you. There is bog that way and it's black dark."

"Very well." The thought of bog made him shudder. "Put a lead on her," he told Paullus, "and let her follow her nose, but don't get ahead of Eirian."

Eirian spoke to two of the High Isle men who were gathered around them and they nodded and set off toward the village at a trot.

The mother was weeping now. Rutilius was stone-faced.

"Show me where they were last," Faustus told the child, and they followed her to the far side of the fire where the village had been dancing up the sun. He held the cloak for Pandora to sniff. She had never tracked a human but she could follow a deer's scent step for step.

"Good girl," Paullus said encouragingly. "We're going hunting. Find!"

"That is *my* man!" Rutilius shouted after them again. "Mind you bring him back to me. You are not to discipline my men!"

347

"Come with us then!" Faustus shouted back, but Rutilius didn't follow.

Pandora led them away from the sea cliffs and the village, nose to the ground, onto the heath where Faustus had never ventured. Behind them he could hear the men Eirian had spoken to coming back, and see the bob and swing of their lantern. They were carrying something between them.

Faustus could smell the bog before they got to it. "This is dangerous," Eirian said. "Give her to me." She took Pandora's leash. "The rest of you stay behind us."

The ground was hummocky and wet now. No village girl would have come out here willingly. Their footsteps squelched as they walked. Eirian kept Pandora close, but let her lead. The lantern light shone on water all around them, with islands of solid ground. There was silence as they walked except for the awful burbling sounds of the bog and the night wind.

"If they've gone into this, they won't go far," Faustus said.

Eirian didn't answer. The lantern light that shone on her face showed her mouth set in a furious line.

They heard them before they saw them, wailing and shouts in the darkness, the girl's weeping and the man's angry voice.

"Hoy! Hoy!"

"Oh Mother, they're in," Eirian said. She turned to the men who were trailing them. "Hurry!"

They came forward gingerly with a coil of rope and a hurdle of willow branches between them. Paullus lifted the lantern and its light reflected off the dark, watery surface of the bog and the figures trapped in it.

"Get her out," Faustus said.

Rutilius's man lifted a frightened, angry face to them. "Help me! Get me out!"

"The girl first," Faustus said.

The girl, white-faced, held perfectly still as they laid the hurdle on the quivering surface and one of the men stretched himself out across it with the rope. Rutilius's man thrashed in the water and began to sink deeper.

348

"Hold still!" Faustus shouted at him. They might still get him out in time.

The man on the hurdle caught the girl's hands and passed the rope over her shoulders. The other man grabbed him by the ankles and together they pulled. It was the same battle that Faustus had fought for Cornutus. The quaking bog wrapped its arms around her waist and held on. Eirian edged Pandora back and gave her lead to Paullus and they watched while the men fought the bog for Adaryn.

Rutilius's man was up to his chin. His hands, covered with the slime of the bog, were raised above his head, pleading. "Get me out!"

"Be still!"

"She did this to me. Leave her and get me out!"

The bog made a horrible sucking sound and Adaryn came partway free.

"Heave!"

"We've got her! Careful now."

They edged back along the hurdle, drawing it to solid ground and pulling Adaryn to stand dripping and slime-covered on a tussock of grass.

"Lay it down again and get him out now," Faustus said, but saw with horror that Rutilius's man had sunk below the surface. Only his hands clawed at the air before they too sank from sight.

"It's too late, Centurion," one of the men said. "We'd never find him in that. If he was even alive, which he's not... not now."

"I told him it was bog," Adaryn whimpered, shaking. "He wouldn't hear me. He said be quiet and lie down or he'd kill me." She bent suddenly and vomited, beer and roast mutton and bog slime. Eirian put her arms around her. "I only wanted to dance," she wept into Eirian's shoulder. "He said to come and dance with him, and then..."

Eirian took Adaryn's cloak from Faustus and put it around the girl. One of the men made the sign of horns at the place where Rutilius's man had gone under, and then at Faustus too. "Remember which one he bade you save first," Eirian told them.

—

"Where is Tubertus?" Rutilius stood over Faustus's desk in the Principia tent, which they now shared.

Faustus was bent over a tablet, writing reports by the light of an oil lamp. His feet were still wet and he was in a foul mood. "In the bog. We couldn't get to him in time."

"*What?*"

"He stumbled into a bog in the dark, dragging the girl."

"They brought that girl back. And you *left* him?"

"I didn't leave him, he went under before we could get to him. I told him to hold still," Faustus added.

Rutilius's face was flaming with anger now. "You pulled the girl out first and let him drown? I will see that you are discharged without honor." He loomed over Faustus's desk. "And first I will have you flogged."

Faustus pushed his chair back and stood up. "You can try," he said between his teeth. "I have twice the men under me here that you have. This is a diplomatic mission and I have been sent to make overtures to these people and your man jeopardized all of that by trying to rape one of their women. *That* is going in my report to the governor."

Rutilius stood seething, fists balled, shifting from foot to foot. "Tubertus was my helmsman."

"That's unfortunate. The girl told him he was heading into the bog. I expect he wished he had listened to her, just before he went under. He got what he had coming."

Rutilius drew his fist back.

"You can fight me if you want to," Faustus said. "And make fools of both of us, brawling like schoolboys. I should like to punch you just now, so try it."

They stood glaring at each other while Septimus and Rutilius's optio watched them warily. Rutilius did not have the high ground and Faustus thought he knew it. He had not kept his men on a leash and he had not gone with Faustus to hunt Tubertus down. He had stayed at the fire, lordlywise, as Eirian called it, and then complained about the results. When Rutilius finally spun on his heel and stalked out, Faustus was almost disappointed. It would have been satisfying to beat him into a pulp. Tubertus was dead because his commander had not imposed the discipline that he should have.

In the morning Faustus walked through the village, with Paullus and Pandora rather than a military escort, making pleas-antries with everyone he met and inquiring after Adaryn. Her father was a cobbler, he had learned from Eirian, with a shop in the village, and Faustus took the last of the hearth gifts provided by the governor for softening up the local important men: a small silver mirror that he had held back because there was only one and it wouldn't do to give one man's wife a gift and not the others. Adaryn was sitting by the fire in her father's shop, wrapped in a blanket, and she looked up with a frightened face when Faustus came through the door.

"Have you taken a chill, child?" he asked gently and she nodded, her eyes wary. He knelt by her chair while her father watched. Faustus noted the hammer in his hand. "I have come to bring Rome's apologies," he told her, looking to her father as well, and her mother and small sister in the doorway that led from the family quarters.

"I didn't," she whispered. "He said I... but I didn't."

"Of course not," Faustus said. Establishing that was going to be important for her sake. Village gossip was vicious every-where. He pulled the little mirror from the pouch at his belt. "This is from the governor of Britain and from the emperor in Rome," he told her. "It is a present to say that they are sorry."

She took it and smiled a little. Her father nodded at him. Faustus gave a small inaudible sigh of relief. If Adaryn's family

351

were at peace with him it would go a long way to counter the black looks behind the polite greetings he had met in the market that morning.

"If that chill doesn't get better, I will send our doctor from the camp to see you," he told her. "If you want him, that is."

"We will see," her father said.

—

At noon Faustus called a parade to pray for the shade of Tubertus, and followed it with a furious lecture on encounters with the natives. He ordered Rutilius's men out on the field as well, and Rutilius, after some thought, complied.

"A man is dead, in a way no one of you would wish for yourselves." He paused to let them imagine the bog. "And all our efforts to befriend the people of these islands in the name of Rome have been put at risk. All because some man felt his cock was more important than the good of the Empire and the governor's orders. Let me tell you that yours are not. If anything like this occurs again, every single one of you will pay the penalty for it." He saw his cohort turn their heads just slightly out of parade stance to look at Rutilius's crew. The three centurions of the Fleet stood stiffly at attention but their faces said that they had absorbed the size of their commander's mistake, and the benefits of imposing Faustus's orders on their sailors before his infantry did. With luck, he thought, the impression he had made would linger the three months until they could sail. If not, there was likely to be outright war the next time something happened.

He dismissed them and walked back to the village, this time alone, to order supplies and make further amends where possible. In his office in the brewery he skipped the usual bargaining and paid the asking price for grain and salt fish and winter cabbages.

"That's costing you some silver to make redress," Madoc observed.

"It's not my silver," Faustus said. "I'll have six more barrels of your beer as well if you please. I'll give you a chit and they'll pay when you bring it round." The wine, even the military ration, had run out a week ago.

"I'll do that. And here's Faelan's girl to see you," Madoc said. Faustus saw Eirian sitting on a barrel.

She hopped down as Madoc went to see to the beer. "Catumanus says the bog has taken that man as a gift," she said. "He spoke to it this morning."

"To the bog?"

"Yes. The bog is alive. It has a mind, I think. Catumanus has told the village that the score is even and no one is to kill you."

"Thoughtful of him," Faustus said, unable to think of any other response.

"Catumanus also knows how many other people would die if anyone did," Eirian said frankly.

Faustus sighed. "Eirian, I know we are unwanted. We will leave as soon as the weather allows it. My men are tired of beer and sick of salt fish. They don't want to be here any more than you want us."

Eirian looked thoughtful. She had an expressive face and Faustus thought that you could watch her emotions chase themselves across it like clouds. "Not them, no. Maybe someone will miss *you*," she murmured.

"Even after everything?"

"You did your best," she said. "I remember watching your ships come up the firth and thinking that you might be monsters under all that steel, and then you were kind to our pig girl. She will sail with you, won't she?"

"If she still wishes to marry Varus."

"She's with child," Eirian said. "She'll have to." She looked wistful. At first Faustus thought she envied the pig girl her marriage, but then she said, "I should like to have sailed in one of your ships. They are very wonderful."

"I could show you one," Faustus said on impulse. "They are under the shed now for the winter." He looked out Madoc's

353

doorway. "It's getting dark and it's going to rain again, I think, or snow, but it's dry in there. Would you like to see them?"

"Oh, yes, please." She beamed at him.

The sky overhead was ashen and the early-setting sun made only a dim glow through the cloud cover. Village and farm were putting down tools, bringing cattle in, closing the shutters. Smoke drifted through roof thatch, carrying the smell of supper. Past the village the world grew darker except for the lights of the Roman camp in the distance. The Watch on its walls called out the first hour of night as the last of the sunglow faded.

The boat shed loomed up in the dark, the pale canvas of its roof catching the faint light of a full moon along its sides. The shed was open at the sea-facing end, the liburnians drawn up and settled beside each other in a row. Their hulls disappeared into the shadows overhead, propped on supports to keep them upright. The bronze rams at their prows jutted like beaks below the newly repainted eyes. Eirian gazed up at them with admiration.

"The man that the bog took, he was a helmsman?" she asked Faustus.

"Yes."

"I expect the ships know," she said. "They are like great beasts," she added. "You can almost hear them breathe."

Faustus had regarded them as transportation and loathsome transportation at that, after their adventure in the Bowl. He tried to see them with Eirian's eyes. A ladder against the side of *Victoria*'s sister ship *Concordia* indicated that Rutilius's crew was still at work on the deck and hold. "Come on," he said.

She followed him up the ladder and they wandered about the *Concordia* in the twilight that came through the open end of the shed. Eirian inspected the carved sternpost, the furled sails and the masts stepped down onto the deck, and the mechanism of the *corvus*, the spike-beaked boarding ramp that could fasten to the deck of an enemy ship. They went below to the darkness of the oar decks and the sleeping quarters, and the hold where supplies would be stored. Eirian's interest was vast and her questions mostly unanswerable by Faustus.

At the end she declared herself satisfied with the tour. "Thank you," she told him on deck again, smiling up at him in a faint shaft of moonlight. The light caught her eyes like specks of the snow that had begun to fall outside. An impulse possessed him that his brain recognized as mad and his body as overpowering, and he bent and kissed her. To his surprise she kissed him back and he flung his intent to apologize into the moonlit shadows.

When he drew his mouth away she prodded a finger at the segmented plates of his lorica. "You are like kissing a great beetle."

She watched while he unbuckled the plates and then he felt her hands exploring his back and chest.

"There is no monster underneath," he murmured. He put his hand on her breast and she leaned into it, slipping her own under his tunic. By that time Rutilius's entire crew and the governor of Britain could have come on board and he would not have known it. He spread his cloak on *Concordia*'s deck and they lay on that with hers over them while the snow came down, silvering the world, and he began to hear as she did the ship breathing around them. He tried to go slowly, thinking that he might be her first, but she drew him into her insistently, greedily, and he let desire drive him. She was slim but muscular where other girls had been soft, and hungry where they had been acquiescent. It was only afterward, when he lay spent on top of her, that he thought, *What have I done?*

Eirian was quiet, possibly thinking the same thing. He was afraid to ask. Finally, she said, "If I don't go home to fix supper they will come looking for me."

"Eirian, I am sorry—"

"Don't," she said. "You showed me the ships, something wonderful. Tomorrow I will show you something, something you haven't seen."

"Eirian—"

"We have three months," she told him. "Don't look past that." She pushed at his chest and he rose and pulled up his breeches while she straightened her gown and cloak. "Meet me where we had the solstice fire," she said. "Tomorrow when the sun comes up." She slipped down the ladder and vanished while he sat on *Concordia*'s deck, cursing himself.

—

Nonetheless, the next day, after the prayers at the standards had been made in the pre-dawn darkness, he went to the sea cliffs and the dead ash of the fire. The snow had stopped and it coated the ground like a blanket and frosted the remains of the bonfire with ice crystals. He had left his lorica and helmet behind and pulled a cloak with a fur-lined hood over his head. The breeches adopted for British winters, coming in the British fashion to the ankles, were wrapped with fur leggings above his military boots. Maybe she wouldn't come, he thought, and then saw her, bundled in her own cloak, making her way along the sea cliffs.

"Come," she said and held out her hand and he took it.

She led him down a frost-rimed path where the sea cliffs changed to tumbled stone and then to a rocky beach exposed by the ebbing tide where the retreating sea had left tidepools behind, filled with strange creatures and bits of kelp. They walked on what would be the seabed at high tide, back past the cliffs, and he saw that a gap had opened in the cliff face. The arched entrance still dripped water and the wet sand smelled of salt and tidal detritus. It made Faustus think of the dwellings of the hill people, and it was cold as their underground houses were. But it was very beautiful, the rock faces of its sides carved over eons, licked by the sea into fanciful shapes and patterns, each layer of stone wearing differently under the water's tongue.

At the end was a shelf of stone jutting from the wall and Eirian climbed up to it and sat. "We have until the tide turns," she said. "Even if you can swim, it's not good to be here when the water comes back. It's dark and too easy to forget which way is up, under the water. That's how the finpeople find you."

Faustus shuddered, only half joking. "Your islands have too many monsters."

"The islands rise up through very deep waters," Eirian said. "No one knows what lives at the bottom."

"The seals know, I suppose," he said.

"If they go that deep. If they do, they keep it to themselves."

"Even from you?" he asked.

"Myself, I don't want to know. But Catumanus says that we who are born here are all part of the water and rock and part of each other, but we have lost the ways to speak between us. It is only sometimes that I can hear them."

Beside her in the dim watery light of the sea cave, Faustus felt his father's shade beat about his head like a frantic moth. *Don't make the mistake I made.* He would not, he told himself. It was only for a little while. He bent his face to hers and kissed her again and was lost again and they wrapped around each other while the waves whispered outside. In the daylight now he could see the clan marks on her upper arms and breasts that marked her as a creature of the island. *A selkie will only break your heart*, Tuathal had said. Her skin was smooth and cold and Faustus half expected to feel her change in his arms, but breast and flank and white throat stayed the same and the long hair spread across the rock did no more than mimic seaweed. He kissed the marks on her breasts and put his hand between her legs where it was warm and felt her shiver against his fingers. His father's shade stilled and they lay entwined in the sea cave until Eirian lifted her head to the sound of the incoming waves.

"We have to go," she said, putting her hand gently to his face. "But we can come back again. Mark when the tide goes out."

They couldn't keep each other. He knew that, and knew that she knew it, and he told himself that it had been just this once. And yet every day he found himself marking the tide and taking the path down the sea cliffs, walking into a dream that he must wake forcibly from in March. He mustn't do what his father had done, but he could have three months. Eirian made certain that they took precautions that he was learning were among the things that women knew how to do but didn't talk about to men.

He asked her if she would take him to the nearby small islands, the uninhabited ones, just for the pleasure of wandering about them with her, and she brought a boat one calm day and a meal to share and they went out into the bay and then north around the coast for an afternoon, going ashore on a small speck of an islet along the edge of the Bowl to eat and watch the seabirds and the clouds rolling across the water. They spread their cloaks on the ground and touched all the now familiar places until they were spent, and then they sat leaning on each other looking out over the water.

"What is that over there?" he asked, pointing to a larger island lifting its head above the waves.

"That one is sacred," Eirian said abruptly. "I can't take you there. Don't ask."

He remembered that she had dismissed Demetrius's questions when he had pointed at the same island and remembered now too her uneasiness when they had spoken of Calgacos. He almost spoke his thought aloud but she looked so distressed that he said instead, "Don't fret. It isn't important."

"I forget who you are sometimes," she said.

He thought of the tall blond man who had spoken to Agricola over a green branch. He thought of other captive leaders, paraded like pets or tame lions and like as not executed afterward. That was what they had done to Vercingetorix. He abandoned the idea that had begun to take shape in his head.

He kissed her again. "I will not ask."

In the meantime, what they were doing was evident to both village and camp and there was grumbling that the commander was doing what he had forbidden his men to do.

"Does she look unwilling?" Septimus had snapped and that had settled the cohort, although Rutilius lost no opportunity to complain. Paullus observed his master with the air of a man watching a game with weighted dice.

Faelan dragged Eirian out of the dairy by her hair and she hit him with her fist and hit him again when he came at her, and her brothers laughed from a safe distance that even a girl could take the old man in a fight now. Faelan put a poultice on his nose and Eirian went to sleep in Catumanus's house until Faelan sent Eogan to say that she might come home because there was no one to cook or see to the house.

The village watched all this with interest and disapproval both. Unmarried women were free to do as they pleased, but those who were too free were suspect. Catumanus consulted the fire in his forge and was silent on the matter.

Winter froze a shield like glass around them, enclosing them, blurring the sight of anything outside it. It was easy not to try to look through that glass. And then the thaw came on a whisper of warm wind and the cries of curlews and oystercatchers.

Eirian climbed the cliff path and looked out over the firth to the mainland and south to wherever Rome was. She could feel the stones under her feet reach up like hands, like roots to anchor her here, to the known and familiar. Faustus had been something she couldn't keep, like the swans that come in winter and fly in the spring. She had known he would go, she told herself.

Rutilius ordered the ships launched and Faustus paid Madoc the last of his fee. He went one more time to the sea cave but Eirian didn't come. He hadn't thought she would. She had said once that when the time came she would not ask for a last misery of parting but keep the old joy instead.

He marched his cohort aboard and tried not to pick out faces on the shore. She would remember him kindly, he thought. He had not made his father's mistake over again, and tried to rip a woman from her land to be a stranger elsewhere. Surely his father had been right for once. And in any case they were bound for Hibernia, which Agricola had said could be taken with one legion, and the thought of a new campaign was a fine excitement singing just under his skin. The ships slipped into the firth and the sails billowed out in the spring sunlight, their wings spread across the water.

XXI

Afterward

Spring, 838 ab urbe condita

The Second Augusta had wintered at Eburacum, a sizable fortress lying in the triangle between the River Abus and its smaller tributary. Coming into port, Faustus felt himself slip entirely the otherworldly tether that had held him in the Orcades and come again into the familiar world of military order.

A trireme flying the imperial banner lay alongside the wharf, a sign that some great personage was visiting. The fort was frenetic with activity and the reason for it became clear when Faustus went to the Augusta's legate to report their arrival.

"The governor's been recalled," Arrius Laenas said. "His replacement's here."

"Recalled?" Faustus stared at him. "*Now?* The emperor gave him triumphal ornaments and a commemorative arch."

"Yes," Laenas agreed. "The emperor seems to have felt that this was the ideal time for him to retire triumphantly. The campaign for Hibernia has been retired as well. Governor Agricola told me before he sailed that the emperor disapproves, and so our new governor, Sallustius Lucullus, disapproves as well." The legate paused while Faustus absorbed that and then said, "The official welcome ceremony is tomorrow, Centurion. Polish up your cohort."

"Why would the emperor recall Agricola just when he's doubled the size of his province for him?" Faustus demanded furiously when, cursing, he had hunted Galerius down in the Augusta barracks.

"There was an imperial directive not to go north of the Clota, you may recall," Galerius said. "Agricola was clever enough to maneuver around that and clever enough to rationalize doing so. Emperors don't like that sort of thing. And they don't like leaving the same man in charge of four legions for too long either."

"Laenas says the Hibernia campaign is off!"

"Tuathal is even unhappier than you are," Galerius said. "Sit down and have some wine and quit pacing, you make my neck ache watching you go back and forth."

"Sorry. What is Tuathal going to do now?" Faustus took the cup Galerius offered him. It was better than any wine he had had for months and he drank appreciatively.

"Do it without us," Galerius said. "He's rounding up an army on his own account and apparently Lucullus has given that his approval. Tuathal is recruiting mercenaries from anyone with an eye for adventure and some gold at the end of it. I'd say he should wait for Lucullus to come round but I don't think he's going to. Tuathal *or* Lucullus."

Faustus stalked back to his quarters to find Paullus trimming up his helmet crest. "We're to parade in honor of the new governor tomorrow," Paullus informed him, "and everyone's parade armor has been sitting here in bags all winter. I've started on yours. And Septimus was looking for you." Faustus noted that Paullus spoke as if he too belonged to the cohort, and he supposed he did.

The entire fort bustled with the hysteria that only the advent of a new commander of unknown temperament could engender. Helmet crests, worn by the ordinary legionary only on parade, were affixed, and tunics inspected for wear and cleanliness. Fresh pilum points were stolen, reissued or traded for a pot of boot polish, cloaks were brushed and mended, hair cut and chins shaved, and every century and cavalry troop trotted out for drill. The ones who routinely mixed left with right were added to the Sick List for spurious reasons or carefully concealed in the midst of their formation where they would be less noticeable.

Constantia, having heard that Faustus had returned, came to see him and brought Pandora a piece of ham.

"For the dog?" Faustus said indignantly. "I've been living on porridge and salt fish all winter."

"It's character building," she said, sitting down in his spare chair. "Governor Lucullus believes in character building. He told Father so."

"What's he like?" Faustus asked her.

"Ambitious, I think."

"Governors tend to be."

"He's different from Governor Agricola. *He* wanted to take the whole island and bring it into the Empire, *for* the Empire. This man wants things for himself, for his own sense of importance. Maybe I'm being unfair. I didn't care for him. He told me it was unbecoming for a female to be in the hospital."

"So have plenty of other people," Faustus observed.

"I haven't cared for them either. I'm glad to see you, however."

"You just like my dog," Faustus said, but in truth he was glad to see her too. Constantia was an easy companion because he didn't love her, nor was she physically available in the way that Abudia's girls were. It would be a while before he went to see them, though. Not until the memory of Eirian had faded a bit.

"You look gloomy," Constantia observed. "Maybe it's all that salt fish."

"Not at all," Faustus said. "I'm only aggravated. We were supposed to sail for Hibernia and now we're not."

"Tuathal was in a flaming rage about that," Constantia said. "Where is he?"

"In the south, pulling together a war band that ought to terrify the usurping king in Hibernia if he can get them across the channel in any kind of order."

"How's he paying them?"

"With a war chest of gold that his mother smuggled out of Hibernia along with his infant self," Constantia said. "It appears that Governor Agricola has known about it all along, which neatly prevents Governor Lucullus from appropriating it."

"That must have been a vast disappointment," Faustus said. "So near and yet so far."

"He's recruited a terrifying combination of highborn young hotheads from the southern families, farm boys with a yen for adventure and scythes for weapons, any number of dubious people who are running from things in Britain that make Hibernia look attractive, and some I suspect are Caledone fugitives from your last battle."

"You've seen them?"

"No, but Father's new junior surgeon came up from Isca last week and he'd seen them. The legion's ordered back to Isca as soon as you've provided a sufficiently ostentatious display of martial grandeur for the governor's command ceremony, so I suspect you'll have a chance."

--

The ceremony was accomplished the following day with no untoward missteps from Faustus's cohort, not even from Bassus, who had been so unnerved by his encounter with the seals that he had apparently lost all ability to count, or so his centurion said, retrieving him at parade practice and pointing him once again in the right direction. On the day of the command parade, however, he performed admirably, so when Faustus was summoned later that afternoon to the Principia he expected only the legate's praise for a commendable performance on short notice.

Instead he found the new governor in residence. Sallustius Lucullus was spare and broad-shouldered, with a businesslike look and a shock of dark hair in a fashionable fringe of curls across his forehead.

Faustus saluted the governor and then the legate.

"Centurion Valerianus," the governor said. "I appreciated your report on the Orcades."

"Yes, sir." He wondered if Rutilius had had anything to say.

"I understand that you are well acquainted with young Tuathal Techtmar. And speak the language of the Britons."

"Yes, sir." So it wasn't Rutilius.

"Excellent. I intend to give you a somewhat unusual assignment in that case. My predecessor contemplated the invasion of Hibernia to restore young Tuathal to his father's seat as high king. While the emperor and I have decided that that campaign would be ill advised, we do wish to render him what assistance we can, as a connection with Rome once he has assumed the throne would be to our advantage." The governor paused, and Faustus had the feeling that he had rehearsed this speech in advance. "And of course he was given certain expectations which we cannot now fulfill," Lucullus continued. "Therefore you are assigned to his campaign in an advisory capacity, as representative of Rome. No doubt you can assist with many details to ensure his good will, should he be successful."

Faustus stared at him and at the legate, whose annoyed expression suggested this development might have been a surprise to him. Faustus refrained from telling them that the language of Hibernia was not the same as the language of Britain. If he could have ordered up the posting himself he would have asked for exactly this. Therefore he found it suspicious, but could not say that either. He said, "Yes, sir," instead and waited to see what else was forthcoming. Nothing else was.

"You will accompany your legion south to Isca Silurum," Lucullus said, "where I have arranged for Tuathal to have space to collect his army and drill them. No doubt you will be a help there too."

"Yes, sir."

"Very well, Valerianus, you are dismissed. I feel certain that you will serve Rome admirably."

Faustus saluted and left, still suspicious.

As the door was closing behind him, the legate snapped, "You intend to send one of my best officers haring off to Hibernia just when I have got him back?"

That was flattering, Faustus thought. He paused outside the door.

"Lartius Marena the Elder wants a favor." Lucullus put just a bit of emphasis on the word "favor." "It seems your centurion has gravely offended Lartius the Younger and both would like something to happen to him."

That served to rivet Faustus to the corridor outside the door, but he heard little else.

"Having Lartius Marena in debt to you for a favor may be inadvisable," the legate suggested.

"So may not obliging him. This seems to me to solve the problem. Out of my command, out of Lartius's sphere of influence. Don't argue with me, Laenas. I'm annoyed enough."

—

Demetrius bade Faustus farewell while the Second Augusta formed up in marching order and the cart with his own belongings rumbled away to the dock. He had dedicated two silver plaques to the gods of Ocean and the *genii loci* of Eburacum in gratitude for so far not having drowned. "I expect they'll see me home safely," he said. "They are very nice plaques."

Constantia kissed Demetrius on the cheek. "Travel safely." She looked wistfully after him and climbed aboard one of the hospital wagons with Aunt Popillia. The new governor was traditionally minded and a stickler for deportment. A woman on a horse had shocked him so deeply that Silanus had irritably ordered his daughter onto a wagon until they were out of sight of Eburacum.

They reached Isca in fifteen days, trailed home by the civilian entrepreneurs who had followed the column during its long campaign.

"Six years," Galerius said. "You won't see a campaign like this again. You'll be able to tell your grandchildren you marched with Julius Agricola."

"And then died trying to knock that appalling band of Tuathal's into something resembling Roman discipline," Faustus said.

Galerius gave a hoot of laughter. "Have you seen them?"

"Not yet, just heard descriptions to make me shudder." Faustus almost confided that his participation was thanks to Tribune Lartius's broken nose, but that was a secret that might have fangs. And Constantia probably shouldn't know. "They're camped at Llanmelin."

"The legate isn't going to like having that many fighting-age men milling about in his territory. He'll like it even less if they look like an actual threat."

"They won't be an actual threat to anyone, including the current king in Hibernia, if we sail before they're ready," Faustus said. "The Hibernians almost all fight in small kinship bands that align themselves according to whoever they strike a bargain with or who has insulted them that week. If we can turn Tuathal's army into something resembling a legion, that will be our advantage. And anyway, the legate has orders from the governor."

"I don't know what the governor was thinking sending one of ours off to stick his nose into a war that the emperor has decided against."

"If Tuathal becomes high king it will be useful to the Empire," Faustus said.

He was not actually sure of that, but both Tuathal's alliance and his reasonable distrust of Rome in light of broken promises were bridges to cross later. He would meet Tuathal's band, and Tuathal himself, and see what he saw.

–

"When I become high king," Tuathal said, "Rome had best remember that I did it without its aid."

"That may be leverage you'll be glad to have," Faustus told him.

Tuathal raised his brows. "Then why does Rome send you to me?"

"To keep her hand in, I expect."

Tuathal considered him. Tuathal had grown some more and was taller than Faustus now, still slender but more muscular. His father's sword on his hip looked shorter measured against his new height, but no less portentous. The gold eyes on the hilt stared out on a world about to shift.

"If you wish to serve as my second, I will welcome you," Tuathal said abruptly. "There must be no question as to who commands. Can you abide that?"

"I would not command that lot for all the gold yet mined," Faustus said. "But I will train them for you."

"Agreed."

There was one more thing to do here before he paraded Tuathal's ragged band of opportunists and tried to make a legion of them. He made his way on foot down to the oak grove, took off his lorica and helmet, and his sword belt with its iron buckle, and laid them in the grass outside the grove. Then he put a bronze coin in the bowl below the spring and sat down to wait. The water rippled over the image of the emperor's head and the inscription around it, IMP CAESAR VESPASIANUS AUG, minted in the reign of the emperor's father, in whose name Faustus had taken his first oath to the army.

Salmon appeared at midnight. "I would have come sooner," he said, "but they make so much noise." He jerked his thumb up the slope at the darkened camp. "It is hard to hear over their presence."

"Are you well?" Faustus asked. "And the Old One and Curlew?"

"Well enough," Salmon said. "When there are not Sun People trampling over our hills and through our gardens."

"We will take them away soon," Faustus said. "I wanted to see the Old One again before we do, if she will still welcome me after all these years."

"She sent me to fetch you," Salmon said. "Come."

Faustus stretched and followed him, winding between saplings growing up through what had been Llanmelin's outskirts, and then the dark trees and scrub. Only the faint smell of peat smoke told him when they had come to the Old One's house in the hillside.

The Old One was even older and frailer now, her hair a fine mist about her face. Curlew was with her and she too looked older, a woman now, although a woman in miniature, with a baby at her breast. They both smiled when they saw him and he knelt down in front of them and bowed his head to the Old One with a strange sense of homecoming.

Curlew motioned him to a seat and gave him a cup of something hot and faintly sweet, balancing the baby in the crook of her arm. Salmon squatted on his heels beside them while Curlew lit a rushlight from the embers in the hearth and set it on the table. She held out the baby for him to admire. It opened solemn eyes and stared at him, a deep blue stare like pools.

"Why have you come to us, Faustus?" the Old One asked softly, and he sipped at the cup, warming himself with the drink and with her use of his familiar name.

"For your blessing," he said. "I am to go to Hibernia with that noisy band that is camped at Llanmelin, and try to put a prince back on his father's throne."

The Old One raised her brows, white now against her dark skin. "It is a small matter to us who rules in Inis Fáil," she said.

Curlew put the baby back to her breast. "But for his sake we may wish his venture well," she said gently.

"Kings rise and fall," the Old One said, "and neither the rise nor the fall is of importance to us, one Sun Lord being much like another. But as Curlew says, occasionally there is one who bears our blood, and him we will watch over if we can."

"I saw something of your kin in the north," Faustus said. "One of them did me a service, the others put dead sheep in our water and sent arrows from the trees. And I thought the while on the matter of blood, and still have not sorted it out."

"Nor will you," the Old One said. "Kinship is not a straight line." She watched him silently for a moment. "The thing that was with you six years ago is with you still, but it fears us, I think. It beats against our walls to get out."

Faustus thought of the way it had beat about his ears while he lay with Eirian. "I have questioned whether it is my own dreaming," he said.

"I think there is little difference," Curlew offered. "What we dream has substance."

Faustus was silent. He dreamed of Eirian. Not every night, but often enough to trouble his sleep.

"It is not only at Samhain that the gates may be open," her grandmother said. "You must give it leave to go and eventually it will find its way."

"I have tried to give it leave," Faustus said ruefully.

"Grandmother is optimistic," said Salmon. "We have tried to give the Sun People leave as well."

"The Sun People most unfortunately are not dead," the Old One snapped.

"I can rid you of the ones at Llanmelin at least, in a few months," Faustus said. He stood, nearly bumping his head on the chamber roof.

"That would be most welcome." Her face softened. "And you are welcome, Faustus, whenever you wish to visit us."

"Thank you, Grandmother."

She pulled a leather thong over her head. "Take this." A small blue stone hung from it, warm from her skin. "So that a part of us goes with you, on your ship to Inis Fáil."

In the middle of the stone was a small white dot like an eye. He put the cord around his neck.

The baby reached for it and Curlew let the child grasp it and then pulled its fingers away. "We will ask the Goddess to bring you back to us, when you have put your king on his throne."

–

The sun was coming up, burning off a thick mist as Faustus and Salmon ducked through the door in the hillside again. Salmon led him until they could see the walls of Llanmelin and smell the cookfires within them and then he raised his hand and was gone, a disappearance so utter and immediate that it left no breath of movement among the trees.

Faustus collected his sword belt and armor and put them on again. "You didn't like it in there," he said to the empty air. "You'll have to get used to that. If you hadn't fought so hard to own her, she might have been more willing. I took your advice this once, and I am not sure I thank you for it." He ran his fingers over the little blue stone at his throat and then set off through the meadow toward Llanmelin.

Author's Note

On Language, History and Myth

The language spoken in Britain during the first century CE would have been dialects of Brythonic. The Gaels of Ireland had not yet come to what is now Scotland, and the language of the Caledones would instead have been similar to that of the southern tribes. The only remnants of Brythonic now are in the languages of Wales, Cornwall and Brittany, and so when choosing names for my Caledones I have looked more to names from Welsh sources than Gaelic ones. The exceptions are Tuathal Techtmar and Calgacos of the Caledones, who live at the edges of history where it often crosses into myth. The only source for the existence of Calgacos is Tacitus's *Agricola* and he may have simply made up a war leader on whom to hang an eloquent pre-battle speech. At any rate, Calgacos is never heard of afterward and Tacitus says nothing about what happened to him after the battle.

Tuathal Techtmar is a legendary High King of Ireland, son of a deposed ruler who came back from exile in Britain to reclaim his father's throne. The first accounts of him appear in medieval sources but it is thought that he actually existed, and the sources put his exile and return in the first or second century, ranging from the time of the Flavian emperors through the reign of Hadrian. Another theory stems from Tacitus's mention of an exiled Irish prince who was to be Agricola's pretext for an invasion of Hibernia, and there is some evidence that he may have been given unofficial Roman support. Because this fits my purposes nicely, I have chosen to adopt it.

373

A man named Demetrius did indeed dedicate two plaques in Greek to "the gods of the legate's residence" and to Oceanus and Tethys at Eburacum, and is very likely the Demetrius of Tarsus who, according to Plutarch, had been sent to Britain by the emperor to study the Druids.

The location of Agricola's great battle with the Caledones is one of those things that historians dispute endlessly because Tacitus was notoriously imprecise in his locations. Tacitus called it Mons Graupius and since no one knows what that means or exactly where it is, I have simply chosen the proposed location that best suits the narrative, that of the mountain called Bennachie in Scotland. Because Mons Graupius would be the Roman name, not the Caledone one, and no one but Tacitus uses it, I have used instead a name that carries some mythological as well as actual meaning and derives from the current common name of the peak where the action takes place, Mither Tap, here given as Pap of the Mother.

No evidence of Roman camps has been found in the Orkneys so far but there have been finds of coins and other artifacts of Roman origin. Tacitus says that Agricola ordered the Fleet to sail around Britain and it is thought that it may have wintered there. I have placed my Roman camp on the shore so that over the ensuing centuries the sea may have taken it.

As for Tacitus, he was Agricola's father-in-law, so add what grain of salt you wish to his account. Unfortunately, it's almost all we have.

Where I cross most definitely into the territory of myth is with the Old Ones, the little dark people of the hills. There was indeed a small, dark, probably blue-eyed, race who lived in Britain before the tall blond Celts, and whose DNA still appears in Britons of today. "Cheddar Man", the Mesolithic body dated to 7150 BCE and found in Somerset, provided the DNA evidence for dark skin and pale eyes. He also, with more advanced testing, proved to have a living relative, a Somerset history teacher who shares his mitochondrial DNA, indicating a common maternal ancestor. These dark folk flourished at least 6,000 years before the Celts first came, and their descendants were no doubt absorbed into the dominant populace long before the date of this novel, even if they did not entirely vanish, making their continued presence as a distinct people unlikely.

Mythologically speaking, however, they are still a presence and their echoes may be heard even today in folklore, in the tales of small folk inhabiting the hollow hills, the Neolithic burial chambers that dot the land, seldom encountered and often vengeful and dangerous when they are. As each new wave of invaders flowed across Britain, these old ones would have faded ever farther into the background, living on the edges of the newcomers' settlements, hunting with the flint and bronze weapons that the newcomers' iron blades so easily defeated; remnants who eventually achieved the status of the fairies, the fae of fireside stories, for whom it is still advisable to put out a saucer of milk now and then. For that reason they inhabit this novel.

And Gratitude

Finally, grateful thanks:

To my husband, Tony Neuron, for general moral support and for creating the frontispiece map.

To Kit Nevile, who is a peerless editor.

To Elizabeth Montgomery, who first introduced me to Roman Britain when we were in college and gave me Rosemary Sutcliff's novels to read, and who in aid of this book coached me on how one might steer a small boat through a storm.

To Jim Doolittle, for the term "reissued", winner of my informal contest for a word describing something acquired by irregular channels in a military camp.

Place Names

Listed below are the Roman names for places mentioned in this book and their modern equivalents. In some cases where the Roman name is not known I have used a form of the current name, particularly for places in Wales. In the first century CE, the Gaels had not yet come to Scotland and the languages spoken in Britain were variants of Brythonic, of which the only remnants today are Welsh, Breton and Cornish. Thus place names in what are now the Highlands of Scotland would have had more in common with Welsh than with Gaelic. In the cases of Bryn Epona and Bryn Caledon, I have devised fictional strongholds based on other British hill forts.

Place Names and Their Modern Equivalents

Alauna: Ardoch
Antium: Anzio, Italy
Aquae Sulis: Bath
Belerium Promontory: Land's End
Blestium: Monmouth
Bodotria: Firth of Forth
Bowl, the: Scapa Flow
Brocavum: Brougham
Bryn Caledon: fictional hill fort of the Caledones
Bryn Epona: fictional hill fort of the Ordovices
Burrium: Usk
Caledonia: Highland Scotland

Calf, the: Cava Island, the Orkneys
Calleva: Silchester
Camelon: name still in use today
Castra Pinnata: Inchtuthil
Clota: Firth of Clyde
Coed-y-Caerau: name still in use today
Corstopitum: Corbridge
Deva: Chester
Dolaucothi (Luentinum): Pumpsaint
Dubris: Dover
Eburacum: York
Gallia Narbonensis: Languedoc and Provence, southern France
German Ocean: North Sea
Great Island: Mainland Island, the Orkneys
Hibernia (Inis Fáil): Ireland
High Isle: Hoy Island, the Orkneys
Inis Fáil (Hibernia): Ireland
Isca Silurum: Caerleon
Ituna: Solway Firth
Llanmelin: name still in use today
Londinium: London
Luentinum (Dolaucothi): Pumpsaint
Luguvalium: Carlisle
Mona: Anglesey
Narbo Martius: Narbonne, France
Oceli: Spurn Head
Orcades: The Orkneys
Pap of the Mother: Mither Tap, Bennachie
Rutupiae: Richborough
Sabrina: River Severn
Taexalorum Head: Kinnaird Head
Tamia: Bertha (Perth)
Tavus: River Tay
Thule: The Shetlands

Trimontium: Eildon
Vectis: Isle of Wight
Venta Silurum: Caerwent
Viroconium: Wroxeter

Glossary

Adonis: mythologically beautiful youth, lover of Venus
Amazons: ancient mythical female warriors
amicus: personal friend
Annwn: Celtic underworld
Apollo: Greek sun god, often associated with wolves
basilisk: mythical serpent hatched from a rooster's egg; it can kill with a glance
Beltane: May 1
Boreas: god of the north wind
century: eighty men
Ceres: goddess of the harvest
cohort: six centuries; ten cohorts make a legion
corona aurea: gold crown, an award given to officers who have held their ground
corvus: literally "crow" or "raven", a boarding ramp with a spike at the end
cuirass: breast and back plates
Damara: Celtic fertility goddess
dexter: right-hand
Diana: goddess of the hunt, fertility and the moon; protector of women in childbirth
donativum: bonus paid to the army
Druids: ancient Celtic priesthood
the Eagles: the Roman army; from the eagle standards of the legions
Epona: Celtic goddess of horses, adopted by Roman cavalry

Fama: goddess of fame and rumors

fascinus: amulet embodying the divine phallus; generally a penis with wings

Fortuna: goddess of fortune (good and bad)

Gaia: among the most common of Roman names, thus a generic name for any woman

genius loci: the spirit or god of a place

gladius: Roman military short sword

the Goddess: Earth Mother in any of her many forms

Gofannon: Celtic god of metalwork

greaves: lower leg armor

haruspex: priest interpreter of omens

hauberk: shirt of ring mail or scale

Hecate: goddess of the Underworld

hypocaust: underfloor hot-air heating system

Juno: wife of Jupiter; goddess of marriage and childbirth

Jupiter: the great god, Roman equivalent of Zeus, patron of Rome

latrunculi: Roman board game of strategy

legate: commander of a legion or other high office

Lemuria: festival and ritual for warding off ghosts

liburnian: fast ship with double oar decks

lorica: armor made of segmented plates

Lugh: Celtic sun god

Lughnasa: Festival of Lugh, August 1

lunula: crescent moon amulet worn by Roman girls

Mars Ultor: god of war in his guise as Mars Avenger

Mercury: messenger god, ruler of wealth, commerce and thievery

Mithras: Persian savior god popular in the Roman army

Morrigan: Celtic battle goddess, one aspect of the Mother

the Mother: Earth Mother in any of her many forms

optio: second-in-command to an officer; a general might have several

paterfamilias: the oldest living male in a household with authority over all the rest

phalera: medal for bravery, a disk of bronze or silver

pilum: legionary's javelin; plural: pila

Pluto: god of the Underworld

Praetorium: commander's house in a fort or camp

primus pilus: centurion of the first cohort in a legion, second-in-command to the legate

Principia: headquarters in a fort or camp

quaestor: official in charge of financial matters

rota: a simple game played on a round board

Samhain: October 31, when the Celtic dead may return to earth

Saturn Sterculius: god of the manuring of fields

Saturnalia: December festival honoring Saturn. Small presents are given, and the tables turned with masters serving slaves

sidhe: in Celtic legend, the hollow hills of faerie; here a dwelling of an older race

sign of horns: invoking the horned god (Pan or his Celtic counterparts) to ward off evil

signifer: legionary standard bearer

sinister: left-hand

Styx: river at the border of the Underworld

tortoise: shield wall formation with shields overhead; defensive structure used in sieges

tribune: military officer, either political appointee or career man

Vercingetorix: Gaulish chieftain who led a rebellion against Julius Caesar

vexillation: troops detached from their regular unit for service elsewhere

vicus: civilian settlement around a military base

Wild Hunt: mythological band of supernatural or ghostly riders

Thank you for reading *Shadow of the Eagle*

If you enjoyed the first instalment of Faustus' epic story, then get ready for…

A DANGEROUS SECRET
A FRONTIER IN FLAMES

EMPIRE'S EDGE

THE BORDERLANDS BOOK II

Coming April 2023